Also by Edward Cox from Gollancz:

The Relic Guild
The Cathedral of Known Things

THE
WATCHER OF
DEAD TIME

Book Three of The Relic Guild

EDWARD COX

GOLLANCZ
LONDON

First published in Great Britain in 2016 by Gollancz
An imprint of the Orion Publishing Group Ltd
Carmelite House, 50 Victoria Embankment,
London EC4Y 0DZ

An Hachette UK Company

1 3 5 7 9 10 8 6 4 2

A CIP catalogue record for this book
is available from the British Library.

ISBN 978 1 473 20036 4

Typeset by Deltatype Ltd, Birkenhead, Merseyside

Printed in Great Britain by Clays Ltd, St Ives plc

www.edwardcox.net
www.orionbooks.co.uk
www.gollancz.co.uk

For Dot and Norm, and everything you gave me.

STRANGE CREATURES

And then, for the longest time, he played the game alone.

Fabian Moor had spent half a human lifespan isolated inside a cube of thaumaturgic metal, surrounded by silver light radiating from four close walls. A claustrophobic sanctuary fifteen feet high and wide and long. Mighty spells had been cast upon it by the greatest of all Thaumaturgists, Iblisha Spiral. The cube had been Moor's haven – or prison; the hub for a universal portal which he had spent the last forty years using to search through the Nothing of Far and Deep for the House of all Houses.

The Great Labyrinth.

It was not meant to be this way. Spiral, the Lord of the Genii, had a grand plan that should have seen Moor returning to the Labyrinth at his master's side. But forty years ago, the magickers of the Relic Guild had proved to be a bigger obstacle than anyone had anticipated. However, even with the help of the mighty Skywatcher Lady Amilee, the Relic Guild wasn't powerful enough to destroy Lord Spiral's plan, or Moor. They had only delayed the inevitable.

At the centre of the silver cube, a strange tree-like creature grew from the floor. With a small degree of pride, Moor gazed upon its leathery, brown-green bark. Roots writhed like a nest of snakes at its base; branches grew from a solid trunk, coiling in the air and sliding over the ceiling. One of the serpentine branches pointed at Moor. He raised his index finger to meet its tip. The tree shuddered at the touch of its creator, but the branch withdrew when Moor held out the terracotta jar in his pale hands, recoiling from the forbidden thaumaturgy it held.

There had been moments when Moor had wondered if he would ever see this jar again. It was one of four, plain and smooth, its lid sealed with wax, filled with the darkest magic. A lifetime ago, Moor had buried them in the foundations of the Labyrinth, where they had remained, waiting for the day of Moor's return when he could reanimate the essences they preserved.

The last of Lord Spiral's Genii, sleeping the long sleep, and it was almost time to wake them up.

There had been moments when the isolation of the long game had threatened to drive Moor insane. The Nothing of Far and Deep was a vast, thick cloud of primordial mist – unimaginably huge to lesser creatures – and the Labyrinth was the only House dwelling inside it. Or so others believed. Moor's task might appear impossible to achieve, like trying to find a single diamond buried in a desert. But he had prevailed. Compromise, adaptation, patience – that was all Moor had required to carry Lord Spiral's ultimate goal across the decades to a time when there was no one waiting to help the people of the Labyrinth.

The Genii War was long over, the Timewatcher and Her Thaumaturgists were gone for good, and the terracotta jar in Moor's hands was the beginning of the future. The days of isolation were at an end, and the silver cube had almost served its purpose. Almost …

The serpentine tree stirred and writhed as a presence filtered through the thaumaturgic walls, disturbing the stolid air. A curious sensation washed over Moor. Someone had summoned him – but not with words, more with feelings that rippled through the silver cube, carrying fear.

Moor laid his hand on the glowing surface of a wall subtly unlike the others. Immediately the thaumaturgic metal's state shifted, changing from solid to pearlescent liquid and finally to clear, shimmering air.

A bedraggled man stood on damp cobbles outside. Behind him, an alleyway of the Great Labyrinth stretched away into misty gloom. He was small, his clothes and skin grubby, and his feral eyes were fixed on the terracotta jar in Moor's hands. Charlie Hemlock, they called him. It was a good name for the poisonous sort of human he was.

'Hello, Charlie,' said Moor.

Hemlock gave a quick nod in return.

Three golems stood in a line behind him. Deformed and withered bodies covered by black cassocks, grotesque faces hidden beneath the wide brims of their hats, these stone servants had lost every aspect of the humans they had once been. Subservient, incapable of speech or thought, they waited for orders. The power stones that energised the pistols in their hands glowed with violet light.

Moor said, 'I trust everything has gone to plan, Charlie? Our prey has caught scent of the bait?'

Shifty and nervous, Hemlock wrung his hands together and looked at a young woman lying unconscious at his feet. 'It won't be long before Marney comes looking for her.' His voice was slightly distorted through the wall of air.

Moor studied the smooth surface of the terracotta jar. 'Perfect.'

The unconscious woman, the *bait*, unwashed and dressed in oversized clothes no better than rags, had short blonde hair streaked with red dye. Such a small and innocent-looking thing, but deceptive in her appearance. Her name was Clara, her clients called her Peppercorn, and she had been touched by magic.

'Marney will be here soon,' Hemlock stressed, anxiety lacing his voice. The prospect obviously disturbed him, as it should. Marney, an empath, one of the last magickers of the Relic Guild ... and the keeper of secrets. She was dangerous and clever, concealing herself well among the denizens of Labrys Town. Moor had found Marney practically impossible to locate, but with Peppercorn Clara's unwitting assistance, the empath had finally been enticed out of hiding.

'So,' Hemlock said, eyeing the peculiar tree behind Moor. 'If that's everything, I'll just take my money and be on my way.'

'On your way?'

'If it's all the same to you.' Hemlock spoke brightly, casually, belying the fear beneath.

Moor clucked his tongue. 'I understand how you feel. I've shown you things that frighten you, and now you're wondering if you have bitten off more than you can chew.'

After a quick glance at the golems behind him, and the woman at his feet, Hemlock shrugged at the Genii. Moor resisted the urge to wrap his thaumaturgy around the venal idiot's body and crush the life from him.

'We need to discuss the next phase of the plan, Charlie.'

Hemlock licked his lips nervously. 'I didn't know there was a next phase.'

'Indeed. Come inside, please.'

Hemlock didn't move. 'Look, I've done everything you asked of me, but I'm through with this now. I'm in over my head.' He frowned at the serpentine tree's coiling branches. 'I'll just take my money and leave.'

'No, no, no,' Moor said. 'The part you are about to play is surprisingly important, given that you are a human.'

'But—'

Hemlock's words choked off. Moor had used his thaumaturgy to pulse a command to the golems. In unison, they aimed their pistols at Hemlock. With a yelp, Hemlock skipped away from them, through the veil of shimmering air, into the silver cube. As soon as he had crossed the threshold, Moor commanded the golems to guard Peppercorn Clara and then returned the wall to its solid state.

His face paling, Hemlock stuck close to the wall. His eyes, wide and panicked, darted from Moor to the jar to the tree creature, and back again.

'Charlie, you are too young to remember the Labyrinth before the Genii and the Thaumaturgists went to war.' Moor waited for Hemlock's fear to acknowledge that he was being spoken to. 'You think of the Timewatcher as an all-loving Mother, yet She abandoned you cold-heartedly. Abandoned us all. This is a dangerous time, for you and me both.'

'W-what do you want?'

The Genii faced the tree. A few more of its leathery branches reached for him. He stroked each of them one by one.

'You know the tale of Oldest Place, yes?' He returned his attention to Hemlock. 'The prison House in which the Timewatcher incarcerated the Lord of the Genii?'

Hemlock stared.

'Marney knows the tale, too, Charlie. Better than most, you might say. She is very important to me. And to the future. But here' – he held up the terracotta jar – 'I want to introduce you to a colleague of mine. Her name is Hagi Tabet.'

Confused, afraid, Hemlock said, 'What?'

'Lady Tabet is to be the new Resident of Labrys Town.' Moor ran his finger around the jar's wax seal. 'And I need you to deliver her to the Nightshade.'

'What are you talking about?' Hemlock whimpered. 'No one can get into the Nightshade. Not even you.'

'That's not entirely true, Charlie. I know of a way, you see. Unfortunately, it will cost you your life.'

Hemlock's simmering panic boiled over. Pathetically, he reached into the sleeve of his coat for a concealed weapon, but Moor stopped him in his tracks. The Genii bound the human in higher magic, rendered him immobile, strangled the voice from his throat. His eyes staring, body and limbs boneless as a rag doll's, Hemlock's feet slid over the cube's silver floor as thaumaturgy dragged him forwards.

Once he was close enough, Moor switched places with Hemlock, watching as the sinuous, leathery branches of the serpentine tree reached out and captured him. They coiled around his legs, removed his dirty, patched coat and ripped open his shirt. Popped buttons bounced off silver walls. Hemlock expressed a scream with his eyes as a branch slid around his midriff and two others encircled his wrists, holding him prone and defenceless before the Genii.

'Calm yourself,' Moor said. 'You have a little time to live your life yet.'

Holding up the terracotta jar again, Moor left it floating in the air, slowly spinning. Hemlock's eyes welled with tears as Moor laid cold hands upon his chest and summoned his power.

'It's a small mercy, Charlie, but you won't remember what I'm about to do. For now, brace yourself. This is going to cause you agony beyond belief.'

CHAPTER ONE

PRESCIENCE

Samuel felt as though he was walking along a mile-high tightrope without a safety net beneath him.

He led his Aelfirian colleagues along an old and abandoned tunnel beneath the mighty clock tower called Little Sibling: the parliament building in the Sisterhood of Bells, the Aelfirian capital House. Behind Samuel came Namji. Hillem and Glogelder brought up the rear. The light from Samuel's lamp danced upon the tunnel walls; the power stone in his revolver glowed pale violet.

Van Bam and Clara were missing. The avatar, for reasons Samuel couldn't fathom, had split them from the group, and who knew where they were now? Samuel felt lost without his fellow magickers by his side. Making matters worse, his magic had been anaesthetised; the shock wave from an explosion of anti-magic had sucked his prescient awareness from his body and he didn't know how long it would take to return.

In Van Bam's absence, Namji had inherited leadership over the group. The occasional glassy *chink* came from the satchel hanging over her shoulder, filled with the paraphernalia of a magic-user.

In silence, the old bounty hunter led them out of the tunnel into a chamber of black-bricked walls, cold and gloomy, unused for years. Water dripped from the dark ceiling and slapped on the floor, making the cobbles slimy and treacherous underfoot.

Tall and slim Hillem deactivated the power stones on his pistols and slid them into the holsters at his hips. Glogelder was less sure of his environment. As tall as Hillem but much thicker set, he kept his clunky spell sphere launcher in his hands. On his back he carried a duffel bag filled with spare weaponry and ammunition.

'This must be the entrance to the dungeons,' Namji said, standing over a trapdoor set into the floor. Hillem and Glogelder joined her.

Samuel placed the glow lamp down. His eyes were drawn to the remnants of a staircase at the back of the chamber. At one time it had led up to a doorway set high on the wall, but the staircase was rotten and broken now and the doorway had been bricked up. Samuel shifted his gaze to the ceiling and felt a knot tighten in his gut.

Soon, in the council halls of Little Sibling far above this chamber, an assembly of the Aelfirian governing bodies would occur. The Panopticon of Houses was convening to decide the fate of the one million humans living in Labrys Town; to decide whether or not it was time to destroy the last remaining portal to the Labyrinth. Without that portal, no supplies could get through to the denizens. Without that portal, the inhabitants of Labrys Town would die. But in reality, the decision wasn't really up for debate or vote. It had already been made.

Manipulating the situation, pulling the strings behind the scenes in the Panopticon of Houses, was a covert, power-hungry band of hierarchs known as the Sisterhood. They blamed humans for the Timewatcher and Her Thaumaturgists' decision to abandon the Aelfir after the Genii War. They wanted to cut the last tie to the Labyrinth, eradicate the Aelfir's lingering faith in the Timewatcher. Destroying the last portal was their goal, and the Sisterhood always got what it wanted.

The one person standing between the machinations of the Sisterhood and the ruin of the Labyrinth was Tal, an elderly Aelf, a veteran of the Genii War and a discredited councillor. He was the Relic Guild's agent in the Panopticon of Houses, a self-proclaimed champion of the Labyrinth, and he alone would take the voice of reason into the assembly. Samuel prayed that Tal could convince the Houses to spare the denizens, to make them see the truth – that the Genii had returned and planned to free Spiral from Oldest Place. But even if Tal was successful, it could still be a hollow victory. Unless the Relic Guild stopped the Genii the Labyrinth would fall anyway, and the Houses of the Aelfir would soon follow.

Where in the Timewatcher's name were Van Bam and Clara?

'Samuel?'

Namji was standing at the trapdoor between Hillem and Glogelder, dwarfed by their size. All of them were looking at Samuel. Their pointed ears, large eyes and small noses and mouths gave their faces the triangular appearance of the Aelfir. But where Namji's face was subtly heart-shaped and Hillem's expression always studious, Glogelder looked like a brute. Old wounds had left so many scars and craters on his hairless head and face that Samuel was reminded of a beaten moon. His broken nose had never been set and his ears were battered.

'We need to carry on,' Namji said. 'We can't afford to hang around.'

Samuel joined the Aelfir. The wooden slats of the trapdoor were damp and rotten, appearing too unstable to bear any weight. This proved to be true when Glogelder grabbed its metal ring and tore half of the wood away with one yank. Throwing the rotten mass aside, he quickly removed what remained.

Hillem retrieved the glow lamp and lowered its light into the hole, illuminating the first few steps of a spiralling staircase of stone.

Unconsciously, Samuel slipped a hand into his coat pocket. His fingers closed around the big, black iron key that rested there and he pulled it out, turning it over in his hands. The bow was cast in a diamond shape. At the end of the long shaft were three blocky teeth. Uncertainty was an unfamiliar state for Samuel and he didn't care for the way it felt. The key had been a gift from the mysterious avatar. It opened a cell in the forgotten dungeons far below Little Sibling, but what the avatar wanted the Relic Guild to find down there was anyone's guess.

Namji, Hillem and Glogelder were looking at him again.

'Samuel,' urged Namji, 'the Toymaker is still in the Sisterhood of Bells.'

The Toymaker, Samuel thought bitterly. An assassin left behind by the Thaumaturgists who had been hunting the Relic Guild ever since they escaped from the Labyrinth. But you never saw the Toymaker himself, only his army of hand-sized insectoid automatons and the deadly thaumaturgic stings at the end of their tails. The same anti-magic that had anaesthetised Samuel's prescient awareness had deactivated the Toymaker's toys. But, again, for how long?

'Has your magic come back at all?' Namji said. 'Do you feel anything?'

Samuel could detect the first signs of his magic's return but it was only a vague stirring in his blood, like the tiniest of embers still alive in a fireplace full of dead coals. It wasn't enough to warn him of any danger lurking at the bottom of those spiralling stairs.

Stuffing the key back into his pocket, Samuel shrugged at Namji. 'Unless you know some spell that can detect danger, we have to go down blind.'

'Speak for yourself,' Glogelder half-joked, casting a wary glance into the dark stairwell. His battered face split into a grin. 'Personally, I'm thinking of ditching the lot of you.'

'I do have my detection crystal,' Hillem offered. 'It won't sense danger, but it will alert us if anyone's down there.'

'No, I've got something better,' Namji said. 'But if we have to do this without prescient awareness, then I'm not doing it unarmed.'

She motioned to Glogelder, who shrugged the duffel bag from his back. Dipping inside, he produced a slim box, roughly six inches thick, twelve wide and eighteen long. The big Aelf passed it to Namji.

Laying the box on the cobbled floor, Namji unclasped it and flipped back the lid to reveal two shallow, padded halves connected by three little hinges. Compartments cut out of the padding held the polished silver parts of a weapon. Namji began pulling the components from the box one by one, quickly and methodically connecting them together, each piece attaching to the next with a crisp *click*.

'She's not a fan of firearms,' Hillem whispered to Samuel. 'She won't carry this thing unless it's absolutely necessary.'

At first, Samuel supposed Namji was constructing a handgun of some kind. The butt had a coarse grip, the trigger a circular guard; but instead of a barrel, the weapon had a length of flattened metal with a groove down its centre. And when Namji finished the piece by connecting a short prod with little wheels at its ends and a thin bowstring of steel cable, Samuel realised it was a pistol crossbow, ornately designed from silver metal, not much longer than his revolver.

'Damn fine weapon, though,' Glogelder said proudly. 'I stole it for her.'

Namji clicked a power stone into the weapon's stock. It whined and glowed with violet light when she primed it. There was a whirr of mechanisms and then the bowstring snapped back into the firing position. Namji pulled the trigger. The bowstring sprang forward and then immediately returned to lock into the spring clip, as quick as a flash.

Impressed, Samuel watched as the Aelfirian magic-user removed the last two items from the box – cartridges of bolts, he assumed. Namji clipped one of them to her belt; the other she slapped into the underside of the crossbow. It was longer than the weapon was thick. With another mechanical whirr, the flight groove opened to allow the cartridge to push up a bolt. The groove closed again and the projectile nestled in place, ready to be fired.

It was a strange kind of bolt, thinner and shorter than a pencil, the shaft and flight made of metal, but the small pointed head was clear glass inside which fluid glowed with pale radiance.

'A spell?' Samuel asked.

'Exactly the same as a magical bullet.' Namji dropped her arm to her side, showing that even when the crossbow was held vertically, the bolt remained in the groove. 'A magnetism spell,' she explained. 'It only lets go when I pull the trigger.'

As Glogelder returned the box to the duffel bag, Namji rummaged around in the satchel hanging from her shoulder and produced a small spell sphere. Without much effort, she crushed the glass between her fingers and flicked the spell into the air. Samuel raised a hand against the white light of a tiny star that appeared before her.

She said, 'If there's danger around, the light should turn orange.'

'Should?'

Namji smirked. 'It's been a long time since I last used one.'

She walked forwards and the light preceded her. When Namji stopped at the edge of the hole in the floor, the star disappeared down into it, illuminating more of the spiralling stone steps.

'Well then,' Namji said, taking a breath and standing on the first stair. 'Let's go and see what the avatar wants us to find.'

Hillem drew his pistols and thumbed their power stones. With the duffel bag once again on his back, Glogelder hefted his spell sphere launcher.

Samuel nodded at Namji, and the three men followed her down into the bowels of Little Sibling.

CHAPTER TWO

AWAKENINGS

Van Bam was dead.

It was true; Clara had seen him die. As the wolf, she had watched, helpless and immobile, as the wild demons of the Retrospective ripped him apart and fed on his flesh. Van Bam was dead.

So why could she hear his voice?

I am blind...

It came from the darkness inside Clara's mind, its deep tone disturbing the nothingness that had beset her being, reawakening emotions and memories and scars.

I cannot see where I am.

There was a strained edge to the illusionist's voice, as though he was speaking while his fingers desperately clung to a ledge above a great abyss. Yet somehow Clara knew he wasn't talking to her.

Help me...

Don't be afraid, said a different voice. A woman. *They didn't get me. I'm still here.*

Clara recognised the new voice. It belonged to Marney, the empath. She had always been inside the changeling's head. Hadn't she?

I cannot hold on, Van Bam said. Weak. Distant.

You're not supposed to, Marney replied, soft yet stern. *Trust me like you used to, Van Bam. I will find you.*

Clara heard a bestial screech from somewhere beyond the darkness in her mind. She began retching. And then pain rushed through her like white fire.

The wolf's eyes snapped open and golden light filled them. She gagged and choked, coughing out viscous fluid as a cold length was yanked from her throat. Vision blurry, the stench of death filling her nostrils, she whined as a second cold length was wrenched from her head. Another screech came from close by. The wolf lay on her side, her eyes focused on a spike of green glass protruding from her stomach. Agony roiled her gut and she vomited blood. Magic flowed through her veins like molten metal.

And the metamorphosis began.

She growled and yelped as her stomach wound healed with ruthless magical contractions which pushed the spike of green glass from her body. It fell free and hit stone with a discordant chime. Her head throbbed as the hole in her skull closed. Clara half-barked, half-sobbed, thrashing while her skeleton reorganised its structure with a series of harsh cracks and jerks. Her silver-grey pelt shrank, each hair drawn back into her skin to leave behind the dark grey material of magically charmed clothes.

She was the human.

Lying upon the hard surface of a huge stone table, not quite under-standing why she was there, Clara stared up into the face of a hulking, obese brute. His head bald, expression cruel, he glared at Clara with one dark eye. Viktor Gadreel. The name came to her like a slap in the face, along with another word: Genii.

Dressed in a priest's cassock, Gadreel was holding a diamond-shaped box as black and polished as obsidian. Thaumaturgic symbols glowed upon its surface with purple light. Two glass tubes, smeared with Clara's blood, sprouted from its sides. Known Things … The box was called Known Things. It contained a secret. It knew how to kill Spiral.

'Still alive, little wolf?' Gadreel said, his voice a rumble of thunder. His fat, slug-like lips were twisted, perhaps in amusement. Or maybe he was surprised, impressed, by Clara's survival. 'But not for much longer,' the Genii added.

As he backed away from the table, the glass tubes lost their solidity, becoming flaccid, gelatinous tendrils that whipped the air as they were sucked into the body of the black diamond box.

Known Things was the Relic Guild's last hope.

Van Bam's voice filled Clara's mind again.

What is happening to me?

Isn't it obvious? said Marney.

The Genii strode towards a wide rent in the air. Like a wound in reality, it was alive with the swirling darkness of a portal. Without breaking his stride, Viktor Gadreel entered the portal and disappeared. The rent closed after him, sealing with a wet noise to become a thin crack which blew away like smoke.

Clara managed to lift herself up on one elbow and saw the pack of wild demons Gadreel had left behind.

Beneath the golden glow of a domed ceiling, the demons fought and jostled over Van Bam's remains. Their grey carapaces were smeared with blood and their long, knife-like fingers were picking the last morsels of flesh from a mound of broken bones, stuffing them into their gaping mouths.

Sobbing, teetering on the edge of unconsciousness, Clara knew she was too weak to summon the wolf again. She looked around the chamber for a means of escape. There! A circular hole in the wall. She remembered that beyond it, a bridge spanned a yawning chasm in a mighty cavern that led directly to a portal out of this place. But the hole was barricaded by debris and broken rocks.

The demons screeched.

The Cathedral of Doubt and Wonder, Van Bam said. *Was it a trap?*

No! Marney's voice was impassioned. *Events unfolded as they had to.*

Had to? Van Bam was angry, desperate, but his voice was fading. *We gave the Genii the location of Oldest Place!*

You were supposed to, Van Bam.

Clara noticed gaps between the rocks that filled the circular hole. She wondered if she had the strength to make a hole big enough to squeeze through, then outrun the demons to the safety of the portal. She tried to slip from the stone table quietly and gracefully, but only succeeded in falling to a heap on the floor. The green glass spike followed her down. It smashed into a thousand emerald shards, the impact resounding through the chamber like a small explosion. The remnants of an illusionist's wand skittered and tinkled across the floor. And the pack of wild demons noticed her.

Losing interest in what remained of Van Bam's body, they crept towards Clara, their movements twitchy like insects'. Mouths filled with teeth and gore, rheumy, fishlike eyes rolling in their sockets, their hunger came for the changeling.

Clara tried to scurry away from them, but unconsciousness called again and fatigue overwhelmed her panic.

Tell me why. Van Bam's voice was growing fainter and fainter. *Why were Clara and I sacrificed?*

Clara is still alive, Marney told him. *And she needs you.*

I-I don't understand.

Have faith in me. I won't abandon you, Van Bam ... Van Bam?

But the illusionist's voice had gone, and the demons were almost upon Clara. Seven of them. One screeched and the others took up the call, anticipating the rush, the tearing and feeding, the promise of hot, fresh blood. They stank of hopelessness and death.

Clara gave up. Perhaps if she closed her eyes, her mind would return to that dark place and she would feel nothing of what was about to happen ...

The demons stopped, their eyes searching the chamber as a scuttling sound filled the air. Accompanied by the *ticks* of metal on stone, violet light shone through the gaps in the barricade. Forgetting Clara, the demons faced the light, clustering together, hissing.

A single rock fell from the barricade and rolled across the floor. The violet glow intensified. The blades of the demons' fingers clacked together. Clara yelped as the barricade collapsed and an army of insectoid automatons rushed into the chamber.

The demons didn't get the chance to mount a counter-attack. As Clara pushed herself away, the automatons – silver, hand-sized, at least a hundred of them – swarmed the monsters. Their lashing tails, tipped with the violet glow of thaumaturgic stings, pierced slimy grey carapaces, flashing as they administered deadly shocks of higher magic.

You never meet the Toymaker, they said. *Only his toys.*

The demons fell, shrieking in pain and rage, buried beneath a writhing mound of silver. When the shrieks ceased, the automatons moved towards the changeling, leaving the corpses of the demons to steam and melt behind them.

Clara, said Marney, *I need your help.*

A part of Clara wanted to laugh at the absurdity of the empath's words. She wanted to say, *I'm a little busy right now, being saved by the one thing that wants to kill me more than the wild demons do.* But she had become transfixed by the Toymaker's toys. They had stopped several feet from her and were coalescing, clambering on top of each other. With clinks and scrapes of interconnecting metal, the silver automatons grew into a humanoid figure six feet tall, broad across the shoulders. A framework man, formed from legs and tails and little silver bodies, a hundred violet lights glowing within it. The last *toy* scrambled over the face and clicked into place, leaving a smooth metal disc where a mouth might have been.

The automaton approached the changeling.

Clara's eyelids fluttered. She struggled against the weight that was pushing her mind down but couldn't stop her eyes from closing. Vaguely, she was aware that the Toymaker had reached her, but instead of feeling any pain there was only a curious sensation of rising, as though the automaton had gently lifted her into its arms.

And in the darkness, Marney spoke again. *Come with me, Clara. We have to find Van Bam.*

Hamir had never enjoyed physical exertion, but the only way he could get Lady Amilee out of her dream chamber was by unceremoniously manhandling her.

Waking up had been relatively easy for the necromancer; his mind had spent only a short time in the Skywatcher's dreamscape, whereas Amilee's had spent four decades there while her body remained in stasis. And now, high in the domed observatory of the Tower of the Skywatcher, Lady Amilee could not be woken. She was barely breathing.

The sarcophagus-like dream chamber was deep and Hamir was smaller, frailer than Amilee. He struggled to lift her into a sitting position before heaving her over the lip of the chamber. The limp weight of her body sent them both falling to a heap on the observatory's dusty glass floor.

Hamir worked quickly. He laid Amilee on her back, feeling for the beat of her heart. It was there, just, weak and slow. Through her diaphanous gown, Hamir could see the bones protruding from an undernourished body which had subsisted for too long on higher magic.

Amilee's chest rose and fell, but almost imperceptibly; her eyelids were open but her eyes had rolled to whites; the diamond tattoo on her forehead, deeply black, emphasised the colourlessness of her skin. Hamir had been around death long enough to sense its approach.

He summoned his necromantic magic.

Swirls of black invading the green of his eyes, he placed his hands upon the Skywatcher, infusing her with the warmth of life, holding back the cold that had beset her. Hamir felt the remnants of her thaumaturgy flowing through a sluggish bloodstream like cooling magma from a spent volcano. He pressed his hands to the sides of Amilee's head and searched for her mind. It was confused, lost, struggling to make the journey from the dreamscape it had created back to the real world. Hamir whispered words of magic that came from the grey place where he existed between light and dark, and he blew them gently into Amilee's mouth.

Instantly, a little warmth returned to the cold body. The approaching death receded a little more. A flame of recognition bloomed in Amilee's mind, but it was not enough to wake her. Not yet. It would take a while for the Skywatcher to gather whatever strength remained to her.

Breathing heavily, Hamir sat down. Pushing grey hair back from his face, he cast a pitying gaze over Amilee. They had once called her Treasured Lady of the Thaumaturgists, patron of the Labyrinth, one-third of the Trinity of Skywatchers. She had been glorious. It was a long time since Hamir last saw a creature of higher magic reduced to such a wretched condition.

He looked around the observatory. It was as dull and neglected as it had been before he entered the sleep chamber. High above, the domed ceiling that had at one time been filled with incalculable stars in a host of skies was now mostly empty space, except for the dot of a single sun struggling to shine. The sun blinked a few times and sputtered before its weak light died completely, and nothing but empty space filled the dome.

Hamir noticed a table close by. It hadn't been there before his journey into Amilee's dreamscape. With a frown, he rose and walked to it. Upon the table lay a thick purple robe, neatly folded. The robe of a Thaumaturgist. Next to it was a stone jug of water with two glasses and a wax paper packet. He opened the packet to find slices of nutrition cake.

Pouring himself a glass of water, Hamir smiled wryly before draining it in one go, then picked up a slice of the cake.

'Hello, Alexander,' he said before biting into it. 'Are you here to gawp or will you present yourself?'

Alexander, Lady Amilee's dead Aelfirian aide – his ghost was somewhere close by, observing, haunting the tower, loyal to the Skywatcher even in death. He didn't reply to Hamir, but he did materialise.

Dressed in a three-piece suit similar to Hamir's, the ghost appeared in drab monochrome. His small mouth and nose and large eyes gave his face the traditional Aelfirian shape. His thinning hair made his pointed ears look overly long. Unblinking, eyes brimming with silver tears, the ghost of Alexander stared at the immobile form of his mistress on the floor.

'She has to live,' he said, his voice whispery. 'She must not die.'

'What did you expect, Alexander? That your Lady would arise bright-eyed and bushy-tailed? You must understand that even for a Thaumaturgist, forty years confined to a sleep chamber takes its toll upon body and mind.'

'And what *you* must understand is that you have no idea what I sacrificed to keep her safe. Now, *necromancer*, will she live?'

Hamir scrutinised the dead aide, then looked at the table and its contents which had so mysteriously appeared. 'How did you provide these refreshments?'

Alexander said nothing.

Hamir was aware that ghosts could make physical contact with the corporeal world, throw things, hurt people – he once knew a person who had been scratched by a ghost. But he had never encountered a spirit so strongly connected to the place it haunted that it was able to interact with its environment with the same tactility as a living, breathing being. Unless it had access to magic.

'Alexander, tell me how you died.'

The ghost obviously heard the insinuation in Hamir's tone. 'What I did, I did willingly,' he said with defiance.

'I'm sure you believe that.' Hamir looked down at the Skywatcher's face. 'So many of us do when Lady Amilee is manipulating us. It's a gift of hers.'

'Show respect.'

'I'm only speaking the truth. I've known our good Lady here far longer than you.'

'Yes. And she told me all about you, *Lord* Hamir, disgraced Thaumaturgist, murderer, creator of abominations.'

'The Progenitor – *that* is the name the Nephilim gave me.' Hamir was already bored with the direction of the conversation and cast suspicious eyes about the observatory. 'Where was your body laid to rest, Alexander?'

The ghost stared at him.

'H-Hamir,' Amilee whispered.

Hamir was quickly at the Skywatcher's side, helping her to sit up.

Amilee coughed. Her teeth chattered and shuddery breath rose from her mouth in frosty clouds. She clutched at Hamir, groaning as she attempted to stand, but slipped down onto the floor again.

The necromancer tried to settle her. 'Your body and mind need to adjust. Take your time, my lady.'

'No,' Amilee said hoarsely. 'There *is* no time. Tell me you have it, Hamir. The changeling blood. Clara's blood.'

Hamir pulled a phial from the inside pocket of his jacket. It was filled with Clara's blood, and he had almost forgotten he was carrying it since escaping from the Labyrinth. Thinking that Amilee wished to drink the blood, to let its magical restorative qualities reignite her thaumaturgy, Hamir made to pop the cork with a thumb. But Amilee laid her hand over his and stopped him.

The Skywatcher stared at the ghost of her aide, her tawny eyes welling with tears. Alexander bobbed his head at his master, his expression a mixture of sadness and relief.

'Follow Alexander,' Amilee told Hamir. 'He'll show you what the blood is for.'

CHAPTER THREE

HIGHER MAGIC

When Sergeant Ennis came to, he was tied to a chair. Rope bound his wrists to the armrests and his ankles to the legs. More rope around his midriff secured his body to the back. And he had been gagged.

The last thing Ennis remembered was the Lazy House. He had gone there to find information on the Relic Guild agent Peppercorn Clara. He recalled being set up. He recalled being tricked, drugged and abducted by an ageing criminal and retired magic-user ... Long Tommy.

He wished the grogginess would clear; willed his instincts to return. He tried to work the gag from his mouth and wriggle his arms free but to no avail. Where was his abductor?

Ennis's prison appeared to be a storeroom, workshop and office all in one. There were no windows. Random items which amounted to not much more than bric-a-brac took up one side of the room, stored on shelves and piled on the floor. On the other side, next to a closed door, a workbench stood against the wall. Tools were scattered upon it, along with a big magnifying glass and a collection of strange-looking metal contraptions. Directly in front of Ennis was a battered old desk. Whatever was sitting on the desk was covered with a stained dustsheet.

Ennis reasoned he was being held at Long Tommy's junk shop, the façade he kept in the eastern district behind which he hid his criminal activities.

The door opened and the man himself entered the room. Somewhere in his late sixties, dressed in a plain shirt, trousers and a worn woollen waistcoat, Tommy glared at Ennis with pale eyes. His grey, unshaved face and silver hair gave him an almost ghoulish appearance in the light of the wall-mounted glow lamp.

Tommy stared at Ennis from behind his desk, his eyebrows knitted angrily. He then produced a snub-nosed pistol from a drawer.

'I've been asking around about you,' he said, his voice full of disdain. 'Nobody seems to know you. My police contacts have no idea what you're up to these days. But I've got my suspicions.' Tommy thumbed the pistol's power stone. It whined and glowed. 'You're off the grid, Sergeant Ennis. No one knows you're here. So I'm going to ask you some yes-no questions, and if I smell any horseshit I'll start putting bullets in you. Understand?'

Serious…

Ennis nodded.

'You're working undercover, hunting for the agents of the Relic Guild, right?'

Again, Ennis nodded.

'You've been told that the Relic Guild wants to ruin this town. That they worship the Retrospective and want to feed the denizens to the wild demons, or infect us with this magical virus they carry. Either way, I'm right, aren't I?'

Another nod.

'You believe our new Resident, this mysterious Hagi Tabet, is working day and night to keep her people safe?'

Ennis made to nod, but faltered.

'Ah, there it is,' said Tommy. 'You're beginning to suspect that nothing is as it appears, aren't you, Sergeant?'

Ennis tensed as Tommy aimed the pistol at him.

Frightened…

'Did you know that the heads of the Merchants' Guild were summoned to the Nightshade and no one's seen them since?'

Emphatically, Ennis shook his head.

'Then did you know that the Resident sent her aide and that bloody animal – the *Woodsman* – into the criminal underworld to carve up a few of the bosses?' Tommy practically growled the last question, angrier about the fate of his fellow criminals than anyone in the Merchants' Guild.

Ennis implored with his eyes. He had no knowledge of these events.

'Our Resident is dismembering this society,' Tommy said, closing one eye and peering down the pistol's sight at the police sergeant. 'And I honestly can't make up my mind whose side you're on, Ennis.'

It was impossible to speak through the gag, though Ennis tried, straining against his bonds, willing his captor to not pull the trigger.

'Damn it,' Tommy whispered. He deactivated the power stone and placed the pistol on the table. 'Your trouble is you're too young to remember life before the Genii War. You don't know what it means to be a magicker of the Relic Guild.'

Desperate...

Tommy stared into the distance for a moment before drawing a deep breath. 'Sometimes the magic of the Labyrinth touches a denizen. It gives them a special gift but takes away their choices in life. It wipes out all those sticky obstacles like family and friends and makes damn sure that a magicker has no responsibilities other than duty to the Relic Guild. They make a promise. To protect the denizens of Labrys Town against horrors you've never seen in your life, Ennis, and the crimes of ... people like me.'

Tommy's eyes fixed on his captive. 'The magic of the Labyrinth chooses well. It doesn't make mistakes.' He snorted a bitter laugh. 'The Relic Guild disbanded years ago, decades – that's what you believe. *You* who are too young to remember the old days, the *good* days, before Spiral ripped everything apart and the Thaumaturgists left us trapped behind hundred-foot walls. Ennis, the Relic Guild aren't responsible for what's going on in this town, but you can bet your faith in the Timewatcher that they came back because we needed them to.'

Dipping into the desk drawer again, Tommy produced an item wrapped in a handkerchief and placed it down beside his gun. He unwrapped the handkerchief, exposing a shard of grey metal in the rough shape of a diamond.

This metal was the reason why Ennis had gone to Long Tommy's junk shop in the first place. The shard had come from the remnants of a destroyed contraption the Relic Guild had built in the cellar of a warehouse on the south side. A strange substance, light yet durable, soft and malleable yet strong. It had obviously held some magical property, and so Ennis had taken it to the old crook and magic-user for identification. Evidently, Tommy was none too pleased about what he had discovered.

'Have you ever seen the Resident's aide, Ennis – this ... Lady Asajad?'

Ennis nodded.

'I've been told she has scarring on her forehead. Is that true?'

When Ennis confirmed it, Tommy pulled away the dustsheet to reveal a small device sitting on the desk, simple but odd-looking. It was comprised of a square metal dish with four metal rods that rose from each corner to meet above the dish, giving the device the appearance of a pyramid's skeleton. A powdery substance filled the dish, as white as talcum in the room's dim light.

'I haven't needed one of these in years,' Tommy said, staring at the contraption. 'It's an alchemist's kit. In the old days, I used one to test the magical properties of the artefacts treasure hunters brought to me. Last night, I used it to test that.' He pointed at the metal shard. Tommy sniffed. 'If you want to know how powerful the magic held in a relic is, all you have to do is place the item onto a bed of iron filings.' He pointed at the square dish. 'The metal rods syphon a little of the magic, swirl it around a bit and then send it back down to the metal dish. The dish heats the iron filings and then releases the magic into them. Whatever the magic turns the filings into, that tells you how strong the magic is. And shall I tell you what your piece of metal turned them into?'

Tommy licked the end of his finger and dipped it into the powdery substance. When he lifted his finger to the light, it sparkled like jewels.

'Glass dust,' said Tommy. 'I bet you don't know what that means, do you?'

Ennis shook his head, struggling to swallow, his mind racing.

'It means that what's in that metal is as strong as magic gets.' Tommy was angry; fearful, too. 'I had one or two run-ins with the Relic Guild in the old days. And the last time they paid me a visit was because of ... *shit* like this! That metal is holding higher magic, Ennis. It's thaumaturgy—'

Tommy broke off, disturbed by a blue glow shining in through the door. He snatched up his pistol, primed the power stone and took aim.

'Who's there?' he demanded.

'Just a friend,' replied the calm, gentle voice of a man.

To Ennis's incredulity, a spectre drifted into the room, a ghost in the rough shape of a person made of blue light. Its centre was the colour of twilight, surrounded by an aura of bright sky-blue and tendrils of light that waved in the air like strips of cloth underwater.

'Ah. Looks as though I've arrived just in time,' the ghost said amiably.

The pistol shook in Tommy's hands. He licked his lips nervously and gave Ennis a quick glance. Ennis, wide-eyed, shrugged at his captor, just as perplexed.

'Now then,' the ghost continued, 'Tommy, if you would be so good as to remove Sergeant Ennis's bonds, the three of us really need to talk. I'm afraid to say that something very bad is about to happen to Labrys Town.'

In a chamber somewhere within the maze-like structure of the Nightshade, Hagi Tabet hung on a web of tentacles. The leathery appendages had sprouted from her back and pierced the floor, walls and ceiling, dividing the room in two, holding the Resident of Labrys Town aloft. Tabet's eyes were closed. In her bony hands she held a records device, of a kind – the profound creation that was Known Things.

Upon the smooth, black surface of Known Things, the language of the Thaumaturgists glowed with purple light. Two glass tubes extended from its diamond-shaped body. One had punctured Tabet's temple, lancing her brain; the other went into her mouth and down her throat. Viscous fluid gurgled through both tubes.

Fabian Moor watched Tabet, waiting, flanked by the birdlike frame of Mo Asajad and hulking Viktor Gadreel. Moor shared the anticipation of his fellow Genii; the moment they had been waiting decades for had finally arrived. The air of impatience surrounding them was palpable.

Moor's eyes shifted to the creature standing in the corner of the room. The Woodsman.

The wild demon's hands rested upon the wicked head of its huge woodcutter's axe. Seven feet tall and menacing, its impressive muscles were covered by a host of ugly red gashes crudely stitched with thick twine. Dressed in a leather jerkin and a kilt studded with rusty spikes, its face was a dark triangle at the front of a long, pointed hood. Upon its feet were calf-length boots made from fresh human skin.

The Woodsman cut an imposing figure, yet he was just one of countless other demons inhabiting the Retrospective, all of whom would soon be raised as a single, unstoppable army. But in that moment, Moor was irritated by the Woodsman's presence and stench.

Marshalling calm, Moor focused on Hagi Tabet and the diamond-shaped box in her hands.

Known Things. It felt churlish to refer to it as a mere records device. It had been designed by Iblisha Spiral: he who had been called First Lord of the Thaumaturgists until he rose against the Timewatcher and became Lord of the Genii. Known Things looked to be fashioned from obsidian, but its black, diamond-shaped shell had been crafted from unused time. Aside from the Timewatcher, only Spiral could manipulate the substance of time in this way.

To contain a personal slipstream, a secret timeline in which all of Spiral's plots and plans were hidden – that was the purpose of Known Things. It had enabled Spiral and the Genii to slip the net, blind their Mother and fellow Thaumaturgists to the uprising until it was too late. But not even those great creatures of higher magic had understood just how deep Spiral's plans went. Defeat in the Genii War had always been part of the strategy.

Tabet looked calm, at ease, as the fluid in the glass tubes fed her the information stored inside Known Things, including that which had recently been stolen from the mind of the changeling: the secret location of Oldest Place, the House in which the Timewatcher had imprisoned Lord Spiral.

Impatience getting the better of him, Moor clicked his fingers at the Woodsman. 'You. Come here.'

Without hesitation, the Woodsman presented itself before the Genii, bowing its hooded head.

'You will go into Labrys Town,' Moor told it testily, 'and you will gather food for the Resident. Now.'

The Woodsman straightened, hoisted its axe onto its shoulder and strode from the room. Its subservience only further agitated Moor.

'Is something bothering you, Fabian?' Asajad said in that coldly amused way of hers. 'You sound a trifle vexed.'

Ignoring her comments, Moor addressed Gadreel. 'You claim the agents of the Relic Guild are dead, yet there were only two magickers present at the Cathedral of Doubt and Wonder.'

'The changeling and the blind illusionist,' Gadreel confirmed. 'The wild demons had their way with them.'

'Then one of the magickers is still on the loose.' Moor clenched his teeth as bad memories of an arrogant, surly, gun-wielding human surfaced. 'His name is Samuel, and he is perhaps the most cunning and dangerous of them.'

Gadreel gave a dismissive grunt. 'One human magicker is no threat to us.'

'A long time ago, Viktor, I believed the same thing. I was wrong.'

'Oh, Fabian, *please* get a grip on yourself,' said Asajad. 'Here we are on the cusp of victory and yet your thoughts idle on unimportant matters. This obsession you have with the Relic Guild is as pointless as it is tiresome, and I will listen to it no more!'

'*Lady* Asajad—' Moor growled, but he stopped as Hagi Tabet inhaled a breath.

She shook on her web, her eyes flitting in their sockets as though caught in a dream state. Blood dripped from the glass tube in her temple. Tabet's cracked lips worked at the tube in her mouth and her words came as a sigh from all places at once.

'I have it.' Each word caused the symbols on Known Things to flare. 'I know where Oldest Place is located.'

The razor edge of his irritation blunted by desire, Moor addressed Asajad and Gadreel. 'Do it now,' he ordered.

Without argument, his fellow Genii faced each other and began speaking the quick, breathy language of higher magic. Together, they conjured a portal. It began as a crack in the air from which spilled a shadowy luminescence. Asajad and Gadreel used their thaumaturgy to widen the crack into an oval of churning night six feet tall, swirling in the space between them. As they maintained the spell, Moor used his magic to turn the oval until it faced Tabet.

'Give us the coordinates, Hagi,' Moor demanded.

Tabet strained. One of her tentacles detached itself from the floor with a sound like a cork pulled from a wine bottle. It stretched towards the portal; the reptilian green-brown appendage snaked through the air, almost cautiously approaching the dark surface. Moor's hand flashed out and caught the tentacle. With his other hand, he produced a scalpel and sliced off the end.

Tabet hissed from all places. The stump dripped a brownish sludge as Moor fed it into the portal. A deep drone filling the chamber announced that Tabet was channelling the information of Known Things through the magic of the Nightshade, and she seized control of the thaumaturgy set in motion by her fellow Genii.

Asajad, her hair black and straight as a fall of oil, her smooth, porcelain-pale face expressionless, moved away from the portal; Gadreel, his fat lips twisted into an uncustomary smile, did the same. Together, they stood alongside Moor.

How long had they been dreaming of this moment?

'Now, Hagi,' Moor whispered.

The tentacle became rigid, as hard as iron, and stabbed into the black like a cable of energy. The droning rose in pitch as Tabet fed the portal with the coordinates of Oldest Place. Sparks and flashes of higher magic danced upon the portal's surface. It crackled along the iron-hard tentacle to crawl over Tabet's suspended naked body, and the symbols on Known Things blazed.

Tabet groaned and swayed on her web. When the dancing sparks of thaumaturgy subsided, her voice came from everywhere. 'It is done,' she said and fell limp, exhausted, but clearly pleased with her work.

Moor could feel Asajad's and Gadreel's gazes upon him, but he only had eyes for the gateway to Oldest Place.

'Maintain the portal, Hagi.' Moor's tone had become breathless, excited. 'It is time to bring Lord Spiral home.'

CHAPTER FOUR

ROGUE ELEMENTS

The star of white light hovered in the air ahead of Namji, banishing the darkness as the group followed the spiralling stairs down into the bowels of Little Sibling. Footsteps whispered around the stairwell. Samuel felt the absence of his magic keenly and wished that Clara were present; the wolf's heightened senses would have made a welcome ally in this place.

With one hand clutching the key in his pocket, the other holding his revolver, the old bounty hunter felt the weight of anxiety in his gut. He was inclined to trust that whoever controlled the avatar knew what they were doing – *had* to trust in that – but as usual there were no straight answers, no resolutions to the mysteries the Relic Guild had been dragging with them since escaping the Labyrinth. At least the key gave Samuel a little hope, a direction, a purpose, leading him to whatever secret was kept in the forgotten dungeons.

After a surprisingly long descent, the spiralling stairs ended in a cramped and damp corridor. Samuel stared into the gloom beyond Namji's magical light. The way ahead felt so uncertain without his prescient awareness. Unknowable. Dangerous.

In this confined space, Glogelder swapped his spell sphere launcher for his pistol. 'So what now?' he said, his thick voice echoing.

Samuel pulled the key from his pocket, holding it as though clutching a protective talisman.

'We find something to unlock,' said Namji.

Leading with her pistol crossbow, she followed the light down the corridor, into the dungeons.

The cobbles on the floor were slick. Beneath the low ceiling, the bricks of the walls were thick with dirt. Moss grew in patches. The group passed darkened cells along the way. Decades ago, the dungeons beneath Little Sibling had been used to hold enemy officers captured during the

Genii War. Prisoners had been interrogated, tortured, executed in the cells; but now the cells were empty and their doors were open.

After a short distance, Namji's magical light hovered before a heavy door of thick metal bars stretching from wall to wall, blocking the corridor. Samuel went ahead of the group with the key in his hand. After a quick inspection which revealed no lock that the key might be used for, or hinges upon which a door might swing open, Samuel realised it wasn't a door at all.

'It's a barricade,' he said.

The metal bars were three inches thick, no more than six inches apart. The frame had been welded to metal plates fixed to the walls, floor and ceiling, and then reinforced with a host of heavy-duty bolts. But had it been constructed to keep people out, or to keep something in? Either way, there was no going back now; the Toymaker would be hunting them again soon. If he wasn't already.

Samuel clanged the key against the bars. The metal was coated with rust, but solid. 'I don't have enough acid to create an opening,' he told the group. 'We could try ice-bullets – might make the metal brittle enough to break.'

'No,' Namji said. With a hand gesture, she summoned the star of light, and it zipped back to hang above her head. 'Get behind me,' she told Samuel.

Samuel stood alongside Hillem and Glogelder, watching as Namji aimed her crossbow. She pulled the trigger and the steel string snapped forward. The bolt sliced the air and its glass head smashed upon the floor at the base of the barricade, releasing a spell with the sound of a gale.

Magic created a ball of wispy energy like a storm. The ball wasn't particularly big, reaching only halfway up the barricade and barely touching the walls, but the spell it contained was fierce. The bars began shuddering, and then the magic cut through them. The lower half started bending, folding, melting, as though collapsing under a pressure so heavy, so immensely dense, that it melted metal. The spell took a while to die. And when it had gone, so had the bottom half of the barricade.

'Vacuum magic,' Hillem told Samuel. 'It's one of Namji's own spells. Very effective. Very brutal.'

Beneath the barricade, the spell had also cut a smooth bowl out of the cobbled floor, and in it molten metal steamed as it cooled.

'You don't want to see what it does to a person,' Glogelder commented with a shudder.

'Let's go,' said Namji.

With the star of light once again leading the way, Namji ducked under what remained of the barricade and into the passageway beyond. Samuel went next, Hillem behind him, and Glogelder brought up the rear. More cells lined the walls, each one open and empty.

They continued until the star stopped and its colour turned from white to a deep, ominous orange. The group halted and raised their weapons.

'Wait,' Samuel said. He could see a vague colour touching the edges of the star's warning light. 'Put it out,' he said.

Namji clicked her fingers and the little star fizzed and fell to the floor as a dying ember.

Purple luminescence tinted the air in the corridor, weak, barely lifting the gloom. It came from the last cell on the left, through a viewing hatch set into the one door that was closed.

'This must be it,' Namji said.

Samuel took the black iron key to the cell. The door was made from thick, sturdy wood and he was surprised to find it unlocked already. In fact, the lock was missing altogether. Where it should have been, a large, neat section had been cut out of the door, just below the viewing hatch, roughly a foot square.

Confused, with the key still in his hand, Samuel pushed the door open with the barrel of his revolver. The Aelfir gathered behind him.

Samuel swallowed. 'Stay where you are,' he said, voice tight.

The cell held a prisoner: a woman, naked, with her back to the door, sitting on the floor upon a circular platform of metal. Her body was emaciated, limbs withered, dirty skin stretched tightly over fragile bones. She was unnaturally still. She couldn't be alive. She looked more like a preserved corpse.

Samuel found his courage and entered the cell.

The purple light was radiating from symbols engraved into the metal platform, which formed a strange design of interconnecting shapes and patterns. Samuel had seen this kind of configuration before and a pang from the past formed ice in his gut.

'What is it, Samuel?' Namji said from the doorway. 'Who is she?'

'I don't know.' Samuel pointed at the source of the purple light. 'But those symbols – it's the language of the Thaumaturgists.'

Namji walked into the room for a better look. Samuel raised an arm to prevent her from going past him.

'This is a prison designed to hold a creature of higher magic.' Samuel stared at the back of the emaciated prisoner. 'The light is a thaumaturgic spell. Whatever you do, don't touch the platform.'

Samuel skirted around the big metal disc to the other side of the cell. The Aelfir joined him, and they all gained their first look at the prisoner's face.

She looked as though she hadn't moved or spoken or seen the sun for decades. Hands nestling in her lap, she stared up at the ceiling, the dead and dry milky orbs of her eyes coated in dust. A toothless mouth hung slack. The leathery skin of her stomach lay in folds. Breasts and ribcage had been removed and her skin had sealed around the missing square of the cell door, cruelly embedded into her chest, complete with an old, black iron lock.

Samuel clutched the key in a fist, staring at the patch of scarring upon the woman's forehead.

'Genii,' he whispered, mouth dry.

'Bugger me.' Glogelder aimed his pistol at the prisoner. 'Tell me what to do.'

'Put your gun down and keep your distance,' Samuel snapped.

'Oh, shit,' said Namji. 'What is going on?'

'Is she dead?' asked Glogelder.

'She doesn't look particularly alive,' Hillem answered.

'How can we be sure?' Glogelder sounded disturbed. 'Maybe we should go back for a while, wait for Samuel's magic to return.'

Namji shook her head. 'There's no time.'

'I'm not sure it would make a difference, anyway,' Samuel growled. 'The last time I faced a Genii, my magic didn't acknowledge the threat he posed.'

There was a moment of silence, and then Hillem said, 'How long do you think she's been here?'

'You tell me.' Samuel looked from the lock in the prisoner's chest to the key in his hand. 'This has to be—'

The Genii drew a ragged breath. The group jumped back as one, aiming their weapons.

The Genii blinked rapidly and her withered eyes spilled tears down her hollow cheeks; her limbs and body shuddered into movement, bones cracking, skin rubbing on skin like ancient parchment. The Genii drew several more short, harsh breaths as though preparing to sneeze, but then she released a scream with the fury of a thousand wild demons.

'Timewatcher save us!' Glogelder shouted. 'What is this?'

The Genii's scream died. She pinched her eyes shut, sobbing in pain. Her wasted form shook so violently that Samuel wondered if she would break apart. The shaking stopped abruptly and her eyes snapped open, black as night and deadly, glaring at the group.

'You took your time,' she croaked from her toothless mouth.

'What about now?' Glogelder said. 'Can I shoot her now?'

The Genii huffed a laugh. She tried and failed to moisten cracked, colourless lips with a tongue as dry and rough as sandpaper.

Samuel pushed down the aim of Glogelder's pistol and motioned for Hillem to do the same.

'Who are you?' he demanded with confidence he didn't feel.

'What does it matter, human?' She tilted her head and one of her hands moved to the lock in her chest. 'Just give me the key.'

Samuel glanced back at the others. Namji shook her head.

'*This* is why you're here?' Samuel said, gesturing at the Genii with the key.

'And I've been waiting for it since the end of the war.' She looked confused. 'How long has it been?'

No one answered her.

'Give me the key,' the Genii pleaded. 'It's the only way to release me.'

'Not bloody likely,' Glogelder growled.

'I tend to agree,' Hillem added.

'Why would I release you?' said Samuel.

'Because your journey ends here if you don't.' The Genii smacked her lips a few times and raised bony hands to her face, working jaw muscles that hadn't been used for years. 'There's no going back. Only forward now.'

Feeling more uncertain than ever, Samuel was glad when Namji moved alongside him.

'Who imprisoned you?' she said.

'Who do you think?' The skeletal face tried to pull an expression of disgust. 'That self-righteous Skywatcher. *Amilee.*'

'Amilee?' Samuel resisted the urge to back away. He shared a look with Namji.

'She trapped me here and spared me from execution at the end of the war. Nice of her, don't you think? Wish she'd just let me die with the others.'

'Why did she do this to you?' Namji asked.

Beetle-shell eyes blinked at the Aelf. 'If you can be this dim-witted in a simple conversation, I very much doubt you'll survive what comes next.'

Bewildered, angry, frightened, Samuel willed confidence to fill the void of his dampened magic. He summoned his experiences, drew strength from his long years of service to the Relic Guild; the stolen relics and artefacts he had tracked, the countless criminals he had interrogated, the host of unlikely situations he had escaped to complete a plethora of missions on the Nightshade's behalf. And a calm settled on the old bounty hunter. Cold as winter.

'If you want this key,' Samuel told the Genii in an even tone, 'you'd better answer my questions. *Why* did Amilee put you here? *What* happens next?'

The prisoner closed her eyes. Dust-filled tears struggled to run down her cheeks, silver in the purple glow of thaumaturgy.

'To forget who I was, but to know what I am, that's why the Skywatcher keeps me here.' She tried to cackle but resorted to huffing sobs instead. 'I remember things sometimes ... many things.' She leaned forward, staring up at the magicker with an imploring expression, though her eyes remained emotionless black holes in her face. 'At one time they called me Lady ... but now I am the Icicle Forest.'

Samuel recoiled as though the Genii's words had slapped his face with bad memories. 'What did you say?'

'I am the doorway.'

Samuel stared, his mouth working but his words missing.

'The Icicle Forest,' Namji wondered. 'I've never heard of it.'

'Nor have I,' Hillem admitted.

'Shut up, both of you.' Samuel's teeth were gritted at the Genii. 'What do you know about the Icicle Forest?'

'I know it will give me death.' She dropped her voice to a whisper. 'The doorway is hiding inside me. Amilee put it there. Give me the key and I'll let you in.'

Samuel looked at the square of wood and the black iron lock that had been so cruelly set into the Genii's chest; then he looked at the key in his hand. *Doorway?* Did she mean there was a portal *inside* her? Was that possible, even with higher magic?

'Why?' Samuel said. 'Why would we want to go *there?*'

'Because everyone dies if you don't.' The Genii twisted her gummy maw into a hideous rictus. 'Only by going to the Icicle Forest can you help your missing friends to kill Spiral.'

Samuel's thoughts raced to Van Bam and Clara. 'What does that mean?'

'The Skywatcher said that some truths are hidden from the skies. There is a rogue element, a missing piece to your puzzle. Unless you find it, you can never hope to use the secrets of Known Things.'

Another blade of winter stabbed at Samuel. 'What do you know about Known Things?'

'I ... I don't remember.'

'Then what is the missing piece? What *rogue element?*'

'It is trapped in the Icicle Forest.'

Samuel flushed with anger. 'Speak plainly!'

'I can tell you no more, human, and your time is running out. Give me the key and I will open the door for you.'

The key's teeth bit into Samuel's palm.

'Giving her that thing doesn't sound like a good idea to me,' Glogelder said.

Namji shushed him. 'What do you think, Samuel?'

'Please,' the Genii sobbed. 'The Skywatcher's message is all I have to give you.' A line of drool dripped into her lap. 'I no longer care about Spiral or the Timewatcher or anyone else ... I just want release. Give me the key or you all die.'

Samuel felt a nudge from his magic.

It wasn't much, still only an ember of its usual fire, but enough to steer his gut instincts, to convince him that bad things would happen if the group didn't move forwards. And there was only one way to achieve that.

'No choice,' he told the Aelfir, and he threw the key into the glowing prison.

'Samuel,' Namji hissed.

Too late.

The black metal sparked as it entered the thaumaturgic light and clanged onto the metal disc a few inches from the prisoner. Clawed fingers tipped with dirty, cracked nails grabbed for the key. A desperate sort of triumph came to the Genii's face as withered arms lifted her prize and a trembling hand slid the head into the lock in her chest. She turned the key with a *clunk* that shook her frail body.

The Genii closed black eyes.

A long breath gurgled from her slack mouth as she slumped. The light radiating from the thaumaturgic symbols shrank into the centre of the disc, intensifying, surrounding the prisoner in a column of purple that stretched from floor to ceiling.

'Get back,' Samuel warned.

The others didn't need telling twice. They followed the old bounty hunter's example until each of them stood with backs flat to the wall, weapons aimed at the prisoner.

Within the column of purple light, the Genii's body collapsed in on itself, as though what little moisture remained to her had instantly evaporated. She crumbled like a dying golem, bones and flesh and muscle becoming a pile of dried organic matter in a few short seconds. The lock disappeared beneath her remains. The Genii's face was the last part of her to collapse; and as it did so, her toothless mouth warped into what looked like a perverse smile of relief.

The Genii's remains began to swirl within the column, slowly at first, then with increased ferocity as though caught by a violent wind. The storm moaned and howled then began to coalesce. The purple glow of thaumaturgy flared with violet light so dazzling that Samuel and the Aelfir had to cover their eyes.

When the light died, the symbols of thaumaturgy carved into the metal had ceased glowing altogether. But within the circle now stood a monument made from compacted organic matter resembling an archway of bone. Within the archway, thick white mist roiled with the sound of a lonely wind.

Samuel stared into the Nothing of Far and Deep, the weight of his revolver in his hand giving him little comfort.

'*Shit*,' he said, his fear returning, wishing more than ever that Van Bam was with him. 'What is going *on*!'

Although Samuel shouted the last word, his colleagues remained silent, tense, until Glogelder said, 'Someone's going to have to explain this to me.'

'Me, too,' Hillem added.

Samuel said nothing and glared at the portal.

'This is good news,' Namji announced, gesturing to the Nothing of Far and Deep almost excitedly. 'This is what the avatar wanted us to find. Lady Amilee left it here. The avatar's master must be the Skywatcher. A Thaumaturgist stayed after the war. She's been helping us.'

'Yeah ... Lady Amilee,' Samuel said, his voice hollow. 'And she wants us to go to the Icicle Forest. I wouldn't be so happy about that, if I were you.'

'Why not?' said Hillem. 'What *is* the Icicle Forest?'

Samuel rubbed at the indent of the key still engraved on his palm. 'Namji, do you remember how Fabian Moor got into the Labyrinth during the Genii War?'

She was quiet for a moment. 'Ursa,' she replied.

'Moor did terrible things to himself to gain access to the Labyrinth,' Samuel said for the benefit of Hillem and Glogelder. 'His physical form was reduced to ashes, to his *essence*, and stored in a terracotta jar, where he was safely hidden from detection. A group of treasure hunters found that jar and brought it into Labrys Town, and an Aelf from Mirage called Ursa was stupid enough to open it.

'Moor's essence was reanimated by blood. By the same process he brought the last of the Genii back, and continuing to drink blood is the only way Moor and his cronies can stay alive now.' Samuel looked at Namji. 'But did you ever hear where those treasure hunters found the terracotta jar containing Moor's essence?'

Namji began to shake her head, but then she looked at the portal. 'The Icicle Forest?'

Samuel confirmed the answer with silence.

'So what is it?' Glogelder asked. 'A House?'

Samuel shrugged. 'I think only the Genii know for sure. There were rumours that Spiral created secret strongholds in the Nothing of Far and Deep, but they were supposed to have been destroyed during the war.'

'Evidently, at least one survived,' said Hillem.

'So what if it's one of Spiral's strongholds?' Namji said. 'Amilee wouldn't send us there if the Genii were still using it.'

'Listen to me.' Samuel rubbed his forehead. 'Years ago, Van Bam and I met one of the treasure hunters who went to the Icicle Forest. He was the only survivor of that trip. Just before he died, he said it was a savage place – *evil* – and you really don't want to know about the wounds he sustained there.'

Nobody spoke. Samuel's heartbeat was loud in his ears. The lonely wind of the Nothing of Far and Deep moaned from the portal.

'You all heard what the Genii said.' Namji's voice sounded strong, resolute. 'This is to do with Known Things. What if Van Bam and Clara are there, waiting for us? What if *they* are this rogue element?'

With a noise of frustration, Samuel opened the chamber on his revolver and emptied it of ammunition.

'I'll tell you this much,' he said darkly, replacing the regular metal slugs with fire-bullets from his utility belt. 'There's no way I'm walking into the Icicle Forest until my magic comes back.'

THE GHOUL

There were four Aelfirian soldiers standing guard, one at each corner of the cold and grey observation room. With rifles hanging from their shoulders, dressed in dark grey army uniforms, they stood to attention, barely moving, never speaking. Their faces were concealed behind black masks with dark-lensed goggles which hid their eyes.

They reminded Marney of giant ants.

Surrounded by the soldiers, Marney sat next to Denton at a sturdy metal table. Behind them, the room's only door was closed; in front of them, the entire back wall was an observation window. The glass had been misted to the colour of storm clouds, and nothing could be seen of the interrogation cell on the other side.

Marney looked at Denton. He faced the observation window, hands clasped together on the table before him. His expression was calm but Marney could sense that he was controlling his anxiety behind a magical shield, just as she was.

Somewhere around a week had passed since Marney and Denton first set off from the Labyrinth. It was difficult to be certain, though; time didn't flow at equal speeds through the Aelfirian Houses. Sometimes jumping from one House to another meant stepping from morning into night, and night into morning. Marney had lost all concept of time on this strange mission to find a fabled realm called the Library of Glass and Mirrors, a dangerous House where the histories of the past, present and future were kept.

She looked at the soldiers. There was nothing aggressive in their statue-like postures, but they had been ordered to detain the empaths. The trouble was, Marney couldn't read them. They were dead to her magic.

Those masks shield them from us, Denton had explained earlier. *They're protected from any magic that affects them mentally – empathy, telepathy, illusions … I don't know what's going on here, Marney, but we'd need thaumaturgy to get past those masks and question these soldiers.*

Here was Cradle of the Rise. The battle had been won in this House almost immediately prior to Marney's and Denton's arrival, but the empaths were detained the instant they emerged from the portal. For their protection, a faceless officer had said from behind a mask. But it hadn't rung true. The Timewatcher's army had defeated Spiral's Genii. Cradle of the Rise was victorious. Yet this did not feel like a House celebrating victory. Anything but.

I don't like it, Denton.

Me neither. The old empath didn't take his eyes off the observation window. *Something is very wrong in this House.*

But we're so close to the end.

Keep faith, Marney.

The journey so far had taken the empaths through many Houses. For the most part they had travelled without hindrance, but the war between the Timewatcher and Spiral had been an ever-present threat around them. Sometimes they clipped the war, protected by the Timewatcher's Aelfirian armies. Occasionally they found themselves in the heart of the fighting, and Marney had seen and done things that she desperately wanted to forget. But always they had kept moving forwards, searching for the portal that would deliver them to the Library of Glass and Mirrors.

However, most people believed the Library to be a myth, a story, a lie; such a mysterious place did not have an entrance at the end of a well-travelled path. Its portal was hidden, and to find it the empaths had been navigating what Denton called the Way of the Blind Maze: an ancient mode of travelling much like finding the combination to a lock. By passing through carefully selected Houses and portals in a specific sequence, the portal to the Library would eventually reveal itself.

Frustratingly, from Cradle of the Rise the empaths were due to travel to the Burrows of Underneath, where, according to Denton, the portal to the Library of Glass and Mirrors would appear to them. Whatever obstacle the agents of the Relic Guild had hit in this penultimate stage of their journey, it felt a little too final for Marney's tastes.

The door opened. A small middle-aged Aelf walked in carrying Marney's and Denton's backpacks. He did not wear a protective mask. The four soldiers snapped to attention and saluted him, almost in unison. The Aelf spared the empaths a glance, a distinct lack of good humour in his large eyes, before addressing the soldiers.

'If any of you ever claims to have seen me, I'll ensure you *disappear*.' It was no idle threat. 'Now get out.'

Without hesitation, the soldiers followed the order. The Aelf locked the door behind them and then placed the backpacks on the table before the empaths. Marney noted that his dark grey uniform was plain, unadorned by any insignia of rank. His hair was thinning, his face careworn. Emotions were weak, fluctuating, impossible for Marney to read.

A satchel hung from his shoulder. He shrugged it off and placed it on the table between the backpacks.

'It is in your best interests to remain silent,' he said. He opened the satchel and pulled out a small wooden box. 'Please, say nothing.'

Leaving the box on the table, the Aelf turned away and walked up to the observation window. He stood before the misted glass with his hands clasped behind his back.

I think it's best if we do as he says, Marney.

Who do you think he is? Marney asked.

Judging by the authority he commands and lack of rank on his uniform, I'd guess he's secret service. Denton sounded intrigued.

Does that make him an ally or an enemy?

Whichever he needs to be, I should imagine. Denton peered closely at the small wooden box. *Let's just see where this leads.*

Denton took his backpack and placed it on the floor beside his chair. Marney did the same, but looked inside hers. She was comforted to find her baldric of throwing daggers sitting at the top, along with an envelope, which she pulled out, holding it tightly.

Denton had given Marney the envelope at the beginning of their journey. It contained coded instructions for their mission – which was to say, everything that Marney hadn't been told about it. At the beginning, she had thought they were searching for information on the Icicle Forest, but she came to learn that there was much, much more to their mission. However, it was too dangerous for Marney to know exactly why Lady Amilee was sending them to the Library of Glass and Mirrors. Denton knew, however; and the only time Marney was to open the envelope was if he fell along the way.

Marney hated that she had been kept in the dark but trusted her mentor. She had witnessed people die to protect the secrets inside that envelope. She herself had killed to keep them unknown to anyone other than Denton. But unless they could leave Cradle of the Rise for the Burrows of Underneath, the envelope's contents were academic. The mission ended here, in this room.

Denton was watching Marney. *Please tell me it is unopened*, he said.

Marney showed him the unbroken wax seal on the envelope before sliding it into the leg pocket of her fatigues. She felt Denton's relief.

'This war has changed much,' said the Aelf, his back still to the empaths. 'Nothing will ever be the same again.'

He placed a hand against the observation window. There was a brief, low drone and the misty effect began to clear from the glass, fading away until it gave a view into the detention cell. And its occupant.

Marney's breath caught.

The prisoner was female. Human-looking, not Aelf. She hovered in the air above a circular metal platform inscribed with a host of strange interconnecting symbols and glyphs that Marney didn't recognise.

The language of the Thaumaturgists, Denton said in awe. *It's a prison formed from higher magic.*

The symbols glowed with purple radiance. The woman hovered on her back above them, turning slowly in their thaumaturgic glare, her arms and legs hanging limp. She wore the dark cassock of a priest, but when her upside-down face came in line with the window, Marney saw the patch of scarring on her forehead that identified her as a Genii.

Marney felt her empathic control slip. *Denton, only a Thaumaturgist is powerful enough to imprison a Genii like this.*

I know.

Marney swallowed. The last time she and Denton had met a Thaumaturgist, it had almost put an end to their mission. Hopefully whoever had created this prison was long gone from Cradle of the Rise.

'It's a rare thing, you know,' said the Aelf, 'to catch a Genii alive.' He remained facing the window. His tone of voice was soft, calm yet commanding. He gestured to the prisoner. 'This is Lady Jubilee. For a creature of higher magic, she was remarkably easy to overcome. So easy, in fact, that I was suspicious of a trap at first. But I think, in the end, she believed too much in her own power. Complacency was her downfall.'

The Aelf turned from the window and faced the empaths. His thinning, unruly hair and pointed ears were highlighted against the purple glow coming from the interrogation chamber. His large eyes were full of secrets.

'I have learned that Spiral's armies tell tales of me,' he said. 'To them, I am a myth, the monster in the shadows waiting to snatch them from their beds. They call me the Ghoul.' He sounded pleased. 'Fear is vastly destructive to an army, and I might be guilty of fanning the flames of my myth.

'The truth, however, is that I am a covert operative in the Timewatcher's army. I hide on the periphery, watching and listening, waiting for special little moments like these.' He looked back at Lady Jubilee in her thaumaturgic prison. 'In this regard, I am not unlike an agent of the Relic Guild.'

He didn't say this to elicit a reaction from the empaths; he was simply stating fact. The Aelf – the Ghoul – was obviously a man of resolve, hardened by the war.

He continued, 'My job is to gather intelligence and then decide how best to use it against the enemy. I have orders to transport Lady Jubilee to the last place she will ever see. And there, before she faces her final fate, she *will* tell me everything she knows of Spiral's plans.

'I answer to very few people in this war. No one stands in my way, my methods are never questioned, and those who are allowed to *see* me very rarely meet a good end.' It wasn't said as a threat. 'Officially, I am not here. Officially, neither are you.'

The Ghoul stared in silence at the box on the table.

Marney, can you read his emotions?

Only a little, Marney replied. *He's been trained to hide what he's thinking and feeling from magickers.*

But he knows that training would offer no defence if we decided to use our magic to control him. He's not carrying a weapon, either. He clearly knows who we are and he's happy for us to see him, *as he puts it.*

Marney considered for a moment. *He's telling us we can trust him? Let's hope so.*

The Ghoul drew a breath. 'Lady Jubilee's misfortune brought me to Cradle of the Rise, and lucky for you that it did. For the last few days my network has been whispering about two human magickers drifting through the Houses, when the war was supposed to have confined *all* humans to the Labyrinth.' He eyed the empaths shrewdly. 'Yet no one appears to know what they are doing, or where they are going.'

But he does? Marney said.

He certainly knows something, Denton replied.

Lady Jubilee's mouth hung open, as if releasing a moan of anguish.

'The Timewatcher and the Thaumaturgists have gained the advantage in the war,' the Ghoul said. 'Our triumph in Cradle of the Rise is just one of many recent victories and Spiral's position is growing weaker by the day. There are plans afoot for a mass offensive, an operation we're calling the Last Storm. It will happen soon, I believe, and the Genii are no longer strong enough to stand against it.' His face darkened. 'However, the Lord of the Genii still has a sting in his tail.'

He turned back to the window. 'It would appear that certain Houses have been subjugated by the Genii in secret. Spiral has been using them to hide reserve forces. One such House is Mirage.'

Marney had to stop herself swearing aloud. House Mirage ... Van Bam and Angel had been sent there on a mission.

Under the table, Denton gripped her hand. *Don't assume the worst,* he told her. *Let's hear what else he has to say.*

'Under the command of a Genii named Lord Buyaal, Mirage became active and launched a surprise invasion on its neighbour. The Burrows of Underneath.' He looked back over his shoulder. 'I'm sure you don't need me to tell you the strategic significance of this House.'

Marney could sense Denton holding back a barrage of questions. She pushed down her own rising sense of panic and squeezed her mentor's hand.

'The Burrows of Underneath might not be completely lost but we can take no risks,' the Ghoul continued. 'We have heard nothing from the Thaumaturgist who was in command there and reports from the few soldiers who made it to us drew a very bleak picture. Therefore, all portals that lead from the Burrows of Underneath to allied Houses have been sealed. And that would include the portal in Cradle of the Rise.'

Marney looked at Denton, but the old empath's eyes were fixed on the Aelf.

The Ghoul added, 'If anyone wished to travel to the Burrows of Underneath from here, they would need powerful magic to break into that portal now. *Higher* magic, I should imagine.'

The Aelf laid his hand on the observation window and a brief drone filled the room. Lady Jubilee jerked in her prison as though she had been shocked, and then the glass became the colour of storm clouds once again.

'I have orders to take you into custody,' the Ghoul said, facing the empaths. 'However, for the time being, I have decided that you cannot yet *see* me.'

He approached the table, slipping a leather wallet from his trouser pocket. 'You and I share a benefactor who outranks the few commanding officers who outrank *me*.' He placed the wallet on top of the wooden box.

Marney recognised it: Denton's sigil wallet. It contained a plate of magical metal. If the right person touched that metal, it would show a diamond inside a circle engraved into its surface: the sigil of Lady Amilee the Skywatcher.

Denton took the wallet and the Ghoul opened the box. Inside was a spell sphere filled with a magical liquid alive with scintillating lights.

The Aelf picked it up. 'I'm told this spell will last for only a brief time.' And he hurled the sphere at the wall behind Marney and Denton.

A noise as if the air had been sucked from the room made Marney's ears pop. The large circle of a portal had appeared on the wall, although it was not like any portal Marney had seen before. It stretched away like a cave filled with rainbow-coloured jewels, illuminated by streaks of pale lightning clashing and dancing in a network of energy. The only sound was a vague hissing.

'I'm going to step outside for a few moments,' the Ghoul said, his expression and voice full of warning. 'If you are still in this room when I return, then you will *see* me. Good luck.'

And with that, the Aelf left the observation room.

In his wake, Marney and Denton shared a look before returning their eyes to the portal.

A shared benefactor? Marney thought to her mentor. *Amilee.*

Denton got to his feet. *Time to get out of this House,* he said. *Take only what you need, leave nothing that identifies us or the mission.*

With the envelope of instructions already in her pocket, Marney pulled her baldric of throwing knives from her backpack and slipped it on.

Denton was staring into the depths of the portal. *Marney, I have no idea what we're about to head into.*

Marney stood alongside him, her emotions locked down tight. *Let's go and find out.*

Early morning and the sun had finally cleared the boundary wall. Mist rose above Labrys Town. The air smelled fresh and clean. For now.

Samuel climbed up a fire escape to the apartment above a baker's shop. Reaching the top, he found the apartment window unlocked. He opened it and climbed inside. Scented smoke greeted his nostrils.

It wasn't much of an apartment: a cheap and dingy dwelling on the east side of town – just a small bedroom and a smaller bathroom. The floorboards were bare and unfinished, the paint on the walls old and peeling. Brown water stains decorated the ceiling. A dressing table had been fashioned from recycled packing crates. The bed with its thin mattress looked about ready to collapse, as did the chair sitting next to it.

The bed had been used recently. Upon the dressing table an incense stick burned. Samuel watched the lazy coils of scented smoke drifting up to the stained ceiling.

Some people believed that smoke would guide the spirits of the dead to Mother Earth and the loving embrace of the Timewatcher. It was an Aelfirian custom and a pointless superstition as far as Samuel was concerned; it only served to make the living feel less guilty about surviving friends and loved ones. But Samuel knew of at least one person who would buy into the concept.

'I know you're here, Van Bam,' he said to the room. 'Do you really want to play this game with me?'

The illusionist didn't reveal himself and Samuel sighed into the silence.

No one had seen Van Bam for the better part of four days, not since he returned from a mission to House Mirage with news of Angel's death. Van Bam blamed himself for what had happened to Angel, and even Gideon had allowed him space and solitude in which he could grieve. But now the wheels of the Relic Guild were turning again and Van Bam was needed.

'I'm not going anywhere,' Samuel said, sitting on the windowsill and folding his arms. 'We've got a mission.'

Silence.

It wasn't surprising that the illusionist had chosen to seek refuge in this apartment. Although Samuel had never been there before, he knew what it was used for. Against their better judgement, Van Bam and Marney had become lovers and this was their secret nest. To find it, Samuel had to track Van Bam's spirit. He'd found a hair in the illusionist's chamber in the Nightshade and used it in the spirit compass. And considering that Van Bam shaved his head, Samuel really didn't want to know which part of him the hair had come from.

Van Bam and Marney had tried to keep their relationship secret from their fellow agents but everyone in the Relic Guild knew, including Gideon, who was never going to be happy about a romantic tryst between his agents. This dreary apartment was a private space where the lovers could meet away from the prying eyes of the Nightshade; where they could feel … normal?

With their duties to the Relic Guild of paramount importance and Gideon looking over their shoulders, Van Bam and Marney's relationship was doomed to fail. Samuel couldn't understand why anyone would wish to pursue such a pointless exercise.

Although, he had to admit, he wished Marney were here now. She would know how to deal with Van Bam's grief.

It didn't matter to the illusionist that his survival had saved the Labyrinth from invasion; he took no satisfaction from the fact he had exposed Mirage and the Genii who controlled the desert House. All that mattered to him was his guilt; he had made it home while Angel had not.

Samuel didn't know what he could say to Van Bam to help him through this, but he did wonder how many more Relic Guild agents would die before this war was over.

Samuel's eyes lingered on the burning incense stick for a moment, and then he looked pointedly at the rickety chair beside the bed.

'Should I light a stick for Gene as well?' he said, a little unkindly. 'Would you feel better if we grieved together?'

There was a light, glassy chime and Van Bam materialised, sitting in the chair with his green glass cane lying across his lap.

'I watched her die, Samuel.' His eyes were puffy, the whites blood-shot, as though he hadn't slept for a while. Stubble grew on his head. 'I promised to get us both back home, but I left her behind.'

Samuel could've told Van Bam that he had been the one to put Gene out of his misery. He could've excused himself by explaining how the elderly, harmless apothecary had been infected by Fabian Moor's magical virus; explained that there was no cure for the virus, and the only way to stop Gene from becoming a bloodthirsty animal who would spread the disease had been to put a bullet through his head. He could've told Van Bam how that incident was plaguing his nightmares every time he slept. But he didn't. He didn't know how to talk about it, even if he wanted to.

'Angel knew the risks of the job,' Samuel said instead. 'She served the Relic Guild for a lot longer than you and me.'

'And telling me that proves what, Samuel?' Apparently there were no tears left in Van Bam, only futile anger. 'What does it change?'

'Nothing.' Samuel summoned what tact he could muster. 'Seems to me you beat the odds to get home, Van Bam. This Genii in Mirage – Buyaal, was his name? Do you think any of us would've fared better against a creature of higher magic? Yes, Angel died, but that's always the risk for us. You stopped Spiral's army invading Labrys Town. Angel's death saved a lot of lives.'

'You were not there,' Van Bam replied, his voice mournful. 'You do not understand what happened.'

'Then explain it to me, Van Bam.'

'I cannot. I ... I have been ordered not to discuss it.'

'Fine.' The Relic Guild was founded upon secrets, even between its agents, and Samuel had long ago given up questioning that fact. 'It's time to come back to us.'

Van Bam stared at him for a long time. He made to speak, stopped, and then finally said, 'Has there been any news of Denton?' A pause. 'And Marney?'

Samuel shook his head. 'We're not allowed to talk about them, either. We don't know where they are or what they're doing. And I think that includes Gideon.'

Samuel couldn't stand the sorrow etched into Van Bam's face and averted his gaze, looking at the incense stick again.

'Look – Fabian Moor is our prisoner and he's going nowhere. Hamir can't get him to talk but his deeds are still playing out in town. We also have a new informant – a lowlife from the eastern district called Long Tommy. I went to see him this morning and he had some worrying information. I need your help, Van Bam.'

Red eyes fixed on the floor, Van Bam nodded.

'I'll wait for you outside.'

Samuel climbed through the window. He paused, straddling the ledge, looking at the illusionist. Two agents dead, two more missing – it felt like the Relic Guild was on the back foot, even though they had Moor in custody.

'I know how you're feeling, Van Bam.' Samuel was surprised to hear the genuine sympathy rise in his voice. 'I ...' Not really knowing what he had intended to say, Samuel stepped out onto the fire escape. 'Don't keep me waiting,' he said, before heading down to the alley below.

A slender silver blade sighed across the square and stabbed into a soldier's throat, just below his black mask. Choking, he fell and died, but not before squeezing off a few rounds from his rifle, shooting his fellow soldier in the legs. She screamed, dropping like a lead weight to the rubble-strewn ground. Marney slid another dagger from her baldric but she didn't get the chance to use it.

The soldier's survival instincts had cut through her pain. She crawled behind her fallen comrade, rolling his corpse onto its side. The barrel of her rifle appeared over the makeshift barrier, and with a bellow of rage from behind her mask, she began firing at Marney. The rifle's power stone flashed with bursts of thaumaturgy, shooting bullets with a low and hollow spitting sound.

Marney rushed back the way she had come, following the crumbling wall of a tavern. Bullets cracked the stonework behind her. She made it to a hole that used to be one of the tavern's windows and dived through, landing painfully on the debris inside. Scrambling to her feet, she pressed herself against the wall next to the broken window, turning away sharply as a bullet sent a spray of stone chips towards her face.

The shooting stopped and Marney took steadying breaths, keeping her emotions locked down behind a magical shield of apathy.

The Ghoul, the mysterious Aelf, had warned the empaths that they were heading into hostile territory, but they hadn't been given a chance to adjust to their change of environment. After Lady Amilee's portal had broken them into the Burrows of Underneath, Marney and Denton immediately faced seven enemy soldiers guarding the portal and the empaths had been separated. The appearance of humans had spooked the soldiers. While Marney managed to escape their clutches, Denton had been captured. The soldiers then abandoned their post, fleeing into the city and taking the old empath with them as a hostage.

Marney closed her eyes and called out for her mentor. *Denton! Denton, where are you?*

Silence. He wasn't close enough to contact mentally and he was getting further away with each passing moment.

From outside, Marney heard the wounded soldier shouting into some kind of transmitter, begging for assistance. Her voice was surprisingly clear through the mask. She cursed viciously, obviously receiving no reply.

Marney needed a plan and quick. She was pinned down, and unless the soldier removed her protective mask she was impervious to empathic magic.

The tavern was in ruins, much like everything else Marney had seen so far in the Burrows of Underneath. Most of the wall opposite her had fallen down, giving her a view of the road that led back to the portal to Cradle of the Rise. No point trying to return there. On the floor, the bodies of two more dead soldiers lay upon the debris of broken stone and plaster, splintered wood and smashed glass. The hilt of a silver dagger protruded from the throat of one; another winked from the lens of the other's goggles.

Marney had killed three soldiers so far. That left the one outside and the three who had abducted Denton.

If Marney allowed herself to feel anything, she was sure it would be despair. The Burrows of Underneath was comprised of a series of huge interconnecting cities within what appeared to be a world-sized subterranean House, home to a hundred million Aelfir. But this city – whatever its name was – felt empty, deserted. There was no trace of emotions at all, as though every living being had been removed. Although that would make *feeling* for Denton easier, if the soldiers took him too far away – to another city, or through a portal that led to Spiral's allies – Marney might lose him for ever.

Gritting her teeth, Marney gathered her daggers, cleaning the blood off them before sliding them into the baldric. She crouched down beside the corpse closest to her. She decided against taking the rifle; she had never been any good with guns. Lifting a protective flap on the soldier's utility belt revealed three small spell spheres about the size of grapes. She selected one and shook it. The clear substance inside emitted the faint glow of magic.

The mask worn by the soldier out in the square protected her against magical manipulation but not from a magical blast. Marney narrowed her eyes at the spell sphere, trying to decide what kind of spell it held. Offensive? Defensive?

'Only one way to find out,' she whispered.

Standing with her back to the wall again, Marney took a deep breath, counted to three and then rounded into the gap in the brickwork, hurling the spell sphere in the general direction of her assailant. She ducked out of the way as the soldier returned fire. The bullets cracked harmlessly against the wall. Marney heard the tinkle of shattering glass, followed by the drone of a released spell, and then ... silence. Unnatural silence.

Marney risked a look outside.

The soldier was on her knees, rifle discarded, surrounded by a dome of translucent energy. She ripped away her mask, revealing an Aelfirian face expressing abject agony. She covered her ears with her hands and threw back her head in a silent scream. Blood poured through her fingers as she succumbed to some kind of sonic explosion.

Marney watched while the solider wept tears of blood and more showered from her nose. She died and toppled onto the corpse of her fellow solider. Feeling nothing, Marney waited for the dome of sonic magic to exhaust itself.

High above, a strange sky – if the Burrows of Underneath could truly claim to have a sky – rolled with dull crimson fog, thick as dirty smoke, forming an uninterrupted blanket of cloud. Colossal, jagged rock formations protruded from the fog like the peaks of a mountain range clinging to the ceiling of a monumental cavern. The atmosphere was humid and heavy, and Marney felt crushed by the vastness of this House.

Again she tried to contact Denton. Again he didn't reply. Her hand moved to the leg pocket on her fatigues, feeling for the envelope inside. Had the moment arrived? Was it time to open the envelope, memorise the instructions and continue the mission alone? Was it time to give up on her mentor?

Marney's empathic magic flared strongly, deadening her emotions so completely that to most people she would have disappeared from perception.

No, it was not time to give up on Denton. As the last of the sonic magic dissipated, Marney approached the two dead soldiers in the square. With her foot, she pushed the woman off her comrade's body. She pulled the mask from his face and studied it. The black material felt almost metallic but was as light as air; the lenses of the googles appeared to be simple tinted glass. Inside, the mask was inlaid with veins of copper wire and a thousand violet lights as tiny as pinprick stars in the night sky. Power stones, Marney reasoned, as small as sugar grains.

The mask moulded itself to the shape of her face when she put it on and she marvelled at how easy it was to breathe through the not-quite-metal material. She heard a gentle buzzing which felt as if it travelled through the bone of her skull to her eardrums. The dark lenses cleared, showing the environment with a clarity that Marney's naked eyes had never beheld.

She stared down the narrow road leading out of the square, flanked by damaged buildings. Dark coils of smoke rose from the city towards the crimson mountain range sky. Marney did not want to guess how many Aelfir had died here.

The buzzing in Marney's head intensified, like static, and through it rose a barely audible voice.

'... assistance required. Please respond.' A man's voice. Gurgling. Distorted. Desperate. 'Is anyone receiving? Urgent assistance—' There was a burst of static, and when the man's voice came back he was uttering a long line of curses. 'What's wrong with these damned transmitters?'

'It's magical interference.' This voice belonged to a woman. 'It's messing with our signal.'

'No shit,' said a second man. 'The others must be dead. That human is still out there somewhere.'

'And she's probably a magicker, too.' The woman sounded angry. 'There's no telling what she could do to us. I say we kill this one. He's only slowing us down.'

Denton. Alive.

'That's not a bad idea,' the second man replied. 'We can make a report when we reach—' Another burst of static.

'Quiet, both of you!' the first man snapped. 'We're taking this old bastard with us, and that's an order. From this point forward, we're on our own. I have no idea what's going on, but screw this House. We keep moving and regroup in Mirage.'

Mirage ... Marney held back thoughts of Van Bam.

The voices fell silent, the static lessened to a low-level buzz and the view through the goggles began to change. Still attuned to the masks of the enemy soldiers, Marney thought as her vision dimmed except for a strip of brilliant clarity. It began at her feet, travelled across the square and headed down the street into the city. At the top of the right lens, a red symbol pulsed faintly. The simple shape of a castle sat beneath a small circle: the House symbol of Mirage. The mask was giving Marney directions to Mirage's portal. To Denton.

Marney sprinted off, vaulting the dead bodies, running deeper into the Burrows of Underneath.

The House smelled of ruin. The hot and greasy reek of smoke and death filled Marney's nostrils despite the mask covering her nose. The air was laced with a residue of magic that prickled against her skin and her every step was dogged by chunks of fallen buildings and shards of glass. If not for the low buzz of the mask, only the silence of utter abandonment would have greeted her ears. The voice of this city was dead.

Passing not one corpse or casualty, Marney wondered if the citizens had been subjugated, as she had witnessed the Genii trying to do to other Aelfir, forcing them with thaumaturgy to switch allegiances to Spiral. Had the inhabitants of the Burrows of Underneath been moved to House Mirage, too, where their numbers would swell Spiral's army by tens of millions?

Perhaps the war wasn't as close to ending as the Ghoul seemed to think.

Marney focused her attention on more immediate matters: Denton was alive, his three abductors were isolated and Marney had one chance to rescue her mentor before he reached the portal to Mirage and faced ... what? Interrogation? Torture? Worse, a Genii?

She picked up speed. The goggles continued to give her directions via a line of clarity which took her through the ruins of a town house and out across a plaza, where a demolished fountain wildly sprayed water into the air and flooded the area. Marney splashed across the plaza and through the shower. The mask sent her right into an alley and then left into a wide street at the end. And it was there that the distorted voices of the soldiers buzzed in her ears again.

'... what do we do?' The snippet was panicked, the reply disjointed, mostly incoherent, but Marney heard the words, 'Higher magic,' and, 'Take cover!'

A burst of static coincided with a dull concussion that came from somewhere just up ahead. Throwing caution to the wind, her leg muscles and lungs burning, Marney sprinted. She approached the end of the street, where two tall opposing buildings had toppled and crashed together to form a clumsy, unstable triangle. The ground began vibrating.

Deep drones of preternatural energy shook the air. Pieces of stone and glass fell from the triangle.

Cautiously, Marney made her way under the precariously leaning buildings and peeked onto a wasteland of rubble. Her emotional control almost slipped when she saw Denton. He and the three soldiers were crouched behind the remnants of a long wall, hiding. On the other side of the wall, brilliant light and deepest darkness clashed in a vicious dance. The roar of magic rose and fell like a siren.

Marney ducked back into cover, removed the mask and let it drop to the ground. The air prickled upon her face.

Denton, she thought.

Marney! His reply was full of relief and fear. *Stay where you are. A Thaumaturgist and a Genii are fighting.*

Marney slid a throwing dagger from her baldric. *Denton, can you break away, grab a gun – anything?*

No – wait! Marney, the soldiers want to take refuge until the fighting is over. We're heading back your way. Hide!

Marney moved quickly. With rumbles of higher magic shaking the ground, she fled back down the street and into the first opening she found – a broken doorway leading to the foyer of what appeared to be a hotel, though it was hard to be certain with the amount of wreckage inside. She slid a second dagger from the baldric, found a hiding place with a view of a smashed window and waited.

A moment later, the soldiers crept by.

One led the group with Denton behind him; the other two brought up the rear, rifles aimed at the old empath's back. Denton shuffled rather than walked, clearly exhausted. There was blood on his face. Marney waited for them to pass before slowly, quietly stepping out onto the street behind them, a throwing dagger in each hand.

She prepared herself.

She attacked.

The first dagger sank into the base of the woman's skull. She fell, dead. As her comrade looked down at her in shock, Marney's second dagger severed the artery in his neck. He sank to his knees, clutching his wound, trying to stem the shower of blood. His wail of anguish was all the more disturbing for the expressionless mask on his face.

As he fell sideways to die, the lead soldier wheeled around in surprise. Denton knocked the rifle from his hands and they wrestled, toppling to the ground. The soldier gave his captive a crack on the nose with his elbow, but not before Denton had clawed the mask from his face.

Marney seized her chance.

Even as the solider drew his pistol and primed its power stone, Marney sent her empathic magic spearing into his emotions. Without mercy, she made the soldier *feel* how right it was to slide the barrel of his gun into his mouth and pull the trigger.

The back of his head burst with a spray of red.

Denton kicked the corpse away from him and got to his feet, stiff and awkward. There was a cut on his forehead and blood poured from his nose, which was obviously broken. He had locked down his emotions as tightly as Marney had. They stared at each other for a moment, as though contemplating the complete lack of emotions shared between them.

Finally, Denton wiped blood from his nose and smiled. 'You know, rescuing me was incredibly reckless. You really shouldn't have taken the risk.'

'Well, I did, so stop complaining and tell me what we do next.'

Denton was about to reply when a boom of magic stole his words away. The Thaumaturgist and the Genii were still fighting, and their battle shook loose debris from the already fragile buildings and sent it tumbling to the street around the empaths.

'We have to get out of here,' Marney said.

'Couldn't agree more,' Denton replied. 'But it's not that easy.'

He led Marney to the end of the street. Together they looked out onto the wild and furious display of thaumaturgy taking place behind the long wall.

'The portal we need is on the other side of that wall,' Denton said. 'A little tricky to get to at the moment, I'm sure you'll agree.'

'Wait,' said Marney. 'That's where the soldiers were taking you. It's the portal to Mirage?'

'Ironic, don't you think? They were about to deliver me to where we're heading anyway—'

A great *crack* of higher magic shattered the air.

Marney stared at her mentor. 'You heard what the Ghoul said, Denton – Mirage has fallen to the Genii, just like this place. And we have to go there to reach the Library of Glass and Mirrors?'

'Not exactly. We've been travelling the Way of the Blind Maze, Marney. By reaching the Burrows of Underneath, we have completed the combination to the lock. That portal won't take us to Mirage. It'll redirect us to the Library. In theory.'

'*In theory?*'

'Nothing is infallible.'

The old empath's face became serious again as he looked back at the fight taking place behind the wall. Another clatter of higher magic sent a swarm of jagged sparks climbing towards the mountain-range sky. Shouts of rage followed, tinged with triumph, as though the battle might have found a victor.

Denton wiped more blood from his face. 'Let's take a closer look,' he said.

When Samuel and Van Bam arrived at the abandoned ore warehouse in the southern district, they found Hamir inside, along with the twins Macy and Bryant.

While Bryant stood watching, Hamir sat at a table slowly filling a syringe with blood from Macy's arm. The twins – tall and broad, blonde-haired, with almost identical faces – ignored Samuel but looked surprised and pleased to see Van Bam. Hamir had no interest in anything other than what he was doing. The elderly necromancer had already filled two syringes, now stored in a wooden rack, and was working on a third. He was collecting the blood that would serve as food for the Relic Guild's prisoner.

Fabian Moor hung in his thaumaturgic prison, his feet several inches above the circle of symbols that had been carved into the warehouse floor. The symbols glowed with purple light and blocked the Genii's higher magic, holding him immobile and powerless. Stripped of clothes and dignity, Moor's head hung limp, his long white hair falling across his chest.

Although the prisoner carried no visible wounds, Samuel knew he had been repeatedly tortured. On one occasion, Samuel had watched as Hamir deployed his special brand of magical agony upon the Genii, and he had no wish to witness it again. He didn't want to know what else the necromancer had done in an attempt to break Fabian Moor, to force him into revealing what he knew about Spiral's war plans.

Samuel approached the twins and the necromancer.

'Is he all right?' Bryant said, gesturing to Van Bam as he swapped places with his sister and offered Hamir his arm.

Van Bam, who had maintained the sombre silence he had been keeping throughout the journey to the warehouse, was standing in front of Moor, his bare feet inches from the prison's glowing symbols. This was the first time the illusionist had laid eyes on the Genii.

'He's fine,' Samuel said.

'Are you sure?' said Macy, rolling down her sleeve.

'Hamir,' Van Bam said, his voice hollow. 'Can you show me Moor's face?'

Hamir paused screwing a syringe onto the needle in Bryant's arm to give Van Bam a questioning glance. He seemed about to enquire after the reason for the request but evidently decided he didn't care, as was Hamir's way. With a whispered word, the necromancer gestured towards the thaumaturgic prison. The purple light intensified and Fabian Moor raised his head with a gasp. The Genii stared straight at Van Bam with unblinking eyes, his mouth hanging open.

'Thank you, Hamir,' said Van Bam. Without acknowledging anyone else in the room, the illusionist stared back at the Genii.

'What's he doing?' Bryant said.

'Preparing,' Samuel replied.

'Well, he doesn't look all right to me,' Macy said. She walked over to Van Bam and began talking to him quietly.

'Preparing for what?' Bryant asked.

Samuel didn't reply; his attention had been caught by a glass box sitting at the back of the warehouse upon the platform of the cellar elevator. Inside the box, a purple mist of protective magic surrounded a strange device: a head-sized sphere of glass filled with murky water and covered in a wire mesh and a host of thumbnail-sized power stones.

When the Relic Guild had first captured Moor, he had been using the device to store harvested shadows.

'Hamir,' said Samuel, 'do we know what that thing is supposed to do yet?'

'No.' The necromancer continued draining blood from Bryant's arm.

'Best guess is still a shadow carriage of some kind,' Bryant said.

'On consideration,' Hamir added, 'I believe it was designed to transport Mirage's invasion force from the Great Labyrinth to Labrys Town.' He looked pointedly at Van Bam. 'An invasion that was thankfully sabotaged.'

Van Bam gave Hamir a slow glare before returning his attention to Moor, while Macy continued to speak to him.

'However,' Hamir continued, 'nothing can be known for certain unless the Genii is made to talk.' He tapped a leather-bound book on the table beside the wooden rack. A gift from Lady Amilee, it contained powerful arts that only Hamir could translate. 'Thus far, even the secrets of the Thaumaturgists have been unable to break him.'

After filling two more syringes with blood, the necromancer told Bryant to roll down his sleeve. He removed a smooth metal cylinder from a bag beside his chair and used it to store all five syringes.

'Now, if you'll excuse me.'

Hamir rose and walked to the elevator platform, taking the cylinder and the leather-bound book with him. Placing the items on the glass box containing Moor's mysterious device, he activated the elevator's control box and descended into the cellar without another word.

Well used to Hamir's ways, Bryant gave a light shake of his head and turned to Samuel. 'So what's going on?'

'I've just discovered the identity of one of Moor's business associates.' Samuel pulled a sour face and headed towards the eye device on the warehouse wall. 'I need to call in Gideon.'

A glass hemisphere fixed to the wall, the device was filled with a milky substance, giving it the appearance of a rheumy eyeball. These devices were scattered throughout Labrys Town, always watching the denizens, always listening to their conversations. If a regular denizen touched an eye, it would connect them to the police; but if a magicker touched one, the connection would be made directly to the Nightshade.

As soon as Samuel laid a hand on the hemisphere, the milky fluid began to churn; there was a buzz and the Resident's voice snapped angrily, 'What is it?'

'We've got a problem,' Samuel said levelly, moving away from the eye.

A moment later, the Nightshade projected Gideon's image from the eye into the warehouse. He materialised wearing a dark green roll-neck jumper and black trousers. His face was gaunt, shaded by stubble, and his sunken eyes glared manically. His hands were covered in the pale scars of a blood-magicker. Gideon looked around the warehouse before his angry gaze settled on Samuel.

'Well?' he demanded.

Samuel took a calming breath. His relationship with the Resident had been abrasive since the day they met, and just seeing his image raised his heart rate.

'Before we captured Moor,' Samuel said, 'we knew he'd been conducting business with various people in the underworld. This morning, I found out that one of them is Gemstone Llem.'

'Did you say Llem?' Macy said. She lost interest in Van Bam and joined the conversation. 'That could be problematic.'

Bryant puffed his cheeks. Even Gideon looked concerned.

Gemstone Llem was a well-known name in Labrys Town's underworld. A boss among criminals, she had made staying one step ahead of the law an art form. The Nightshade had been watching her for years, waiting for her to slip up, but Gemstone Llem never did. Until now.

She was the daughter of an Aelfirian ambassador and a high-ranking human merchant. She spent most of her time in the Gemstone Isles, the House her father came from, while abusing her mother's merchant contacts to conduct shady business in the Labyrinth that was very hard to trace back to her. When the war started, Llem, along with many other Aelfir, had been stranded in Labrys Town as guests of the Resident. None of them was allowed to return to their Houses until the Thaumaturgists decreed it was permissible again to use the portals outside the town in the Great Labyrinth.

'Shit,' Gideon said, irritated.

Llem was problematic because she knew how to hide behind her Aelfirian heritage. Given that Aelfirian visitors were already afforded far more courtesy than the denizens, there would be a diplomatic quagmire to navigate if the Resident wanted to question her officially. Coupled with the fact that Gideon needed to maintain a good relationship with the Merchants' Guild for when contact with the Aelfirian Houses was re-established, bringing charges against Llem without embarrassing her parents would be tricky.

It wasn't that Gideon *couldn't* have her dragged to the Nightshade; he was the Resident, and in Labrys Town his law held sway no matter where an Aelf came from. And the situation was certainly serious enough to justify some heavy-handedness. But a lot of the Aelfirian exiles were already angry at Gideon for allowing the delegates from Mirage to return home while they had to remain – and they would only get angrier if word of Mirage's treason got out. The Resident had to be careful and Gemstone Llem would be aware of that. Ruthless and clever, she knew how to make herself untouchable. To a point.

Gideon made an angry noise. 'Are you certain she's been dealing with Moor?'

'As much as I can be,' Samuel replied. 'I went to see Long Tommy. He says that Llem's scared. Apparently, when we captured Moor it left her in the lurch and she's looking for a magic-user to undo their business arrangement.'

'Why?' Gideon demanded. 'What kind of business was it?'

'Tommy didn't know.' Samuel shrugged. 'Sounds like unfinished business, though. All Tommy could tell me was it involved a property somewhere in town.'

'What property? Warehouse? Apartment?'

'If we want to find out, we need to talk to Llem.'

'That's not very helpful, is it?' Gideon said spitefully.

Samuel felt his hackles rise. 'I can only tell you what I've been told, Gideon.' He gestured angrily at Fabian Moor. 'It's not my fault if you've had no luck talking to *him*!'

'Shut up and let me think, you idiot.'

Macy and Bryant tensed, ready for the Resident and his agent to add to their list of many confrontations, but Samuel bit his tongue and Gideon fell silent.

The Resident's eyes darted from side to side as he conversed with Sophia, the former Resident who now served as his spirit guide.

'Obviously we haven't got time to take the official route,' Gideon said. 'Yet we can't exactly go accusing Llem of fraternising with a Genii.'

It was a good point. There weren't many denizens who knew that Fabian Moor was a Genii; most believed he was a wild demon who had sneaked into town. If word of Llem's arrest got out and the general populace learned the truth, it might induce panic across Labrys Town.

'Me and Bryant need to be careful here,' Macy said. 'Llem knows us.'

Which was the problem with having agents working undercover in the underworld. Macy and Bryant's magical gift of inordinate strength meant they got a lot of work as bouncers or bodyguards with various clubs and criminals, and for many years they had been a valuable source of information. The trouble was, to keep that line of information flowing, the twins could rarely act directly upon what they discovered without revealing their affiliation to the Relic Guild.

'Unless you think this is worth blowing our cover for,' Bryant said to Gideon.

Again, the Resident conversed with Sophia.

'I've got an idea,' said Samuel.

'*You*, Samuel?' Gideon grinned cruelly. 'Well, this I simply have to hear.'

Ignoring the Resident's acerbic manner, Samuel looked over at Van Bam, who was still staring at the Genii in his prison.

'Can't do this the official way,' he said, 'and Moor won't tell us anything. So if we're going to get to Llem quickly, we need to be underhanded.'

'Make your point,' Gideon snapped.

It was Van Bam who replied, his grief replaced by anger. 'He means that we have to do this the Relic Guild way.'

The illusionist turned from the prisoner and gave Samuel a nod. Whispering, he tapped his green glass cane upon the floor and a crystalline chime spread across the warehouse. Van Bam's image wavered, his clothes altering, his skin colour changing. In an instant, the illusionist shifted his appearance into the perfect likeness of Fabian Moor.

Gideon chuckled darkly. 'I like your thinking. Do it.'

Denton and Marney stood on either side of a slim breach in the wall. Higher magic rumbled, followed by shouts.

'You shame the Timewatcher!' It was a woman's voice. Hard. Full of rage. 'You shame your fellow Thaumaturgists!'

Furtively, the empaths took stock of the situation.

On the other side of the wall, a Genii was sprawled on his back upon rubble, a blanket of wavering energy holding him down, crushing him. A Thaumaturgist loomed over him. One of her hands was balled into a fist, glowing with higher magic that stretched out to a point, as though she held a sword. Defeated, the Genii could do nothing but lie prone before her power.

Several yards beyond them was the stone archway of the portal to House Mirage – the final piece in the puzzle of the Way of the Blind Maze that would, somehow, redirect Marney and Denton to the Library of Glass and Mirrors.

'You deserve no mercy, Lord Buyaal,' cried the Thaumaturgist.

Buyaal, Marney thought. The Genii who had taken control of Mirage.

'You brought misery and suffering to the House I protected.' The Thaumaturgist raised her sword of higher magic, preparing to stab down. 'You are a traitor!'

A clap of thunder disturbed her.

A dark hole appeared in the air twenty feet above the scene. By the time Marney realised the hole was a portal, a second Genii had dropped through and fallen onto the Thaumaturgist.

She had no time to defend herself. With a bellow of rage, the Genii – huge, hulking, powerful – brought both his massive fists down into her face like an animal in a berserker rage. He hit the Thaumaturgist again before grabbing her around the throat and hoisting her into the air. Her face a bloody ruin, she kicked wildly as the Genii squeezed. His hand flared with magic and the Thaumaturgist's body fell to the ground in a heap, separated from her head.

Marney locked down her emotions and steadied her nausea.

The Genii glared at the head in his hand for a moment before casually tossing it away. He wiped sweat from his bald pate and then dispelled the magic that held his fellow Genii to the ground.

Lord Buyaal, the usurper of House Mirage, dusted down his priest's cassock and gave his hulking rescuer a surprised look.

'Lord Gadreel,' he said. 'I thank you for your timely intervention.'

'Do you?' Gadreel's voice was a rumble of brooding thunder. 'It's not as if I was given a choice.'

Buyaal looked taken aback. 'Who sent you?'

'Who do you think, you imbecile?' Gadreel jabbed a meaty finger at his fellow Genii. '*You* are not supposed to be here. *You* were supposed to send troops to the Great Labyrinth.'

Buyaal didn't reply. Marney and Denton shared a worried look.

Gadreel added, 'Lord Spiral would like an explanation.'

Buyaal swore. 'I lost Mirage's doorway to the Great Labyrinth,' he admitted, voice heavy. 'Two human magickers got in the way.'

'*Human* magickers?' Gadreel said dangerously. 'Of the Relic Guild?'

'Yes. The man escaped and ruined our plans. The woman, I killed.'

Marney's empathic control almost crumbled to dust. She turned away from the hole in the wall, pressing her back flat to the brickwork, taking deep, steadying breaths. Angel. Dead.

Denton had also turned from the scene. He tapped a finger to his temple then pressed it to his lips, shaking his head. Although the air still prickled with spent thaumaturgy, creatures of higher magic might easily detect a mental conversation between two empaths.

Marney peered through the hole again.

Gadreel was glaring at his companion. 'You allowed a *magicker* to better you, Buyaal?'

'He had help,' Buyaal snapped.

'I do not care!' Gadreel bellowed, and his already impressive size seemed to grow, loom – so much more powerful than the Genii before him.

'Wait,' Buyaal said, raising his hands against the threat. 'As you can see, I've delivered the Burrows of Underneath to our Lord.'

'You truly believe your actions here can compensate for losing the Great Labyrinth?' Gadreel rumbled. 'Do you realise how large this House is – how many more cities it holds?'

'I had to act quickly,' Buyaal countered. 'Our plan was revealed, and—'

Gadreel cut him off. 'Millions of enemy Aelfir have fled to the other cities and Lord Spiral no longer has the time and resources to flush them out. You have achieved nothing here, Buyaal. And you would be dead now if I hadn't arrived.' Gadreel drew a deep, angry breath. 'Lord Spiral has ordered me to clean up your mess. The Burrows of Underneath *and* your troops are now under my control.'

With a guarded tone, Buyaal asked, 'Then what does Lord Spiral wish of me?'

'*You* will return to House Mirage,' said Gadreel. 'And there you will wait until you receive further orders ... or punishment for failure.'

'It wasn't my fault, Viktor. You have to listen to me—'

'Tell it to Lord Spiral! Leave. Now.'

Without another word, Buyaal stormed over to the portal, activated it and disappeared into darkness, travelling back to Mirage. Gadreel looked down at the Thaumaturgist's decapitated body. He spat on it and then summoned his higher magic.

His deep voice rising and falling with the breathy sighs of the language of the Thaumaturgists, Gadreel cast a spell which he hurled into the sky to form a huge orb of slate grey. The orb shattered into thousands of shards, a screaming flock of Genii magic. The flock dispersed, racing away in all directions, radiating a sense of hate and loathing as it went. Marney had seen this kind of magic before; the Genii used it to subjugate their enemies. This was how they turned the Aelfir's love for the Timewatcher into devotion to Spiral.

Gadreel watched his spell disappear across the Burrows of Underneath, apparently pleased with his work. He then sliced his hand through the air, creating another dark rent. He widened the portal before stepping through and disappearing himself. The rent sealed to a black line, which finally blew away like smoke in a breeze.

The prickle of higher magic in the air lessened. The silence was heavy. The empaths didn't move for a moment, as though reluctant to believe that the Genii had truly vacated the area.

'Let's go,' Denton finally said, and he led the way through the breach in the wall.

As they carefully navigated the rubble-strewn ground towards the portal, Marney averted her gaze from the bloody ruin that had been a Thaumaturgist. When they reached the stone archway, Denton activated the portal. Its darkness churned with the drone of magic.

The old empath wiped blood and sweat from his face. '*If* we've done this right, the portal will take us to the Library of Glass and Mirrors.' He sounded uncertain. 'If we haven't …'

'It'll take us straight to Buyaal,' Marney finished, her emotions numb. 'He killed Angel, Denton.'

'We have bigger, more immediate concerns,' Denton said, not unkindly. 'Like finding out if we've navigated the Way of the Blind Maze correctly.' Denton held out his hand and Marney grasped it. 'Let's get this bloody mission over with.'

Together, beaten and tired, emotions protected behind shields of apathy, the empaths headed into the portal.

CHAPTER FIVE

THE PROGENITOR

A fine, warm drizzle misted the humid air. Thick clouds smudged the light of Ruby Moon into a patch of dull red. The mossy, black-bricked walls and cobbled floor of an alleyway led to a T-junction.

Clara felt afraid and confused.

She didn't know how she had returned to the Great Labyrinth, but she was more concerned with the golem facing her in the alleyway, no more than thirty feet away. Its misshapen form covered by a wide-brimmed hat and priest's cassock, it aimed a silver pistol at Clara, the power stone primed and glowing.

Clara lifted her hands before her face. 'No!'

But the golem didn't shoot.

A rustle of movement came from the shadows of a buttress halfway between Clara and the golem. A coat appeared, tossed into the alleyway. The golem's pistol flashed and spat, sending a bullet fizzing into the garment. Bitter magic whipped and moaned, freezing the coat in mid-air. Even as it hit the cobbles and shattered into a hundred shards of ice, a woman left the cover of the buttress. She spun into the alley and threw a dagger at the golem. The pistol clattered to the ground. The golem stumbled. Its hat fell to the floor, revealing its grotesque face and the silver blade stuck in its eye socket.

Clara recognised the woman. 'Marney!'

The empath ignored the changeling, throwing two more daggers into the golem with expert precision. Marney readied a fourth blade but didn't release it. The golem twisted and jerked spasmodically, its body and limbs bending to hideous angles. Hissing filled the alleyway with the acrid stench of dispelling magic. Finally the golem broke apart, collapsing to the cobbles, now nothing more than chunks of stone within its cassock.

'Marney?' Clara said.

Saying nothing, the empath approached the remains, dagger in hand.

'What's going on?' Clara peered up through the drizzle at the red bruise of Ruby Moon. She looked down at her hands, clenching and unclenching fists. She didn't feel right. Somehow, she felt incomplete. 'How did I get here?'

Again Marney didn't reply as she inspected the remains of the golem. Clara froze when a second golem rounded the corner into the alleyway, its pistol primed and aimed at the empath.

Clara shouted a warning, leaping to the cover of a buttress, but Marney had already rolled to one side, a silver dagger flying from her hand. It hit the golem high on its sunken chest, sending its shot wild. Clara flinched as the bullet cracked the alley wall, releasing ice magic which spread over the brickwork like frost on a windowpane. Before the golem could fire again, Marney finished it off with two more daggers to the head. The empath's adversary lost the spell that animated it and broke apart.

Clara stared at the scene for a moment. 'Tell me what's going on.'

Without giving the changeling the slightest acknowledgement, Marney collected her throwing daggers and took off. She turned right at the T-junction and disappeared into the Great Labyrinth.

'Marney!' Clara shouted after her. 'Wait!'

'I'm right here, Clara.'

Clara wheeled around.

Marney stood in the alley, looking exactly as she had a few moments before, dressed in a black jumper and trousers, wearing a baldric of throwing daggers like a waistcoat. Her brown hair, lined with grey, was pulled back and tied into a tail. Her face carried the lines of a woman somewhere around sixty.

Clara looked down the alley to where the empath's doppelgänger had disappeared, and then back at this new version of her.

'What ... ?'

With a slight smile, Marney walked past Clara. She stopped, staring down at the remains of the golem at her feet.

She said, 'In about fifteen minutes, you and I will meet for the first time. I will hide secrets in your mind, and then Fabian Moor will abduct me.' She looked back at the changeling. 'This is the night you joined the Relic Guild, Clara.'

Clara rubbed her forehead. '*What?*'

'Well, perhaps it's truer to say that this is a memory of that night.'

'Whose memory?'

'Mine. Or the template of it.' Marney looked amused. 'What's the last thing you remember?'

Clara thought for a moment. 'The Toymaker. I think he rescued me.' She shook her head in disbelief as she remembered a hundred small but lethal automatons connecting together to form a single construct. They said that you never saw the Toymaker, only his toys. And now Clara knew why: the Toymaker *was* his toys. 'But why help me? He's been trying to kill the Relic Guild ever since we escaped the Labyrinth.'

'He had a change of heart,' Marney said drily. 'The Toymaker works for Lady Amilee now. As we all do.'

Amilee – she had been behind everything. Clara felt tightness in her chest. 'Amilee let Van Bam die?'

'No, Clara.' There was no emotion in the empath's voice, as though she had disconnected her feelings. 'What Amilee did was find a way – the *only* way – to give us a chance of defeating the Genii. Van Bam is dead but not gone.'

'I heard his voice.'

'You heard his ghost.'

'He was talking to you.' A tear fell from Clara's eye and she wiped it away. 'You said we have to find him.' She looked around at her environment, still not feeling quite connected to it. Anger flared. 'I don't understand.'

A rumble of thunder came from the sky. Protracted, rising in volume before fading, it reminded Clara of a growl. It was only then that she realised the incompleteness she was feeling was due to the fact that her magic was no longer inside her. The wolf was gone, and Clara began to panic.

'Calm yourself,' Marney said, looking at the sky nervously. Thunder growled again and the drizzle became rain. 'Come on.'

Taking Clara by the arm, Marney led her to the T-junction, where they turned right into a long alleyway which stretched into the gloom.

'Where are you taking me?' Clara said shakily.

'We'll know when we see it.' Marney looked agitated. 'There are memories within memories in this place, Clara. I'm a projection, a copy of myself. *I* am what I planted in your mind.'

Absently, Clara touched her lips, recalling the moment that Marney had hidden information in her mind with an empathic kiss. 'So all this is inside *my* head?'

'And we're not alone,' Marney said warningly. At another rumble of thunder, she looked back nervously. 'Right now, you have to stay calm and focus your thoughts. I need you to think about Van Bam.'

Clara yanked her arm from Marney's grip and rounded on her angrily. 'What's going on? Van Bam is dead!'

The rain turned into a torrential downpour, almost instantly drenching the magickers. Marney had to raise her voice against its hiss.

'Do as I say, so Known Things can pick up on the information we need.'

'What are you talking about?' Clara shouted. 'Known Things is *gone*!'

'No, Clara. Not quite.'

'Listen to me, Marney – we're already too late!' The changeling's words were underlined by rumbles from the sky. 'Viktor Gadreel killed Van Bam and took Known Things away with him.' Her anger became distress. 'He stole the location of Oldest Place from my mind. The Genii know how to free Spiral.'

'Trust me.' Marney held Clara by the shoulders. 'Known Things will still show us how to kill the Lord of the Genii. Where do you think you are right now?'

Clara baulked, looking around. '*This* is Known Things?'

'I'll tell you everything I know but we have to keep moving.'

Both of them soaked to the skin, Clara allowed Marney to lead her off again. Above, the clouds flashed, thunder came with a strange bestial roar and the rain fell harder.

Marney said, 'When you were disconnected from Known Things, you should have died. But you didn't.'

The metamorphosis, Clara recalled: changing into the human had healed her wounds.

'Known Things searched your memories for information, Clara, but it's a two-way process and your mind has retained a copy of its entire contents.' Marney waited for a peal of thunder to pass before again shouting over the rain. 'That was the trade-off. To gain access to Known Things, you had to give the Genii the location of Oldest Place.' She looked back down the alley and then urged Clara to quicken her pace. 'Spiral has to be free before he can be killed.'

'And *I* freed him?' Clara was mortified. She longed to feel the wolf's courage inside her. '*That* was Amilee's plan?'

'You have to listen to me,' Marney repeated. 'Your connection won't last for ever. I don't know how much time we have, but we need to discover how to kill Spiral before Known Things fades from your memory.' More thunder. 'Van Bam's ghost is trapped in here with us, Clara. We have to find Van Bam to find the Nephilim.'

Clara almost stopped again. The clashes in the sky now sounded more like distorted howls that burrowed deep into her being. It disrupted Clara's thoughts and she struggled to comprehend this bizarre situation.

'What have the Nephilim got to do with this?'

'Everything!' Marney replied. 'The Nephilim are our last hope, Clara.'

The rain fell in great fat drops. Clara's bare feet splashed through an inch of water already covering the cobbles. She couldn't shake the disturbing notion that the howls of thunder were chasing her.

'You don't have to understand,' Marney continued. 'Just keep thinking about— Wait! Yes, there it is.'

Up ahead, a patch of radiance had appeared in the alleyway, hovering in the air, glowing through the downpour; a glassy substance the same deep green as Van Bam's illusionist's cane.

'Well done, Clara!'

Not knowing what she had done, confused and still feeling somehow detached from her environment, Clara hurried with Marney towards the green light.

They stopped in their tracks as the rain abruptly ceased, replaced by an ominous stillness.

The clouds disappeared from the sky, boiling away in an instant. It was as though time had sped up, revealing stars and the bright, sterile glare of Silver Moon. The temperature dropped. Drenched and shivering, Clara's breath frosted in the air.

'What's happening?'

Before Marney could answer, a great, stony *crack* came from behind her. The magickers wheeled around. The alleyway was long, stretching back as far as Clara could see. Although the sky was clear, the roar of thunder raced down the alleyway towards them, caught between a bestial howl and a human scream. A powerful stench came with it: blood, death ... the damp pelt of a wolf. The alley walls began collapsing. Black bricks fell, forming a lethal vortex that followed the roar of thunder towards the magickers.

'*Shit!*' Marney hissed.

'What is it?'

'Your magic, Clara. It's no friend to us here. *Run!*'

Taking Clara's hand, the empath practically dragged her down the alleyway towards the radiance. The covering of rainwater had become thick and slushy, freezing, threatening to trap the magickers before the deadly storm.

'Don't stop thinking of Van Bam, Clara,' Marney shouted. 'Think of Van Bam *and* the Nephilim.'

The Nephilim ... the name inflamed memories in the changeling, memories of blood-magic, of giants and hidden doorways. She saw Van Bam, a pack of wild demons ripping the flesh from his bones; and as she did so, the environment became starkly, frighteningly real. The green light grew, stretching across the alleyway like gelatinous emerald.

'You did it, Clara,' Marney shouted. 'That's our way out.'

And as the howls and screams of Clara's magic brought a storm of ice and bricks rushing towards them, the magickers reached the emerald portal. It enveloped them in green light that whisked them away from the Great Labyrinth.

The ghost of Alexander led Hamir through the Tower of the Skywatcher to a spacious chamber decorated with sheets of white satin. The walls, floor and ceiling were entirely covered, and it was hard to make out where one sheet ended and the next began. Hamir imagined he had entered a cavern within a cloud. At the centre of the chamber, the material had been twisted into a series of pillars that stretched from floor to ceiling, forming a wide circle.

Hamir glanced at Alexander, who had remained just inside the door. The ghost seemed reluctant to move any further into the chamber, perhaps fearful of the grisly monument inside the circle of satin pillars. It sullied the pure, clean whiteness.

Hamir raised an eyebrow. 'Is that your corpse, Alexander?'

The door slammed shut behind the ghost with an angry gust of wind. 'Why don't you just get on with it, necromancer.'

Hamir stepped inside the satin pillars.

Alexander's corpse stood like some perverse presentation in an anatomy lesson. Held upright by a framework of metal encompassing his legs and supporting his back and neck, both his arms were missing at the elbows, the stumps healed around glass tubes through which dark fluid travelled. Alexander had been sliced open from throat to groin, the skin pinned back, all traces of blood cleaned away. His ribcage had been removed, along with his stomach and intestines and bowels – most of his other organs, too. In fact, as far as Hamir could see, Alexander's body only retained its heart and lungs. More glass tubes sprouted from these organs and ran into a line of small metallic hemispheres fixed to the floor. The dark fluid flowed like blood through veins.

'And you say you made this sacrifice willingly?' Hamir said.

Alexander's ghost now stood alongside Hamir. Unable to gaze upon his flesh, he focused on an oval frame standing next to his body. Resting upon another metallic hemisphere, it was as tall as a man and made from a pearlescent substance that Hamir recognised as thaumaturgic metal.

'How long have you been this way, Alexander?'

'That is none of your business.'

Above the corpse's ashen face, with its slack, tongueless mouth and hollow eye sockets, Alexander's scalp and the top of his skull were missing. A hundred needles stuck into the pallid walnut of his brain were connected to a network of thin copper wires that converged into the base of a metal box hanging from its stand just off Alexander's shoulder.

'Fuel,' Hamir said.

Alexander's body was acting as an organic power stone, kept in a radically slowed state of decomposition, maintaining the slightest current of energy flowing through the Tower of the Skywatcher.

'This is necromancy of the lowest and foulest kind,' he said to the ghost. 'The Timewatcher forbade the Thaumaturgists from ever using this kind of magic. Lady Amilee must have been desperate indeed to resort to this.'

'She was strong when others were weak,' Alexander retorted. 'And you should be grateful for that.'

'Should I?'

'You know what to do, necromancer. And you don't need my help to do it.'

With silver tears shining in his eyes and anger on his face, the Aelfirian ghost faded and was gone.

'Charming,' Hamir muttered, and removed the phial of Clara's blood from his inside pocket. He'd been carrying the phial since this whole damned scenario began, and now he was glad of the chance to be rid of it.

Approaching Alexander's corpse, Hamir was at first perturbed by its complete lack of aroma, but then impressed by Lady Amilee's surgical skills. He could feel heat coming off the copper wires connecting the brain to the box hanging beside the body. Like the oval frame, the box carried the pearlescent quality of thaumaturgic metal.

Hamir looked at the phial in his hand.

Changeling blood was priceless to the art of spellcraft, a magical catalyst which could empower the most mundane spells almost with the potency of thaumaturgy, if only for a short time. Yet Lady Amilee could not possibly expect this single phial to return her tower to its former glory. So what *did* she expect? What could the gruesome engine that Alexander had become achieve with this blood?

Hamir reached out and touched the box. The thaumaturgic metal reacted by rippling and then swirling into a miniature whirlpool that created a dark hole in the structure. Hamir popped the cork from the phial and fed the open end into the hole. The metal hardened around the glass and the box drank Clara's blood, leaving behind not one drop or smear inside the phial.

The copper wires began to glow, the heat increasing, flowing through the thin strands into Alexander's exposed brain. Organ tissue sizzled. A little smoke rose. Alexander's mouth closed and fell slack again. His body jerked and entered a series of rhythmic spasms, as though the corpse was pumping the energy of the changeling blood into the veins of Lady Amilee's tower. The dark fluid in the glass tubes became as clear as water, shimmering with magic. The oval frame beside the corpse began singing with a high, clean peal.

Hamir backed away.

The frame's pearlescent metal started to brighten; the light thickened into lines that stretched across the space within the oval like slowly spreading cracks in glass. The lines connected, merged, filling the frame with a sheet of multicoloured light. With a nerve-shredding din, the sheet shattered and was sucked away, leaving behind a churning whiteness.

'The Nothing of Far and Deep,' Hamir whispered.

The distant sound of a lonely wind moaned around the chamber of white satin. Alexander's corpse continued to spasm. Hamir retreated further as a portal opened in the primordial mists and a strange vision emerged.

It was an automaton, but not a design Hamir had ever seen before. Made from a framework of a hundred moving pieces, a host of tiny violet lights shone from within its body. A smooth metal disc of silver appeared to serve as a mouth on an otherwise featureless face. And in its framework arms, the strange automaton carried a small, unconscious woman.

Clara.

With crackles of energy and a puff of smoke, Alexander's body ceased pumping heightened magic through the tower. The power of the changeling blood exhausted, the portal deactivated and the Nothing of Far and Deep disappeared.

Hamir was speechless. The automaton stood motionless before him and the necromancer got the impression that it was waiting for orders. He considered approaching to check that Clara was alive but decided against it. The changeling looked very still in the automaton's arms. She wore simple dark grey clothes that he could see were imbued with magic.

'Let me introduce you to the Toymaker,' Amilee said.

Hunched over, dressed in purple robes, the Skywatcher entered the circle of satin pillars, moving with the gait of an elderly human. Her face was ashen and she struggled for breath.

Hamir looked back at the automaton. 'The Toymaker?'

'His story is a little complicated,' Amilee said. 'But don't worry, Hamir – Clara is alive, if not entirely well.'

Hamir attempted to process the last few minutes. 'Would you care to tell me what in the Timewatcher's name is going on, my lady?'

Amilee approached the Toymaker and stroked Clara's hair. 'Such a young and naïve creature,' she whispered. 'I am truly sorry for the weight of the burden I have hung around your neck. And for what is to come.'

Hamir frowned. 'My lady?'

'Later, Hamir,' she said, turning from the Toymaker. 'Clara needs our care.'

'Why did my magic attack us?' Clara said into the darkness.

'Actually, it was protecting *you*,' Marney's disembodied voice replied.

'Strange way of showing it.'

'Not if you consider all the facts, Clara. Known Things was created by Spiral, and his presence is in here with us. Your magic doesn't like that, and rightly so. It sees Known Things as an invader.'

'So what happens if my magic reaches us?'

'It's not a case of *if* but *when*,' Marney replied. 'Eventually, your magic will destroy your connection to Known Things, wipe it from your mind. So you have to *learn* what we need to know before it catches us.'

The dark was complete. Clara couldn't see Marney or anything else, though she felt more stable than before. Her legs were solid beneath her and her thoughts were clearer, despite the absence of her now rogue magic. It brought courage and acceptance, and a curious realisation that, even though she had been carrying Marney's presence in her mind since this whole dilemma had begun, she didn't really know the empath at all.

'Where are we?' Clara asked.

'You tell me,' Marney replied from the dark. 'You brought us here.'

It felt to Clara as though a cool breeze was blowing through her mind, bringing with it more and more clarity. She wondered if it was Marney's doing; empathic magic calming her emotions and anchoring her to the situation.

Above, the darkness blushed with a vague pinkish hue, like the first signal of a rising sun in an otherwise starless sky.

'Why are the Nephilim so important?' Clara asked.

'Because they are the closest thing to Thaumaturgists that we have left,' Marney answered. 'But the Nephilim disappeared, Clara. And only Spiral knows where they are.'

Clara considered this. 'Van Bam said he met a Nephilim, years ago.'

'He did, but I really don't know much about it.' The sky was slowly growing brighter, and Clara began to make out an etching of Marney's face in the gloom. The empath stood close by, her expression concerned. 'It's hard to remember things sometimes.'

'His name was ... Bellow,' Clara said. '*Gulduur* Bellow. Is that why Van Bam's ghost is connected to the Nephilim? Because they met?'

'I ... maybe.' Marney sounded contemplative. 'All I know for sure is that Spiral imprisoned the Nephilim herd shortly before the Genii War. For some reason, he's keeping them alive, hidden. Van Bam met the only one to escape Spiral's clutches. But there are hundreds more of them, Clara, and if we release them – if we're *very* lucky and they agree to help us – they might just be strong enough to destroy Spiral and the Genii.'

The pieces were clicking together for Clara. 'Known Things is a records device,' she realised. 'Every secret Spiral needed to keep from the Timewatcher is stored in here. Including what he did with the Nephilim.'

'You're catching on,' Marney said, amused; and then, less so, added, 'Concealing the location of Oldest Place was never our most important agenda. Finding out where Spiral hid the Nephilim's prison is.' She looked disturbed. 'You're holding Spiral's deepest and darkest secrets in your mind, Clara, and we're right in the thick of them. All we have to do now is figure out where to look—'

Marney broke off. Clara's breath caught.

The darkness erupted with hues and colours like a thousand rainbows unfurling. A vast nebula dotted with the clean light of a million silver stars danced in the sky with kaleidoscopic storm clouds, clashing and mixing before cascading to surround the magickers with a scintillating wall of energy.

Clara gave a Marney a look both confused and astounded, but the empath only had eyes for something else.

A small man had appeared. He sat cross-legged on the floor, head bowed, dressed in ripped and stained robes of purple. A configuration of symbols formed a circle beneath him. The pattern – strange inter-connecting shapes – was not something Clara had seen before, yet somehow she recognised it.

'The language of the Thaumaturgists,' Marney said.

The small, dishevelled man was so still that he might have been dead. His raven hair hung limp.

'Who is he?' Clara asked.

'Someone you know,' Marney replied.

A star fell from the nebulous sky, a bright point of silver blue that raced down and stopped abruptly before the man. It hovered three feet from the ground, bobbing gently. With a sharp intake of breath, the man looked up and stared at it. The hair fell away from his face revealing a tattoo of a black diamond on his forehead. He was young, eerily beautiful, and a tuft of dark beard sprouted from the point of his chin. Clara didn't recognise him until she stared into the soft green of his eyes.

'Hamir?' she said.

'But not as you know him, Clara.' Marney sighed, the sound full of disappointment. 'Hamir has served as the Resident's aide for longer than any human alive can remember. The agents of the Relic Guild used to joke that he was as old as the Nightshade itself, but the truth is he is far older.'

Hamir, bedraggled and broken, stared at the star before him. His shoulders shook as he wept.

'This isn't the necromancer you know,' Marney continued. 'This is Lord Simowyn Hamir.'

'Simowyn?'

'His true name, Clara. The name of a disgraced Thaumaturgist.'

Clara didn't know Hamir very well; she'd not had the chance to before the Relic Guild went on the run from the Genii. Looking at him now, so young and broken, the diamond tattoo of the Thaumaturgists on his forehead, she reasoned that none of her colleagues would have guessed he was a creature of higher magic.

'What happened to him?'

Again, Marney gave a disappointed sigh. 'The Progenitor,' she said. 'Have you ever heard that name before, Clara?'

'No.'

'There aren't many people left who remember the story, but the Progenitor is the name the Nephilim adopted for the rogue Thaumaturgist who created them.'

A tendril of light reached out from the star, stretching towards Hamir and rising above him. He watched it as though hypnotised by a snake preparing to strike.

'Hamir *created* the Nephilim?' Clara said.

'With dark methods that Thaumaturgists are forbidden to use.' There was disgust in Marney's voice. 'The Nephilim are hybrids, Clara – half-Thaumaturgist, half-human. Hamir abused a hundred denizens in his experiments. One hundred women. Using foul magic, he impregnated them with the souls of dead Thaumaturgists and forced them to give birth to the Nephilim. Not one of those women survived.'

Clara flinched as the tendril of light struck, stabbing into the black diamond on Hamir's forehead. His eyes squeezed shut, his mouth opened in a silent scream as the silver-blue light darkened to red. Clara felt no remorse for him, nor was she surprised by Marney's revelations. She couldn't exactly explain it but the information felt familiar, as if, here in this strange place, all things were indeed known to her.

Marney said, 'This must be the day Hamir was punished for his atrocities. What we're seeing happened centuries ago – a thousand years, more or less.'

A thousand years, Clara wondered. Back when the Labyrinth was new. She felt confused and said, 'Known Things was designed to hold Spiral's plans for the Genii War. How does Hamir's punishment fit in?'

'Memories within memories, Clara.' Marney didn't take her eyes off Hamir. 'They should have killed him for what he did,' she added bitterly. 'But instead, they drained the higher magic from his body and took away his thaumaturgic mark. There's no greater punishment for a Thaumaturgist, they say.' She scoffed. 'Hamir was stripped of power and sent to the Labyrinth, where he became the servant of the Residents.'

Clara looked at the cloudy rainbow walls and sparkling lights that surrounded her, then back at Hamir and the star of torturing light. '*Who* punished him?'

Marney, her eyes steely, didn't seem to hear, and all the while the black diamond tattoo smouldered and burned away from Hamir's forehead. Blood ran down his face into his open mouth. As it drained Hamir's thaumaturgy, the star's colour changed from red to purple.

'You got off lightly, you bastard,' Marney growled.

'Lucky for you that he did.'

It was a man who had spoken, though he was nowhere to be seen. Clara shot a worried look at Marney but the empath appeared unfazed by the voice.

'It's all right, Clara.'

On the other side of Hamir, a man emerged from the nebulous sparkling wall. Dressed in a simple russet habit, his unruly hair and thick beard long and grey, he approached the prisoner. His face was kindly but his eyes were shrewd as he looked from one magicker to the other.

Marney said, 'I was wondering when you'd make an appearance.' Her tone was even.

The man smiled. 'I thought it best to introduce myself.' A soft voice, tone bordering on amusement. 'There are one or two things about this place of which you need to be careful.'

Marney snorted.

'I know you,' Clara said, unable to hide her incredulity as Known Things whispered to her.

There had once been a Skywatcher known to the creatures of higher magic as Honoured Lord of the Thaumaturgists, though the Aelfir called him the Wanderer. His true name was Baran Wolfe, and he had been a member of the Trinity of Skywatchers, a select and favoured band among the Timewatcher's Thaumaturgists, a band which had also included Yansas Amilee and Iblisha Spiral.

History said that the Genii War began when Spiral murdered Wolfe; but history failed to acknowledge that Wolfe was not killed outright.

Spiral drained him of power, ripped the silver wings from his back and forced him to become the caretaker of secrets, the perverted and tortured wretch Voice of Known Things. Of course he would be present here.

'Hello, Clara,' Wolfe said softly. 'It's a pleasure to meet you. You also, Marney.'

Marney glared at him. Clara was intrigued, fascinated by a sudden and overwhelming sense that she knew this Thaumaturgist.

'I was present at Hamir's trial.' Wolfe watched the star of light. His face became serious. 'And I wasn't alone.'

Marney explained for Clara. 'Whenever a Thaumaturgist defied the Timewatcher, the Trinity of Skywatchers convened a court called the Council of Three.'

'Amilee and Spiral,' said Clara. 'They were there, too.'

'Their voices always carried more weight than mine,' Wolfe said distantly. 'Especially here on Mother Earth.'

'Mother Earth?' Clara said, surprised.

'The Council of Three tried all offending Thaumaturgists at the Timewatcher's House.'

Clara took in her surroundings again, a sense of awe rising within her. '*This* is Mother Earth?'

'A representation of it,' Wolfe replied. 'Creatures of lower magic aren't capable of seeing Mother Earth. Not while they're alive.'

'Why are you here?' Marney demanded.

Wolfe raised an eyebrow. Clara tried to fathom why the empath sounded so bitter towards the Skywatcher.

'The two of you have no time to waste,' Wolfe said, 'yet you are about to go running in circles, blind and desperate.'

'You want to help us,' Marney said, unimpressed. 'Is that it?'

'You sound as though you don't want my guidance. But I think we both know that you need it.'

Hamir's body jerked. The star had apparently finished draining the higher magic from him. The tendril, now less like light and more like a purple gelatinous umbilical, slipped from Hamir's forehead with a wet sound. Hamir groaned. The process had also drained him of youth. His raven hair now grey, the diamond tattoo replaced by an ugly red wound, he fell face down onto the symbols beneath him looking like the elderly necromancer Clara knew.

The soon-to-be-aide of the Residents faded and disappeared. The little star fizzed with higher magic as it sucked the gelatinous tendril into it.

Wolfe said, 'You cannot find the Nephilim with wishful thinking and blind luck. In fact, you'd be more likely to damn yourselves.' Face grave, he stood before the purple star and it rose up to his eye level. 'The machinations of creatures of higher magic are not meant for your understanding. There is information stored in Known Things that could crush your minds beyond redemption. *Ghosts* that you really don't want to stumble upon.' His smile returned. 'Fortunately for you, I am quite the experienced guide.'

Wolfe blew upon the star. With a creaking sound like water freezing, its colour changed to emerald green and its shape became a thaumaturgic diamond.

'You know how to find the Nephilim?' Clara said.

'I certainly know in which direction you must go,' Wolfe replied.

Marney continued to aim her steely glare at him. Clara felt perplexed.

'Explanations will have to wait for later, I'm afraid,' Wolfe continued, and he plucked the green diamond from the air. 'But a warning – never forget where you are. This is Spiral's domain and you could not handle knowing everything that he does. Search only for the Nephilim.'

Above, the multicoloured sky dimmed and the stars began winking out one by one, leaving behind black holes. Clara felt an emptiness inside her as the voice of the wolf growled thunder.

The Skywatcher's expression became utterly humourless and his pale eyes bored into the changeling. 'If your magic wipes Known Things from your mind before you find the Nephilim, there will be no point in you waking up. There will be no one to stop Spiral and every House in existence will fall before him. The Lord of the Genii's plans go deeper than even his followers know.'

So saying, Wolfe hurled the green diamond over the magickers. Clara followed its arching path and watched as it hit the scintillating wall with a glassy chime. The diamond ruptured the cloudy colours with a great gout of darkness which rolled up into the air like waves parting a sea. A night sky was revealed, in which shone the clean, bright glare of a moon.

The darkness descended, hissing like red-hot metal dipped into water as it formed the silhouettes of crooked buildings and towers lining a long, wide street. The green diamond glinted in the sky, the only star to accompany the moon.

Baran Wolfe had disappeared but his voice was carried on a cool, gentle breeze that came from the new landscape.

'I will find you again ...'

And then nothing.

Clara felt as though she stood on the threshold between two different worlds, and she watched as the scintillating, multi-hued representation of Mother Earth continued to darken. Thunder rumbled again, and this time it was underlined with a distinct howl.

'We should go,' Marney said quietly.

Clara followed the empath down the street of the city in silhouette. The darkness rolled and sealed shut behind them.

CHAPTER SIX

LORD OF THE GENII

A sea of red and blue stretched to the horizon, writhing, angry, rolling with clashing waves shining every shade found between dusk and dawn. Thick lines of black stone tried to form something solid in the sea, but the waves tore them to pieces which sank into the depths of perpetual flux. Giant, house-sized bubbles of deep purple rose and burst with sparkles of unused time, spiralling as they were borne up to a livid sky where ulcerous clouds bled the rains of continual shapelessness back down into the sea.

This was Oldest Place.

Fabian Moor recalled a description he had once read of the House, written by a poorly educated human historian: *A damned place of fire and poison.* How little the creatures of lower magic understood.

The air was surprisingly still and clement given the storm-like conditions; but there was nothing breathable about it, not even to a creature of higher magic. Hovering above the sea, Moor had cast a spell, a protective cocoon that wrapped him in fresh air and shielded him from the never-ending downpour of unused time. Mo Asajad and Viktor Gadreel had done the same while keeping their escape route open. Their faces masks of concentration, skin glowing with thaumaturgy, Moor's fellow Genii laboured to maintain the portal back to the Nightshade. The black, churning disc hung in the air between them.

After Known Things had given Hagi Tabet the relevant information, it had been relatively easy to find Oldest Place. Leaving, however, just might take a greater degree of luck.

Moor looked out across the red and blue sea. In the near distance, a grand formation of higher magic rose, connecting the volatile sea to the ulcerated sky like a spout of static-dashed darkness. There was something dangerous about it, almost sorrowful, and Moor's blood quickened.

'Preserve the portal,' he told Asajad and Gadreel. 'Be prepared to leave.'

And he drifted off towards the formation of magic.

He flew slowly, cautiously, high enough to avoid the eruptions of the sea. Oldest Place was a ruthless House that would not forgive the Genii any wrong move.

It was said that the Genii War had not only ended countless lives, but also the Timewatcher's compassion. Without mercy, She had broken those who rose against Her, and then She abandoned those who had stood beside Her. She destroyed the surviving Genii, flinging their corpses into the primordial mists of the Nothing of Far and Deep before disappearing with Her Thaumaturgists for good.

Yet despite the magnitude of Her wrath, the Timewatcher had chosen not to execute Lord Iblisha Spiral. For him, the great enemy and instigator, She had created this prison House. And now Moor understood the bitter depths of Spiral's punishment.

The location of Oldest Place had been regarded as the Timewatcher's most closely guarded secret. Theories and speculations had run rampant among the humans since the end of the war. Some claimed that Oldest Place had been set to drift in the great void of space; others that it had been shrunk to the size of a snow globe and stored away in the Timewatcher's private vaults on Mother Earth. Or perhaps it was in the very bowels of the Timewatcher's most loveless creation, the Retrospective, where Spiral sat on his throne and fed upon the souls of the dead like some ignoble demon.

So many guesses and lies. A plethora of myths, spawned from lesser minds, each as wild and unfounded as the next. It therefore came as no surprise to Moor that no one had guessed the true location of Spiral's prison.

Oldest Place was beneath the Great Labyrinth. Or more accurately, perhaps, to the side of it. On the periphery, in a gap between the real and the unreal – that was where the Lord of the Genii had been imprisoned; and the denizens of Labrys Town had never known how close to him they had always been. The House of all Houses, the one realm for which the greatest Thaumaturgist had been willing to go to war to conquer; the final irony of Spiral's sentence was to be incarcerated literally within touching distance of what he coveted most.

It was almost poetic, and Moor flushed with anger as he looked down at the sea below him.

Unused time had been manipulated to create Oldest Place – the same substance from which the Timewatcher had created the Labyrinth – but here She kept it in an unstable state: a ceaseless, repetitive loop that ensured time never really passed in this House. Except for the formation of magic rising from the sea. As Moor approached it, he realised that it hadn't been made from unused time. It was something else entirely.

The static-dash darkness formed a wall of sorts around the plateau of an island of black stone which rose from liquid time like an industrial chimney. Whispered voices, far-off moans and wails, reached Moor's ears. He kept his distance, hovering in the air, considering what he saw.

Human mythology might have claimed that Oldest Place reduced Spiral to a monstrous king of demons, but the truth was far more wretched. Oldest Place had been designed with one simple function: to keep Lord Spiral's body alive so his mind could be tortured by the Timewatcher's retribution for eternity.

Again, angry whispers and distant wails reached Moor's ears.

To relive the atrocities of the Genii War, to be reminded of the deaths he had caused, the Houses he had destroyed and his every act of betrayal over and over and over again – that had been Spiral's existence for the last forty years. The island and its wall of strange, dangerous magic was a cell. It had been created from *dead* time.

Moor felt a pang of doubt. He hovered, summoning the courage to move closer.

No one but the Timewatcher – and Spiral – could manipulate the substance of dead time. But was Moor's higher magic powerful enough to fool it?

He drifted a little closer to the wall. Once before, Moor had managed to fool the Timewatcher's thaumaturgy. He remembered how it had felt, respected how small he was compared to it. If he had one advantage in Oldest Place, it was that the Timewatcher never knew that some of the Genii had survived the war. She had thought this prison her best-kept secret and that there was no one left who could find it and spring Spiral from his cell.

Moor understood straight away that if he touched the wall of dead time physically, he would be crushed beyond existence. If he let his own thaumaturgy latch on to it too tightly, it would absorb his power entirely. He required subtlety. He required patience.

As the world around him roiled in flux, Moor conjured a phantom of himself, an astral copy which drifted gracefully away from his body and headed into the wall of dead time.

At first, it almost snatched his spirit away faster than he could control. The buzz of static shook his mind. With supreme concentration and perfect calm, Moor slid his magic over the rapid flow of energy, followed its currents until he found a way through the wall into pandemonium.

His phantom eyes were filled with ghosts: countless screaming sprites and wailing apparitions, spectres and ghouls trapped by the Timewatcher's spell, rushing and spinning, crushed together, spiralling into a vortex of madness that rose above the island, contained by dead time. The voices were too clamouring and fast for Moor to comprehend, and again he had to bolster his own thaumaturgy lest the ferocity of the ghosts sweep him up into their tumultuous din. He heard enough, however, to ascertain that the voices were shrieking about death and loss, violence, injustice and rage. It was the voice of the Genii War Moor could hear; the chaos of the dead, forced to recount their agonies in a never-ending loop.

How many millions had died in the war? How many souls had the Timewatcher trapped in Oldest Place instead of allowing them an afterlife?

And to think She had led them all to believe that She was their loving Mother.

Below the vortex of ghosts, nestled on the smooth island plateau, was a small, plain jar. Made from terracotta, its lid sealed with wax, the jar's very presence forced Moor to control mixed feelings of excitement and anger. The Timewatcher had forbidden Her Thaumaturgists to use this kind of dark magic, yet She had used it Herself to preserve the physical essence of Her First Lord, Iblisha Spiral.

Was there no end to Her hypocrisy?

A roar, much louder than the tumult of voices, filled Moor's mind. In the vortex, the giant face of a man formed from wispy radiance. Bald-headed and thickly bearded, his eyes shone with violet light. His mouth opened and his maniacal bellow appeared to be directed at the Genii's phantom. *My Lord*, Moor thought to it; but the face, tortured by the voice of war, didn't respond and shattered into pieces that the storm of ghosts carried away.

Moor's heart raced. To witness Lord Spiral's helplessness was too much to bear. With his body stored as ashes in the terracotta jar, he was powerless to prevent his mind from being ripped and torn for eternity. Yet Fabian Moor, Spiral's most trusted Genii, still found hope in the knowledge that the Timewatcher had not planned on anyone finding Oldest Place.

Carefully, masterfully, Moor's thaumaturgy searched for strands of dead time that weren't so raw and primal, areas of the wall which the Timewatcher had tamed with Her magic. They were fleeting, always moving, but Moor managed to capture what he wanted.

A bolt of energy streaked out to surround the jar with a sphere of spinning magical lines. Immediately, Spiral's mind reappeared as a giant face. With a wail of anguish, it raced down to the jar as though desperate to protect its body. When the face was close enough, Moor engorged the sphere. It sprang open like a trap and closed around Spiral's mind, holding it inside along with the jar.

Moor waited for several seconds.

The ghosts continued to race and wail above.

Nothing retaliated.

With a delicate use of higher magic and unwavering patience, Moor lifted the sphere and brought it towards the wall of dead time. Surrounded by the Timewatcher's spells and manipulations, the contents passed through without hindrance, the wall detecting no irregularities.

Moor returned to his body and gently coaxed the sphere out into the still, unbreathable air of Oldest Place. Separated now from their prison, Lord Spiral's body and mind were perfectly preserved by the spinning lines of magic.

Suspicious, Moor waited, ready for Oldest Place to react, to rise up with some magical retribution; but nothing changed. The sky still bled; the red and blue sea roiled. Its prisoner gone, the island, the cell of dead time, incarcerated only the voices of countless ghosts, trapped for eternity.

Moor allowed himself a small moment of triumph. Unimpeded, he drifted back towards Asajad and Gadreel, the sphere flying ahead of him.

Oldest Place had lost its prisoner.

Ennis had been hearing stories of Lady Amilee for as far back as he could remember. This Thaumaturgist – a Skywatcher – had been the patron of the denizens, vital to the Labyrinth in the old days. But like the rest of the Thaumaturgists she had slipped into legend and become a mythical figure long before Ennis was born. He had never really stopped to consider that Lady Amilee might be real. But she was – the last of the Thaumaturgists – and the blue ghost was her avatar, sent to Labrys Town as the harbinger of disaster.

A flash of light came from the workshop's doorway, followed by a line of hard swearing. Ennis shook his head. Sitting behind the counter out in the junk shop's display area, he continued waiting for Long Tommy to finish his feats of magical engineering.

Earlier, Ennis had watched Tommy work on the shard of strange thaumaturgic metal. Jars filled with powders and potions of varying colours surrounded the old shop owner on his workbench. From a note-book, he followed handwritten guidelines transcribed from the avatar's instructions. Over the green flames of magical fire, Tommy had melted the metal in a bowl of black Aelfirian glass, while whispering alien words and adding ingredients Ennis couldn't identify – and didn't want to, judging by the stench they created.

The metal had shed pearlescent light as it liquefied and the atmos-phere in the workshop became odd; not hot, as Ennis had expected, but filled with a pressure that tingled upon his skin, like it was trying to seep through his pores. It evoked a disquieting feeling in Ennis, and he hadn't been able to shake the notion that the metal was sentient, and that it recognised him.

Tommy, however, had remained unfazed. He had been dealing with magic for decades and it was fascinating to watch him work. Even so, when he put on welder's goggles and warned that the light was about to get too intense for the naked eye, Ennis had seized the chance to leave the room, relieved to escape the uncomfortable atmosphere.

He had been waiting in the main shop for almost two hours.

Ennis had arrested a few magic-users in his time but never actually witnessed spells being cast. Given that Tommy was also working with thaumaturgy, Ennis reasoned that, under normal circumstances, what he was allowing to take place in the old junk shop was grounds enough to get them both executed under the Resident's law. But these were not normal circumstances, and the Resident's law didn't seem to count for much these days.

Ennis shivered.

Another name the avatar had brought back from the past was Fabian Moor. It was little wonder that Ennis had been so confused over the last couple of days. He had a gift for piecing together information, solving the most bemusing of puzzles, connecting the unlikeliest of links and arriving at the truth. But even he couldn't have guessed that Fabian Moor and three other Genii had survived the war and taken control of the Nightshade. And soon, the denizens of Labrys Town would understand the reason for the Genii's return.

Spiral was coming.

'Prepare,' the avatar had warned. 'The Lord of the Genii will care for no one. Do as I say, or *every* denizen dies.'

Ennis rose from the chair, anxiety making him restless, and began to pace the shop.

Where was Lady Amilee now? Why send only her messenger when the denizens needed *her*, their patron, a Thaumaturgist? The avatar had been evasive when asked questions, its answers often cryptic. 'Events will unfold as they have to,' it had said before it disappeared. It was now apparent that Lady Amilee and her avatar expected an old-time crook and a lone policeman to perform the task of *preparing* Labrys Town.

Or every denizen dies...

Those words echoed around Ennis's mind, preoccupying his thoughts as he paced. He didn't notice Tommy emerge from the workshop at first.

'Something on your mind?' Tommy said sourly. He was carrying a wooden box. The welding goggles were pushed up on his forehead.

His eyes were circled by pale skin; the rest of his face was tinged red, as though sunburned. 'I have no idea if I've done this right.'

He dumped the box on the counter and dipped inside it. The first items he produced were two thumb-sized bullets cast from the thaumaturgic metal, their surfaces polished to a mirror finish.

Ennis stared at them. 'It took you over two hours to make two bullets?'

'Cut me some slack,' Tommy growled. 'I'm a little out of my depth here.'

Ennis picked up one of the bullets. It weighed next to nothing, and its texture felt curiously solid and liquid at the same time. It was too large for a pistol but too fat to be a rifle slug.

'I had to add some lead into the mixture,' Tommy explained. 'The avatar said it wouldn't matter. They'll do the job well enough.'

'Let's hope the avatar was right,' Ennis replied, laying the bullet down beside the other. 'This ends very badly if it was wrong.'

'I've seen all kinds of crazy shit in this town over the years. Rights and wrongs, trust and suspicion ... I suppose you just grow a sense for knowing when someone's telling the truth.' He stared at the bullets. 'I always used to think that the Relic Guild and the Nightshade were the scariest things in this town. But years ago I had a run-in with Fabian Moor, the first time he was here, and I soon changed my mind.'

'You've led a strange life, Tommy,' Ennis said.

'You don't know the half of it. If the avatar says those bullets can kill a Genii, then I believe they can. Here ...' Tommy delved into the box again, this time producing a pistol in an old holster of cracked brown leather. He drew the weapon and handed it over. It was of a design Ennis had never seen before: blocky, as heavy as it looked, and with two barrels and two triggers.

'A custom-made piece,' Tommy said, scratching the stubble on his cheek. 'As powerful as a rifle but easier to conceal. I bought it years ago from someone who was desperate for cash. Funny – I thought I'd got a bargain at the time.'

'You couldn't sell it on?' Ennis asked, turning the pistol over in his hands.

'I was conned. It has a unique power stone, you see. Won't work with any other kind. Give it a go, see what happens.'

With a frown, Ennis thumbed the power stone set behind the barrels. It whined into life, but instead of glowing with the usual violet light, the stone shone red.

'It's charmed,' Tommy said, his tone both amused and accusatory. 'Only a magicker can activate it.'

Ennis froze. Glaring at Tommy, he deactivated the power stone.

'I bloody knew it!' Tommy said bitterly. 'As soon as you walked into my shop, I knew there was something off about you.'

'So you know,' Ennis growled. 'Good for you.'

Tommy scoffed. 'And you actually had the cheek to treat *me* like a criminal. So what kind of magicker are you? Mental? Physical?'

'Does it matter?' Ennis cracked open the pistol and angrily fed a mirror bullet into each barrel. 'It's none of your business.'

'Oh, I think we're well past keeping secrets from each other, don't you, Ennis? Who else knows what you are?'

Ennis didn't reply. Anxiety boiled in his gut.

'No one, I bet.'

'We have to stay focused,' Ennis muttered. 'If we don't succeed, *nothing* will matter.'

'Fine,' Tommy snapped. 'Keep your bloody secrets.' He pursed his lips. 'But whatever your magic is, I hope it makes you as good a shot as the man who sold me that gun. You only get two chances to kill a Genii.'

Ennis slapped the barrels shut, slid the pistol into its holster and placed it on the counter. 'Don't worry about me. Just remember to make good on your end.'

'I'm scared, not stupid. I'm about to call in every favour I'm owed, lean on every person who'll listen to me, and all because a ghost and a copper told me to. That sort of thing doesn't go down too well in the underworld.'

'You want to switch places with me?'

Tommy barked a laugh. 'I reckon I could do with some magic in my veins right now. Here, I've got something else for you.'

Dipping into the box again, he revealed a sheathed knife and drew it. The blade was long, with the same mirror finish as the bullets.

'I tried a little experiment,' Tommy said. 'I brushed the remnants of the thaumaturgic metal over the blade. There was enough to give it a decent coat, and it's as sharp as anything.' He resheathed it. 'Thought it might come in handy – you know, as a backup.'

'Thanks.'

'No idea if it'll work, mind.' Tommy placed the knife back in the box, followed by the holstered pistol loaded with thaumaturgic bullets. 'I've been the scourge of this town once or twice in my life, but I don't think I've ever been its saviour.'

'We haven't saved anything yet.'

'Well, you're certainly as miserable as every other magicker I ever met.' Tommy broke into a broad grin. 'Thinking of it, if you'd been born in my day, you would've been an agent of the Relic Guild.'

'Is that right?' Ennis said dismissively, and he reached into his jacket pocket. 'Here, I've got something for you, too.' He passed Tommy a folded piece of paper. 'Instructions,' he explained, 'on how to find a secret apartment hidden in the central district. It used to belong to Old Man Sam.'

'Old Man Sam?' Tommy dropped the paper before he'd read the instructions. 'The bounty hunter?' He stared at Ennis as though the police sergeant had somehow read his mind – or stolen his memories. 'You've got to be kidding me.'

'As far as I know, no one else alive has a clue that apartment exists,' Ennis said, taking the box from the counter. 'If things go to plan, I'll meet you there afterwards. If they don't …'

'You can buy me a drink on Mother Earth.' Tommy offered his hand, his face earnest. 'For what you're about to do, Sergeant – good luck.'

Ennis stared at the hand for a moment before shaking it. 'You, too, you old crook.'

The Retrospective. Created by the Timewatcher at the end of the Genii War as punishment for Spiral's surviving allies. Hundreds of thousands of enemy Aelfir had been consigned to its perversions, their minds shattered beyond redemption, their bodies torn and corroded and ground into compost to seed the foundations of dead time. And they had risen as bloodthirsty animals, ever-multiplying legions of wild demons. They stalked the nightmarish plains that had formed from the raw material of their broken Houses. The Retrospective was the heart of hate.

But the heart had stopped beating.

The violent sky no longer bellowed and spat bolts of lightning; the noxious clouds no longer wept tears of acid; the fiery winds had ceased whipping and burning across the barren landscape. The Retrospective's fury had fallen to silence.

Wild demons gathered, an endless congregation of every shape and size of monstrosity imaginable. Corrupted beyond mercy, they observed an unspoken truce in the bestial war which had raged between them since the Retrospective's creation. They had come to bear witness, these incalculable monsters, to pay homage to a monument of flesh which hung over a hill of red, scorched rock.

Humans. At least a hundred of them, young and old. Stacked one upon another, their skins fused together, their limbs twisted and bent to form the framework of a sacrificial tower fifty feet high. Not quite dead, the humans' weak, dying moans were all that broke the demons' congruent stillness. Tears and sweat and blood and waste dripped onto the hill.

Fabian Moor observed from the safety of the Nightshade, looking out through a portal onto the endless swarm of wild demons surrounding the hill: giants as sturdy and gnarled as trees; *things* that looked like insects and arachnids; mammoth bloated slugs; four-legged beasts; humanoids designed for causing agony. None of them making a sound. Above, great demons flew on leathery wings, circling the tower of humans in a wide arc. All of these monsters waited, staring, preparing for the return of the high lord they had once followed. And would follow again.

With the Retrospective in his control, Lord Iblisha Spiral would bring the Houses of the Aelfir to their knees, subjugate their devotion. He would raise an army of billions, dwarfing even the number of demons to be found in this cursed House. The Genii would march on Mother Earth, taking their army to the Timewatcher, who would then know true despair.

The mind of Lord Spiral flew round and round the tower of humans as a silent phantom, a shapeless wisp, darting between airborne demons, hungry to find form again. Beneath the tower, the terracotta jar containing his essence sat on the hilltop. With only his spectral presence, Spiral had already achieved what it was said only the Timewatcher could do: he had tamed the Retrospective.

Moor turned to Asajad and Gadreel. Behind them, Hagi Tabet hung on her web of tentacles, Known Things in her hands, glass tubes in her mouth and temple. Her eyes watered as she stared into the Retrospective.

Asajad locked gazes with Moor. Her customary impudence was gone. For the first time that Moor could remember, Asajad looked afraid. Did she fear that the rite would not work? Or did she fear the return of her lord?

Gadreel, however, looked excited. His expression was as intolerant as always, and his one eye, dark and dead as a sea serpent's, gazed upon the tower of humans as though admiring the handiwork of the Genii. His fat lips were twisted into his approximation of a smile.

As for Moor, he was in no doubt that the winning move in the long game was about to be played.

'My friends,' he said triumphantly. 'The Genii War is won.'

Moor struck out with his thaumaturgy, sending a lance of energy into the Retrospective. It hit the jar. Terracotta shattered.

A dome of ash grey ballooned. A drone spread across the battered landscape, tremulous with the accumulation of enormous power. The wild demons stirred. The phantom of Spiral's mind raced down and dived into the grey dome.

Like an abscess bursting, the dome erupted into a great dirty sandstorm that roared into the air, tearing into the tower of flesh.

With their last breaths, the humans screamed as the blistering sandstorm raged upwards, shredding and tearing, drinking blood and devouring flesh. Blossoming with a deep crimson colour, the storm chewed its way through the humans as quickly and efficiently as fire burning paper. When it reached the top and finished feeding, the storm hung as a dull red cloud. The remnants of the humans rained down on the hill in a shower of bones.

The wild demons screeched and bellowed, swarming the hill, reaching out for the burning cloud above them. As if they were praying, Moor thought. When the cloud descended, it fell like a boulder, leaving behind red streaks as it dropped from the sky. It crashed into the swarm with an almighty explosion. A shock wave rolled with fire, spreading out across the Retrospective, incinerating every demon in its path. And it came for the Nightshade.

Hagi Tabet whimpered.

'Fabian,' Asajad said. 'Close the portal.'

'Why fear it?' Gadreel growled. He stood proudly as the shock wave neared. 'Lord Spiral returns.'

Moor was frowning. He could perceive the hate and hunger hurtling towards the Nightshade. It was twinned with a madness so deep-rooted that he realised it would not stop until it devoured everything in its way. Including the Nightshade and its occupants.

'Something is wrong,' Moor whispered, a sense of dread rising within him.

'Nonsense,' said Gadreel.

'Fabian!' Asajad screeched. 'Close the damned portal!'

A scorching wind blowing upon his face compelled Moor into action. He closed the portal as Spiral's fire came dangerously close. Silence returned to the Nightshade.

Gadreel glowered his disappointment, but Moor and Asajad stared at each other, troubled. Not all was as it should be with the Lord of the Genii's reanimation.

CHAPTER SEVEN

ICE GIANT

With the Sisterhood of Bells far behind them, the agents of the Relic Guild arrived at a strange and cold House where they were surrounded by countless trees, tall and crooked and encased in ice.

'So this is the Icicle Forest,' Namji said, shivering and buttoning up her jacket.

'Looks like we got a one-way ticket,' Glogelder said. The expression on his scarred and pitted face was balanced between bemusement and fear as he watched the portal close and disappear.

Hillem said nothing, just slid his pistols into the holsters at his hips and, ever the student, began examining the tree closest to him.

Samuel scanned the area, holding his ice-rifle tightly, his breath frosting in the air. Whichever way he looked, he could see nothing through the dense, barren trees encased in glimmering frozen shells. Above, up through the leafless boughs, an unbroken grey blanket covered the sky. Overcast and dim, the Icicle Forest was shrouded in unwelcoming twilight.

The sloping forest floor was unnaturally smooth; there was no undergrowth, no tree roots or fallen branches protruding from the thick covering of fresh snow. And when Samuel dug at the untouched layer with his boot, he uncovered no dead leaves or mulch; just more snow, hard and compacted, glinting with tiny blue stars.

'Samuel,' said Namji, 'do you sense anything?'

The old bounty hunter shook his head. His prescient awareness had returned to him – and he was thankful for that, especially because it was currently dormant and issuing no warning of imminent danger – but even so, Samuel remained tense and alert. There was no breeze in this House. No sound. No scent.

Glogelder grumbled. 'So we don't know where we're going or what we're supposed to do.' Adjusting the straps of the duffel bag on his back, he looked up and down the slope, then checked the power stone on his spell sphere launcher. 'Would've been nice if our instructions were a bit more detailed.'

Samuel shook away images of the Genii Lady Amilee had imprisoned in Little Sibling.

'I've got something that might help,' Namji said. She sat down on the snow, laying aside her crossbow, and reached for her satchel. 'Give me a moment.'

From the satchel, the Aelf removed a folded piece of parchment, which she opened and laid flat on the ground, followed by a small spell sphere the size of a human eyeball filled with clear liquid. She cracked the sphere like an egg, releasing the liquid, which radiated a deep blue glow as it poured into a thick puddle upon the parchment. Discarding the broken glass, Namji used her index finger as a scriber, drawing magical symbols with the glowing ink.

'Look at this,' Hillem said. He was still studying the tree and had broken away some of the ice covering the trunk. 'The ice is more like a shell, brittle like dead bark. And the tree underneath isn't wood.'

Samuel saw that Hillem had uncovered a shiny substance like resin, red with veins of blue and mottled by a deep purple. Samuel laid his hand upon it, surprised that it felt warm yet somehow insubstantial. Hillem checked another tree, and then another. Intrigued, Glogelder shouldered his launcher and investigated for himself.

'They're all the same,' Hillem said.

Samuel pulled his hand away as the tree's warmth prickled against his skin, raising the hairs on the back of his neck.

'What are they?' Glogelder asked.

No one had an answer.

'There,' said Namji. 'That should do it.'

Whispering a few words of magic, she held the parchment up before her face and blew upon the blue script. The parchment burst into flame in her hands, burning brightly and quickly. As the ashes fell to the ground, black smoke rose and unfurled into a bird as black as soot, flapping dark wings, soaring up through the trees towards the dreary sky.

Namji retrieved her crossbow and stood. 'Now we have eyes above,' she said.

Samuel, Hillem and Glogelder waited. Eventually, Namji's eyes glazed, not quite looking at her colleagues but perhaps through them. Her eyes moved from side to side as though seeing some distant place, far beyond her companions. She was looking down on them through the eyes of her spell, Samuel realised. It was a trick he had seen Van Bam use before.

'What do you see?' he asked.

'We're in a depression,' Namji answered. 'The forest fills a giant bowl about a mile across. I can see a clearing halfway down, like a strip of bare land. Looks like a pale ring dividing the trees.'

Samuel tried to imagine what Namji's magical conjuration was seeing. 'Anything else?'

'The forest starts again and continues until you get to the centre. There are walls there. *Big* walls, far taller than the trees. Four of them, I think. Boxing something in.'

'Can you see what?'

'No – the spell can't travel far enough ahead of me. We'll have to get closer for a better look.'

'Well then,' said Hillem, 'if that's all there is besides trees, it must be our destination.'

'Brilliant,' Glogelder muttered. 'No idea what we're looking for, but we're going to find it anyway.'

Samuel shared the Aelf's apprehension. 'How long does your spell last?' he asked Namji.

'Long enough to lead us to the centre,' she replied. 'I'm blind on the ground, though. Someone will have to lead me.'

Hillem placed Namji's hand in the crook of his arm.

'For now, just head down in a straight line,' Namji said. 'I'll get more of an idea where we're headed once we reach the clearing.'

'I'll take point,' Samuel said. For the hundredth time, he checked that both power stones on his ice-rifle were primed. 'Glogelder, you bring up the rear. And no one get in front of me.'

They set off into the trees, heading towards whatever Lady Amilee had sent them here to find.

The way was easy enough, though no sign of a well-worn path presented itself. The further Samuel walked, the more he realised that something was missing from the Icicle Forest. It wasn't just the strange trees and eerie silence, the lack of scent and breeze. There was a distinct absence of life. This place had once been a secret Genii stronghold, created by Spiral during the war. Odd that a creation of the most powerful Thaumaturgist who had ever existed should feel so dead and empty. But there it was. The very chill in the air felt somehow hollow, as though the House's heart had been ripped out.

But *something* was here.

A missing and important piece to a seemingly endless puzzle, the Genii had said. Her message lingered in Samuel's thoughts. Van Bam and Clara, wherever they were; Samuel and the Aelfir; the denizens of Labrys Town ... *everybody* faced annihilation unless this *rogue element* was found.

Namji called out directions, steering the group gradually to the right and onwards down the steady slope. Every now and then, as he guided Namji through the tall and crooked trees, Hillem paused to break the brittle veneer of ice covering one of the trunks. None were wood, and Hillem wondered aloud about the function of the trees, and why there was so much snow on the ground, yet none falling from the heavy snow clouds above.

'Does it matter?' Glogelder bemoaned. 'Still won't tell us why we're here – or bring back the feeling in my feet.'

The cold grew ever more bitter as they trudged on.

Samuel recalled the time he met the treasure hunter who had come to the Icicle Forest to find the terracotta jar containing Fabian Moor's essence – at least, he had met what remained of the man. Llewellyn was his name, and he had described this House as *evil*. Something in the Icicle Forest had mauled Llewellyn, broken him. Only magic had sustained his life, and if the Relic Guild hadn't put him out of his misery, not even that would have kept him alive for much longer.

Yet the Icicle Forest did not stir Samuel's magic enough to give him that dull, sickly feeling in his gut that warned of danger at the end of the path he was on. Samuel hoped – *prayed* – that it meant whatever power had made this House evil had perished during the last four decades.

After about fifteen minutes of walking, the group reached the clearing Namji's spell had seen. It wasn't the empty space she had supposed. Where the trees stopped, a series of standing stones began. Craggy, ovular and slate-grey, too many to count. Apparently placed at random in the snow, they were of varying sizes, the smallest reaching to Samuel's waist, the biggest taller than Glogelder. If Namji was right and this clearing formed a ring within the forest, then Samuel guessed the standing stones must fill it entirely.

Glogelder walked up to one and rapped his knuckles against it. It sounded as solid and stony as it looked. 'What are these things?'

'What are you talking about?' said Namji. 'What's down there?'

Hillem described the area.

'Funny,' Namji continued, 'I can't see any stones from the sky.'

'What about the centre of the forest?' Samuel asked.

'The walls are too high and close together. We'll have to get nearer to see inside.' She pursed her lips. 'I'll tell you what's strange, though. The sky isn't really a sky. It's thick, almost solid – no clouds. And it's moving. Like … like the Nothing of Far and Deep.'

That made sense, Samuel decided. The Nothing of Far and Deep was where Spiral had supposedly hidden all his secret strongholds. Perhaps the Icicle Forest was akin to a giant bubble inflated inside its primordial mists. But why was it dark grey instead of white?

Hillem, however, looked confused by Namji's revelation and gestured to the ground. 'If there are no clouds in the sky, then where did the snow come from?'

Glogelder made an exasperated noise. 'You really pick your moments to think about the stupidest things. Who cares!' Clearly agitated, the big Aelf had a dangerous look in his eye. 'I don't like this place being so quiet – so let's keep moving, shall we?'

With Hillem still guiding Namji the group set off again, weaving between the standing stones, snow crunching beneath their feet. The forest began again on the other side of the clearing, where the strange trees grew more dense and close, and a wide, darkened path burrowed through them like a tunnel. But they hadn't cleared the standing stones before Samuel's prescient awareness flared as a bad feeling in his gut.

'Wait,' he said, raising a hand. The group halted behind him. 'Namji, can you see anything moving towards us?'

'No. Why?'

Samuel's magic grew a little warmer. 'I think we're being watched. And by nothing good.'

Instantly alert, Glogelder raised his spell sphere launcher and scanned the area. With a pistol in each hand, Hillem stepped away from Namji. The three men formed a triangle around her, looking out through the standing stones, searching for anything lurking there.

'Are you sure you can't see anything?' Samuel demanded.

'No,' Namji replied. 'There's nothing, I— *Oh!* She staggered, holding her head. Blood trickled from one nostril and her eyes gained focus as she wiped it away. 'My spell,' she said breathlessly. 'Something severed my connection to it.'

High above, Namji's magical bird dispersed as a puff of black smoke against the grey. As Samuel's magic began to gather heat, Glogelder said to Hillem, 'There's your snow.'

Flakes were falling from the Nothing of Far and Deep. Thick, glinting red and blue, they came fluttering into the clearing and onto the forest. A breeze picked up, bringing with it the acrid stench of magic. Eerily, the snowflakes avoided contact with the group, almost falling in flocks that spiralled down to settle on the standing stones. The end of Samuel's rifle managed to snag a single flake. It clung to the barrel for a moment, sparkling, before stretching like a long line of mucus and dropping to the ground.

In but a few moments, each standing stone had a pile of glimmering snow upon it.

'It's moving,' Glogelder announced.

He was talking about the standing stone closest to him. It was shaking, rocking from side to side, making a low groaning sound. With a hard *snap*, a crack appeared in its side, and then more of the stones began to shake and groan.

'They're not stones,' Samuel announced, his voice coming from that cold and distant place where his magic ruled his instincts and intuition.

The others looked at him.

'They're cocoons—'

A fist punched out of one of the stones, sending shattered pieces flying into the snowstorm. Samuel's prescient awareness went berserk.

'*Run!*'

'Do we dare look?' said Mo Asajad.

Silence.

In the Nightshade, the Genii stared at the wall where the portal into the Retrospective had been. A sense of unease crawled over Moor's skin, blemishing his elation that Lord Spiral, after all these long years, was finally, blessedly free. His rebirth had caused such a violent and un-expected cataclysm. The madness with which it had exploded ... Did they indeed dare look into the Retrospective again?

'What happened, Fabian?' Asajad's usual cold, mocking demeanour had disappeared. She spoke with anger. She spoke with fear. 'What did we witness?'

'Lord Spiral's reanimation, of course,' Gadreel answered.

No, no, no, Moor thought as he and Asajad looked at their hulking comrade. *That was no simple rebirth.*

'It was reanimation,' Gadreel affirmed joyously, not a shred of doubt in his tone.

'It was more than that, Viktor,' said Asajad. 'Had the portal not been closed, Lord Spiral would have devoured us all.' Concern and confusion lay heavy on her face. 'Is there something you are not telling us, Fabian?'

'No.'

'You are sure? You always were deeper in his confidence than the rest of us.'

It was true. Iblisha Spiral had trusted Fabian Moor above all other Genii, and there were many things Moor knew that his comrades did not. But had he been naïve to believe that he knew everything of his master's plans?

'Please, Fabian,' Asajad said. 'Tell me I am paranoid.'

'What did you expect?' Gadreel said angrily, as though Moor and Asajad were deliberately trying to ruin his moment of triumph. 'You remember the power of Lord Spiral, yes? You comprehend that he has spent the last forty years incarcerated in a House where the Time-watcher's retribution tortured him perpetually? And yet you didn't expect his rebirth to carry such rage and power?' His one eye looked disgustedly at them. 'Perhaps the long game has left you *both* paranoid.'

Moor and Asajad shared a lingering look.

'There are secrets.' Hagi Tabet's voice came from all places at once.

Hanging on her web of leathery tentacles, the black diamond of Known Things in her bony hands, Tabet looked down on her comrades, her eyes watery and unfocused.

'There are things we do not know,' Tabet said. The thaumaturgic symbols on Known Things glowed purple with each word. 'I have been reading the memories of the changeling. The Relic Guild has received help from Lady Amilee.'

'*Amilee?*' said Asajad.

Gadreel looked at Moor. 'What is this?'

'Impossible,' Moor whispered. 'The Thaumaturgists followed the Timewatcher to Mother Earth after the war. They are ... *gone!*'

'Amilee remained,' Tabet said. 'In this I am not mistaken.' A tear rolled down her cheek. 'From the shadows, she has been steering the Relic Guild.'

Moor's worry deepened. 'Did she know that we planned to free Lord Spiral?'

Fluid gurgled along the glass tubes connecting Known Things to Tabet's mouth and temple. 'I believe so.'

Moor hissed out a breath.

'It does not matter,' Gadreel announced with supreme confidence. 'Whatever plots and plans the Skywatcher made to stop us, she has failed. Our Lord is returned to us!'

Asajad ignored him. 'Hagi,' she snapped, 'where is Amilee now?'

'The changeling did not know. But there is more ...' Tabet's eyes flitted from side to side, scanning information from the box in her hands. 'I have found a secret place inside Known Things, and what it contains frightens me—'

Tabet choked off, as if the words had been stolen from her throat. The room was filled with the stench of age, hopelessness and death.

Tabet gasped from everywhere. 'Oh my … he is here!'

The portal to the Retrospective opened.

It began as a dark line on the wall, splitting the repetitive pattern of tiny mazes. The line widened to the size of a doorway, through which the House of dead time could be seen.

The sky undulated with toxic clouds, alive with lightning. The scorched and barren landscape stretched into the distance; and there, standing in uniform rows, were millions of wild demons. A menagerie of the grotesque, they flanked a narrow stretch of blackened ground. Waiting, disciplined, the demons didn't move or make a sound.

A roar of thunder came from above and a cloud burst open with a shower of lightning bolts. A figure fell from the sky, a man gliding on wings of silver. He landed gracefully on the stretch of ground between the ranks of demons. His wings folded upon his back and he strode towards the Nightshade.

Tabet whimpered. Gadreel stood proudly. Moor and Asajad stepped back.

Naked from the waist up, the man wore a long black skirt that reached to the ground. It swirled with each step, revealing bare feet. His torso was muscular. His head was shaved smooth but his beard was thick, as dark as his skirt. And as he neared the portal, Moor could see the triumphant expression revealing long white teeth. Power radiated from him, the highest of magic.

The Genii dropped to their knees.

Lord Iblisha Spiral entered the Nightshade.

'My Genii. My *friends*.' His voice could command universes, his presence too vast for even the grandest halls. 'Arise.'

His heart hammering, Moor stood. Asajad and Gadreel flanked him. Tabet seemed frozen on her web.

'All these years.' Spiral's eyes leaked power in violet vapour. 'All those plans within plans.' He looked at each of them in turn. 'Lord Gadreel. Lady Asajad. Lady Tabet. *Fabian*. It is a blessing to see you again.'

'Welcome home, my lord,' Gadreel said, bowing.

'Home?'

A strange smile touched Spiral's lips, which disappeared when he regarded Hagi Tabet. He appeared to find shame in Tabet's withered, naked form, disappointment in the web of tentacles. The light of his eyes flared angrily when he saw Known Things in her hands. But when he spoke, his voice betrayed nothing but benevolence.

'Lady Tabet. Yours is the greatest sacrifice, I think. Look at what you did to yourself to bring me *home*.'

'It was an honour, my lord.'

'And I will not forget that.'

As Spiral moved towards Tabet, Moor frowned. There was something about the Lord of the Genii that didn't look quite ... *solid*. Spiral placed his hands over Tabet's almost lovingly, and his touch made her gasp.

'Thank you,' Spiral whispered, and he wrenched Known Things from her grasp.

The tubes shattered, leaving a jagged shard in Tabet's temple. Sobbing, she spat out pieces of broken glass, dribbling blood down her body. Moor spared a glance at Asajad and Gadreel. Gadreel clearly revelled in his lord's return; Asajad's countenance remained concerned. Tabet began swinging on her web, her sobs building momentum towards a scream.

'Sleep, Hagi,' Spiral said, and with a light burst of thaumaturgy he rendered Tabet unconscious.

Holding Known Things at arm's length, Spiral began whispering the language of the Thaumaturgists. The symbols decorating Known Things pulsed with light to each word. And then they began to move. Losing form, the symbols merged into two pools of purple radiance that flowed from the box, over Spiral's hands and slithered up his arms to slide across his chest and abdomen. Spiral threw his head back as though shocked. The Genii backed away as Spiral's wings fanned and rose above him like scythes. Finally, the purple light formed into words of higher magic, setting like tattoos as black as obsidian.

'Freedom,' Spiral growled, and he crushed Known Things to a cloud of dust as fine as smoke.

Moor resisted the urge to shy away as his Lord's power swelled, threatening to break down the walls.

The dust settled. Spiral folded his wings, his beautiful face cruel and determined, as he glared at his Genii.

'Now it begins.'

'Keep moving!' Samuel shouted above the howling wind.

Glogelder launched a spell sphere. It exploded with fiery magic, roaring like a savage orange furnace, shedding black, choking smoke. Yet the blast did little to impede the monsters. Through the blizzard of glittering snow they came as a horde, chasing the Relic Guild down the track that cut through the trees and led to the centre of the Icicle Forest.

The cocoons in the clearing had hatched demons the likes of which Samuel had never seen before. Humanoid, quick and powerful, their bodies and limbs glowed with violet light fractured by a network of dark veins. Their heads were featureless black ovoids bearing swirls of purple for faces. They died easily enough; each time Samuel's rifle shot a crystal-hard dart of ice, a demon shattered into a thousand iridescent pieces which spiralled up through the snowstorm towards the sky; but Samuel's prescient awareness told him that a never-ending line of these creatures was chasing them. It told him to run, and to keep running.

As the old bounty hunter followed the directions of his magic, Hillem turned and fired his pistols. He was hardly a marksman, but the horde was so densely packed together it was difficult for him to miss. Eerily, the glowing demons had no voices, and the only sound to join the howling wind was the stomping, rushing noise of a stampede. And it was gaining on the group.

With clenched teeth, Namji aimed back with her crossbow as she ran, shooting a bolt at the ground behind the group. A dome of vicious vacuum magic ballooned, droning in the wind. It devoured and crushed any demon who passed through it, sucked in any that tried to go over or round it, shredding each of them into fountains of light, buying the Relic Guild enough time to get ahead in the chase.

While Samuel, Namji and Hillem sped on, Glogelder sent two more spell spheres arcing high over the dome of vacuum magic. They detonated with the roar of magical fire.

Samuel took consolation from the fact that his magic banished the weight of his advancing years, filling his muscles and joints with the energy of youth, and he pumped his legs as hard as he could. Either side of the track, the forest was too dense, the trees growing too close together for the demons to overtake and head the group off. Samuel's magic told him their only chance was to reach the centre of the Icicle Forest.

One of the great walls that Namji had seen from the air loomed at the end of the track. Fifty feet high at least, it looked to be a single piece of smooth, grey stone; and mercifully there was an arched opening cut into its base. Before long, Samuel reached the wall, sped through the archway and entered the House's centre.

Boxed in by four walls, surrounded by level, snow-covered ground, was a formation of red rock. It resembled a miniature mountain, its colour a stark contrast to the whiteness. Samuel could see no paths or cave mouths that might lead into the mountain, but his magic urged him towards it.

'Come on!' Samuel shouted, but a cry from Hillem stopped him in his tracks.

'Glogelder!'

The big Aelf was still on the forest track. With Namji's vacuum magic depleted, the horde of demons once again thundered behind him, a mass of violet power, quickly catching him up. Glogelder shrugged the duffel bag from his back and let it fall to the ground. Namji made to use her crossbow, but with a prick from his magic Samuel stopped her. Glogelder turned, fired his spell sphere launcher at the duffel bag and then continued to run with a shout of warning.

The spare ammunition and spell spheres inside the bag exploded with force enough to shake the ground. A fiery shock wave sped down the track after Glogelder, and Samuel knew he wasn't going to outrun it.

'Glogelder, no!' Hillem shouted.

Driven by his prescient awareness, Samuel shoved Namji out of the way and dragged Hillem clear. The shock wave punched Glogelder through the archway, sending him flying through the air like a rag doll. A great gout of fire spewed after him. As the fire receded, Glogelder hit the ground with a sickening thud, flipping over and over in the snow until he stopped ... at the feet of a giant.

Gaunt and pale, dressed in a brown habit, the giant stood ten feet tall at least. His hair was an unruly mess, hanging about his shoulders, and his eyes were orbs of pure, shining blue. Behind him, a dark cave had appeared at the base of the miniature mountain. Samuel aimed his rifle even though his magic warned of no fresh danger.

'I'd stop gawking, if I were you,' the giant said with a surprisingly calm and gentle voice. 'Get inside.'

The stampede of demons could already be heard rushing down the track again.

'Move!' Samuel shouted, but Namji and Hillem didn't need to be told. The three of them sped through the blizzard towards the opening.

The giant's huge hands were smeared with blood and he began weaving symbols in the air as the Relic Guild ran past him. Once they had entered the cave, Samuel turned and saw the giant release a mighty spell that sped away from him, carving a furrow in the snow. The magical energy raced down the track and smashed into the oncoming horde, destroying every demon in its path. Samuel detected the tang of spent thaumaturgy in the air.

'Oh, shit,' Hillem whispered.

The group's saviour entered the cave, carrying Glogelder's limp body. The big Aelf looked as small as a child in the giant's arms. His coat, blackened and charred, still smouldered. The opening disappeared behind the giant, reverting to solid red rock, and a soft glow came from the back of the cave.

Hillem was the first to speak, his voice pained. 'Is ... is he dead?'

'No.' The giant gave him a reassuring smile. 'Your friend is a little beaten and broken, but I'm sure it's nothing I can't fix.'

Namji stepped forward, her face awed. 'Gulduur?' She sounded stunned. 'Gulduur Bellow?'

The giant regarded her for a moment before his bright blue eyes widened in recognition. 'Namji!' His smile became a broad grin. He looked at Samuel. 'You are travelling with a human. A human magicker. This is a *good* day.'

Samuel's magic might have fallen dormant, but he still had to resist aiming his rifle as the giant approached him.

'I am so very pleased to meet you,' said the giant. 'I wonder – would you mind helping me complete a puzzle?'

— CHAPTER EIGHT —

MISINFORMATION

All was still. The buildings had no detail. Without doors or windows or signs, they rose as dark, blocky shapes on either side of the street as though they had been carved from shadow. The street itself was paved with damp and grimy cobbles and could easily have been mistaken for any street or lane or alleyway in Labrys Town. A moon hung in the sky, fat and full and bright. The only star shining amidst the silvery glare was the green diamond.

With each step Clara took, she felt more grounded in this strange mindscape that belonged to both her and Known Things. Marney walked beside her. Neither woman knew where they were headed.

'What happened to Gideon?' Clara asked Marney.

The empath gave her a sidelong look. 'I'm not sure. Just be thankful his voice isn't in your head any more.'

'It wasn't as bad as you might think,' Clara replied truthfully.

Gideon, the ghost of an ex-Resident and Van Bam's spirit guide – Clara's, too, for a time. No one really understood why his voice had appeared in Clara's mind. His presence had been cold and mocking, malicious at times, but he had always worked for the good of the Relic Guild. So long as he was given the respect he demanded. Clara had stopped hearing his voice at the precise moment Van Bam died, and she still felt the emptiness he left behind.

'Who knows?' Marney said. 'Maybe Gideon's ghost took the final journey to Mother Earth.'

'I hope so,' Clara replied, not least because she needed to believe that even though the Timewatcher had abandoned humans and Aelfir alike, She still welcomed their dead souls into Her House.

'The truth is, Clara, Gideon was an easy man to hate.' Marney's words had a bitter edge, suggesting she didn't much care what had become of the ex-Resident. 'I never knew anyone who wasn't intimidated by him

– well, except Samuel, maybe. Those two had more than a few run-ins back then.' She shivered. 'I spent a lot of time hiding from Gideon up here in your mind. He was very tenacious trying to find out what I knew.'

Clara frowned. 'But how did you know so much? Van Bam and Samuel couldn't work out how you discovered the location of Oldest Place. Only the Timewatcher was supposed to know.'

'It's complicated, Clara,' Marney replied. 'There is so much about the Timewatcher and the Thaumaturgists that humans and Aelfir aren't supposed to know.'

'But you do?'

'Not exactly.' A faraway expression came to Marney's face, and she looked up at the sky. 'During the Genii War, it was a strange time in the Labyrinth. Some of us in the Relic Guild learned far more than we ever wanted to.'

Up above, the green diamond moved in the sky, dropping to a lower position, brightening before dimming.

Marney continued, 'When Fabian Moor first came to Labrys Town, he was working under very specific orders. Spiral had planned for the war meticulously. He had divined as much detail as he could, until he reached the stage where the outcome of the war pivoted on one specific moment. There was a House – it doesn't exist any more, but you might've heard of it. Mirage?'

'That's where Namji came from. Where Van Bam met the Nephilim.'

'Exactly. Mirage had planned to invade the Labyrinth, and that was the *moment*, Clara. If the invasion had been a success, it would have started a chain of events leading to Spiral's victory.'

'But obviously the invasion failed,' said Clara.

'And that began a chain of events which led to Spiral's defeat. As soon as that invasion failed, Fabian Moor knew his lord and master would lose the war. From that moment on, Moor began following Spiral's second plan.'

'Second plan?'

'Spiral had seen it all, Clara. He divined that the Timewatcher would abandon the Labyrinth and the denizens after the war, and that She would go back to Mother Earth and not return. He knew that She would create a prison for him – Oldest Place – and that someone in the Relic Guild would come to know its location.'

'You?'

'Not directly.' Marney sighed. 'Amilee created an anomaly, something that Spiral couldn't divine.' She smirked. 'You and me, Clara. Amilee made damn sure that Spiral didn't see us coming.'

In the sky, the green diamond flashed and dropped a little lower.

Clara said, 'So Amilee has known that the Genii would come back to free Spiral since ... when? The end of the war?'

Marney shrugged. 'Amilee has always kept her secrets close. She's been hiding, waiting, and there must be a damn good reason why she hasn't shown herself yet.'

'She sends her avatar instead.' Clara thought of the blue spectre with a touch of frustration. 'That thing could really do with learning how to speak plainly.'

Marney chuckled. 'Ah,' she said, 'I think we've reached our destination.'

The green diamond had now dropped so low that it glowed like a lamp on the darkened street. The magickers rushed to it and discovered a house that was not smeared with darkness. Light shone through grimy windows, glinting off damp cobbles. Voices came from within, too low to understand. Marney pushed the door open and led Clara inside. But the strange world of Known Things did not greet them with the interior of a house.

It was a silver room, perfectly square, its metal walls radiating sterile light.

Clara gasped.

'I know how you feel,' Marney muttered.

At the centre of the otherwise empty metal room, Fabian Moor stood staring at the wall. As pale as an albino, he wore the black cassock of a priest. Long white hair framed his face. A fresh burn wound on his forehead wept. He was unaware of the magickers.

'Another memory,' Clara said, keeping her voice low.

Marney nodded. 'But not one of mine.'

'Then whose? Baran Wolfe?'

'Like I said, it's complicated.' Marney studied the memory of the

Genii. 'Forty years ago, the Relic Guild believed it had killed Moor. I was the only one who knew different. I was the only one who knew that there was more to his mission than we had discovered. I just didn't realise it at the time.'

Moor spoke. 'Yes, my lord.' He bowed his head. 'I understand.'

'One last order, Fabian.' The new voice came from a shadow that had appeared on the wall. Male, commanding, it flooded the silver room with a sense of disquiet.

It's Spiral, Marney's voice said in Clara's mind, as if speaking aloud might somehow direct the Genii Lord's attention to her. *This must be one of his memories.*

Clara quashed the nausea that threatened to rise in her gut.

'Anything, my lord,' Moor said.

'When you reach the Nightshade, see if you can bring Simowyn Hamir to our side.'

'Hamir?' Moor looked up. 'He is important to you?'

'As of this moment, no,' the shadow said, 'but he could prove useful in the future.'

'My lord?'

'Do you doubt me, Fabian?'

'Never!' Moor bowed his head again. 'But ... but given Hamir's past, can he be trusted?'

'Simowyn is a whim. Either gain his compliance or kill him. He is a secondary consideration. Understand?'

'As you wish, my lord.'

The shadow moved across the wall, oily, spreading over the metal. 'Prepare yourself.'

Fabian Moor screamed and fell to his knees. The silver walls blazed, blinding Clara to much of what happened next. Moor appeared to collapse in on himself, his cries silenced abruptly as he imploded. When the light receded, the shadow had gone, and so had Moor. All that remained was a small terracotta jar sitting on the spot where he had stood. A jar containing a Genii's essence.

'Hamir,' Marney mused, almost to herself. 'Spiral must've been interested in him because of the Nephilim. Hamir did create them, after all.'

'Well, I don't think Hamir's a factor any more,' Clara replied. 'He didn't escape the Labyrinth with us. He was left behind and the Genii probably killed him.'

'We don't know anything for certain. We can't be sure that Hamir's dead.' Marney aimed a curious look at Clara. 'Just as we can't be sure that I am.'

'I ... What?'

Marney glared meaningfully. 'I remember the night you joined the Relic Guild. I remember talking to you in the Great Labyrinth, but then I was inside your mind. I have no memory of what happened to the ... *real* me after we met.'

With a sinking feeling, Clara couldn't bring herself to meet the empath's eyes. 'Moor abducted you.'

'Well, I know *that*,' Marney said offhandedly. 'I let him take me – to throw him off *your* scent.'

Clara reached out and squeezed Marney's shoulder. 'Once Moor discovered you'd given me the location of Oldest Place—'

'He no longer had a use for me, and there was no reason to keep me alive,' the empath finished. She smiled sadly. 'But we don't know that he killed me. Not for sure.'

Clara didn't know what to say, but obviously Marney detected what she was thinking from her emotions.

'You think I'm a ghost like Van Bam.'

'I'm so sorry, Marney.'

'Funny ...' The empath rubbed her forehead, clearly confused. 'I don't *feel* dead. Known Things makes everything so real—'

The sudden sound of weeping filled the room. Deep and sonorous, it tugged at Clara's heartstrings and she flinched as the silver wall from which Spiral had spoken cracked open, parting with the groans of tearing metal. The weeping grew louder.

The tear in the wall widened to form the entrance into a huge cavern. Marney shrugged at Clara, and they stepped inside.

A giant wept. He sat on the plateau of a huge boulder surrounded by magical fire in a great bejewelled cavern of red rock. Wearing only a simple brown habit, the giant faced the high ceiling, where gems and veins of precious metals glinted like stars and nebulae in the night sky. Then he bowed his head, hiding his face in tangles of unruly hair, and his tears came with dry huffs. It was the saddest noise Clara had ever heard. She and Marney kept their distance.

'Is … is that a Nephilim?' Clara said.

'I think so,' Marney replied. 'I've never seen one before, so— *Look!* A man had materialised on the boulder. 'It's him.'

The giant dwarfed Baran Wolfe. Even in his seated position, he and the Skywatcher would have been face to face were the giant's head not bowed. Silently, Wolfe reached out and laid a hand on the giant's head, calming his tears.

'What's he doing?' Clara wondered.

'I don't know, and I don't think I care,' Marney replied stiffly.

Clara frowned at her. 'What's wrong? Why don't you like Wolfe?'

'Because I'm a Thaumaturgist,' Wolfe called from the boulder. 'But not just any Thaumaturgist. I am Lord Wolfe the Wanderer. My death started the Genii War. Marney is angry with me for that, perhaps even blames me for what occurred at the war's conclusion.'

'Not just you,' Marney said hotly. 'I blame *all* your kind. You abandoned us after we gave you everything.'

'Ah, yes.' Leaving the giant, Wolfe walked to the edge of the boulder. 'It seems a strange decision to abandon the Labyrinth and walk away from you, but the Timewatcher's reasoning was always a little hard to fathom. And let us not forget that I was not present when our Great Mother made Her decision.'

Silver wings sprang from Wolfe's back and he leapt from the boulder, soaring down to land elegantly before the magickers. Clara covered her eyes as the wings folded and stirred up a swirl of dust.

'But I hope,' Wolfe said to Marney, 'that we can call a truce and work together, especially in light of the task ahead. Yes?'

Marney nodded, though her expression remained sour.

'And what about you, Clara?' Wolfe looked at her as though he knew her. 'Any feelings about *my kind* that you'd like to get off your chest?'

Immediately, Clara recalled events she wished she had never experienced. 'Sometimes I don't know who to be angry with first, but definitely not you.'

'Oh?'

'Amilee showed me a vision of your final moments at the Falls of Dust and Silver.'

'Ah.' Wolfe's eyes were sad. 'The House in which Spiral tricked the Nephilim herd. The House in which Spiral used me to make his first strike against the Timewatcher.'

'I know how you felt,' Clara said. 'The sense of betrayal you experienced, the shock, the fear for the future, the pain ...' She swallowed. 'I felt your agony when Spiral had the wings ripped from your back.' She spared a quick glance at Marney. 'The war, and what happened after, wasn't your fault.'

Wolfe seemed surprised by Clara's words. 'Empathy from the changeling but not the empath?'

Marney didn't say anything.

'Thank you, Clara,' Wolfe said. 'Now let's see what we can do about righting a few wrongs.' He looked back at the giant sitting on the boulder. 'This impressive fellow is indeed a Nephilim. His name is Gulduur Bellow.'

'*Bellow?*' Clara blurted.

'I found him in Mirage shortly before the war began,' Wolfe said. 'He had lost his herd. The only Nephilim to escape Spiral's trickery. This is only my memory of Bellow. I've no idea what became of him after we met.'

'Wait,' said Marney. 'You were in Mirage *before* the war, and you didn't stop what they were planning?'

'It wasn't as easy as that, I'm afraid. I could sense that trouble was brewing in Mirage, though I couldn't tell what. Please remember, my mind was troubled at the time, namely with the *many* nefarious plans of my fellow Skywatcher Iblisha Spiral.'

Wolfe faced the boulder. The Nephilim was looking up at the bejewelled ceiling again. Through slits in Wolfe's habit, Clara could see his silver wings resting against his back. She felt happy that he had them again.

'I asked Gulduur Bellow to watch Mirage for me,' Wolfe continued. 'I asked him to stay and wait for someone who would need his help getting home. Lucky for us all that he agreed.'

'Van Bam,' Marney said, her tone emotionless. 'Bellow saved him, and he was able to warn the Labyrinth of Mirage's invasion plans.'

'Precisely.'

Marney stared at the cavern floor, lost to thought.

Clara said, 'So meeting Bellow connected Van Bam to the Nephilim in some way?'

'Perhaps,' Wolfe replied, but he was addressing Marney. 'A secret was told to your illusionist friend. A secret I'm certain has not been heard by many humans.' He looked back over his shoulder. 'Do you know why the Nephilim are nomads? Do you know why they travel from realm to realm, never staying in one place for long?'

Clara recalled something Van Bam had told her. 'They're searching for a House.'

'The Sorrow of Future Reason,' Marney said.

Up on the boulder, Gulduur Bellow began weeping again, the sound whispering around the cavern.

'The Nephilim's tale is an unfortunate one,' Wolfe said. 'The Time-watcher forced them to bear the burden of the atrocities that led to their creation. She forbade them a House of their own and ensured they were shunned wherever they went. Abominations, we called them. But I learned in Mirage that they are far, far from that.'

Wolfe was quiet, contemplative, for a moment. 'And so the Nephilim crafted their own legend. They believed they travelled towards a future when the Timewatcher would bestow forgiveness and create for them a House they could finally call home. The Sorrow of Future Reason. I trust you know its House symbol?'

Clara could see it in her mind's eye: a spiralling pattern with a straight line running from one side to connect to a square. Inside the square, and on its right side, were mirrored triangles. The symbol almost looked like an arrow.

Gulduur Bellow lowered his head. He wrapped his arms round his huge body and began moaning.

'Before I became Voice of Known Things,' said Wolfe, 'I promised Bellow that I would help him find his herd. Perhaps now I can make good on that promise.'

'Then stop wasting time,' Marney said unkindly, unperturbed that she was talking to a Thaumaturgist, albeit the ghostly memory of one. 'Tell us what to do.'

Wolfe's smile returned, and with it a sparkle of light flashed in his eyes. 'Do you ever wonder why the secrets just keep piling up and no one has a straight answer?' he asked Clara.

'It had sort of crossed my mind, yes.'

'I know Lady Amilee of old, and I know her well. If she needed to keep her plans concealed from Spiral's powers of divination, she would have been *very* selective about the information she gave you. Remember, while you were connected to Known Things, it could've drained any or all of your secrets. At that stage, a lack of knowledge was a weapon.'

'But now she's not connected to Known Things,' Marney said. 'And it wasn't looking for me.'

'Exactly so,' said Wolfe. 'Thus, at this moment, while a copy of Known Things remains in your mind, Clara, you are free to discover your *straight answers*.'

Clara frowned at the Skywatcher. 'I don't suppose you could just tell us what we need to know?'

Wolfe looked at Marney and said cryptically, 'Secrets within secrets, memories within memories. There is a place inside Known Things where Spiral keeps his deepest secrets – secrets he wouldn't even share with his most trusted Genii. It is one of the places I warned you about. The information there is dangerous, but it is where you must go to discover Van Bam's ghost. And the fate of the Nephilim herd—'

Gulduur Bellow screamed a curse. Clara flinched and backed away. The echoes of the Nephilim's voice bounced around the cavern, carrying the undercurrent of a growl like distant, bestial thunder.

'You must leave,' Wolfe stated. 'I will show you the way and meet you later.'

He gestured towards the ceiling. From among the multitude of glittering jewels, the green diamond shook free and fell into the Skywatcher's hand, singing with a glassy whine of protest.

'Your guiding light,' Wolfe said grimly

'No!' Bellow's voice was as harsh as the crack of a whip. The giant stood to his full, impressive height on the boulder. He glared across the cavern, his eyes flashing with the power of storm clouds. 'This must end!'

'Oh no,' said Clara.

The Nephilim was changing. He grew to twice his size, his habit ripping and falling away as rags to reveal a body covered with black and silver hair. Claws as long as swords sprouted from his fingertips and his face stretched to a monstrous wolf's snout. He opened a mouth filled with teeth and howled with the sound of a hurricane.

'Leave,' Wolfe commanded, and he hurled the green diamond at the cavern wall. It punched a large hole in the rock which led into darkness. 'I will see you again soon.'

Clara covered her ears as the Nephilim mutated into a howling darkness that began to break the boulder into chunks, swallowing debris, sucking jewels from the rock. Wolfe extended his wings and vaulted into the air. Marney grabbed Clara's hand.

His wings shedding silver light, Wolfe flew at speed into the dark mass that Gulduur Bellow had become, and he blazed with thaumaturgy that screeched like a thousand blades unsheathed at once. The whole cavern shook, preparing to be ripped apart and devoured by Clara's magic.

Wolfe's voice came from the storm as a gentle sigh. 'Go ...'

Once again, the magickers fled deeper into Known Things.

CHAPTER NINE

THE HEAD OF THE SNAKE

Transcendence.

Moor and Asajad were right. Lord Spiral's reanimation was no simple rebirth, as it had been for his Genii. Certainly, Spiral's pent-up power had called for a bigger sacrifice, which Moor had anticipated; but upon release from the terracotta jar, Spiral's essence had claimed much more than flesh and blood to achieve form.

'It is just as I foresaw,' Spiral had said earlier. 'My armies will be self-replenishing. My domain will grow and grow ...'

The Lord of the Genii had merged with the Retrospective. The magic which had created it was now as much a part of him as he was a part of it. The House of dead time was irrevocably fused to his soul. Iblisha Spiral's desires were carried by every wild demon; his heart beat in each change of the land and weather; the fiery wind whispered his name. And yet he could manifest at will outside the Retrospective.

Moor and Gadreel stood with their lord in a huge warehouse located in Sunflower, a sub-House of the Aelfheim Archipelago. Lady Asajad was absent, having been sent on an errand by Spiral. Moor didn't know the details of this errand and his disquiet was growing.

Two long rows of pallets flanked the Genii and their lord, each thirty feet long and fifteen wide, holding huge quantities of cargo. Sixty pallets, Moor counted, upon which wooden crates or sacks or metal storage containers were stacked high. Food stocks, materials, medical supplies – everything the denizens of Labrys Town needed to survive.

'It astounds me after all that occurred,' Spiral said, 'that the Time-watcher still retains compassion for humans.' His violet eyes regarded a large stone archway at the back of the warehouse. The last portal to the Labyrinth, via which the Aelfir had kept the denizens alive since the end of the war. 'Would it not have been kinder to simply put them out of their misery and destroy the Great Labyrinth?'

'Yes, my lord,' Gadreel replied, far too eagerly for Moor's liking.

'Yet we must be grateful that She did not.' Spiral summoned his higher magic. The symbols on his body darkened to a void-like black and his presence became somehow insubstantial. 'I, however, do *not* share Her compassion. The humans have had time enough.' His voice carried the distant tumult of many demons shrieking. 'And I want them to suffer.'

Spiral released his magic. It stole Moor's breath as it rushed by him. There was a crack of energy as the stone archway crumbled to a heap of powder and the last portal to the Labyrinth was destroyed.

Moor stole a glance at Viktor Gadreel. The hulking Genii was pleased with his master's actions, his one eye glinting darkly.

Spiral's eyes weren't quite focused, he appeared to be looking into some unknown distance beyond his Genii. He turned and faced the entrance to the warehouse, where ten Aelfirian police officers stood frozen. They had come to accost the Genii who had suddenly appeared and frightened away the warehouse workers, and Spiral's thaumaturgy had rendered them immobile.

'Soon,' said Spiral, 'when the humans are gone, I will absorb the Labyrinth into the Retrospective. I will crack open the Nightshade like an egg and consume the power it holds. Imagine what I will achieve with that magic!'

'You will be unstoppable,' Gadreel rumbled.

Spiral was talking about the First and Greatest Spell, the highest of all magic; that which had been used to bring the Labyrinth into existence. Imbued into the Nightshade, it was the power of creation, of travel, of boundless possibility – it was the power of the Timewatcher.

'The Retrospective and I cannot be complete without the First and Greatest Spell,' said Spiral. 'With it, *we* will become *limitless*.'

For the first time in forty years, Moor's faith was blemished by doubt, and he wonder if *we* included the Genii.

'My lord,' Moor said with a frown. 'What of Hagi Tabet?'

'Ah.' Spiral's face was contemplative. 'Lady Tabet has served me without question and I feel blessed by her devotion. But her symbiosis with the Nightshade *is* complete. It cannot be undone. Her sacrifice is, regrettably, unavoidable.'

Moor surprised himself by wondering if Spiral was telling the truth.

At that moment, a rent appeared in the air. It brought the tumult of violence along with the stench of corruption and hopelessness. The rent widened and Mo Asajad emerged from the Retrospective into the warehouse. The portal sealed behind her.

'It is done?' Spiral asked, appraising her carefully.

Asajad gave a small nod. Her trademark cold smile didn't touch her thin, colourless lips. 'It is, my lord.'

'Good,' Spiral purred. 'Your virus will spread like wildfire among the denizens. There will be no safe quarter in Labrys Town.'

Moor's anxiety resurfaced. 'My Lord, forgive me, but why waste time toying with the humans?' His tone was guarded, careful to show respect. 'Why not take the Labyrinth and the power of the Nightshade now?'

Spiral regarded Moor. 'You have doubts, Fabian?' he said quietly.

'He does, my lord,' Gadreel answered, clearly exasperated. 'Lord Moor is a little frightened of humans. They have ... *tricked* him, and on more than one occasion.'

'Is this true, Fabian? *You*, whose diligence ensured we are all standing here now, on the brink of great things – *you* are troubled by the humans?'

As Moor struggled for an answer, Gadreel said, 'Unfortunately so.'

'My concerns are justified,' Moor stated, noting that Asajad was uncharacteristically forgoing the chance to mock him. 'The Relic Guild had help, both during the war and now. My lord, not all the Thaumaturgists departed with the Timewatcher. Yansas Amilee remained.'

Spiral's displeasure was made apparent by the symbols on his body taking on a dull purple hue. He glared at Gadreel, as though unwilling to take Moor's word for it. 'Is this true?'

'Apparently so,' Gadreel answered, head bowed. 'Hagi discovered Amilee's involvement from Known Things before ... before you destroyed it.'

'Did she now?' Spiral said quietly. 'And what else did Lady Tabet discover?'

'Nothing, my lord. We were in agreement that the Skywatcher was seeking to prevent your return and she has clearly failed.'

'Clearly.' Spiral pursed his lips. 'Strange that I should not have predicted this.'

'I'm sorry, my lord,' Moor said, 'but we do not know where Amilee is now.'

'Oh, but can't you guess, Fabian?' A stark lack of concern returned to Spiral's beautiful and terrible face. 'Our *Treasured Lady* is a slippery snake, but there is only one place where she would hide.'

Once again staring across the warehouse at the frozen police officers, Spiral's thaumaturgy swelled. 'Amilee alone cannot stand in my way, and it is time to formally announce my return.'

The Lord of the Genii unleashed his power, gripping one of the officers and dragging her to him. The restraining magic disappeared and the policewoman struggled in Spiral's arms, shouting with incoherent panic as he forced her head back, exposing her throat, and sank long teeth into her flesh. She began to spasm in his embrace, jerking with every draught he took from her veins. Finally, Spiral let her body fall to the floor and wiped blood from his lips.

'A curious thing, this virus we carry,' Spiral said, looking down at his victim. Her teeth were clenched and her whole body shook violently. 'So empowering, so ... contagious. It is fitting that the Retrospective and I both need blood to remain strong, so we can grow and spread together.'

Moor had seen the virus change creatures of lower magic many times before, but never with the speed induced by Spiral's bite. The policewoman began to issue a series of shrieks, caught somewhere between coughs and barks. The ragged wound on her neck had stopped bleeding and black veins began snaking from it, spreading over her skin like a dark web. The woman's large Aelfirian eyes became jaundiced and her gums receded, making her teeth look long. With a bestial cry, she jumped to her feet, her posture stooped like an animal on the prowl. She glared at Spiral and the Genii with eyes filled with hate and the need to destroy and rend and taste blood. But even in such a bloodthirsty state, she dared not attack her infector.

Spiral motioned with his hand towards the remaining police officers, dispelling the magic that kept them frozen. They didn't bother priming the power stones on their weapons; instead, as one they fled from the warehouse, shouting warnings as they ran. With more cough-barks, the infected policewoman pursued them on all fours and quickly disappeared through the door after them.

She would spread the virus to every Aelf in Sunflower. Moor wondered how long it would take for Spiral's empowered virus to reach its conclusion, turning the organic matter of all the infected to stone, leaving behind docile, servile golems.

A cry came from outside. A fresh victim. A new carrier for the virus.

'You, my Genii, deserve to taste sweeter blood than that of humans,' said Spiral. 'Go. Feed. Run amok among the Aelfir and gather your strength. For afterwards we shall bite the head off the snake.'

'I wasn't expecting this,' said Marney.

Clara agreed.

The magickers had arrived at a run-down and gloomy theatre. They stood at the back, looking out over row after row of seats occupied by the silhouettes of audience members. There were perhaps five hundred of them – a full house – and they faced a stage where moving scenery depicted a strange scenario.

A collection of frameless paintings spun and rocked, representing an angry, rolling ocean. The backdrop was a slate-grey sky backlit by flashes of lightning. Stage right, a huge purple sheet flapped in the wind, embroidered with a bright golden sun sending out spears of light. Stage left, sheets of deepest black coiled and twisted like a column of smoke. Downstage, a small, narrow tent had been erected. It reminded Clara of the fortune teller's tent she had once visited at a fair in Labrys Town, except for the fact that it was clearly made from skin.

Somewhere offstage, boards wobbled to create rumbles of thunder. As lightning flashes illuminated the audience, Clara caught sight of demonic deformities, and she realised that not one individual present was human or Aelf. Tasting blood in the air, she stared at the stage.

'What's it supposed to be?' she asked.

'I think it's a representation of the Genii War,' Marney replied. 'The sun is the Timewatcher. The darkness is Spiral.'

'What about the ocean?'

'I don't know.'

Clara had the impression that the empath wasn't being entirely truthful. In fact, she was beginning to wonder if Marney was being as *selective* with information as Lady Amilee had been.

Casting a wary eye over the theatre, Clara said, 'There's something I don't understand about Van Bam. Why is he trapped in here with us at all?' Marney frowned at her. 'Don't get me wrong – I'm glad he is. I sort of feel like we saved him.'

'*Saved* him?'

'The Nightshade,' Clara explained. 'Its magic has always selected who becomes Resident, right? But the Genii disrupted that process, and I'm pretty sure Hagi Tabet wouldn't be a welcoming host for Van Bam's spirit. Ordinarily he would have become her guide, but his ghost wound up in here with us instead – which I'm grateful for. But why? How?'

Marney took a little too long to reply for Clara's liking. 'One mystery at a time, Clara. Let's find the Nephilim first, then maybe we can ask Van Bam himself for an answer.'

Evasion? Clara wondered as the empath pointed at the stage.

'Right now,' Marney continued, 'I want to know what that tent is for.'

'So much confusion,' said Baran Wolfe.

The magickers wheeled around. The old Skywatcher had materialised, as bedraggled and peaceful a presence as always and showing no ill signs from his battle with Clara's magic. He gestured to the stage.

'I wouldn't even begin to guess how many memories are mixed up in this little show.' He looked pointedly at Marney. 'Would you?'

'Just tell us what to do next,' Marney said evenly.

The painted ocean rolled and the demonic audience watched, still and silent.

'Listen to me carefully,' Wolfe said. 'Known Things does not function in a predictable way. You are inside *unused* time. Known Things is an amalgam.'

'All right,' said Clara. 'So it absorbs everything into ... one mashed-up brain of information?'

'Eloquently put.' Wolfe chuckled. 'And that *mashed-up brain* currently resides in your mind. Memories and information don't necessarily have to belong to any one person.'

'It could come from me, you, Marney, Van Bam, Spiral – or all of us at the same time.'

'Very good.' Again, Wolfe looked pointedly at Marney. 'When I became Voice of Known Things, it was near impossible to resist Iblisha Spiral's power and he crushed everything I ever was from me. Almost.'

The Skywatcher switched his gaze to Clara. 'Mercifully, I retained a seed of who I was and what I had done before Known Things, including the guarding of a secret that I knew would change much if Lady Amilee could keep it from Spiral.' Wolfe's expression became coldly satisfied. 'The Lord of the Genii does not know that a single Nephilim escaped his trickery.'

'Gulduur Bellow,' Marney said. 'But Bellow's only one. We need the whole herd.'

'And *you* are only one magicker, yet look at all you have achieved, Marney.' Sadness touched Wolfe's features. 'I don't know what became of Bellow, and I don't remember what he can change. I lost too much of myself to Known Things.' He brightened. 'But I remember enough to spare you both the confusion of wading through this dangerous amalgamation of memories.' Wolfe pointed at the tent of skin. '*There* is where you will discover the Nephilim herd. But I warn you – that tent also holds some of Spiral's more personal records.'

Clara swallowed. '*Personal* records?'

'I cannot say how they will manifest to you, but please remember … The Lord of the Genii was once called First Lord of the Thaumaturgists, and I *Honoured* Lord. We both served the same master.'

Looking over the demonic audience at the tent onstage, Clara felt unease squirm in her gut. Scenery moved; boards wobbled thunder. 'What are you saying?'

'He's talking about the Timewatcher,' Marney stated without emotion.

Wolfe sighed wistfully. 'Iblisha Spiral and I have both kept Her company. We know Her face. We know Her voice. And Known Things knows our memories.'

'Oh …' Clara felt strength draining from her legs.

The Timewatcher. A symbol, a myth – the great and powerful Mother who abandoned Her children. Clara had never stopped to consider that the Timewatcher was real.

Wolfe continued, 'Spiral once loved the Timewatcher so *so* dearly, and his memory of Her forced him to bury that love deep inside Known Things – along with the plans that he entrusted only to himself.' Wolfe's face became oddly poised between amusement and a resolve which showed some of the power he'd commanded as a creature of higher magic. 'Unfortunately for Spiral, when he forced me to become Voice of Known Things, he made me the curator of this place. He could hide nothing from me.'

'Then why do we need to go into the tent at all?' Clara said, fearful of what she might find there. 'If you know Spiral's secrets, then you know where the Nephilim are.'

It wasn't the first time that Clara had pointed this out; and not for the first time, Wolfe addressed the cryptic answer to Marney.

'All things are known in the end, and nothing is ever as it first appears. I cannot do this for you.'

Lightning illuminated the audience.

'Once you enter that tent, there is no coming out,' Wolfe said. 'While we have been speaking, your magic has been devouring the world outside. The inside of this theatre is now all that remains of Known Things in your mind. I will hold your magic back for as long as I can, but eventually it will devour me, too, along with the contents of that tent. And now you should leave.'

The audience stirred, moving in their seats with bestial grunts and groans. Clara and Marney watched them, frightened that they might rise and attack. When they finally settled again, the magickers discovered that Wolfe had disappeared.

'That's annoying,' Marney said.

Thunder growled, deeper than anything made by boards, and the sound itched against Clara's skin, overwhelming her fear of the tent.

'Let's go,' she said.

Cautiously, they set off down the aisle. The taste of blood in the air became stronger and Clara fought the urge to gag, just as she fought the urge to look at the faces of the demonic audience.

'I don't know about you,' Marney said as they climbed the steps to the stage, 'but I really don't want to walk into that tent.'

The scenery moved and clashed. Lightning blazed again, somehow making the tent look taller.

With the magickers onstage, the audience began an eerie applause of slow, wet-sounding claps. Stage lights shone in Clara's eyes and she could see nothing of the monstrosities in their seats. The claps became synchronised until they unified into one sharp *crack*, repeated over and over, aggressive, urging, slowly increasing in tempo.

Marney pulled back the flap of skin, revealing the tent's dark opening. 'After you,' she said.

'Thanks,' Clara said drily, and she ducked inside.

As the flap fell closed behind them, all sound from the theatre died. The reek of blood disappeared.

Lit by candles, the interior of the tent was larger than it had appeared from the outside. The walls moved in and out as though breathing, though thankfully they appeared to be made of canvas, not skin. A collection of tarnished copper pots sat on a floor of flat, hard-packed earth, all filled to spilling point with uncut green gems. A run of clear ground led to the back of the tent, where a full-length dress mirror stood in a silver frame.

Clara headed towards it. Marney appeared reluctant at first, pausing for a heartbeat before following.

The mirror didn't quite reflect their images. Its surface wavered almost fluidly, struggling to retain a permanent state. Clara caught glimpses of herself and Marney surrounded by cauldrons filled with green gems; but she also saw somewhere else. It might have been an alleyway.

'What is it?' she asked Marney. 'A portal?'

'Maybe. I think so.' Marney looked confused. 'I'm not sure.'

In one of the cauldrons, a green gem had begun to glow. It made Clara think of Van Bam. Not really understanding why, she picked it up and weighed it in her hand. The glow intensified as it changed shape into a smooth, neat diamond. And she could almost hear the deep, soothing tones of the illusionist.

'Clara,' Marney hissed, sounding frightened. 'What are you doing?'

But Clara was listening to some instinct inside her that drove her actions. She raised her arm and hurled the diamond at the mirror.

The mirror shattered outwards, trapping images of the magickers in a thousand flying portraits, sharp and jagged. Clara raised her hands. Marney yelled. But before the storm of broken mirror touched them, the shards froze in the air momentarily before being sucked back by the black vacuum that had appeared within the frame.

Clara barely had time to shout before she and Marney were also picked up and dragged into the darkness beyond the mirror.

GLASS AND MIRRORS

Ocean.

Marney knew what the word meant. She had heard her fellow agents talk about them before, how they had sailed on them, swum in them, caught fish from them; but Marney had never seen one herself. And now, too drained and exhausted to cope with adding any new experiences to a mind already full to bursting, she protected her emotions behind a shield of apathy, feeling nothing for the ocean that surrounded her.

But she could tell by the look of awe and wonder on Denton's face that they weren't gazing upon the usual definition of the word.

The empaths stood on a tiny island of flat, clear glass. There was no sign of the portal which had delivered them there. Neat steps led down to a promontory that sat flush with water as clear and still as the glass beneath their feet. The ocean reached to the horizon, calm beneath a sky blanketed by gently rolling clouds of deep purple.

Daylight appeared to shine from the air itself, warm and welcoming; but night lay beneath the ocean's surface. It was a dizzying view from the island, down into depths where millions of stars shone amidst glowing nebulae in an alien sky. This expanse of water was like a barrier dividing two realities.

'The others must know about Angel,' Marney said to Denton, her voice dispassionate. 'Van Bam will blame himself for her death. I know he will.'

'I think you're right,' Denton replied. At the mention of Angel's name, he, too, encased his emotions in magical apathy. His nose was broken and cuts and scrapes and dried blood covered his face. 'But that's not our concern right now.'

In the near distance, rising like a monumental palace, was the mythical place that Marney and Denton had come to find: the Library of Glass and Mirrors.

Big enough to be a citadel, it was made entirely of translucent crystal which reflected the sky and sea in a clash of deep purple and twinkling stars. It was the largest structure Marney had ever seen, dwarfing the Nightshade many times over, maybe spacious enough to hold a hundred thousand residents or more. She could make out a few spires and domes, but much of the Library's detail was lost due to dancing lights and translucency.

It was said that inside this place, everything that could be known *was* known – the histories of past, present and future. Assuredly it was the most breathtaking vision, the most wondrous House Marney had seen on this nightmarish mission, yet she felt nothing.

'Marney,' said Denton, 'do you remember how I told you that the Thaumaturgists fear the Library?'

Marney nodded.

'I choose to believe that the Timewatcher is wise and has no need to abuse the histories this place keeps. Spiral, on the other hand, would if he could.'

A vague sense of intrigue bloomed in Marney. 'But he can't?'

Denton didn't answer directly. 'The Library is undoubtedly the greatest and most dangerous of all resources. Thus great and dangerous power protects it.' He pointed to a small vessel that had appeared, sailing towards the island with a dark figure standing at its prow. 'The Thaumaturgists and the Genii are not the only creatures of higher magic, Clara.'

As Marney watched the vessel, she realised it was jaunting towards the island with a series of snappish movements that left streaks of light behind it, but caused no disturbance on the surface of the water. The figure looked frozen, statue-still, coming closer all the time with frightening speed.

'Who is it?' Marney asked.

'A Librarian. I think. I hope.' Denton shrugged. 'The truth is, I don't know much more than you do about this place and its inhabitants.'

'Are they expecting us, at least?'

'Since legend says the Librarians know everything, I'd hope so. But on the off-chance they don't ...' Denton pulled the sigil wallet from the leg pocket on his fatigues. 'Let's pray they hold Lady Amilee in high regard.'

'Now that we're here,' Marney said, with the vessel almost upon them, 'I don't suppose you can tell me what we're looking for?'

Denton shook his head. 'I've dedicated my life to the pursuit of knowledge, but I never realised how terrible knowledge could be until now.' He looked at her, his eyes sad. 'The Librarians went to great pains to hide the portal to their House, and with good reason, Marney. Do not let curiosity get the better of you. Understand?'

The vessel reached the promontory and revealed itself to be a flat platform of glass as clear as the island itself. The lone passenger – the Librarian – stood with hands tucked into the sleeves of a black robe, face hidden by a deep hood. He made no attempt to disembark.

Marney, thought Denton.

I know, Marney replied tiredly, *let you do the talking, right?*

Actually, I was going to warn you that I have absolutely no idea what happens next. But trust me.

The empaths walked down the steps, and as they approached the vessel, the Librarian spoke.

'I greet you on friendly terms.' A high male voice, officious in tone yet soft. 'Do you reciprocate?'

It struck Marney as an odd way to begin a conversation, but Denton remained unfazed. 'We do,' he said smoothly, and offered the Librarian the sigil wallet. 'Our credentials.'

The hand that appeared from the robe wasn't quite real to Marney's eyes. It seemed to be made of light, but not bright light; rather a hardened luminescence that resembled pale scales. The Librarian took the wallet from Denton and promptly threw it into the water without so much as opening it. It wasn't an aggressive act. The wallet sank down towards the stars at the bottom of the ocean.

'We know who you are,' the Librarian said without the slightest inflection that might indicate his mood. 'And we know why you are here.'

Marney tensed as the dark opening of the Librarian's hood turned towards her.

'What is written about you in the Library of Glass and Mirrors is curious. We Librarians are ... intrigued by your arrival.'

He gestured that they should join him and the empaths stepped onto the glass vessel. Marney lowered her apathetic shield enough to allow her empathic magic to search for the Librarian's emotions. What she felt was as alien as any other creature of higher magic she had tried to read, and it threatened to overwhelm every sense she had. She withdrew her magic hastily, and Denton gave her a warning look.

'I suggest that you sit,' said the Librarian, turning and staring back towards the crystal citadel rising from the ocean. 'The uninitiated can find the crossing a little turbulent, and if you fall into the water, you will never stop falling.'

The empaths did as the Librarian instructed, Denton groaning as his old joints complained. Once they were seated, the platform set off for the Library of Glass and Mirrors.

The crossing made Marney feel a little sick. The strange lunging motion of the glass platform combined with the dizzying emptiness of space below turned her stomach and forced her eyes closed. She was relieved when they reached the towering glass monument and the vessel slid smoothly into the huge arch of a tunnel cut into its base.

Marney's breath caught. The tunnel ceiling was far overhead and lit by something resembling huge luminous dandelion heads, millions of them, their soft light waxing and waning as they drifted serenely. The lights, pale and violet, only seemed to emphasise how surprisingly dark it was inside the Library's transparent structure. They were mesmerising.

So beautiful, she thought to Denton.

Careful, Marney, Denton replied. *The Librarian can probably hear our magic.*

I don't care, Marney said, transfixed by the dandelion lights, allowing awe to bleed through her apathy. *Look at them, Denton!*

The old empath chuckled in her mind.

As the vessel slid further into the Library of Glass and Mirrors, the strange drifting lights formed into configurations that somehow conveyed a message to Marney, perhaps a gentle greeting. She felt as though there were no walls or barriers, and that she was floating down into the great void of space beneath the ocean.

She grew curious about the Librarian, standing so still on the vessel. *Why does he cover himself?* she asked Denton. *Why hide from us?*

I think you've got it wrong, Marney, Denton replied. *I'm not entirely sure the Librarians are corporeal beings. He isn't hiding. I suspect he's letting us see him.*

'That is quite correct,' said the Librarian with that soft, officious tone. 'I adopt this image so you see me. So you accept me.' He moved up to the edge of the vessel. 'And you will see me again shortly.'

Marney yelped as the Librarian stepped off the edge and disappeared. Denton looked perplexed. The dandelion lights died and the stars in the depths went out.

'Denton?'

'Don't worry. I'm sure this is normal.' But he sounded concerned in the dark.

The vessel stopped. A tingling sensation filled Marney's gut, as though she were rising or falling – she couldn't tell which – in an elevator. It was a disconcerting feeling, for although she was beset by the sensation of motion, the deep purple hue that suddenly broke the darkness above was getting neither closer nor further away. Marney decided they were rising, and the purple was a view of the sky outside. There was something about the sky that Marney recognised.

'Denton, if the Librarians are creatures of higher magic, then the Library isn't inside the Nothing of Far and Deep, is it? Or out among the Houses of the Aelfir?'

'No, it isn't.' Denton hesitated, watching his protégé, gauging her reaction. 'The Library of Glass and Mirrors is inside the Higher Thaumaturgic Cluster.'

His answer didn't tell Marney anything she hadn't already guessed, but it still inspired her to tighten her emotional defences again.

The Higher Thaumaturgic Cluster, inside which the Timewatcher resided on Mother Earth. What felt like a lifetime ago, Lady Amilee had shown it to Marney from a distance, a great purple cloud in space bigger than the Nothing of Far and Deep. But Marney had only seen it from afar, and now ...

'We're *inside* the Higher Thaumaturgic Cluster?'

'Yes – and it wouldn't surprise me if we were the first living humans ever to see it from the inside. This isn't exactly the reality we're used to—'

A soft, warm radiance abruptly banished the purple sky. The platform reached its destination, sitting flush with a floor of clear glass in a gigantic hall that looked to Marney like the inside of a hollow tower. The walls glowed gently with all the colours of the spectrum. Above, the dandelion lights had returned, drifting and filling conical heights.

'This is interesting,' Denton murmured.

The temperature had dropped and Marney pulled her jacket tighter around her.

A series of identical mirrors had been set into the multi-hued walls, each six feet tall and oval, too many to count. Their surfaces didn't look quite solid; Marney's reflection rippled slowly, almost wavering like sheets drying in the breeze. It was a hypnotising effect and she rubbed her eyes.

'Stay here,' Denton told her.

Marney couldn't say for sure whether the Librarian had been in the hall when the empaths arrived, but he was there now, standing before one of the mirrors. Denton approached the figure, and they conversed in voices too low for Marney to hear. They didn't speak long before the Librarian stepped to one side, and the rippling surface of the mirror changed.

Marney saw an impossibly large library room in the mirror, stacked floor to ceiling with books, stretching far into the distance. Row after row of reading tables lined the centre, along with what appeared to be lamp posts topped with spherical glow lamps shining with blue light.

'I might be some time,' Denton said. 'Wait for me here, and try not to worry.'

Marney sank further into magical apathy.

Denton's smile was tired. 'I'll be as quick as I can, and then we can go home.'

With a nod to the Librarian, Denton approached the mirror and stepped into the reflection as though it was an open door. As he walked away into the library room, the mirror's surface reverted to show Marney's rippling reflection. She looked dishevelled, and dark circles ringed her eyes. She didn't care.

'You are not offended that you cannot accompany your friend.'

Marney was aware that she was alone with the Librarian. She wasn't sure if his words were a question or a statement but answered nonetheless. 'It's less dangerous if only one of us knows why we're here.'

'I agree with you.'

The Librarian remained standing by the mirror doorway. Marney felt no threat in his scrutiny, and she gazed around the hall to lessen what was fast becoming an uncomfortable silence. So much hardship, so many struggles to reach the Library of Glass and Mirrors. It hardly seemed feasible that Marney had actually arrived. Almost dreamlike.

'Would you like to ask me a question?' the Librarian said.

'These mirrors – they're all portals? To other rooms in the Library?'

'Sometimes, yes. Sometimes they lead to entirely different libraries, some of which no longer exist and others yet to achieve existence. At least from your perspective. Do you understand?'

Marney didn't. She shivered and wrapped her arms around her.

'Forgive me,' the Librarian said. 'You are cold.'

The empath jumped back as a black iron brazier rose from the glass floor. The strange flames that filled it were like moving shards of mirror holding the reflection of fire. But the warmth they gave was very real and banished the chill from Marney's body. She couldn't suppress a mighty yawn.

'How long has it been since you last slept?'

Marney thought about it. She had spent so long jumping from House to House that the days and nights had blurred into a grey twilight where time no longer had meaning. 'You know, I really don't remember.'

'Your journey has been hard and you are tired. Perhaps you will rest now.'

Something bumped gently against the back of Marney's legs. A lounger had materialised behind her. Covered with thick cushions and upholstered in soft velvet, it was the most comfortable and inviting resting place Marney had ever seen. She yawned again.

'Please,' said the Librarian. 'You have nothing to do but wait for your friend. Sleep.'

Marney made no argument and climbed onto the lounger. Instantly, her eyes closed and her mind drifted away. As she fell asleep she heard the Librarian say, 'Afterwards, we will talk about your future.'

The door exploded inwards, wood ripping from hinges, and Fabian Moor strode into a grand reception hall.

The manor house was in the western district, and the occupants had already heard whispers that Moor had escaped the Relic Guild. Even so, the four henchmen guarding the entryway were unprepared for this morning raid.

Moor thrust out a hand, releasing his magic. Four silver streaks raced away, one after the other, each finding a different target. Cold swirls of air froze the henchmen into statues of solid ice before they could even draw their weapons. At the back of the hall, two more appeared, one running down either side of the double staircase. A third up on the balustrade aimed her pistol. Moor turned her to ice and sent out a burst of magic that knocked the other two unconscious before they reached the bottom of the stairs.

'Show yourself!' Moor shouted up to the hall's high ceiling. 'Do it now! Or I will kill every person in this house to find you!'

A woman appeared at the top of the stairs, flanked by two armed bodyguards. She wore a green gown of expensive material and held herself regally. Jewels glittered on her face, tiny multicoloured stones stuck to her skin in patterns resembling ritual tattoos.

She glared down at Moor with fearless eyes. 'Not many people can escape the Relic Guild's clutches,' she said. Her tone was effortlessly neutral. 'I'm impressed.'

'Spare me,' Moor said, his skin glowing with energy. 'You and I have business to conclude, Gemstone Llem.'

She stared for a moment longer before walking away with her remaining bodyguards, saying, 'Follow me.'

Behind the illusion, Van Bam sneered. He was in exactly the right mood to play the part of a Genii.

Focusing his magic to maintain his mask while simultaneously keeping Samuel, Macy and Bryant invisible, Van Bam as Fabian Moor ascended the stairs and followed Llem and her cronies. The illusionist could see the truth behind his own magic, and his fellow agents climbed the stairs ahead of him as wispy green skeletons. Samuel took the lead, his prescient awareness alert for hidden dangers, his pistol loaded with ice-bullets.

On the upper floor, Llem led the way through ornate double doors into a plush and spacious office. This house was rented by her father. Fortunately for the Relic Guild, he and his staff had returned to the Gemstone Isles before war had broken out and Llem's mother didn't live here. Aside from Llem and what remained of her hired help, the house was empty.

She sat behind a leather-topped wooden desk. Her bodyguards flanked her, hands resting on weapons holstered beneath their suit jackets. Llem's jewels sparkled in the warm golden light of a glow lamp sitting on the desk, mostly hiding the expressions on her human-looking face. In fact, the only indications of Llem's Aelfirian side were her point-ed ears. She seemed confident, but Van Bam could see the fear she was trying to hide in her hazel eyes.

The green skeletons of Macy and Bryant found two henchmen hiding inside the room, behind the opened doors. The twins punched them unconscious and threw their bodies out of the office while Van Bam created the illusion of higher magic glowing from his hands. At the same time, Samuel took aim over Van Bam's shoulder and pumped an ice-bullet into each of Llem's bodyguards. They froze with a whirl of icy wind. Van Bam flexed his hands, and, right on cue, Macy and Bryant slammed the doors shut behind him.

Llem barely flinched, but she no longer tried to hide the fear in her eyes.

'Now we are alone,' Van Bam said. 'I trust there will be no more interruptions?'

Llem glanced casually at the frozen statues either side of her and managed to retain some composure. 'We had a deal,' she said. 'You left me in the lurch.'

'I was indisposed.' Although Van Bam had mastered Fabian Moor's image, he had not heard his voice – no one in the Relic Guild had – and he hoped Llem didn't notice any discrepancy. 'I have been told that you are seeking to reverse the work you have done for me.'

'And that surprises you? I didn't think you were coming back, and

I didn't want to get lumbered with the blame for what I'd done. But now' – she opened a drawer and produced a key, which she threw on the desk – 'it's all yours.'

Van Bam looked at the key; it could've opened any one of thousands of houses in Labrys Town.

'The address,' he demanded.

Taking a pencil, Llem scribbled it down on a piece of paper, which she folded and placed on top of the key. The green skeleton of Macy picked them up and brought them to Van Bam. Llem appeared unperturbed by the objects floating in the air. The illusionist looked at the address. A house in the northern district. But what was kept there?

'*All* my requests have been met?' Van Bam said.

'Exactly as you *demanded*.'

'You are sure, Llem? I do not like surprises.'

'Surprises?' Llem's face betrayed more of her fear. And some anger now. 'I don't even fully understand what I've done for you, Moor. Everything about this job has been a nightmare. I want to wash my hands of it.'

'Then everything is prepared?'

'The House is protected, the *merchandise* is in place and no one will be missed.'

Van Bam looked at the key in his hands, mulling over what that might mean. He decided that he had all the information he needed. 'You have served me well, Llem.'

She scoffed. 'A good magic-user of mine lost his life setting up that place.'

'You seek recompense?'

'Only to never have this deal come back on me.' It was clear that she was struggling to maintain her courageous façade. 'I don't care what you're doing, but if the Relic Guild gets wind of our association, I'll be dragged to the Nightshade.' She feared the Relic Guild more than the man before her. She didn't know Moor was a Genii. 'I don't want to see you again. Ever.'

'Easy terms to agree to,' Van Bam said. With the green skeletons of Samuel, Macy and Bryant following him, the illusionist headed for the door. 'And if I were you,' he called back, 'I would keep a very low profile.'

It was strange. Marney couldn't remember waking up. She couldn't recall rising from the lounger to eat from the table laden with exotic fruit which had appeared beside the brazier of mirror-flames. She poured herself a glass of water; it tasted sweet, cool in her throat. She bit into a semicircle of what appeared to be blue melon. It had no smell but wasn't entirely tasteless. It left a bitter tang in her mouth, surprisingly refreshing as it sated her hunger.

Denton had yet to return but the Librarian was there – silent, still, watchful, hidden in his black robe. His presence felt natural, calming, nothing like as intimidating as the other creatures of higher magic she had met.

'How long was I asleep?' Marney asked him.

'For as long as you needed to be.'

Marney decided that was as good an answer as she was going to get and finished the slice of melon. 'You're not the only one, are you?' she said, pouring another glass of water. 'Librarian, I mean. There must be more of you, surely.'

'There must be.'

Once again, he used an ambiguous tone, and Marney wondered how much she, a creature of lower magic, could ever truly understand the Library of Glass and Mirrors, or any other House inside the Higher Thaumaturgic Cluster. *This isn't the reality we're used to*, Denton had said. Perhaps everything Marney had been shown, including this hall of many mirrors, was only a simplified representation that the eyes of a lower creature could perceive.

'I am curious,' said the Librarian. 'You have magic that allows you to control *feelings*.' He said the last word as though it encompassed an alien concept.

'I can manipulate emotions, in myself and others. I'm an empath.'

'How interesting. Then, for example, you can detach yourself from your emotions to better accept incongruous situations, such as the one in which you presently find yourself.'

'Yes.'

'Yet you are not using your magic now.'

Marney froze, her hand inches from picking up another slice of blue melon. She had spent so long keeping up a guard, protecting herself from the horrors of war behind a magical shield of apathy, that she had almost forgotten what it felt like to be without it. But the Librarian was right: she had dropped her empathic defences entirely. Her emotions were raw and exposed.

'Please, tell me how you are *feeling*,' said the Librarian.

Marney wasn't sure at first. She looked around the hall, at the changing colours in the glass walls, at the mirror portals that occasionally gave glimpses into other rooms and realms, and a sad smile came to her face. 'Guilty,' she realised.

'I am not sure I understand why,' the Librarian said.

Marney did. She understood all too well. 'A friend of mine was murdered. Her name was Angel. She was a healer. She was travelling with another friend – Van Bam. An illusionist.' Tears came to her eyes. 'When I heard about Angel, I didn't want to admit it, but my first reaction was relief. Relief that she had been killed and not Van Bam. You see, Van Bam and I, we're … we're—'

'Lovers,' the Librarian finished.

Marney dared not confirm lest weeping overtake her. She wiped tears from her eyes, seeking no help from her magic, deciding to feel something honest for once.

'You should not feel guilty, but you will anyway,' the Librarian continued, a strange inflection to his voice which she couldn't interpret. 'Love is such a potent and visceral reaction. It is, perhaps, the one incomprehensible emotion that all races share.'

'I wish I could believe that,' Marney said. 'I haven't seen much love in this bloody war.'

'You are a fascinating creature, Marney. Surprisingly complex.'

For the first time since he appeared in the hall, the Librarian moved, walking to stand on the opposite side of the brazier. He held his hands, covered in scales of hard light, before the mirror-flames – as an act of normality to comfort her, Marney surmised, not from any need for warmth.

'This Library holds a record of your visit,' he said. 'It holds an account of the path that led you to the Library. But of your future, there is next to nothing.'

Marney narrowed her eyes at him. 'What does that mean?'

'Either that much of your future is yet to be written, or that it has been hidden as completely as you are able to hide your emotions.'

'But I thought you knew everything – the past, the present, the future ... *everything*.'

'Kindly, I would tell you that the Library of Glass and Mirrors is beyond the comprehension of humans and Aelfir. Perhaps it is simpler to say that this place can know *all things*, but not *everything* is knowable. At this present moment, of course. From either of our perspectives.'

Marney tried to bend her mind around that. 'And there's something unknowable about me?'

'Just so.'

Marney opened her mouth, struggled with words for a moment, but in the end could only think of asking, 'Why?'

'Intriguing, is it not?' the Librarian replied. 'This makes you a rare and fascinating creature indeed, and it is the sole reason why I decided to help two humans at the behest of Yansas Amilee. The Skywatchers are good at hiding things, and who knows where your future will lead?'

'Sometimes it's difficult to imagine anything beyond the war,' Marney said, suddenly uncomfortable and needing to shift focus away from the topic. 'Are you even aware of what's going on around you?'

'Yes, we are aware.'

'Whose side do you stand on?'

'An interesting question,' the Librarian said, apparently oblivious to Marney's discomfort. 'There are many Houses inside the Higher Thaumaturgic Cluster. Not all of them are as devoted to Mother Earth and the Timewatcher as humans and Aelfir, and most don't care about the war between Her and Her greatest son. And they will continue not caring until a victor emerges.' Although the Librarian's face was hidden by a hood, Marney had the distinct impression that he was smiling at her. 'As for me, I stand in the Library of Glass and Mirrors, of course.'

'Do you know?' Marney licked her lips, ignoring the echo of Denton's voice, warning her to curb her curiosity. 'Do you know who wins the war?'

The Librarian took a long time to reply. 'The only thing I will tell you for certain is that a day is coming when you will hear Her voice. And on that day, you will understand why your future has been hidden.'

'*Her* voice?' Did he mean the Timewatcher?

'Your friend is returning.'

One of the mirrors began rippling like water. Marney gawped, feeling like a child caught in the act of misbehaving. The reflection in the mirror changed to show the library with the long line of blue glow lamps, and Denton stepped out into the hall. He looked a little daunted at first, as though struggling to remember where he was. Marney was sure that only a handful of hours could've passed since he entered the mirror portal, yet there was heavy stubble on his face as if days had gone by. Bruising covered his broken nose and circled his eyes.

He looked at his protégé and blinked.

'Denton,' Marney said, her relief bringing fresh tears to her eyes.

Denton looked around the hall, shaking his head, confused.

'Are you all right?' Marney made to go to him, but he stopped her with a raised hand.

'You have what you came for,' the Librarian said.

After a quick, nervous glance at Marney, Denton nodded. Marney sensed that he had shut down his emotions.

'Then your time here is at an end.'

The Librarian walked to the edge of the hall and gestured to one of the mirrors. Marney's heart skipped a beat as it cleared to show a lush forest in an Aelfirian House. At the end of a track she could see a wooden door set into a frame made from two gnarled trees – a doorway to the Great Labyrinth.

'Your way home will not be as traumatic as your journey here,' said the Librarian. He looked back at Marney. 'I wish you luck, whatever your future holds.'

And with that, he sank down through the glass floor of the hall and was gone.

Quashing a feeling of longing, Marney managed to tear her eyes away from the image of the forest. Alone now with her mentor, she used her empathic magic to control her anxiety while she watched Denton pace, muttering to himself.

'No, no, no. It wasn't meant to be like this,' he said, clearly disturbed. 'Surely she knows another way.'

'Denton,' Marney said, her voice small. 'What is it?'

'Your envelope,' he snapped. 'Give it to me, Marney.'

It was an order, and he marched towards her with an outstretched hand.

Hurriedly, Marney pulled the envelope of secret, coded instructions from the leg pocket on her fatigues, and Denton snatched it from her. Without pause, he threw it into the brazier. The envelope sank into one of the mirror-shards of fire and immediately burst into flames.

Agitated, his magic barely concealing his fear, Denton rounded on Marney, held her by the shoulders and stared into her eyes.

'Do you trust me?' he said.

'Of-of course,' Marney replied shakily.

'There are things I cannot explain to you, Marney. Lady Amilee expects far too much of us and … and she has *very* good reason.'

'Denton, what's wrong?'

'I need you to trust me more than you ever have before.' His tone was ice. 'Can you do that?'

Marney did her best to emote a sense of calm to her mentor. He batted it aside with a hard shell of apathy.

'I have seen too much, and I need you to understand that what I am about to do is for the good of everyone, for *all* of us, for every House and every living soul. Do you understand?'

'Denton, you're frightening—'

He cut her off with a shout. 'Will you trust me as you've never trusted me before?'

'Yes!'

'Then forgive me.'

To Marney's surprise, before she could stop him, Denton pulled her forward and placed his lips on hers. There was a flash of empathic energy inside her mind, a vibrant, shocking blue. She felt the truth of Denton's words when his voice whispered, *I'm sorry*, and then Marney's mind fell as limp as her body in her mentor's embrace.

In the northern district, an estate of residential dwellings surrounded a park; a collection of moderately sized two-storey houses more expensive than those in the eastern district, but nothing like the grand manors of the west side. A chapel of the Timewatcher served as a centrepiece for the park. Sunlight reflected from its stained-glass windows and the sonorous tones of a priest could be heard chanting midday sermons.

Van Bam, looking like himself again, stood in the shade of a tree along with Macy and Bryant, keeping an eye out for any denizens who might get in the way. The area was well populated but the few passers-by didn't linger; and Van Bam's illusionist magic ensured the Relic Guild couldn't be seen. Above, the sky was clear and blue.

The twins looked tense as they watched a detached house on the other side of the park but Van Bam felt relaxed. The green glass of his cane felt cool and reassuring in his hands; the newly cut grass smelled fresh and felt real beneath his bare feet. It was the first time Van Bam had experienced any kind of inner peace since Angel's death. But it wasn't a peace that could last.

Ambient thaumaturgy flashed brightly from the downstairs windows of the house. Van Bam scoured the area; no one else was around to see it. A moment passed, and then several more violet flashes came.

Bryant glanced uncertainly at his sister. 'Do we go and help him?'

'Not bloody likely,' Macy said. 'I'm not going anywhere near that place while Samuel's magic is up and there's a gun in his hand.'

'He will tell us when it is safe,' Van Bam said.

The light of a power stone blazed silently from the upstairs windows, repeating several times before falling to darkness. Soon after, Samuel opened the front door and beckoned his fellow magickers into the house.

'Golems,' Samuel said coldly as they joined him inside. 'A lot of them, but no infected.' His prescient awareness had obviously dulled sufficiently to allow him to holster his revolver. 'They must've been here for quite a while.'

The air was laced with the acrid stench of dispelled magic and spent thaumaturgy. On the staircase and along the hallway, chunks of stone lay scattered in small piles. Van Bam could see more golem ruins through the doorways to the rooms off the hallway.

'Funny, though,' Samuel added. 'None of them was armed.'

'This place has to be something other than one of Moor's feeding nests,' Macy said. 'Otherwise why would he need Gemstone Llem's help?'

'Even so,' Bryant said, 'these golems used to be infected denizens. You've all heard the noise they make. Why did no one hear them and report a disturbance?'

It was a good point. Van Bam tapped his cane against the carpet, summoning his illusionist magic. Almost as soon as pale green light radiated from the glass, spreading in waves through the air, Van Bam detected the dampening spell which had been cast upon the house. It prevented sound from escaping the walls and would've hidden the building from perception – even that of magickers. Van Bam explained what he had discovered to the others, adding, 'The perception magic must be weak or fading if it did not affect us.'

'But *what* was Moor trying to hide with it?' Macy said.

'I can answer that,' Samuel growled. He drew his rifle from its holster on his back. 'The rest of the house is clear, but there's something you need to see in the cellar.'

He led the group down the hallway to the kitchen. Sunlight shone through a window and glinted off pans hanging above a large oven. Water dripped from a tap. Van Bam and the twins stayed behind Samuel as he approached the cellar door. He paused, listened to his magic and then opened it, revealing the cellar stairs along with a pronounced reek of rotting vegetables: the distinctive smell of those infected by Fabian Moor's virus.

'It's all right,' Samuel said, switching on the stairwell lights. 'Well … sort of.'

The group followed Samuel down into a spacious cellar with a high ceiling. Light prisms fixed to the walls like pyramid studs glowed with pale radiance. They made their way towards some kind of construct at the rear of the cellar. At first, Van Bam thought it was sitting behind a series of support pillars that divided the room in two; but a closer look revealed wooden poles engraved with glyphs and wards.

'Stop,' Van Bam said, recognising some of those symbols with a shiver. 'This is necromantic magic.'

Macy and Bryant looked at Samuel.

Samuel shrugged. 'I'm telling you, I'm not sensing any danger. But you need to see the rest.'

Leading the way beyond the engraved wooden poles, he showed them the grim display on show.

The powerful stink of rotting meat arose from a hole in the ground the size of a dinner plate. A metal tripod dangled a small glass box over the hole from a thin wire. The object inside the box looked like a rotten shelled egg, but closer inspection revealed it to be something far stranger. Green-brown in colour, the egg had a leathery surface like the skin of a reptile.

'What is it?' Bryant asked.

Samuel didn't reply and pointed to the ceiling.

'By the Timewatcher,' Macy said.

Bryant replied to his sister with a choice curse.

There were denizens bound to the ceiling by magic, like some perverse mural. With a sickened feeling, Van Bam counted five of them, probably homeless people stolen from the streets. They twitched, their mouths opening and closing as though to release silent moans. From the black veins that webbed their skin and the jaundiced look to their eyes, it was clear they had been infected by Fabian Moor's virus. Evidently, whatever magic held them to the ceiling also subdued their bloodthirsty madness and prevented the virus from reaching its end and turning them into golems.

The reek was palpable.

Macy coughed, covering a retch with the back of her hand. 'Can anyone explain to me what's going on here?'

'Nothing good,' Van Bam whispered. 'Samuel – you are certain your magic is dormant?'

Samuel affirmed by giving the illusionist a sour look. Van Bam wondered if a separate dampening spell had been cast upon the cellar.

As a test, the illusionist whispered to his magic, thinking to conjure the illusion of a bird. The chime of the cane was flat and discordant. Van Bam's bird briefly flared into existence, then sputtered and died.

Her expression troubled, Macy was opening and closing her fists, as if realising her gift of magically enhanced strength had deserted her.

'What is this place?' Bryant wondered. Casting a wary gaze at the denizens on the ceiling, he crouched to inspect the egg hanging from the tripod. He peered into the hole beneath it and made a disgusted noise. 'It's filled with rancid meat,' he said, gagging.

Samuel hadn't taken his eyes off the ceiling. 'Meat from what?'

'Whatever has been set up here,' said Van Bam, 'necromancy is Hamir's province, not ours. I suggest we leave.'

'Agreed,' said Macy.

But before the group had begun to move, the symbols engraved into the wooden poles began to give off a faint light and Bryant said, 'Wait!'

The wire that dangled the egg from the tripod was glowing with heat. Bryant moved closer to it, Samuel aiming his rifle behind him. The glass box cracked and then shattered, dropping the egg down into the hole. The sound of bubbling and boiling followed.

Samuel began, 'I don't like this—' but was cut off by an ear-piercing screech.

A host of tentacles erupted from the hole. Leathery, green-brown in colour, they shot up and stabbed into the bodies of the infected denizens. Two more tentacles whipped out and punched Van Bam and Macy off their feet, out beyond the line of poles. Winded, Van Bam got to his hands and knees. He heard the drone of magic, and then Bryant screamed.

Magical barriers had stretched between the poles, a translucent sickly grey, crackling with energy, separating Van Bam and Macy from their fellow agents. Van Bam's gut wrenched as he saw through the magic that one of the tentacles had pierced Bryant's back, then emerged from his chest and lifted him from the ground. More tentacles had coiled around his wrists and legs and were tugging at him, as though trying to pull his limbs off.

Macy rushed towards the magical barrier. The skin of her hands sizzled and smoked as she punched at the energy and she fell back with a cry of pain.

Samuel's teeth were gritted as he searched for some way out of the trap, desperate without the guidance of his dampened magic. He gave Van Bam a despairing look before Bryant issued a final scream. Blood spurted as Bryant's limbs began ripping from their sockets. Another tentacle punched through the back of his head and smashed out through his face. Samuel fired his rifle. The dull orange storm of fire-magic bloomed behind the barrier of energy.

Macy bellowed her brother's name.

CHAPTER TEN

FIRST AND GREATEST

Samuel had been through too much in his time; he was too old, too tired to be perturbed by anything that life had left to throw at him. He wondered if that was a shame as he sat there facing Gulduur Bellow, a giant, an elder from a race of blood-magickers who Samuel had always been taught to fear: the Nephilim.

After saving the Relic Guild from the demon horde, Bellow had taken them into a spacious cavern within the red mountain. Its walls were unnaturally smooth and the domed ceiling was streaked with thick veins of the same red and blue resin-like substance from which the trees of the Icicle Forest had been fashioned. Samuel had seen nothing in this House that he would consider fertile ground, yet trees of fruit and bushes of berries grew from the cavern's red rock floor. They formed an orchard of sorts, divided by a stream of clear, sweet water that began at a spring flowing from a crack in a boulder and disappeared beneath the far wall to end who knew where.

Like the rest of the Icicle Forest, this cavern had been created by higher magic.

Fed and watered by their host, the companions now sat upon boulders close to the orchard. Bellow was so large, so fierce-looking with his intense blue eyes, but he conducted himself with a welcoming, unimposing manner, encouraging the group to share with him the details of the journey that had led them to this point.

The giant listened raptly as Samuel and Namji told him about the Genii's return and their plan to free Spiral from Oldest Place. He appeared fascinated to learn of the Relic Guild's escape from Labrys Town and their mission to find Known Things, a bizarre relic and supposed weapon that could destroy Spiral.

'And all of this on the orders of Lady Amilee?' Bellow said.

'Indirectly,' Samuel replied. This close, he could see the scars criss-crossing Bellow's exposed skin, the telltale marks of a blood-magicker. He wondered if Bellow's entire body was decorated with them. 'We haven't seen Amilee yet, only her avatar.'

'That doesn't surprise me.' Suspicion and intrigue laced the giant's voice but he didn't elaborate, and then proceeded to tell his own tale.

Bellow had a passion for stories. With an almost excited keenness, he told the incredible history of the Nephilim, of their creation and their creator – the Progenitor, a rogue Thaumaturgist. He lamented the centuries of lies and legends that had painted his people as evil abominations; and how this perception had been encouraged by the Timewatcher to hide what She considered an embarrassing secret. The Nephilim were hybrids, Bellow said – a magical fusion of Thaumaturgists and humans. And the foul magic used to create them had killed one hundred denizens.

Although Samuel remained unfazed by Bellow's story, Hillem was in his element, sitting closest to the giant, asking questions from time to time, listening with open amazement on his young face. When Glogelder first regained consciousness, healed by blood-magic, he had panicked at the sight of the giant, which had amused Bellow. Now the big Aelf looked settled and as unfazed as Samuel, content to eat his fill of fruit, and sulking about the loss of his spell sphere launcher – his favourite weapon – which had been broken beyond repair during the fight.

As for Namji, she and the giant were friends of old.

When Bellow told the tale of his journey to the Icicle Forest – which began when he alone escaped Spiral's plot to trap the Nephilim herd in a hidden prison – Namji said, 'I thought you had died, Gulduur.' She approached the giant and took his massive hand in hers. 'I waited for you, but you never came back.'

'I lost some of my memories,' Bellow replied apologetically, staring at the tiny hand holding his. 'After I fought the Genii Buyaal, I destroyed Mirage's doorway to the Great Labyrinth, and then there is a blank spot. The next thing I remember, I was roaming the desert, healed and whole, but lost and confused.' He turned his bright blue eyes to Samuel. 'But I recall helping Van Bam to escape, and I regret that I couldn't save your friend Angel.'

Samuel felt a pang of dark nostalgia. 'It was a long time ago.'

'And a hard time for us all,' Bellow said. 'You see, I lost the fight against Buyaal. I fought him and his Aelfirian army for as long as I could, but in the end I fell, suffering what most would call mortal wounds, but …' He gave a sad sort of chuckle. 'The Nephilim would tell you that it is their curse, but apparently we are destined to be healed and resurrected from *all* wounds.'

A charged pause.

'You can't die?' said Hillem.

'No, I wouldn't put it that way,' Bellow replied. 'I believe that death doesn't come for the Nephilim in the same way it comes for others, and my people are simply yet to meet theirs. Who knows – maybe the Progenitor made it this way. There is still much concerning my herd's origins that I do not know.'

'So Buyaal couldn't kill you,' said Namji. 'And neither could Spiral?'

Bellow's expression became uncertain. 'Who is the greater force between the Nephilim and the Thaumaturgists? It is not a question that has ever been properly answered. Although if anyone was capable of destroying the Nephilim, you would think Spiral could do it.

'I have often wondered if the Genii Lord removed the Nephilim because he *couldn't* destroy them, or if he had some other plan for my people. Who can guess Spiral's reasons?' Bellow's tone darkened. 'All I can tell you for certain is that if I had faced Buyaal and his army with my entire herd, there would have been no competition.'

Glogelder sat forward. 'But they weren't with you,' he said through a mouthful of apple. 'Spiral trapped your people and only you managed to escape. How did you do it?'

'By the skin of my teeth.' Sadness returned to the giant. 'Spiral had found something my people were defenceless against, a method of subduing the Nephilim – a weapon, I suppose you could call it. He wielded the higher magic which had been stripped from the Progenitor.' He looked up at the red and blue veins of the cavern ceiling, his voice coming from distant memory. 'It blazed with the light of our origins. How could the Nephilim deny the source of their creation? Spiral hypnotised them with the Progenitor's thaumaturgy.'

'But not you,' Samuel said.

Bellow looked at him, as if suddenly remembering he wasn't alone. 'I recognised what Spiral had and realised that he had tricked us in time to resist the *pull* of the Progenitor's power and escape. But not soon enough to warn my herd, to save them. And they have been lost to me ever since.'

Samuel had met several creatures of higher magic in the past. Aloof, hard to fathom, capricious, each and every one of them. But Bellow seemed different; he was personable, welcoming, open and honest, and he spoke as though he addressed peers, not lower creatures who could in no way match his power. Was that because of the Nephilim's human side? Samuel wondered.

'Spiral has a lot to answer for,' the old bounty hunter said, in what he hoped was a consoling tone. 'But how did you end up in the Icicle Forest?'

'Ah, my story continues,' Bellow said, his large face brightening. 'Lady Amilee found me roaming in the desert of Mirage. She helped me to order my mind. I asked after you, Namji, and Amilee assured me you were safe.'

'I never saw her,' Namji said. 'I hid in Mirage until allied soldiers found me during the Last Storm.'

The Last Storm, the day the Genii War ended. But not, Samuel realised, the day the Timewatcher won after all.

'I think Amilee sent those soldiers to me,' Namji added.

'It's unsurprising that the Skywatcher didn't show herself to you then or to any of us now,' Bellow said bitterly. 'There is as much trickery in Amilee as there is in Spiral. She promised to reunite me with my herd. She said she could finally deliver the Nephilim to their home.'

Home, Samuel wondered. He deadened thoughts of Labrys Town, of the denizens ... of Councillor Tal, a lone Aelf standing against the Panopticon of Houses to save a million lives.

'You're talking about the Sorrow of Future Reason,' Hillem said, almost excitedly. His fascination with the situation was beginning to irritate Samuel. 'That's the House you've been searching for, isn't it? I thought it was a myth.'

'Myth?' Bellow considered that. 'The Sorrow of Future Reason is more like *hope*. For a thousand years the Nephilim searched for a home, and I honestly thought our search had come to an end. But once again, Yansas Amilee displayed her gift for deception.'

Samuel frowned. 'She led you to the Icicle Forest.'

'And she abandoned me here almost as soon as the war ended.'

'Why?'

'There's an interesting answer to that,' Bellow growled. 'The *Icicle Forest* – a pretty name for such a damned place, don't you agree? Spiral really lost no love when he created this House.'

'But he didn't create it properly,' Namji added, moving back to her boulder seat. 'If you ask me, the Icicle Forest isn't stable. It's chaotic, like it's ... *in flux*.'

'And why bother creating all those monsters?' Glogelder said. 'What's their purpose?' He shivered. 'I don't envy you being stuck in here with them outside.'

'I should hope not,' Bellow said with a smile. 'Spiral created this House from unused time, which means he had grown powerful enough to do the Timewatcher's work. But those monsters, Glogelder – they're not monsters at all. They are Time Engineers, servants of the Timewatcher, magical labourers who Spiral stole and subjugated. They are the builders of Houses.

'You are right to say the Icicle Forest is unstable, Namji, and purposely so. It is trapped in a loop in time, perpetually recycling itself. Spiral's magic has driven those poor Time Engineers to insanity. They are perversions of what they should be.'

'But that doesn't explain why you're here,' Samuel said impatiently. 'Look, this is all very interesting, but every one of us has been manipulated by Lady Amilee and I'm pretty sure she sent us here to find you, Gulduur. But why? Surely we're not all trapped here now.'

'I'm not trapped here – I've been waiting for you.' Bellow broke into a wide grin that revealed blocky teeth. 'I suspect you're a man who prefers brevity of information over a good story, Samuel.'

'Yep, and as miserable as you like,' Glogelder put in.

Hillem told his friend to knock it off but Bellow laughed, standing up and towering over the group. 'Although she failed to tell me that it would take decades, Amilee said that a human magicker would come, one who would walk with me on the path that would lead to freeing the Nephilim herd.' He looked at Samuel. 'I mean no offence, but I had hoped it would be Van Bam.'

'We don't know where Van Bam is,' Samuel said coolly. 'He's with another magicker – Clara – and they're both missing.'

'I'm sorry to hear that.'

'All part of Amilee's plan, I suppose,' Samuel grumbled. 'You said something earlier about needing my help to solve a puzzle?'

'Indeed.' The giant looked at each of them in turn. 'Come with me,' he said, walking off into the orchard. 'I want to show you why the Icicle Forest was created.'

Ennis had always known he had been touched by magic. For as long as he could remember, he had felt a connection to Labrys Town that no one else seemed to share. There was something in his blood that steered his thoughts, honed his instincts and senses. Ennis thought of his gift as *truth-seeing*; the ability to find clues and links that no one else could perceive, to read important information in apparently innocuous conversations and body language. And he was rarely wrong.

In his youth at the orphanage, Ennis had gained the reputation of a grass. He read the schemes and mischiefs of the other orphans no matter how hard they tried to hide them, and Ennis never failed to inform his superiors. Childhood was a lonely time. But there had never been any spite behind his informing; Ennis had simply been defending those on the receiving end of these schemes. The truth was, he loved this dirty shit-hole that he called home, and there was a desire in his blood to protect its people.

But the use of magic was punishable by death in Labrys Town and it had been that way since the Genii War ended and the Retrospective came. Small wonder, then, that Ennis wound up joining the police force, where his magical gift could easily be mistaken for honest detective work. But Long Tommy said that if Ennis had been born a couple of generations earlier, he would have become an agent of the Relic Guild. Was that true? Was Ennis fulfilling the duties of the Relic Guild now?

In the central district, at the very heart of town, Ennis stood amidst the panic taking place in the large foyer of police headquarters. A crowd of denizens were shouting and arguing with officials who were losing an increasingly desperate battle to maintain calm. A group of armed police officers rushed out of the building onto the streets where panic was beginning to rise into a storm of pandemonium.

Labrys Town was in trouble.

The denizens believed that the Relic Guild were making their move, spreading their plague and preparing the town for the chaos and perversion of the Retrospective; but Ennis knew differently.

Pushing his way through the crowd in the foyer, he ascended the stairs to the upper levels. He crossed the open-plan office, usually bustling with activity but eerily deserted now – apparently even the administrative staff had been called to attend the mounting crises. Reaching the top level, he strode down a long corridor with doorless rooms on either side. Inside the rooms, police watchers lay on reclining chairs, their faces hidden by black bowl-like receptor helmets. The watchers were tuned in with the eye devices on the streets of Labrys Town and would feed any troubling information to the street patrols. Ennis reasoned that troubling news was currently plentiful.

He reached the closed door to Captain Moira's office and heard her agitated voice coming from inside.

'I don't care how thinly we're spread, the denizens need protecting.' She barked a curse. 'This damn virus has already become an epidemic. If *anyone* shows signs of infection, your orders are to shoot them *dead*. Now *get out!*'

The door opened and three officers rushed from the room without so much as looking at Ennis. They headed off down the corridor to the lower levels.

'Where in the Timewatcher's name have you been?' Moira snapped when Ennis entered the office. 'I haven't seen you for days!'

'I've been following your orders,' Ennis replied calmly.

'Obviously without much bloody success.'

Moira had taken off her uniform jacket and her shirtsleeves were rolled to the elbows. With sweat stains at her armpits, she looked dishevelled and tired. Ennis glanced at the eye device fixed to the office wall. The fluid inside the glass hemisphere was still: a sure sign that the eye was inactive and no one was watching or listening to their conversation.

'I asked you to find the Relic Guild,' Moira said, simmering. 'I trusted you, Ennis. I gave you free rein to do whatever you thought necessary. And so far I haven't received one single report. Care to explain?'

'Things got complicated,' Ennis replied. 'There's more to this than you realise.'

'Oh, really?' Moira gritted her teeth. 'More than the virus outbreak that we can't control in the northern district? Or perhaps you haven't heard that the deliveries of cargo have stopped coming through the portal outside the Nightshade? While you were off discovering *complicated things*, did you happen to notice that the underworld has risen up against the police and the warehouses in the southern district are being raided?'

Venting . . .

Ennis experienced a moment of relief at the news of the warehouse raids. Long Tommy had managed to convince the criminal underworld of the real situation and was making good on his side of the plan. Food stocks and weapons were being stolen and hoarded in the central district, where the denizens would make their last stand. Now Ennis just had to convince the police captain.

'The denizens are panicking,' Moira continued. 'We don't have the manpower to deal with an emergency of this size, and now I can't contact the Resident.' She pushed her fists down onto her desk, struggling for calm. 'Ennis, maybe I sent you on a fool's errand. I think I already know where the Relic Guild is. They have taken control of the Nightshade.'

'The Relic Guild isn't the problem,' Ennis said.

Anger returned quickly to Moira's face. 'Have you been listening—'

'Shut up,' Ennis snapped and continued before his captain could object. 'You asked me to do a job, and I did it. What I discovered goes far deeper than rogue magickers.'

'*Sergeant* Ennis—'

Ennis drew his pistol, thumbed the power stone and took aim at his captain.

'What do you think you're doing?' Moira whispered, her voice a dangerous growl.

There were secrets in this town, things that Ennis simply could never guess, not even with his magical gift. But once the avatar revealed them to him, it had all clicked into place. The way forward became clear. Ennis and his magic knew what to do next. The need to protect the denizens surged through his blood.

'Moira,' he said softly, 'on the night the Relic Guild disappeared, two of them were found in this police station, in a secret room beneath the building. It's important that you take me to it. Now.'

She stood proudly, defiantly. Her eyes flitted to the holstered pistol sitting on her desk and Ennis knew what she was thinking.

'Don't,' he warned, his aim steady. 'You trusted me once, and for good reason, so trust me now.'

'*Trust* you, while you have a gun pointed at me?'

'The denizens won't stand a chance unless you do as I say.'

Moira looked warily at the pistol aimed at her, and then she studied Ennis's face, as though finally recognising the sergeant she had been so willing to trust.

'What have you discovered?'

Calculating...

Ennis gestured at the door with the pistol. 'We don't have much time. Take me to this secret room and don't even think about calling for help.'

With the weapon aimed at her back, Moira led the way out of the office and to the end of the deserted corridor, where they stood before a recess. A small square of its back wall was covered with a hundred tiny mazes.

'Believe it or not, there's a door in this wall,' Moira said drily. 'But we haven't been able to find it, let alone open it.'

'Stand back,' Ennis said.

Keeping the pistol trained on Moira, he laid his free hand upon the square of mazes, praying that everything the avatar had said about a magicker's touch was true. He felt warmth on his skin, and then there was a deep *click*. The outline of a door appeared and slid to one side, revealing an elevator.

'After you,' Ennis said, again gesturing with the pistol.

With a frown, Moira entered.

'Explain your actions to me, Ennis,' she said as they descended for a short time before the elevator opened onto a narrow, gloomy corridor.

Nerves fluttering in his stomach, Ennis told Moira to follow the corridor to the end, adding, 'We've been wrong about the Relic Guild. The night they were down here, they were trying to help us.'

'Hard to believe,' Moira replied darkly. She glanced back at the pistol. 'I've seen no evidence to convince me that they're anything but the enemy.'

'That's because we've been listening to the wrong people,' Ennis replied. 'The truth is, Captain, the Nightshade turned against the denizens the moment a new Resident arrived. But there was a safeguard built into the Labyrinth, an emergency procedure to get us out of situations like this.'

The corridor turned left and came to an end. Ennis placed his hand against the wall, which was also decorated with small mazes. A door appeared and swung open with a click. As soon as the police officers stepped into the chamber beyond, the door closed and disappeared behind them.

The air was unnaturally still and oppressive inside the chamber. A single ceiling prism gave pale light. The pattern of mazes was repeated on each cream-coloured wall to almost hypnotising effect. Ennis deactivated the power stone and holstered the pistol. Moira didn't appear to notice; she was transfixed by a head-sized sphere of glass sitting atop a slim pedestal. It was filled with a thick substance alive with sparks and streaks of purple lightning like a trapped storm cloud. Moira couldn't take her eyes off it.

'Captain, you're old enough to remember life before the Genii War,' Ennis said. 'You must recall names like Fabian Moor?'

'Yes,' Moira replied distantly.

'Our Resident and her aides, they're not who you think they are. They're the Genii, Captain. They came back, and they've freed Spiral from Oldest Place.'

Moira managed to drag her eyes away from the scintillating lights to give Ennis an incredulous stare. 'What did you say?'

'It's true.' Ennis pointed at the sphere. On either side of it, the glass was indented with handprints. 'That thing is the emergency procedure.

If the Nightshade is incapacitated, it falls to us – the police – to instigate it. Once set in motion, it will activate Labrys Town's defences and send a distress signal to someone outside the Labyrinth. I don't know who, but someone who can help.'

Moira's mouth worked silently for a moment. 'What?'

Anxiety gnawed at Ennis. 'But here's the problem. The Nightshade isn't incapacitated. Hagi Tabet controls it, and she's a Genii. We can activate the defences but Tabet won't let any distress signal leave the Labyrinth. For that to happen, she has to be removed from the Nightshade. She has to be killed.' He stared at the sphere. 'It takes two people to initiate the emergency procedure.'

'What are you talking about, Ennis?' Perhaps Moira thought he was insane; perhaps she was frightened by the truth in his words. 'I'm not touching that thing.'

'I never expected this to be easy for you to accept,' Ennis said. He felt the tingle of magic upon his skin. 'But maybe someone else can convince you.'

The ceiling prism fizzed and died and the chamber was filled with blue luminescence. Moira backed away to where the door had been as a ghostly presence materialised. Tendrils of sky blue waved in the air around a vaguely human shape the colour of twilight. Void-like eyes leaked tears of vaporous black.

'Greetings, Captain Moira,' the avatar said. 'The denizens need you.'

There was a road in Labrys Town called Resident Approach. It stretched from the central district to the furthest reach of the northern district, all the way to the home of the Resident, the Nightshade.

The northernmost end of Resident Approach was lined by a host of statues – fifty-four of them, to be precise. Each statue represented a former Resident of Labrys Town; they were monuments to the men and women who had governed the denizens, dating back a thousand years. And in their hands, each held a spherical eye device.

Beneath the light of Ruby Moon, a troubled wind blew down

Resident Approach as though the Timewatcher Herself had sighed with displeasure. The statues began to shake. The eyes fell from their hands, rolling into the road like oversized marbles. The milky fluid inside them pulsed with violet light. Stone began to crack with sharp barks. Debris clattered to the ground. Metallic hands emerged from the statues, followed by silver arms and torsos and legs. As the stone shells shattered, an army of automaton sentries revealed themselves and formed ranks on Resident Approach.

Eight feet tall, created from thaumaturgic metal, the automations reflected the red light of the moon from the smooth plates covering their faces and chests. Their exposed internal mechanisms – intricate cogs and pistons – whirred and pumped. As one, the army marched, heading southwards.

And from the eye devices they left in their wake came a commanding voice, a woman's voice that could be heard emanating from all the eyes in every district of Labrys Town, repeating the same message over and over, and she said:

'*This is an emergency. All denizens must proceed to the central district. This is an emergency ...*'

Gulduur Bellow led the group through his orchard to the cavern wall where a simple doorframe of unfinished wood had been set into the rock. The door itself was a cream-coloured panel decorated with a repetitive pattern of tiny mazes.

'It looks like a wall in the Nightshade,' Samuel said, surprised. He moved closer. A small square hole in the middle of the door exposed the red rock on the other side.

'Lady Amilee assured me that this door leads to the very centre of the Icicle Forest,' Bellow said. 'I believe this House is so hostile because Spiral designed it to protect what is kept there.'

'Fabian Moor,' Samuel realised. 'This is where his essence was found.'

'How curious,' Bellow said with a deep frown. 'Amilee mentioned nothing of Fabian Moor. She claimed there was a portal of some kind on the other side of this door. A way out of the Icicle Forest that would lead me to my herd.'

'You haven't looked?' Namji asked.

'No. The door cannot be opened.'

'Looks like there's a piece missing,' Glogelder said, peering closer at the maze-covered panel.

Bellow pointed to a bowl-like depression scooped out of the floor. It was three feet across, and above it a small cream square bearing a single maze hovered in eerie violet magic.

'Amilee left the pieces of this door for me to construct, like a puzzle,' Bellow said. 'I completed as much of it as I was able, but as you can see …' The giant approached the missing piece. He attempted to snatch it from the air but his hand passed through it as though it was no more substantial than smoke. 'The Skywatcher made damn sure that the puzzle could only be finished by a human magicker.'

'Me?' said Samuel.

'Not specifically, but yes,' Bellow replied. 'It's a clever spell, cast by higher magic but one that higher magic cannot break.' He gestured to the floating square. 'But *lower* magic should not have a problem.'

Scowling, Samuel stood alongside the Nephilim but was reluctant to put his hand into the magical light and take the final piece of the puzzle. 'Are we sure about this?' he said. 'Right now, I'm not feeling particularly inclined to trust Amilee.'

'Samuel,' Bellow said with a tired air, 'I've been waiting forty years for you to come, and you *will* do this. You could try to defy me, but do you really want to test your prescient awareness against a Nephilim?'

Glogelder gave a throaty laugh at Bellow's oddly amiable threat, but Namji and Hillem became tense.

'Listen to the gift you were born with,' Bellow added kindly. 'Is it warning you *not* to do this?'

Samuel pushed his hand into the light. The tingle of magic raised the hairs on his arm as his fingers closed around the last piece of the doorway. Solid. He pulled it free, the light disappeared and Bellow urged him to complete Amilee's puzzle.

It fitted snugly into the panel. There was a fizzing sound. The lines around the piece disappeared, merging perfectly with the pattern of mazes. Nothing else happened.

'So what now?' Hillem said.

'The doors in the Nightshade are difficult to find,' Samuel replied. 'But when you know where they are, they will open to a magicker's touch.'

Samuel drew his pistol and laid his hand upon the panel. With a click, it swung inwards. Silver light shone from the chamber beyond. Samuel's prescient awareness remained dormant.

'At last,' Bellow whispered.

Stooping to pass through the doorway, the giant led the group into the chamber. It was smaller than the cavern, but the same red and blue veins lined the rock of its smooth walls and domed ceiling. And at the centre, bathing the group in sterile light, was a huge cube of glowing silver metal.

'What in the bloody Timewatcher's name is *that*?' Glogelder grumbled. 'Can't *anything* be straightforward?'

'It looks like thaumaturgic metal,' Samuel said.

'Is that a good thing or a bad one?' Namji wondered.

'Let's find out,' Bellow replied, and he began walking round the silver cube, studying it, clearly happy to have something new to do for the first time in decades. Hillem, as curious as ever, joined him. Samuel, Namji and Glogelder kept their distance.

The cube was about fifteen feet high, wide and deep, and the magical energy in its light made Samuel's skin tingle.

'Do you know what gets on my nerves?' said Glogelder. 'Why do Amilee and her bloody avatar have to be so vague? Surely it would be simpler to just tell us what we have to do.' He gestured to the Nephilim. 'And what we'd find.'

'I don't think anyone's playing games with us, Glogelder,' said Namji. 'This must be about timing – doing the right thing at the right moment.'

'Well, if you ask me, Thaumaturgists are a strange bunch. Not to mention annoying.'

'And dangerous,' Samuel added as he joined Bellow and Hillem. 'What have you found?'

'It's definitely thaumaturgic metal,' Bellow said happily. 'And I think it's hollow.'

The giant touched the cube. Its state began to change, shifting from solid to pearlescent liquid and finally to shimmering air. The cube did indeed have a hollow interior.

Chunks of grey stone on the silver floor inside reminded Samuel of the remnants of golems after their animation spells had died and they fell apart. Lying face down and naked among the debris was a woman.

Icy needles stabbed Samuel's chest. 'Shit,' he hissed, ignoring Namji's warning cry as he rushed through the wall of shimmering air into the cube.

There was an ugly, weeping puncture wound on the woman's lower back and her skin was mottled with ice burns. Samuel dropped to his knees and rolled her over, already knowing that he would see Marney's slack and pallid face.

'No, no, no,' he pleaded, cradling her head. 'Marney, can you hear me?' She didn't respond. Her eyes were closed. Samuel began patting her cheek. 'Marney, please … wake up. Wake up.'

He felt Namji's gentle hand on his arm.

'Let me look at her.'

Samuel laid Marney down and allowed the Aelfirian magic-user to check her over, then he looked at Hillem, Glogelder and Bellow. The cube's side had solidified behind them.

'We never knew what happened to her.' The flames of anger crackled in his voice. 'We assumed the Genii had killed her.'

The Aelfirian men looked startled. Bellow pursed his lips.

'I'm so sorry, Samuel,' Namji said softly. 'I think she's dead.'

Samuel had known she was going to say it, but he wasn't prepared to accept it. 'You're wrong,' he stated.

'I can't feel a pulse,' Namji told him. 'I don't think she's breathing.'

'I don't care.' Samuel's voice was as cold as winter. 'You must know some healing spells.'

'Let me try,' said Bellow. 'Please, give me some room.'

Namji moved out of the giant's way, but Samuel remained at Marney's side. Bellow crouched, laying one massive hand on her head, the other on her chest. Marney's face looked pale and lifeless.

For the first time in many years, Samuel prayed to the Timewatcher.

'Hmm,' Bellow murmured. 'A spark of life remains in her, and I could heal her body.'

Samuel felt a rush of relief. 'Do it.'

'Her mind is gone.'

'Just heal her body,' Samuel insisted. 'We'll worry about the rest later.'

'No, you don't understand,' Bellow said gravely. 'Her mind is *gone*. She would be a shell, nothing more. Healing her is pointless.'

'Try anyway.'

'Forgive me.' Bellow's blue eyes burned into Samuel's. 'It is time to say goodbye to your friend.'

'You listen to me, *Nephilim*,' Samuel said through clenched teeth. 'You heal this woman to the best of your abilities or I *will* test my magic against yours.'

Bellow's expression became dispassionate.

'Samuel,' Namji hissed. 'Don't!'

'Yeah,' said Glogelder. 'Let's just stay calm.'

Samuel glared at Bellow, unafraid, defiant, angry, heartbroken. 'Marney is one of us. She sacrificed herself to give us a chance to defeat the Genii. Without her, *you* would have been waiting in this place *for ever*! We're *not* giving up on her.'

Bellow's face softened, and for a moment he considered the human before him as if seeing something he hadn't noticed before. 'Very well,' he said.

From the sleeve of his habit, the giant produced a curved knife and nicked the end of his finger, just deep enough to draw blood. He used it to scribe symbols on Marney's forehead, her chin, and her chest. He then began whispering words of blood-magic, which he blew upon the symbols. The blood dried instantly and Samuel was sure he saw a little colour return to Marney's face. And then, blessedly, the empath inhaled a lungful of air and her chest began rising and falling with steady breaths.

Samuel hoped she might open her eyes, but she didn't.

'Remember,' Bellow said solemnly, 'without her mind, she will never be more than she is now.'

Samuel ignored him, removed his coat and wrapped Marney in it.

'Good.' Sucking the last of the blood from his fingertip, Bellow looked around the cube. 'Perhaps now we can concentrate on getting out of the Icicle Forest.'

The giant moved to the silver wall opposite the one through which the group had entered and studied it in silence.

Glogelder puffed his cheeks. 'Never a dull day, is there?' He nudged Hillem, suddenly grinning. 'Who do you reckon would win a fight between them?'

'Shut up, you oaf,' Hillem said. He looked shaken.

Namji said, 'Samuel, are you all right?'

'I'm fine,' he replied shortly. He stood up, Marney in his arms, wrapped in his coat. She felt cold against him.

Had Amilee known they would find Marney like this? Was it part of her plan?

'Strange,' Bellow said. 'This wall is a different design from the others. It isn't fixed to this cube. I suppose you could say it isn't really here.'

'Then where is it?' said Hillem, standing alongside the giant.

'Everywhere and nowhere,' Bellow replied. 'This wall is a conduit to other places. Perhaps it is the portal Amilee spoke of.'

Bellow touched the wall, which changed its state but instead of becoming shimmering air it turned into a cream-coloured maze-patterned wall of the Nightshade. Bellow pulled his hand away, as though the feel of it was uncomfortable.

'There is another door hidden in this wall,' the giant announced. 'It is charmed with the same spell as Amilee's puzzle. Higher magic cannot open it.'

Holding his friend tightly, struggling to order his thoughts, Samuel found himself recalling the night Fabian Moor had abducted Marney. The old bounty hunter had witnessed the event; he had seen the Genii open a portal that led to a chamber filled with silver light.

'I know what this is,' Samuel stated. 'Fabian Moor must have returned to the Icicle Forest after the Genii War. He must've been in here while you were out there, Gulduur.'

The giant looked bemused. 'Why would Amilee wish for that?'

'I don't know, but if that wall is a portal, it must be how Moor got back to the Labyrinth.'

'Then it could actually be a door to the Nightshade?' Namji asked. 'Perhaps the last place Moor travelled to.'

'Why would Amilee want to send us there?' Hillem said. 'The Genii control the Nightshade.'

'Samuel,' said Bellow, 'what is your magic saying?'

'Nothing. But that doesn't mean the Genii aren't there. My magic can't detect them.'

Bellow thought for a moment. 'Regardless, I, for one, am sick and tired of trying to guess what that cursed Skywatcher expects us to do next. So let's just find out, shall we?'

'I'll second that,' said Glogelder, drawing his pistol.

Bellow stood to one side. 'Samuel, please open this door.'

'Here,' said Hillem, 'give Marney to me.'

Samuel stared at him but made no move.

'Trust me,' Hillem continued. 'I'm not the best shot in the world, and if there's trouble waiting for us, I'd rather your gun hand was free.'

'Bloody true enough,' Glogelder added, priming his pistol's power stone. 'No telling what we're walking into.'

'They're right, Samuel,' Namji said, hoisting her crossbow. 'We need your magic and your guns more than Marney does right now.'

Conceding to reason, Samuel placed Marney in Hillem's arms, albeit reluctantly. He drew the ice-rifle from the holster on his back, priming its power stones. His magic still giving no warning signals as he touched the wall of the Nightshade. The door responded with a click before swinging open.

Flashes of purple light assaulted the group.

There were many rooms inside the Nightshade that Samuel had never seen – doubted that even Van Bam had ever seen – and he didn't recognise the chamber he walked into now. It wasn't particularly large, around thirty feet square, and at its centre was a fat column of purple energy, droning and spitting, rising from a dome of grey metal on the floor and connecting to a second dome on the ceiling. The energy was surrounded by a ring of black monoliths that reflected the light like obsidian glass.

'At least there's no Genii,' Glogelder muttered.

Bellow walked towards the column. 'I've heard it said that the magic of the Nightshade is sentient. And now I understand why.' There was a strange, distant edge to his voice as he stared up at the column of energy. 'My entire life I have suffered under the prerogatives of She who cast this Thaumaturgy. I know Her *touch*.'

It was as though the giant spoke to himself. Samuel shared confused looks with the Aelfir.

'This is the higher magic with which the Great Labyrinth was created,' Bellow continued. 'It is the First and Greatest Spell.'

With Marney in his arms, the awe on Hillem's Aelfirian face was evident. 'How can you be sure?' he said.

'Because I have seen it before,' Bellow replied. 'Because the wisdom of the Thaumaturgist whose soul was used to create me still resides within my being. And it recognises the Timewatcher's magic.'

'Bugger me,' said Glogelder.

Namji turned to Samuel. 'Did you know it was here?'

'Yes, but ... not like this.' Samuel was speechless for a moment. Perhaps life could still surprise him after all. He had always supposed that the Nightshade had *absorbed* the First and Greatest Spell, carried it in its walls and foundations – not that it was a living spell held deep inside the building. 'As far as I'm aware, no one knew it was here.'

'Amilee obviously did,' said Bellow.

Samuel felt dwarfed by the spell's presence. He didn't know how much more he could take.

Worriedly, Hillem asked, 'The Genii control the Nightshade, so they must control this magic, too.'

'No.' Bellow's voice was whispery. 'This is the roots of the Spell, pure as the day it was cast, unsullied, uncorrupted, still bearing the Timewatcher's touch. Given the nature of the charm on the door, I do not think the Genii can enter this room, or know what it holds.'

Samuel looked back the way they had come to find the door closed, impossible to discern on the wall. His prescient awareness became a warm, bad feeling in his gut. It told Samuel that the door no longer connected to the Icicle Forest, and beyond it now lay the rest of the Nightshade, and beyond that, Labrys Town. He wondered, briefly, how the denizens – the one million humans the Relic Guild had promised to protect – were coping under Genii occupation, and how Councillor Tal was faring against the Panopticon of Houses, before his magic warned of the terrible things waiting to happen if he opened the door again.

'I think I've found the way out of this chamber,' Bellow announced.

The Nephilim had moved inside the ring of black monoliths and now stood facing one of them. Samuel joined him and saw that the monolith's surface was rippling like night reflected in water, absorbing the purple flashes of the First and Greatest Spell.

'Another portal?' Samuel said.

'So it would appear. What does your magic tell you now, Samuel?'

That this new portal was infinitely safer than the door through which they'd entered the chamber.

Samuel looked back at Namji, Hillem and Glogelder. His gaze lingered on Marney's unconscious form in Hillem's arms. Timing, Namji had said; it was all about doing the right thing at the right moment ...

'This portal is the way forward,' he told his colleagues. 'We go through.'

His words were met with silent agreement.

'Splendid,' Bellow said excitedly. 'Would you like to go first?'

CHAPTER ELEVEN

SPLINTERS OF HER FIRE

A labyrinth. But not the endless maze that surrounded Labrys Town. This was something Clara had never seen before.

There were no bricks or cobbles. The ground was spongy underfoot, with patches of what looked to be thick black grass growing from it – or maybe it was hair. The alley walls – leathery, skin-like – flexed in and out with sighs that did not belong to the wind. This was a living, breathing labyrinth.

'I can sense emotions,' Marney said. 'There's someone else in here with us.'

'Can you tell who?' Clara asked.

Marney slipped a throwing dagger from her baldric. 'Maybe it's more than one person.'

The magickers stood at an intersection, clueless as to which direction to take. A fine, humid mist hung in the air. Above, glowing clouds of deep purple hid any moons or stars.

Baran Wolfe's warnings played in Clara's mind. They had reached an area of Known Things where Spiral kept his darkest and most personal records. The memories here – the memories of the most powerful Thaumaturgist who ever existed – went far beyond Clara's comprehension, beyond Marney's, beyond that of any creature of lower magic. And somewhere among these treacherous secrets nearly a thousand Nephilim were trapped with Van Bam's ghost. Clara hoped she and Marney could find them without experiencing anything else that might be kept in this place.

'There,' Marney said, using the dagger to point down the alleyway ahead. A green glow illuminated the gloomy mist. 'Our guiding light.'

They headed towards it at a cautious pace.

Marney looked more comfortable with the blade in her hand, and

Clara took solace in the fact she was as deadly with her daggers as Samuel was with his guns. The changeling wished her own magic was with her rather than out there somewhere, trying to rid her mind of Known Things. She missed her heightened senses and longed for the confidence that came with being the wolf.

The magickers followed the green light further into the labyrinth. It drifted further away until finally disappearing down a left turn. It waited for them to round the bend and then continued on down a new alleyway to the right.

The sound of breathing grew deeper. The leathery walls shivered, breaking out in gooseflesh.

Again, Wolfe's warnings plagued Clara. 'Can you sense anything?' she asked Marney, keeping her voice low. 'What's in here with us?'

Marney took a moment too long to answer. 'I don't know.'

Ahead, the green light turned left again.

Clara pursed her lips. 'What aren't you telling me?'

'Clara—'

'No! Don't evade the question. Not this time. I saw the way Baran Wolfe looked at you, Marney. I heard the way you spoke to each other. It's not that you dislike *him* – you just don't like that he knows what you're hiding from *me*.'

'There are a lot of things I haven't told you – or anyone else, for that matter – because … because I'm only just beginning to remember some of it myself.' Marney's tone was troubled, her body language edgy. 'You'll understand when I do, Clara, but … I think I know where we're heading.'

The green light led them down a long, straight alleyway. Clara flinched as a voice came from behind, borne on a stiff breeze of hot breath: *I have listened to you.*

The words were not spoken. They came as a collection of senses that invaded Clara's being so she *felt* rather than heard them. Her mind's eye was filled with deep purple shot through with rays of golden sunshine. Feminine, powerful, beautiful yet terrible. And judging by her reaction, Marney had felt the voice, too.

'Oh, that's too much!' The empath put out a hand to steady herself, but thought better of touching the breathing wall. She stumbled, dropped the dagger and quickly retrieved it.

The voice came again: *I have listened to you, and I will listen no more.*

Clara groaned. Marney stumbled again. A nauseating weakness drained the strength from Clara's legs and she could only imagine how the overwhelming emotions in the voice might be augmented for one with empathic magic.

'I ... I can't block it,' Marney whispered.

But the voice wasn't addressing the magickers. And it was answered by a masculine presence.

Think of the example you have set. You weaken our position in the Higher Thaumaturgic Cluster.

So much anger, frustration – centuries of bitterness that had caused a darkness inside a soul millennia old.

The woman replied, *I will not adapt the peace and unity I have created simply because you come before me with demands, Iblisha.*

I am your favoured son, and I come before you to beg you to see reason.

'It's Spiral,' Marney said from between clenched teeth. 'He's talking to ... to ...' She broke off, clutching her stomach.

'The Timewatcher,' Clara finished, and she was crushed by the weight of a displeasure that drove her to her knees. Tears sprang to her eyes.

Enough!

Please, Spiral said, *you will wreck your House. You will bring ruin to the Thaumaturgists.*

And the Timewatcher, the host of Mother Earth said, *Ruin? No, Iblisha, and you shame yourself to say so. Or do you reveal something of your true nature that I have failed to see?*

Rule them. Make them worship how their lives and freedom are preserved only by the grace of your higher magic.

The Aelfir do not need my intervention to express their love for us. Remember that. I will force no one.

No one? A flare of barely contained anger. *Can you not see the hypocrisy in your words?*

The Timewatcher drew a breath, burning with the promise of a fiery tempest. *Never question me again, Iblisha. Be gone from my presence.*

Weeping came next, the deep and heavy remorse of Spiral's tears, burrowing straight into Clara's core. She understood that she was feeling the sound of Spiral deciding upon a course of action that would shatter a love and devotion he had once held dear.

Through tear-blurred eyes, Clara looked at Marney. She, too, was on her knees, holding her head. Her body jerked with every sob that Spiral gave. With a shout of pain, Marney faced the sky. A dull blue light glowed from her eyes, spilling from her ears and nostrils as luminous vapour, shining from the cave of her open mouth.

Clara managed to get to her feet, stumble to Marney's side, then grabbed her hand. The blue light receded at the changeling's touch, though the empath's eyes retained a twilight hue.

'We have to keep moving,' Marney shouted through the crippling torment of Spiral's anguish.

'Come on!' Clara yelled, pulling Marney to her feet.

The green light waited, pulsing urgently, as the magickers ran towards it. Spiral's heartbreak followed them, but the further they ran, the less like a *feeling* it became. Clara imagined it slithering from her body to become an audible sound, bouncing off the leathery alley walls. It rose in volume, perhaps coming closer, until the green light led Clara and Marney into a courtyard and disappeared.

The weeping stopped.

Clara swore.

Marney prepared to throw a dagger.

A man stood in the courtyard, naked and completely stripped of skin. Pale moonlight shone through the purple clouds and glinted from his raw and wet muscles. He grinned skeletally at the Relic Guild agents, pointing a bloody finger at them.

'You sneaky little magickers …'

'… By creating the Retrospective and abandoning the Labyrinth,' Lady Amilee was saying, 'the Timewatcher unwittingly handed Spiral everything he needed.'

Hamir was only half-listening to the Skywatcher; his attention had been divided by the Toymaker. The strange automaton had carried

Clara to a padded table in a whitewashed room in Amilee's tower. While Hamir and her ladyship stood talking over the unconscious changeling, the Toymaker had broken apart into a hundred insectoid automatons. They now clung to the walls and ceiling, apparently guarding Clara's body. The violet light of their thaumaturgic stings glowed at the ends of their tails.

Amilee said, 'The Timewatcher is utterly unaware that the Genii have returned.'

The room wasn't particularly big – long but not wide. The table Clara lay upon had been pushed against the wall at one end of the room. A second empty padded table mirrored its position.

'Hamir, are you listening?'

'Yes, I can hear you.' There was something about the glowing silver insectoids that made Hamir suspicious. 'I've never seen an automaton like this before.'

'Does it matter?'

'Please, my lady, indulge me. What is the Toymaker?'

Looking tired and frail, Amilee sat on the edge of Clara's table. 'He was created by the Thaumaturgists, and they gave him to the Aelfir at the end of the Genii War,' she said. 'The Toymaker is a guardian of sorts. His duty was to protect the last portal to Labrys Town. To *deter* anyone who tried to use it for anything other than sending cargo to the denizens.'

'Ah, an assassin,' Hamir mused. 'But now it obeys your commands.'

'Thankfully, through my avatar, I was able to alter his directives. I suppose you could say he is now Clara's bodyguard.'

There it was again, the way Amilee referred to the construct – *he, him, his* ...

'There's something more to the Toymaker than the average automaton,' Hamir said. 'I'm beginning to suspect that it – *he* – has a soul?'

'You still have keen perception, I see.'

'You might have drained the thaumaturgy from my body, my lady, but you did not make me stupid. *Who* did the Toymaker used to be?'

Amilee's tawny eyes considered the host of hand-sized automatons dotted around the room. 'A former Thaumaturgist,' she said. '*This* is what became of Lord Buyaal.'

'Buyaal?' Hamir's features fell. 'The Genii from Mirage? The Genii who murdered Angel?'

'It was decided that his punishment would be to serve the Time-watcher's final prerogative,' Amilee explained. 'He would keep safe the very people he once tried to help Spiral destroy. He can be nothing other than this construct, and he cannot refuse the commands of a Thaumaturgist.'

'Who else knows the Toymaker is Buyaal?'

'Apart from you and me, the Timewatcher and the Thaumaturgists who created him, no one. He doesn't even know it himself. He has no comprehension that he used to be someone else, or any interest in that idea. The Toymaker can only follow orders and serve. All things considered, Hamir, I think it would be wise if we kept his true identity between us.'

'Fair enough,' Hamir replied, though he didn't know who Amilee expected him to tell seeing as only he, her, a miserable ghost and an unconscious changeling inhabited the tower. Van Bam was dead and the Skywatcher had remained tight-lipped about Samuel's fate. 'Then what of your avatar?' he asked. 'That annoying blue spectre has a spirit at its foundations, too. Who did it used to belong to?'

Amilee waved the question away. 'We have more important matters to discuss, Hamir.'

The necromancer looked at Clara, so deathly still and pale on the table. 'Indeed...'

Earlier, Amilee had explained Known Things to Hamir: a brilliant records device created from unused time. Although gaining access to it had cost Van Bam his life, Clara had survived a connection to it and somehow managed to retain a copy of its contents in her mind. She was now searching Known Things for a cure to the Genii plague.

Hamir wondered how the changeling was coping with Spiral's dark machinations in her mind, but he was more troubled by the cure she was searching for: the Nephilim. Hamir's greatest shame, his greatest crime, the one act that had haunted him for a thousand years – could it really come back to save them all? Were the Nephilim truly their last hope?

'My lady,' said Hamir. 'Why haven't you contacted Mother Earth? Surely if the Timewatcher knew that the Genii had returned and freed

Spiral, then She wouldn't hesitate to come back and deal with them. And I very much doubt She would place Spiral in prison a second time.'

'Do you think I didn't try to warn Her?' Amilee rubbed a hand over her bald head. She blinked once, slowly, as though desperate to sleep. 'The truth is, the Genii War damaged the Thaumaturgists more than anyone realised. They didn't return to Mother Earth merely because the Timewatcher had lost Her mercy. They did so to heal their wounds. The Thaumaturgists are weak, Hamir.'

'So they do what?' Hamir said. 'Consolidate their position? Protect themselves against the other Houses in the Higher Thaumaturgic Cluster – those who might take advantage of this weakness? It makes no difference, my lady. However powerful Spiral became, he could never match the Timewatcher's strength. Contact Her!'

'You don't understand,' Amilee replied sadly. 'She does not *want* to be contacted. I have but the dregs of my former thaumaturgy left to me and am no longer able to cast the simplest of spells. But even if it were otherwise, I still could not undo the Timewatcher's bidding. The skies are closed to me, Hamir. The Higher Thaumaturgic Cluster is lost to us.' Amilee scoffed. '*She* has blinded *me* to Mother Earth.'

Yansas Amilee, once among the Timewatcher's most favoured children, now cast aside by her Mother. So many centuries had passed since Hamir had last been a member of the Pantheon of Thaumaturgists that he struggled now to remember Mother Earth, or the sound of the Timewatcher's voice. Perhaps he had dulled the memories over the years, forced himself to forget all the terrible and dark things that had occurred before his punishment.

'And so the Nephilim really are our only hope,' he muttered. 'How ironic.' He gazed at the many parts of the Toymaker. 'Considering how they have been treated over the centuries, I cannot imagine the Nephilim will be very keen to help us.' He glanced at Clara. 'Assuming we can find them, of course.'

'We will find them because we have to,' Amilee said distantly. 'And they will help us because they will have no other choice.' Her eyes bored into the necromancer's. 'Hamir, you were right to say that Spiral was never as strong as the Timewatcher. But he knows a way to match Her power – surpass it, in fact. All he needs to do is steal the Timewatcher's magic.' She inhaled a shuddery breath. 'If only I was strong enough to claim a sliver of that power for myself. But it is bound to the Nightshade.'

Hamir leaned against the empty table opposite the Skywatcher. 'I'm not sure I follow you.'

'The Retrospective,' Amilee began. 'If Spiral merged his essence with it, fused his very soul to its foundations, he would claim mastery over it and its legions of wild demons. He could open the Retrospective's door on any Aelfirian realm. The Aelfir would have no defence, Hamir – their lands and people would be devoured, absorbed as raw material and added to a House of dead time. But Spiral's power is currently limited. Certain Houses would remain hidden and beyond his reach.'

'Houses in the Higher Thaumaturgic Cluster,' Hamir said. 'Like Mother Earth.'

'Indeed. However, should Spiral devour the First and Greatest Spell, the Retrospective will far exceed the already extraordinary limits of its initial design.'

'The First and Greatest Spell?' Hamir struggled to find words for a moment. 'Could the Retrospective absorb that kind of energy?'

'With Spiral's help, most definitely.' Amilee's ashen face became fearful. 'Imagine the size to which the Retrospective could grow with that magic, Hamir. How *powerful* Spiral would become. By hiding themselves away, the Timewatcher and the Thaumaturgists have ensured they will not see Spiral coming until he has brought destruction upon them. Nor will any other House in the Higher Thaumaturgic Cluster – after all, who else besides Mother Earth ever cared for the welfare of the creatures of lower magic? There is no one watching over the Houses of the Aelfir any more.

'Spiral would be free to devour one world of higher magic after another, growing stronger and stronger, moving on to realms and realities that even *we* might struggle to comprehend.'

The full weight of the implications hit Hamir. The Timewatcher had sacrificed a part of Her being when She cast the First and Greatest Spell to create the Great Labyrinth and Labrys Town. That magic had once stretched out to connect every Aelfirian House. It represented hope, peace, unity; it protected the denizens and saved the Aelfir from self-destruction. It was fundamentally the most powerful spell ever cast.

If Spiral really could harness the First and Greatest Spell, he would absorb a part of the Timewatcher Herself. If he could pervert Her power of creation and travel, fuse it to the corruption of dead time, then ...

'Ultimately, there would be nothing *but* the Retrospective,' Hamir realised. 'Spiral could consume ... *everything*.'

'And he will remake existence to his own design,' Amilee said darkly. 'He will become the Watcher of Dead Time, Hamir. Not the Nephilim, not even the Timewatcher Herself could stop him then.'

'Then surely we are already too late,' Hamir said, gesturing to Clara. 'Once the Genii discovered the location of Oldest Place, they would have freed Spiral immediately. And Spiral would not have delayed implementing his plans.'

'We *do* have time, Hamir,' Amilee said. 'To claim the First and Greatest Spell, the Retrospective needs to devour the Nightshade. And Spiral cannot allow that to happen until he has killed the denizens.' She reached out and took Clara's limp hand in hers. 'His hatred and spite will not allow a million humans to die quickly. But die they will, nonetheless, or his plan will fail.'

When she offered no further explanation, Hamir became suspicious.

It had once been accepted that the Skywatchers had always been deeper in the Timewatcher's counsel than any other Thaumaturgist. It had been common knowledge that Amilee, Spiral and Wolfe knew Her secrets; and the necromancer spied a secret hiding in Amilee's eyes now.

'My lady,' Hamir said evenly. 'I think we can agree that you no longer have any reason to protect the Timewatcher's confidence. So tell me, what is it that Spiral knows about the denizens – that *you* know – that I do not?'

Amilee let go of Clara's hand and rubbed the diamond tattoo on her forehead. She appeared reluctant to speak at first and Hamir thought he was going to be answered with evasion, but then she said, 'What I am about to tell you must remain between the two of us.'

Again, Hamir wondered who she expected him to tell. 'You have *my* confidence.'

Amilee paused, choosing her words carefully. 'The love and loyalty the denizens have for the Timewatcher is part of their conditioning. They have no choice but to retain their faith in Her.'

'Excuse me?'

'You heard right, Hamir.'

'The Timewatcher *conditioned* the humans?' He almost laughed. 'She who preached equality, unity, went to war with Spiral to preserve them – She *forced* them to love Her?'

'She did it to ensure peace,' Amilee said defensively. 'The humans were unpredictable, dangerous, but susceptible to subjugation. They never questioned their high position among the Houses, never sought to abuse it because they couldn't. They are conditioned to serve and protect the equilibrium. They made perfect custodians for the Labyrinth.'

'But not of their own volition,' Hamir countered. 'Tell me, how did She *condition* them?'

'The magic of the Labyrinth is the magic of the Timewatcher,' Amilee said. 'The First and Greatest Spell saturates each denizen of Labrys Town, leaves a splinter of itself in their souls. It … *encourages* devotion. They might curse the Timewatcher's name, but they could never turn against Her.'

'Ingenious,' Hamir said, stranded between feeling impressed and sickened. 'And they never knew it. Cruel, but ingenious.'

'But here's the relevance to Spiral's plan,' Amilee said testily. 'When a denizen dies, the splinter in their soul returns to the First and Greatest Spell.'

Again, Hamir read the implications, and they pushed aside the astounding discovery that every denizen had been unwittingly living a lie throughout Labrys Town's entire history.

'The First and Greatest Spell cannot be complete again until it has reclaimed its splinters,' he said. 'Ergo, Spiral will not devour the Nightshade and the Labyrinth until every denizen is dead.'

'Not just the denizens,' Amilee replied coolly. 'Because of *you*, the Nephilim also carry a splinter of that magic in their souls. After all, you did make them half-human.'

'Ah …' Hamir pushed down old and stormy memories that tried to rise. A thought came to him. 'If Spiral needs these *splinters*, then why did he imprison the Nephilim rather than destroying them?'

'Because he can't. Not yet.' Amilee walked to the head of Clara's table and stroked the changeling's cheek affectionately, gazing down onto her sleeping face. 'Our greatest advantage is that Spiral does not know my plans. But he *does* know that the Nephilim's fate is in your hands, Hamir.'

The necromancer blinked. 'Would you care to explain that?'

'Don't you ever wonder why the Timewatcher didn't execute you for your crimes?' Amilee faced him. Some of the Skywatcher's old anger had returned to her tawny eyes. 'Why did She place you in exile, shamed and drained of thaumaturgy, but alive?'

'You think I wasn't justly punished?'

'You never knew what your punishment was, you fool! The Timewatcher cursed you, Hamir, and lucky for us all that She did. She bound the Nephilim to your life. They will only die when you die.'

Hamir raised an eyebrow. 'Excuse me?'

'Your creations, your *abominations*, were sentenced to live shunned and reviled for as long as their Progenitor lived. The Nephilim bear the curse of *your* crimes, Simowyn Hamir, never to be true masters of their own fate.'

Hamir didn't often consider himself dumbfounded, but he found himself so now.

Amilee continued, 'But the curse can be broken. To free the Nephilim and bring them to our side, we have to reunite you with the thaumaturgy that was drained from you.'

In the stunned silence that followed this declaration, the hundred automatons of the Toymaker skittered. Hamir felt the prickle of a ghostly presence enter the room. Alexander materialised by the door, head bowed and hands clasped before him.

'Forgive the interruption, my lady,' he said. 'I thought you should know that your guests have arrived.'

'Excellent,' said Amilee.

Hamir started. 'Guests?'

'Come,' Amilee said, walking from the room with invigorated purpose. 'It's high time you took responsibility for your demons, *Lord* Hamir.'

'You dare to merge your memories with mine,' the skinless man said. Blood dripped from raw hands clenched into fists and slapped against the leathery ground. 'You come to this place seeking knowledge, yet your minds would be crushed by the *truth*!'

It's Spiral, Marney said in Clara's mind.

It can't be, not really, Clara replied, fear sinking to her bones. *Everything is memory and information. I mean, he can't do anything to us. Can he?*

I don't know.

Spiral laughed bitterly at the magickers, his wet countenance stretching sinew and tendons, revealing bloodied teeth.

'Look at you,' he said disgustedly. '*Humans.*'

Behind Spiral, a door had been set into the flesh of the courtyard wall. A simple, innocuous wooden door branded with a peculiar House symbol. The dark charred mark depicted a swirl connected by a straight line to a square with mirrored triangles. Clara knew the symbol, as did Marney. The Sorrow of Future Reason, a myth, a legend that belonged to giant blood-magickers.

'Shall I tell you why the Timewatcher gave you the Great Labyrinth?' Spiral continued. 'Because you were *weak* and *broken*. She sowed poison seeds in you and ensured that you never abused the power *She* imbued into your House.'

Marney groaned and stumbled. Clara caught her arm, helping her to stay upright.

The unnerving blue light was radiating from Marney's eyes and mouth again. This time, the luminosity also leaked from her nose and nostrils as a host of wispy spheres like glowing dandelion heads. They dragged the light clear of the empath, moving away fast as though caught by high winds.

The skinless Lord of the Genii watched angrily as the tiny spheres travelled over him like a swarm of bees to be drawn into the wooden door. The symbol for the Sorrow of Future Reason glowed blue for a brief moment. The telltale *click* of a lock opening followed.

'What is this?' Spiral growled. 'More trickery?'

'I ... I remember,' Marney hissed to Clara.

Undoubtedly, behind that door was the answer to finding the Nephilim herd, to finding Van Bam's ghost. But when Clara recalled how the Timewatcher's voice had affected her, how real it had felt, she understood that this grotesque personification of Spiral could be as real as he wanted to be; and there was no way he would allow her and Marney to pass.

'You think you know your place in the Timewatcher's heart?' Spiral raged. 'You do not understand what She has done with the First and Greatest Spell!' He spat blood as he shouted. 'But I will take it from you. I will take it from you all!'

Get ready to run, Marney told Clara. Steady on her feet now, the empath held a throwing dagger in each hand. Clara wished Samuel were here with his guns.

'Do you truly believe that we are equals?' Every word Spiral uttered was laced with insanity. '*You* are the Timewatcher's curse. *You* are the cancer that ruined *my* people.'

Spiral's exposed muscles bunched. Clara didn't need her heightened senses to guess his intent.

'There is no place for you on Mother Earth. The Timewatcher is a *liar*!'

Spiral attacked, and Marney's hands flashed out. The daggers struck home: one stabbed into Spiral's chest; the other took his eye. Gouts of violet blood burst from the wounds and Spiral screamed more in anger than pain. Marney didn't let up her assault; she half-emptied her baldric, throwing dagger after dagger at the abomination, each one sinking into raw muscle.

Clara tried to reach the door but skidded to a halt as Spiral expanded his size and blocked the way. He became taller, wider; black hair, matted with blood, began to sprout all over his torso and limbs, pushing the daggers from his flesh. His scream morphed into a protracted howl.

'Shit!' Clara cried. 'My magic ...'

Above, lightning flashed, clouds churned and rain began to fall in fat, heavy drops. Spiral's howls became vicious barks of thunder as his face snapped forward into the muzzle of a wolf. He stood upright, fingers splayed and tipped with long talons; wicked teeth flashed, snapping at the air. Marney threw two more daggers at him but the blades bounced off the thick pelt and fell useless to the ground. Spiral came for the humans he despised so much.

'Stand aside,' said a new voice.

Clara and Marney moved to the side wall. Spiral stopped his advance. Rain washed blood from his pelt in red rivers. He cocked his head to one side, considering the Skywatcher walking into the courtyard.

'Ah, my dear Baran Wolfe,' Spiral said, growling with the thunder of Clara's magic. 'The *least* of us, the *compassion* of the Timewatcher.'

'Too long have you kept me trapped inside Known Things.' Wolfe's voice carried menace; his eyes a distinct lack of mercy. 'I no longer speak the truths only *you* wished me to speak. And I shall tell you a truth now, Iblisha Spiral, Lord of the Genii ... our time here is over.'

Spiral's laugh sounded more like barking. 'I preferred you when you were on your knees, begging me for mercy.'

'Then make me beg.' Wolfe's hands glowed with higher magic. 'The Last Storm is yet to end, Iblisha.'

Silver wings sprang from Wolfe's back and he leapt into the air. Spiral vaulted and met the attack. As they crashed together, Wolfe released the thaumaturgy he had summoned and the Skywatchers exploded into a cloud of burning purple.

'Run!' Marney shouted.

Clara followed the empath across the courtyard, sprinting beneath the blistering cloud of higher magic, while the symbol for the Sorrow of Future Reason blazed and smoked. The door opened of its own volition as the magickers approached and they sprinted through, sparing not one backward glance. Clara yelled, expecting pain, expecting the disorientation of a portal, anything but what she actually found.

A room in a library.

The door slammed shut behind them, silencing the Skywatchers' battle.

Long and narrow, the room stretched away into a distance further than the eye could see. Shelving filled with innumerable books covered the left and right walls, disappearing into the gloom high above. At the centre of the room, countless reading tables had been pushed back to back, and between them stood lamp posts topped with spheres of welcoming blue light. And they, like the room, appeared to stretch into for ever.

Breathing hard, Clara gave Marney a questioning look. 'I bet there's a really interesting explanation for this.'

Marney smiled wryly as she looked around at the infinite books on display. 'Clara, you asked me how I learned so much about Known Things and Spiral, and everything else that's been happening. The truth is, the knowledge was given to me in exactly the same way that I gave it to you.'

Clara touched her lips. 'With a kiss—'

The magickers wheeled around as the door shook in its frame. A distant howl of bestial thunder filtered into the library room. The sound subsided, the door stopped shaking, and thankfully Clara's magic didn't break through. She reasoned that the last memory of Baran Wolfe the Wanderer was now dead.

'This is the Library of Glass and Mirrors,' Marney said.

The name meant nothing to Clara.

'It's a long and old story,' Marney continued. 'I never knew everything, Clara – well, that's not strictly true, but it's complicated.' She became wistful, as though having to order her thoughts through a surge of old memories. Marney chuckled, perhaps at herself, perhaps at the absurdity of the situation. 'There's someone inside Known Things other than you and me, Van Bam, Spiral and Wolfe. And it's someone *I* brought with me.'

One of the spheres of blue light floated away from its position atop a lamp post. It drifted down towards the floor, expanding with an array of gently waving tendrils the colour of the midday sky over Labrys Town. It grew bigger, its centre darkening and forming the shape of a person. Eyes like patches of starless night leaked smoky tears.

'The avatar,' Clara said in surprise.

'That's not what I call him,' Marney said. She looked close to tears as she approached the blue spectre. 'I bet he's never given you a straight answer, has he, Clara? I bet he's only ever given you enough to lead you onwards, and then expects you to come to your own conclusions. It's an annoying trait he's always had.'

'Oh, I seem to remember that you knew how to mystify me on occasion,' the avatar replied. There was affection in its voice. 'It's good to see you again, Marney.'

Marney's voice cracked. 'Hello, Denton.'

CHAPTER TWELVE

THE GHOST OF BLUE LIGHT

Samuel had found that cold place inside him where his thoughts and instincts were as deadly as the rifle in his hands. He focused on nothing – not Marney's condition, not the revelations that just kept getting stranger and stranger – nothing but the present moment.

The portal in the protected chamber of the Nightshade where the First and Greatest Spell was hidden had injected the group into the Nothing of Far and Deep. Samuel, guided by his prescient awareness, had led the companions along a tunnel with wispy white walls, beyond which blue and red lightning crackled through thick, churning primordial mists. No one had spoken, no one had speculated as to which House they were headed towards.

His magic had not been required, however, as the pathway led to a surprising destination.

A circular cave. Its smooth wall, floor and ceiling carved from a dull grey substance, not quite rock, not quite metal.

'Interesting sort of place,' Bellow said. The Nephilim's blue eyes shone in the gloom. He looked invigorated.

As the rest of the group shared worried looks, the wooden door through which they'd entered the cave slammed shut on the Nothing of Far and Deep. Glogelder tried and failed to open it again.

'Locked,' he announced gruffly.

'There is magic in the door,' Bellow said. 'I don't think we're supposed to leave that way.'

'Brilliant,' Glogelder said sourly. 'Another one-way trip.'

Hillem looked up at the domed ceiling, the unconscious Marney still in his arms, curiosity on his face. 'What is this place?'

'Samuel?' said Namji.

The old bounty hunter stood apart from the group, staring through an opening on the opposite side of the cave, recognition rising within him. 'Follow me,' he said.

He led the way out to the base of a mountain just as unnaturally smooth in its formation and made from the same grey metal-rock. A path led from the cave mouth down to a bridge, spanning a yawning chasm that sank into depths of utter darkness. At the end of the bridge, before a great cliff wall that enclosed the area in a mighty semicircle, a grand tower rose, black as night and capped by a dome of tarnished silver.

'The Tower of the Skywatcher,' Samuel said flatly. 'This is Lady Amilee's House.'

'Are you sure?' said Namji, standing alongside him.

'I couldn't be mistaken. But …' The environment looked dreary and lifeless, diluting Samuel's sense of nostalgia. 'Something bad must've happen here. This place used to be … majestic.'

'Majestic or not,' Bellow growled, 'I will be glad for an audience with her ladyship. There are one or two things I would like to say to her.'

The giant set off across the bridge. Samuel and Namji made to follow him but Glogelder stopped them.

'Wait.' With a troubled expression, the big Aelf gestured to the tower. 'There's a real Thaumaturgist in there?'

'Maybe,' Hillem said happily.

'It's really not as impressive as it sounds,' Samuel said. He holstered the ice-rifle and took Marney from Hillem. She was light and pale, still wrapped in his coat. Perhaps Amilee would know a way to wake her up. 'Let's go.'

As the group headed over the bridge, sickly clouds drifted across the sky like dirty smoke. Samuel remembered how those clouds used to sparkle with a host of colours, and how the sky had been filled with the countless stars of other Houses. He recalled the emerald falls that cascaded from the clifftop down into the chasm beneath the bridge, filling the air with a fine rejuvenating mist. And lastly, Samuel remembered how the dome of the Tower of the Skywatcher had glared with silver light, like a star of its own. What had happened to this place?

When they caught up with Bellow, the giant had stopped to study a construct standing guard at the end of the bridge.

'It's an automaton sentry,' Samuel said warily, though he detected no danger.

Namji shivered. 'I remember these things.'

'Ah, I have heard of automatons,' Bellow said. 'They were created by the Thaumaturgists – as servants, yes?'

'And soldiers, bodyguards – whatever they needed them to be,' Samuel answered. 'This one is part of Amilee's private army.'

Hillem said, 'I read somewhere that they're near impossible to beat in a fight.'

'Not this one.' Bellow rapped his knuckles upon the automaton's featureless faceplate. It didn't move. Its pistons didn't pump; its cogs didn't spin. Although the automaton was eight feet tall, it still looked puny beside the Nephilim. 'This poor fellow has no power.'

'Good,' Glogelder mumbled.

The group continued on across a gigantic disc of metal-rock that sprouted from the end of the bridge. The tower rose from the centre of the disc, its huge doors already open. Samuel led the way inside.

Two glass elevator chutes rose from the centre of the vast entry hall and disappeared into the ceiling, and pale luminescence shone down from above. The light barely lifted the gloom at the edges of the hall, but did so enough to illuminate the rest of Amilee's automaton army. Standing dysfunctional in evenly spaced alcoves, there were at least fifty of them.

The tower doors boomed shut.

'Here comes our reception party,' Bellow said.

One of the elevators was active. It descended and a glass door slid open. Two people joined the group in the hall.

Samuel's breath caught. 'Hamir,' he whispered.

But the necromancer – not dead as Samuel had supposed after all – didn't reply or make eye contact, and almost hid behind the second person.

Lady Amilee approached the group. She was stooped, her gait slow and unsteady. She looked as tired and old as her House, nothing like the magnificent Skywatcher Samuel had last met.

The Aelfir remained close to the doors as Samuel stepped forward with Marney in his arms. Gulduur Bellow, for all his talk earlier, had no interest in addressing Amilee. He approached Hamir with a curious look on his large face. Hamir practically shied from the Nephilim, as though embarrassed to be seen. He stared at his feet as Bellow towered over him.

'I am relieved that you have made it this far, my friends,' Amilee said, her voice dry, dusty. 'But we have much work to do. Samuel, please – you must take Marney to Clara.'

'What?' Samuel almost dropped the empath in his arms. 'Clara's here?'

Amilee didn't reply. Samuel frowned at the sadness in her eyes as she stared at Marney. He looked around at his Aelfirian companions, at the Nephilim staring down at the necromancer, and finally back at the Skywatcher.

'Where's Van Bam?'

'Where's Van Bam?' Clara said.

'You'll find him soon enough.'

'What's going on?'

The avatar transformed. Its light began to dim and shrink, forming into the shape of an elderly gentleman, still tall and burly even though he had to be pushing eighty, dressed in a creased and tatty three-piece suit. A threadbare waistcoat strained its buttons struggling to cover his generous paunch. The rumpled wide-brimmed hat sitting on his head had seen better days. The expression on his ruddy face was kind and welcoming, but the glint in his old eyes held mischief.

'It's good to see you *both* again,' he said.

Marney embraced the old man, squeezing him tightly. Tears sprang from her eyes. She looked like a child clinging to her father.

Denton, Clara thought. She had heard that name before. Samuel and Van Bam had mentioned him, and always fondly. An old agent of the Relic Guild, an empath like Marney. But Denton hadn't survived Fabian Moor's first incursion into Labrys Town during the Genii War.

As Denton held Marney, his eyes found Clara's. 'You have travelled your path bravely and wisely, and all for the greater good.'

'I sort of didn't have a choice,' Clara replied evenly. 'So, all this time, *you* were behind the avatar?'

'All a part of Lady Amilee's plan.' Denton stroked Marney's hair fondly. 'My ghost has been serving the Skywatcher for many years. And quite willingly.'

'They've been waiting for us, Clara.' Marney looked up at him. 'This all started back during the Genii War, when Denton and I went to the Library of Glass and Mirrors. I couldn't remember until now.'

'And with good reason,' he said. 'Amilee has worked hard to hide her plans from the skies, from Spiral's vision.'

The way the two empaths stared at each other with such affectionate recognition, sharing years of experiences, made Clara realise that for all she had been through, it would be a long time before she was embedded in the Relic Guild's history. But she was tired; she was bruised and beaten; she had watched Van Bam die, heard the voice of the Time-watcher, been hunted by her own magic, and enough was enough.

'You know,' she said with strained patience, 'Samuel told me once that empaths take a long time to get to the point. I don't suppose you'd like to prove him wrong, would you?'

Denton chuckled. 'Samuel might not be the best role model you could choose, Clara, but I take your meaning. You are long overdue an explanation.'

Gently, Denton coaxed Marney away from him so they could both address the changeling. 'Before the war even began, Spiral had divined many of the Timewatcher's future actions. He knew that She would abandon the Labyrinth and the Houses of the Aelfir. He foresaw the coming of the Retrospective. Most importantly, he divined the creation of Oldest Place, but he could not foresee exactly *where* the Timewatcher would hide his prison.'

'But what he *did* discover,' Marney added, 'was that a record of certain things he couldn't see would be held at the Library of Glass and Mirrors.'

'And I guess this is where you two come in,' Clara said, urging the story along.

'Fabian Moor knew that his lord and master had planned for both winning and losing the war,' Denton said. 'Though we didn't realise it until late in the game, Moor had been biding his time, waiting for the Relic Guild agent who would go to the Library of Glass and Mirrors and return with the location of Oldest Place.' Denton grinned. '*Me.*'

'But he didn't get what he wanted from you,' Clara pointed out.

'No, because Denton gave it to me,' said Marney. 'I didn't know it at the time, and I only started remembering on the night Fabian Moor returned.'

'And then you gave it to me,' Clara said drily. 'But does anything you did matter any more? The Genii know the location of Oldest Place and Spiral is probably free by now. Why didn't anyone stop his plans back then?'

'Divining the infinite variables of the future, even for a Skywatcher, is more complicated than we could ever understand. So much is hindered by luck, chance, opportunity.' Denton removed his hat and began twisting it in his hands. 'Spiral's arrogance was his downfall. He was so certain that Known Things was a perfect creation, that *no one* would be able to glean his secrets. Sadly for him but lucky for us, Known Things wasn't as watertight as he believed.'

'The Library held a record of Known Things,' Marney said, as though she was constantly surprised by memories she was suddenly recalling. 'Unbeknown to Spiral, he had revealed more about *his* future plans than he'd intended to. And what Denton discovered was that Spiral never expected to win the war.'

'There was nothing much to go on,' Denton added. 'Scraps and fragments of Known Things' contents, more like *ideas* – and certainly not enough for Lady Amilee to convince the Timewatcher that Spiral had planned for losing the war, had perhaps always *meant* to lose it. But coupled with the information stored inside a message sphere sent by Baran Wolfe shortly before his death, Amilee slowly pieced together a vision of Spiral's future. She divined that at some indeterminate point the Lord of the Genii would return. But by the time Amilee knew this for certain, the next stage of Spiral's plan had already been set in motion. The Timewatcher and the Thaumaturgists had disappeared from all of our lives and there was no one left to stand in his way.'

'Except Amilee,' Clara said.

'She stayed because she had to,' Denton said. 'She put her countermeasures into action because she knew that Spiral *had* to return. Only when freed from Oldest Place could he be destroyed.'

Clara nodded. 'But not by us.'

'Without the Timewatcher, without the Thaumaturgists, Amilee waited for the Genii to make their move. And then she made hers, using what remained of the Relic Guild as unknowing participants in her scheme.'

'And as it turns out,' Marney said, 'nearly everything the Relic Guild did during the Genii War served to gather the information and time that Amilee needed to form her plan. Now it's up to us to do the rest.'

'All right,' said Clara. 'I understand, but ... please tell me this leads to the Nephilim.'

'Ah, yes, our lost saviours,' Denton said. 'I learned at the Library of Glass and Mirrors that the whereabouts of the Nephilim was stored inside Spiral's not-so-perfect records device, but that we would have to get inside it to find them.' He gave a flourish of his hand, encompassing the room. 'And the information is stored right here, in the last dregs of Known Things, wrapped in my memory, which I planted in Marney's mind, and she in turn hid in yours, Clara.'

His good cheer evaporated as the door rattled, followed by the bestial cry of Clara's magic.

'I regret that I never got the chance to say goodbye,' Denton said quickly to Marney. 'After I planted the information in your mind, I told Amilee what I'd learned and she doctored my memory. We needed to prevent Fabian Moor from finding out just how much I'd discovered at the Library of Glass and Mirrors. We needed to force his hand.'

'We really did try to kill him on that night, you know,' Marney said. 'He almost got me.'

'It might be difficult to stomach, Marney, but Moor's survival – and yours – ensured Spiral's vulnerability. Amilee needed to keep the location of Oldest Place secret until such a time as she could understand and exploit Spiral's weak spot – the Nephilim – and she ... *we* had simply run out of options.'

'I know.'

'I have always been so damn proud of you.'

Marney sank into his embrace and fresh tears filled her eyes. Clara watched, wondering if she was witnessing a moment that had been waiting to happen for forty years.

'You have to leave, don't you?' Marney said.

'My part in this little game is over.' Denton put his hat on and winked at Clara. 'Adventures into the unknown are waiting for me.'

Clara smiled sadly.

'Take me with you,' Marney said – pleaded. 'There's nothing left for me now, I could—'

'No, no, no – your part in this hasn't ended yet, Marney.' The door rattled again and Denton's face became grave. 'Though I don't envy you the path you're about to walk. Goodbye, my dear, *dear* friend.'

Marney held him tightly, as though she never wanted to let go.

Denton looked at Clara, a strange glint in his eye. 'I can lead you to the secrets of the Nephilim but I can't prepare you for what happens next. Good luck, Clara.'

Even as Marney wept in Denton's arms, the old empath broke apart into thousands of tiny blue lights. Drifting like dandelion heads, they swarmed together, flying up to re-form into a glowing sphere atop its lamp post.

Clara gasped. To her astonishment, Marney now stood in someone else's embrace.

'Van Bam!'

It was definitely the illusionist, though much younger than the man Clara knew, somewhere in his mid-twenties. He was dressed in his usual dark trousers and shirt that appeared to be made from the night sky. His head was as smoothly shaved as always, but there were no metal plates covering his brown eyes as he gazed lovingly at Marney. He pulled the empath into a passionate kiss.

Clara couldn't take her eyes off them. A feeling rose inside her – perhaps from magic emoted by Marney – and it told Clara all she needed to know. Marney and Van Bam had been lovers, and not even their decades of separation had dulled their feelings. Seeing them now clinched in a kiss somehow made sense to Clara. They looked right – as though they were supposed to be together.

'Thank you for finding me, Clara,' Van Bam said as he and Marney broke their kiss.

'No problem.' Clara smiled lopsidedly. 'Figured you'd do the same for me.'

'I am impressed by how easily you have adapted to our symbiosis. It was not so easy for me and Gideon.'

'Well ...' Clara blinked. 'What?'

Van Bam stared at her for a moment, scrutinising her, before returning his gaze to Marney. 'You have not told her, have you?'

Marney placed her hand upon his cheek. 'I thought it would be better coming from you.'

'Told me what?' Clara asked.

With his eyes still on Marney, Van Bam said, 'The Nightshade has been watching you.'

Clara's frown was deep. 'What's going on? Where're the Nephilim?'

'Clara,' said Van Bam, his voice deep and comforting, 'the Nightshade is a sentient building. For generations, its magic has selected who among us will govern the denizens. And from the moment you stepped within its walls, the Nightshade recognised you.'

Van Bam and Marney looked unconcerned as the door rattled with a howl of rage. They only had eyes for each other.

'What are you talking about?' Clara demanded.

'Don't you see?' Marney said. 'That's why you could hear Gideon's voice. That's why Van Bam is in your mind now. He's your spirit guide.'

'The Nightshade chose you, Clara,' Van Bam said. '*You* are the Resident of Labrys Town.'

Clara almost laughed at the absurdity of the statement, but her rogue magic hit the door with such force it split wood. To the sound of vicious snarling and gouging talons, the door groaned and bowed inwards.

Van Bam kissed Marney again, quickly, desperately, before turning to Clara. 'Here,' he held out a fist. 'The final shard of Known Things.' He opened his fingers to reveal the star of green light shining on his palm. 'Take it. It will tell you everything you need to know about the Nephilim.'

Clara stared at it and licked her lips uncertainly.

'Take the bloody thing!' Marney shouted as the door buckled and began to fall apart.

Confused, daunted, but compelled by the deafening howl that filled the library, Clara clasped Van Bam's hand. As the door exploded into a million splinters, the changeling tumbled into an abyss filled with green light and the whispers of blood-magic.

Samuel carried Marney to a whitewashed room high in the Tower of the Skywatcher. Clara was there, lying unconscious on a padded table. And she wasn't alone. Samuel placed Marney down on a table matching Clara's, then stared around at the next surprise in this apparently endless game of secrets.

Clinging to the walls and ceiling, the one hundred pieces of the Toymaker watched over Clara. The assassin who had been tracking the group since their escape from the Labyrinth was no longer a foe, but rather Amilee's servant and the Relic Guild's ally. Samuel was dubious, but his magic detected no danger from the hand-sized automatons. The only member of the group who showed no fear of the silver insectoids was Bellow, who studied them with fascination.

'Gulduur,' Amilee said, prompting him towards the changeling and the empath. 'If you would …'

Marney was not as lost as people had supposed. She had transferred a copy of her mind into Clara's; *that* was what Marney had done with a kiss on the night Fabian Moor returned. Now she and Clara were searching the contents of Known Things, which the changeling had somehow gained access to. Samuel didn't really understand and he didn't care to; he only understood that his fellow magickers were searching for the salvation of everyone.

Leaving Bellow to work his unique brand of thaumaturgic blood-magic in an attempt to reunite Marney with her mind, Amilee led Samuel, Namji, Hillem and Glogelder to the small reception hall outside the room. And there they discussed the revelations that Amilee had been sharing with them on the way to this floor of the tower.

'The Nephilim?' Namji said. '*They* are the secret weapon that will destroy Spiral?'

'Only the Timewatcher truly understood how strong the Nephilim are,' Amilee said. 'I sometimes wonder if they frighten even Her.' She looked back at the closed door to the room where Marney and Clara lay. 'Now all we have to do is find them.'

Considering that he had just met his creator, Bellow had remained remarkably calm and compliant. Hamir had taken his leave from the group a while earlier, and Samuel couldn't blame him. The truth of Hamir's origins was finally out after all these years, but Samuel didn't really care.

He didn't care that the elderly necromancer was a disgraced Thaumaturgist, stripped of rank and power for murdering a hundred humans, and who had become the legend the Nephilim called the Progenitor. He didn't care that the group had reached the sanctuary of Amilee's tower and the Skywatcher was finally providing some answers. That the Nephilim herd, nearly a thousand creatures of higher magic, were just waiting to save all of the Houses in existence meant nothing to Samuel. Not at that moment. Because Van Bam was dead. And the pain of it stabbed into Samuel's soul.

'What about you, my lady?' Hillem said respectfully. 'Surely having a Skywatcher on our side still counts for something in this fight?'

Amilee smiled wanly. 'You're not exactly catching me at my best. Beyond what I have already done, I am now largely powerless.'

Much to Samuel's chagrin, the rest of the group seemed keen to bypass Van Bam's death and focus on the task ahead. Hillem stood alongside Namji, both of them unfazed by meeting a Thaumaturgist for the first time. Or maybe it was because the Skywatcher looked so frail and old and unimposing in her purple robes that they spoke to her so directly. Glogelder, who had apparently given up on being daunted by anything, helped himself to the nutrition cakes and water set out for them on a glass table.

Samuel sat next to the big Aelf on one of the cushioned sofas that formed a semicircle in the reception hall. He recalled visiting Amilee's House in his younger days, and how the tower's rooms had appeared magical, providing whatever a person needed at any given moment – a little like the rooms in the Nightshade. He also recalled Amilee's miserable Aelfirian aide, Alexander, who now haunted the tower as a ghost.

'Beg your pardon, my lady,' Glogelder said through a mouthful of food. 'What exactly have you done – besides leading us on a merry chase, that is?'

Amilee considered Glogelder, perhaps trying to decide if his manner was disrespectful or just as gruff as his appearance suggested.

'I did the only thing I could,' the Skywatcher said stiffly. 'At the end of the war, I remained in my tower while the rest of my kind fled back to Mother Earth. I created a mindscape – a garden – a personal slipstream much like Spiral's Known Things. And there I made plots and plans of my own, and hid them from divination.'

'And then you sent your avatar with instructions for us,' said Namji. 'Which weren't always particularly clear, my lady.'

Amilee clasped her hands before her. 'I was never as strong as Spiral – none of us were. And I think we can agree that he proved just how powerful a Skywatcher he became.' She looked at Samuel but he averted his gaze. 'I had to conduct my plans in a clandestine fashion otherwise Spiral would have divined my counteractions from the skies and stars.

'Forty years I hid in my garden, watching, listening, planning, waiting for a time when the Genii returned and the Relic Guild were needed again. I spent too long in my own personal slipstream and it sapped the last of my thaumaturgy. What little remains of my magic is bound to my tower. If I leave, I will die.'

'Is there nothing you can do?' Namji asked.

A distant look came to Amilee's eyes. 'My magic will rekindle itself in time, but that will be too much time to be of help to you.' She fell into a moment's reverie before snapping out of it. 'But everything I have done has led us to this moment, and I will help you to exploit the heart of Spiral's weakness. He does not know that *we* hold the key to the Nephilim's prison.'

'Could they really do it, though?' Hillem said as he poured himself a glass of water. 'I mean, if Spiral has control of the Retrospective, can *anyone* beat him now?'

'Have no doubt that until he claims the First and Greatest Spell, the Lord of the Genii is not impervious to death,' Amilee replied sternly. 'Time is a factor, but Spiral believes he has more time than he does. We have the secrets of Known Things.' Her tawny eyes bored into Samuel's, and this time he did not avert his pale blue glare. 'And yes, it cost us dear to get them.'

The Aelfir tensed, looking at Samuel to gauge his reaction. With fatigue in his ageing body, hollowness in his soul, the old bounty hunter turned his gaze to the floor. He felt Glogelder lean away from him as Amilee approached. Gently, she reached under Samuel's chin and lifted his face to meet hers. He saw some of the splendour, some of the beauty of the Skywatcher he had known in his youth. The black diamond tattoo of the Thaumaturgists on her forehead seemed to blaze from her pale skin like a symbol of hope.

'You were just a boy when I first met you,' Amilee said, a small smile on her lips. 'A wild little thing, you were, full of wonder and such *spirit*! How is it that you grew into such an angry and embittered man, Samuel?'

'It happened easily enough,' Samuel replied, though not unkindly. 'The Timewatcher took *everything* from us.'

'The Timewatcher was wrong to abandon you. She and the Thaumaturgists should have stayed, and we should have grown strong again together.' She narrowed her eyes. 'But answer me this – would you hesitate to make the same sacrifice as Van Bam if you knew it could save every person you once promised me you would protect?'

Samuel clenched his teeth, battling his anguish. 'You know the answer to that.'

'I do, and I know it well, *agent* of the Relic Guild.'

Samuel stared at Amilee and, much to his own surprise, found himself saying, 'It's so hard to believe in my duties sometimes. Spiral and the Genii aren't the only ones who want to harm the denizens. Whether we stop Spiral or not, the Aelfir are planning to cut the Labyrinth off, let its people die.' He felt hopelessness rising. 'It makes me wonder what the point of all this is. There's only one man trying to stop the Aelfir – Councillor Tal – and he—'

'Samuel,' Amilee said gently. 'The fate of Labrys Town and the Houses of the Aelfir is in your hands. Free the Nephilim and perhaps the future will not appear so bleak.'

'I think I agree with you,' said Gulduur Bellow, stooping to pass through the doorway into the hall and join the rest of the group.

'How's Marney?' Samuel asked quickly. 'How's Clara?'

'I have done all I can,' Bellow said. 'Which is to say, I believe I have been successful. Clara and Marney will wake imminently, I think, and they should be themselves.'

The weight of relief almost crushed Samuel.

The blue orbs of Bellow's eyes stared at Amilee. 'Where is the necromancer?'

'Hiding, if he knows what's good for him,' Glogelder said.

A look from Hillem stopped him saying more.

'Hamir is an ally,' Amilee stressed. 'And we cannot do this without him.'

'I do not want to harm him, if that is what you think.' There was a flat, stoic edge to Bellow's usually genial voice. 'Surely after all I have been through, you would not begrudge me a conversation with the Progenitor.'

There was a distinct challenge in the words that only served to emphasise how weak Amilee appeared and how large and strong the Nephilim was.

'No,' said Amilee. 'I think you're owed that, at least. But you need to understand – *all* of you – that Simowyn Hamir is the only one who can free the Nephilim, and you, Gulduur, are the key that opens their prison—'

Before Amilee could say more, a long, piercing howl came from the room behind Bellow. The giant ducked back in, closely followed by Samuel. The others came soon after.

Clara was awake and in wolf form. She stood on the table, sleek and muscular beneath her silver-grey pelt, and her size shocked Samuel. He had forgotten how big she was.

'Clara, calm down,' he said softly.

The wolf bared her teeth and growled at the hundred automatons clinging to the walls and ceiling around her.

Samuel's prescient awareness stirred. 'You're safe,' he promised her. 'It's all right.'

The light of magic illuminated the wolf's pelt for a moment, and then she shrank and morphed sinuously into a young woman wearing dark grey clothes and a hood.

On her knees, breathing heavily, Clara looked straight at Samuel. 'I know where the Nephilim are,' she said, then, '*Shit!*' She clutched her head and fell back on the table, writhing in pain.

Namji rushed to her, opening her satchel to administer some healing spell. Bellow approached Marney when the empath groaned, curling into the foetal position as she began to sob.

Glogelder shouted a curse and Samuel wheeled around. The ghost of Alexander had appeared beside the big Aelf.

'There is a problem, my lady,' he told Amilee, his spiritual face pained. 'Your House is under attack.'

— CHAPTER THIRTEEN —

SISTERHOOD

Uproar. A hammer banging a gavel. A demand for order.

Councillor Tal closed his eyes and fought for inner calm.

After the Timewatcher and Her Thaumaturgists abandoned the Houses, there had been genuine concern among the Aelfir that they would return to the Old Ways: a time when realm fought realm in perpetual wars that raged for so many generations no one could remember why they had started. To prevent this, the Aelfir came together and maintained a peaceful equilibrium by creating the Panopticon of Houses.

'*Order!*'

Based in the Sisterhood of Bells, the Panopticon became the governing infrastructure where all Houses had a voice. But as with any establishment purporting to be a democratic union, an imbalance arose over the years: a state of inequality revealing that some Houses were more important than others. Rumours surfaced of a secret band of hierarchs who controlled the Panopticon from deep within its heart. Powerful, hidden, these hierarchs were known as the Sisterhood. And the Sisterhood spared no love for the place where humans dwelt.

'There will be order in the House!'

Power; the kind that steered people's lives, controlled their beliefs, manipulated governments to their own ends – *that* was what the Sisterhood craved. It had a pernicious agenda to stamp out the Aelfir's lingering faith in the Timewatcher, their fear of Her, and to finally burn Her fading stigma to ashes. The Sisterhood's first strike towards achieving their goal was to openly disobey the Timewatcher's final prerogative with impunity: to disregard the edict commanding the Aelfir to ensure that the denizens of Labrys Town received everything they needed to survive. And the only person standing in the Sisterhood's way was the disgraced politician and veteran of the Genii War, Councillor Tal.

'The House will remember the reason for this session!'

In the mighty clock tower of Little Sibling, the parliament building for the Panopticon of Houses, Tal stood on a podium at the centre of the huge auditorium of the Commons Hall, surrounded by hundreds of Aelfirian leaders sitting in stepped rows of bench seats. It looked as though a representative of every major House was in attendance, just as the Sisterhood had planned. From the podium, Tal faced the raised bench where the three Speakers of Justice sat.

Speakers Cam and Tillane sat on either of Speaker Olivior, not one of them old enough to remember the Genii War. Olivior banged her gavel and continued to call for order, but the Panopticon remained in uproar.

Tal had already been forced to listen while the Speakers read out the long list of charges brought against him. Nothing more than a formality. The Sisterhood had already bent half the Houses to its way of thinking and was using fear and misdirection to manipulate the rest. The reason for this session was to sway dissenting opinions and engineer a vote that would lead the Panopticon to authorise the destruction of the last remaining portal to the Labyrinth. That decision would ensure the deaths of one million humans and kill once and for all any lingering reason to have faith in the Timewatcher.

It was up to Tal to turn the Panopticon against this foolhardy course of action, to convince hundreds of rulers and ambassadors – many of whom already saw a guilty Aelf on the stand – that the Genii had returned.

But the focus of this session had taken a strange deviation and disquiet ruled the Commons Hall.

'*Order!*'

Earlier, Speaker Olivior had said to Tal, '*You* were in charge of the Aelfheim Archipelago when the humans appeared from the portal in Sunflower.'

To which Cam added, 'And not only did you allow them through the portal, but also to escape your custody.'

'Thus causing the deaths of many Aelfir,' Tillane pointed out.

With voices magically amplified to reach every ear, they were speaking lines Tal knew had been pre-scripted for them. The Sisterhood had long ago decided that Tal would be the scapegoat who opened the way for their plans, and the Sisterhood had charmed the tongues of the Speakers.

'What you say is true,' Tal had stated in a tired sort of way. He was too old and had seen too much during the Genii War to feel intimidated by his accusers, or by the judgemental murmurs that filtered through the gathering; or to fear whatever punishment they had planned for him at end of this charade. 'However, I would ask why the Speakers of Justice appear to have no interest in discovering *why* the humans used that portal?'

His question had been ignored. The three Speakers discussed further accusations aimed at Tal, loudly debating his incompetence and obvious sympathy for humans. Tal had scoured the gathering – so many faces, old and young – and tried to locate the members of the Sisterhood. He couldn't see them but he knew they were there, hiding among supposed *peers*, already certain of the outcome, poised to celebrate their coming success.

'Ah, yes,' Olivior had said, after Tillane had rifled through his notes and handed her his findings. 'Am I to understand that the Toymaker did not appear to protect the portal?'

'He *did* appear,' Tal replied. 'And he was responsible for the deaths in Sunflower.'

Cam sneered, 'Was he also responsible for the deaths that occurred when the Retrospective followed the humans here? The truth is, no one has claimed to have seen the Toymaker other than you, Councillor. Do you know anything *else* that we do not?'

Tal had felt the old fire burn in him then, the blazing pieces of a soul shattered and broken by the Genii War. 'I know lots of things that you don't,' he replied with an icy growl.

'It seems to me,' Tillane announced primly, officiously, addressing the hall, 'that even the Toymaker, who was created by the Thaumaturgists themselves to serve the Timewatcher's final prerogative, has given up on the humans. What does that tell the esteemed Houses of the Panopticon?'

At that, loud exclamations – mostly of agreement – had broken out in the Panopticon as though the answer to Tillane's question was obvious: if the Timewatcher and the Thaumaturgists no longer watched over the

Labyrinth, why should the Aelfir be responsible for the humans?

But that was not the cause of the uproar now; that had come a little later.

Tillane had continued, 'The Retrospective has already attacked the Aelfir once, and I believe it is only a matter of time before it will do so again.'

Cam agreed, adding gravely, 'The greatest of our magic-users have confirmed that the Retrospective followed the humans here. It is leaking out through the portal in Sunflower, and we have only one option left if we are to protect our Houses.'

'Yes. Most regrettably.' Olivior aimed a baleful glare at Tal. 'Councillor, I really can't decide if you are guilty of gross negligence or if you deliberately set out to *help* the humans.'

Tal had heard enough of the lies by that point. '*My friends!*' His bellow had startled the Speakers and shocked the Panopticon into a hush. 'You accuse me of helping the humans, and I tell you that I *did*! And I would do so again with all the passion left in my old heart – *because* I know what you do not.' As Olivior called to order the disgruntled voices that arose with the statement, Tal pointed an angry finger at the Speakers' bench. 'The humans fled the Labyrinth in desperation, seeking our help. They are the magickers of the Relic Guild, and they bring a dire warning—'

And that was as far as Tal got before the cause of the uproar presented itself.

A messenger burst into the Commons Hall, bringing urgent news to the Speakers that had quickly spread among the gathering. Something was wrong in the Aelfheim Archipelago. Disease had beset the inhabitants, a potent virus that had spread among them like wildfire, reducing any it infected to savage animals. And the disease was spreading to neighbouring Houses.

Now, as Tal witnessed the discontent rumbling through the Panopticon, listening to Olivior's hammer failing to bring order, he recognised that a time of reckoning had come to the Aelfir; and this proved to be true when the grand doors burst open and four strangers entered the Commons Hall. They looked human. Almost.

'*Silence!*' the lead man roared.

His voice descended with such weight that no one dared deny its power. It achieved what Olivior could not.

Each of the strangers bore scarring upon their foreheads. Three of them were dressed in the black cassocks of human priests: a hulking brute with a bald head and one eye; a fragile-looking woman with long black hair; and another man as pale as an albino, his hair straight and white, his face somehow dispassionate yet cruel.

The lead man stood proudly ahead of the three. Bald-headed and thickly bearded, he wore a long dark skirt. His naked torso was covered in black tattoos – symbols Tal recognised as the language of the Thaumaturgists. His eyes burned with violet fire.

'Who speaks for your *petty council*?' he demanded.

Olivior rose from her chair. Cam and Tillane stood beside her.

'We are the Speakers of Justice for the Panopticon of Houses—' Olivior began, but she got no further.

The man swept a hand before him, stroking the air almost gently. This simple action ripped the throats from Olivior, Cam and Tillane. Spraying blood, they fell dead to the floor.

The Panopticon panicked. Several armed guards rushed in. But before they could fire a single shot from their rifles, the other three strangers had turned and used magic to suck the life from them. Each guard collapsed without a sound.

With another spell, the lead man controlled the rising panic in the hall, panic that threatened to turn the august representatives into a stampede of fleeing Aelfir. He forced every member of the Panopticon down into their seats. With faces expressing terror and confusion, the gathering had been locked into position by magic that also squeezed the voices from their throats.

The abrupt silence was unnerving.

'Tell me!' the man shouted. 'Who will speak for you *now*?'

Tal was surprised to find that the effects of the restraining spell had not touched him. He looked at the fear-riddled faces of his peers, speechless, immobile in their seats – those who had been so ready to condemn him, rulers and ambassadors from just about every major Aelfirian House congregated under one roof – and a strange calm descended on him as the pieces of his broken soul knitted together.

The end had come.

'I will speak for us,' Tal said, his voice clear as he calmly stepped down from the podium.

The man looked amused by the elderly Aelf walking across the hall towards him – and surprised, perhaps. 'Are you afraid?'

Tal shook his head, surprised by the truth in the gesture.

'Do you know who I am?'

'Yes, I know you.' Tal stopped a few paces short of the tattooed man. 'You are the former First Lord of the Thaumaturgists, the Skywatcher Iblisha Spiral.'

'Oh, I am much more than that now.' The Genii Lord pursed his lips thoughtfully.

Behind him, his Genii eyed the Aelf suspiciously. Tal recalled intelligence he had received during the Genii War, descriptions of Spiral's most trusted generals. The pale Genii with the white hair – it had to be Fabian Moor.

'I thought you might be stupid,' Spiral said, 'but you know my true name. This must mean that you are important, at least among your own kind.'

'I am Tal.' He couldn't stop his voice shaking, but not from fear. The aura of power that radiated from Spiral squeezed him from all angles and crackled over his skin. 'But perhaps you know me by a different name.' He did his best to draw himself up. 'During the war, your armies called me the Ghoul.'

Spiral considered him for a moment before chuckling. 'I *do* know that name. How perfect.' Fabian Moor glared at Tal with unashamed loathing. 'You terrified the Aelfir. They said you were the slayer of Genii. But to me, you were no more bothersome than a flea.'

'That's good enough,' Tal replied, still desperately trying to keep his voice from shaking.

'Oh, I understand – you think of yourself as the flea that bit the giant. Fair enough. I say *bravo* to you.' Spiral's aura pressed in, hot and fluid. 'Tell me, do you think your endeavour to stop me was worth it now?'

If Spiral was free from Oldest Place, did that mean the Relic Guild had failed? Or was it yet another part of Lady Amilee's plots and plans against the Lord of the Genii?

'It was worth every minute,' Tal said hoarsely.

'I'm sure you believe that.' Spiral looked around at the gathered House rulers, sitting still and silent under his thaumaturgy. 'I'm going to indulge you, Tal the Ghoul, just this once. Is there something you wish me to know?'

Tal sensed his death coming, and the part of him that had already died during the Genii War embraced it.

'There will always be those who will stand against you,' he stated. He struggled to meet Spiral's fiery eyes and bared his teeth in an angry sneer at the Genii behind him. 'We will continue to fight you and your kind, and *never* kneel to you.'

'No?' Spiral's beautiful face became terrible. 'Your mistake is believing that I covet the fealty of the Aelfir. I do not. What I want, *Ghoul*, is sacrifice. Raw matter. Land masses. You people and your Houses are the fodder that will feed the Retrospective. Together we will grow and expand until the only state of existence is a House of blood and dead time.'

Observing the exchange, the Genii expressed mixed reactions. The hulking brute seemed on the brink of religious fervour. The woman, however, remained studiously neutral. Tal noted that concern flittered across Fabian Moor's face.

'You are a fool to think that resisting me is an option,' Spiral said. 'Come, Tal the Ghoul. Kneel before me as you said you never would. Be my witness as I show you how the future of the Aelfir begins at the Sisterhood of Bells.'

Tal felt as though his soul had been ripped from him as Spiral drove him down onto his knees with the slightest flicker of the magic at his command. Such power!

'Your Mother abandoned you!' Spiral shouted. He appeared to expand as he addressed the Panopticon, his aura causing the walls of the Hall to groan. 'Now welcome your Father!'

The Genii Lord threw back his head and spread his wings behind him like sharp silver fans. The doors to the Commons Hall disintegrated; the wall around them collapsed. The debris was sucked away into the damned land which suddenly appeared, filled with poisonous clouds, and a wind of fire raged like a furnace as it poured into the Hall.

Wild demons followed the wind.

A host of nightmare monsters rushed into the auditorium, screeching, baying for blood. There were no screams of fear and pain from the Panopticon as the fire crisped their flesh. Held silent and still, they could do nothing but endure the torture, waiting for the demons to charge into their midst and tear into them with tooth and claw and jagged appendages. Even during the Genii War, Tal had never witnessed such wanton slaughter.

Blood-soaked stone and wood shook and split and shattered. The ceiling exploded into infinite pieces. Rubble and broken bodies were whipped up into the fury of a tornado. The Retrospective ripped Little Sibling apart. The Sisterhood of Bells would come next, and then … no House or living being would be safe from the carnage.

Except Tal. Except Spiral and his Genii. They had been spared from the danger, kept safe within a bubble of higher magic that lessened the tumult of destruction taking place around them.

There was no compassion on Spiral's terrible face as he folded his wings and glared down at the Aelf on his knees before him.

'Now then, Tal the Ghoul,' he said quietly. 'What am I to do with you?'

DEATH SENTENCE

The scent of death clung to Samuel's clothes and hair. The lingering odour of rotting vegetables was foul in his nostrils and the stench of charred meat laced the air and coated the inside of his mouth with a bitter, oily film.

In the house in the northern district, Samuel sat on the floor of the cellar, a little singed but largely unhurt – at least physically. His back rested against one of the wooden poles engraved with necromantic symbols. Bryant's remains, along with those of the denizen who had been infected with Fabian Moor's virus, lay as ash upon the floor. The leathery tentacles which had exploded into life like a great sea beast rising from the ocean to rip Bryant limb from limb were chunks of useless inanimate grey stone.

The necromantic spells cast in the cellar still trapped Samuel behind magical barriers that stretched between the poles and dampened his prescient awareness. Even without his magic, Samuel felt secure that the danger had passed, though his rifle, lying across his legs and loaded with fire-bullets, brought comfort.

'Interesting,' said a voice.

With a start, Samuel peered around to see Hamir standing in the cellar, studying the barrier that separated them. He hadn't heard the necromancer approach.

'You took your bloody time,' Samuel growled.

'In case you hadn't noticed, I've been a little preoccupied of late,' Hamir replied in that annoyingly amiable way of his.

Samuel got to his feet, slid the rifle into the holster on his back and faced the necromancer through the barrier. 'Can you get me out?'

'I think I know what I'm dealing with.' Hamir ran his hands over one of the poles. 'But ... give me a moment to be sure.'

As Hamir studied the symbols engraved into the wood, Samuel felt a heaviness in his heart. 'How's Macy?'

'Understandably distraught. Now let me concentrate, please.'

Samuel folded his arms across his chest and glared at Hamir.

After Samuel destroyed the tentacular creature with magical fire, Macy had turned wild with grief over the loss of her twin brother. She, like Bryant, had been born with inordinate strength; but the dampening spells in that place ensured she could not break through the magical barriers to save Bryant. She had only been able to watch as Samuel's bullets incinerated her brother to ashes along with everything else.

Macy had lost her mind in that moment, shouting at Samuel, blaming him for Bryant's fate. 'I'll kill you!' she screamed. 'Murderer!' Van Bam had his work cut out convincing Macy to leave the cellar so they could fetch Hamir. He had succeeded, eventually, but as they left she had made a dark promise to Samuel that she was coming back for him.

'This is a primitive sort of necromancy,' Hamir said as he walked from pole to pole, studying symbols. 'Almost amateurish, in fact. Certainly not crafted by Fabian Moor.'

'Magic-users were hired to create this place,' Samuel said. 'I don't know why.'

'Hmm.' Hamir considered for a moment. 'Van Bam tells me there was a creature made of tentacles. Is that right?'

'It came from some kind of egg. When it was dropped into a hole filled with rancid meat it ... *hatched*.'

'And there were also infected denizens held to the ceiling.'

Samuel wondered if the information was important, or if Hamir was simply sating his own morbid curiosity. The necromancer was such a strange man, full of mystery and secrets, and Samuel had long ago learned that it was quicker to just allow Hamir to take his own sweet time.

'I believe what you faced was a golem of sorts,' Hamir explained. 'I've seen them used before and they are not particularly graceful.' He looked up at the shadows of people burned into the ceiling. 'The blood of the denizens, infected with a virus or not, would have fed the creature – and this is clear evidence confirming that what you have found in this cellar was not made by Moor's own hand. A creature of higher magic could create such a golem simply and quickly, and thaumaturgy alone would sustain it.'

Samuel huffed impatiently. 'That's all very interesting, Hamir, but what was it for?'

'Harvesting memories,' Hamir stated. He paused, perhaps following his own line of thought, recalling past experiences. 'Specifically, in this case, memories belonging to people who are a little more resilient to interrogation than the average person. Magickers, for example.'

It made sense. Moor believed that agents of the Relic Guild held unconscious information in their psyches that would allow him to infiltrate the Nightshade and thus gain control of the Labyrinth. Hamir had decided that he was wrong, but obviously the Genii hadn't given up trying.

A thought came to Samuel. 'Why would a Genii need to hire magic-users to do his work for him?'

'I don't know.' Hamir stared at Samuel, through him, and his soft green eyes began to swirl with darkness as though ink had been dripped into them. 'Stand back, please.'

Hamir laid his hands upon the poles either side of him, whispering words of necromancy. The symbols engraved on every pole in the cellar began glowing and the wood smoked. The light died and the sickly grey magic of the barrier sputtered, crackling with energy before disappearing.

'There,' said Hamir, his eyes returning to normal. 'Primitive *and* simple.'

'Good.' Freed from his confinement, Samuel looked around the cellar, wondering how many more agents of the Relic Guild would die because of Fabian Moor. 'I'm going to get drunk,' he announced.

Hamir sucked air over his teeth. 'I understand your need to grieve – and perhaps to avoid Macy – but Gideon has summoned you to the Nightshade.' He blinked at Samuel. 'Denton and Marney have returned.'

Gene was dead, Angel was dead ... and now Bryant.

The Relic Guild sat in silence around a long conference table in the Nightshade. Gideon was at the head, as brooding and menacing as ever. Macy sat next to Marney, staring into the table as though her glare could burn holes in the wood. Her face was pale and her eyes were red. On the other side of the table, Samuel was keeping as much distance between himself and Gideon as he could create. Taciturn as always, he stank of smoke and blood, and his eyes avoided Macy. Hamir was absent, as was Denton. Van Bam was opposite Marney, his eyes, red from tears, seeing only her.

The one spark of emotion left in Marney was a vague desire to be alone with her lover. Other than that, she was struggling with a curious sense of detachment that allowed her to feel nothing about the situation and the deaths of her colleagues; but her state had not been induced by her magic.

Upon returning to the Labyrinth, Denton had immediately been summoned to a private meeting with Lady Amilee at the Tower of the Skywatcher. No one else knew the nature of his and Marney's mission, and Amilee had given strict instructions to Gideon that no one, not even the Resident, was to ask questions of the empaths. That was just as well, Marney had reasoned, for there was very little she could tell them.

Something was missing in Marney. She remembered all too well the journey to the Library of Glass and Mirrors, she had a slight recollection of reaching her destination, but of the Library itself she could recall nothing. Not one memory of what they had discovered there remained to Marney. It was as though information had been stolen from her mind. And she meditated upon this mystery while the group waited in silence for Denton's return.

Gideon shifted in his chair. Restless, his hands balled into fists on the table, he ground his teeth, and Marney could feel every nuance of the angry frustration he emoted. But worse than that, she could also sense his boredom, and a bored Gideon always led to confrontation. Marney steeled herself. She knew what was coming next.

A sneer twisted Gideon's face as his dark eyes glared at Samuel. 'Tell me,' he purred, 'how many of my agents have you put out of their misery now, Samuel?'

Van Bam closed his eyes and groaned. Macy tensed. Samuel returned the Resident's glare.

'I make it two,' Gideon added spitefully. 'Is that right? Or are there more than just Gene and Bryant?'

'Shut up,' Macy hissed. She bristled, practically radiating the power of her magical strength.

Van Bam added, 'Please, Gideon.' His voice was soft, reassuring, concerned. 'Now is not the time.'

Gideon shrugged and his tone became one of mock-contemplation. 'We have lost agents before and we will lose them again, I suppose. But I imagine there must be other magickers out there right now, hiding among the denizens, simply *itching* to replace our fallen friends. For a thousand years the magic of the Labyrinth has catered to the Relic Guild in this way, so it's not all doom and gloom.'

Macy looked ready to punch someone, anyone. Marney sank back in her seat, wondering if there had ever been a time when Gideon was able to respect other people's feelings. She doubted it.

'Your lack of compassion doesn't mean that *we* can't grieve,' Samuel said from between gritted teeth.

'I'm not so sure I agree, Samuel.'

'Well, it wouldn't be the first time you were wrong.'

With an easy smile, Gideon sat back in his chair and placed his hands behind his head – a deliberate show of calm indifference, designed only to antagonise Samuel further. 'I think you'll find that my position as Resident means I can tell you exactly what to feel, and when to feel it.'

'And I think *you* will find that the Resident is a spiteful bastard who should learn when to keep his mouth shut.'

Before Van Bam could offer calming advice, Gideon barked a harsh laugh at Samuel. 'Listen to me, you mawkish idiot. Outside the Labyrinth a war is being fought between creatures of higher magic. In case you've forgotten, the Genii want nothing more than to crush each and every one of us, and one of their number is still in our midst.' Gideon's expression became dangerous. 'So push your grief aside and remember your damned duty to the denizens.'

Macy banged a fist on the table, cracking wood. 'I'll beat you both to pulp if you don't shut up,' she growled.

'Is that right?' Gideon snapped.

'Stop it, all of you,' Marney said softly, tiredly.

Her colleagues' eyes turned to her.

How many times had Marney witnessed this dance? A great hate had always existed between Gideon and Samuel, a hate which the rest of the group was forced to endure, calming things when they got too heated. For Samuel's part, Marney thought he was content to be left alone and to have as little to do with Gideon as possible. As for Gideon, he did nothing to hide his disdain for Samuel, almost relishing those moments when he could poke him with a stick, which he invariably did every chance he got.

But Macy ... she was hurting, more than the rest of them. Gideon and Samuel had no right to drag her into their petty squabbles.

'Oh my,' the Resident said with mock surprise. 'The *pupil* speaks!'

'Samuel's right, Gideon,' Marney continued, unfazed. 'We *should* grieve. We should take the time to remember Gene and Angel.' She reached out and laid her hand on top of Macy's fist. 'And Bryant.'

Macy unclenched her fingers and gripped Marney's hand, closing her eyes against fresh tears. Samuel looked away. Gideon's expression turned sour, but before he could offer some choice retort his eyes began darting from side to side and his shoulders slumped. Obviously he was receiving some kind of mental admonishment from Sophia, his spirit guide and former Resident.

'Perhaps,' Van Bam said, 'we could hold a wake for our friends.'

'*When* time allows,' Gideon asserted. 'Which might come sooner rather than later.' His tone had lost much of its spite and the tension in the atmosphere broke a little. 'I sent a message with Denton for Lady Amilee. I have requested permission to execute Fabian Moor.'

Van Bam stared at the Resident with a surprise that was shared by Samuel. Macy looked grimly please by the news.

'Execute him?' Van Bam said. 'Do we know a way to do it?'

'Hamir says that Amilee's little book of secrets holds details of how to kill a creature of higher magic.' Gideon made a noise of frustration. 'We must have foiled Moor's mission, insofar as we know what it is. And we've had that cursed Genii in our custody for long enough. He has revealed nothing of Spiral's plans, no matter how much he is tortured, and I for one would like to be shot of him. I'm confident Amilee will grant permission for his execution.'

'I want to watch,' Macy said adamantly, as though daring anyone to refuse her.

'Me, too,' Samuel added.

Van Bam remained quiet, and Marney felt his remorse that anyone should find gratification in death, even that of a Genii. She longed to reach out, to lay a hand on his cheek, to feel his skin against hers.

Clearly humoured by Samuel's and Macy's reactions, Gideon said, 'That makes three of us.'

With a soft click, the outline of a door appeared on the conference room wall. The door swung open revealing the large form of Denton.

'Denton,' said Gideon. 'Is vengeance at hand?'

The old empath looking distracted. He was crushing his hat in his hands as he always did when he was troubled. Marney sensed immediately that he had closed off his emotions. He made no attempt to speak or look at anyone.

'Denton,' Gideon said sternly. 'What is the wish of the Skywatcher?'

He stared at the Resident as though suddenly realising he wasn't alone. 'Lady Amilee has agreed to Fabian Moor's execution … in principle.'

'In *principle*?' Gideon said. 'What does that mean?'

'Our Lady has ordered me to speak to the Genii first,' Denton replied. He looked directly at Marney and she felt the remorse he emoted to her. 'And she wants me to speak with him alone.'

'This is a bad idea,' Samuel said.

Along with Hamir and Gideon, he stood in the Nightshade's observation room, feeling uneasy. Van Bam and Marney had decided not to attend – and Samuel could guess the reason why – while Macy had simply left the Nightshade after the meeting, saying nothing but probably wishing to be alone to contemplate her brother's death.

'I have to agree with Samuel,' Hamir said. 'Everything we have discovered about Moor's mission to Labrys Town is based on supposition. We know nothing for certain.'

The back wall of the room acted like a magical window, projecting a view provided by an eye device in an abandoned ore warehouse in the southern district. Fabian Moor sat cross-legged in the purple light of his thaumaturgic prison, eyes closed and apparently asleep. Against the wall to the Genii's left, the strange device he had used to harvest shadows sat in its glass containment box upon the elevator platform. Surrounded by wire mesh and small power stones, the glass sphere was filled with murky water and appeared inactive.

'It makes no difference what we think,' Gideon said, his voice hard but not spiteful. 'Lady Amilee has given her orders, and since when did the Relic Guild ever defy the Skywatcher?' To which he added darkly, 'No matter how much we might disagree with her.'

Samuel always found Amilee's decisions hard to fathom, and especially so on this occasion. He had always thought the safest course of action would have been to execute Fabian Moor as soon as the Relic Guild captured him, not to try to interrogate him – and certainly not to waste time with a final conversation when interrogation failed.

The warehouse's shutter door rose with a series of metallic clacks and Denton came into view. He took off his wide-brimmed hat, which he placed on a table next to a wooden rack filled with phials of blood that had been used to feed the Genii. Denton approached the eye in the warehouse, staring directly into the observation room. His face was unusually grave as he pulled a leather pouch from his jacket pocket and emptied a small pile of dust into his cupped hand. Discarding the pouch, Denton threw the dust at the eye. The image fizzed with static, but returned a moment later to show the old empath approaching Fabian Moor.

'What was that?' Samuel demanded.

'The audio function has been deactivated,' Gideon replied, casting a frown around the room. 'I can't reactivate it.'

'What's he up to?' Samuel swore. 'I should've gone with him.'

'To do what, Samuel?' Gideon snapped. 'Hold his hand?'

'This is obviously a part of Amilee's instructions,' Hamir said before Samuel and Gideon could start arguing again. 'Evidently, we are allowed to *see* but not *hear*.'

Although Denton kept his back to the group, he was obviously speaking to the Genii. Moor opened his eyes and looked up at the empath. A quirky smile played across his lips as he listened.

Gideon cursed. He had clearly tried and failed to reinitiate the audio function again. 'Amilee has done her job well. The Nightshade won't obey my command.'

Whatever Denton was saying, it caused Moor to pull an impressed face.

'That's more than I ever got out of him,' Hamir said, suspicion lacing his voice. 'Interesting. I sincerely hope Amilee knows what she's doing.'

'I've been saying that for a long time,' Gideon whispered.

'Denton knows what he's doing,' Samuel said, as much to convince himself as the others.

Moor leaned back and considered Denton for a long moment. And then, to everyone's astonishment, he spoke.

'Hamir,' Gideon snapped. 'Can you tell what he's saying?'

The necromancer shook his head.

'Van Bam can read lips,' Samuel said.

'Well, Van Bam isn't here, is he?' Gideon growled. 'He's probably off fooling around with Denton's damned pupil.'

Samuel tried to read Moor's lips himself but could only guess that he had said the word *mirrors* before touching a fingertip to his temple and saying something that might have been, *I know.*

But the moment was interrupted by someone else arriving at the warehouse. With hatred on her face and a pistol in her hand, Macy stepped through the door.

'What in the Timewatcher's name is *she* doing there?' Gideon hissed, moving towards the image.

Macy aimed the pistol at Moor, shouting at him. Denton, clearly reacting to unforeseen circumstances, approached Macy with one hand raised in a calming gesture. She didn't listen. She squeezed off three shots at Moor. The Genii shook his head, amused and perplexed by Macy's actions as each bullet hit the light of thaumaturgy and disappeared.

'She is blinded by grief,' Hamir said.

'Damn idiot!' Gideon shouted.

Macy's expression glazed and she dropped the pistol. Evidently

Denton was using his empathic magic to control the emotions steering Macy's actions. Like a sleepwalker, she turned and began heading out of the warehouse.

'Wait a moment,' Hamir said, staring intently at the image. 'Look at the Genii.'

Moor mouthed the word *no*, and Macy stopped. She jerked as though she had been tugged from behind before falling into a sitting position. Some invisible force dragged Macy across the warehouse floor, through the purple glare of the thaumaturgic prison and into Fabian Moor's arms. The Genii pulled her head back, exposed her throat and sank his teeth into her flesh.

As Samuel and Gideon looked on in horror, Hamir exclaimed, 'Impossible! He's using higher magic!'

Denton was beside himself, and he was obviously begging Moor to stop. Macy barely struggled. Her mouth open, her expression one of shock rather than pain, she could do nothing as Moor fed on her blood.

'Why is this happening, Hamir?' Gideon demanded. 'That prison is supposed to suppress thaumaturgy!'

'I must have missed something,' Hamir said, sounding helpless. 'Some flaw in the prison's design ...'

Samuel's heart urged him to rush to the aid of his fellow agents; but cold logic reminded him that the full fifty-mile length of Labrys Town separated the Nightshade and the warehouse.

'Run,' Samuel hissed. 'Denton, *run!*'

But the old empath only watched as Moor finished feeding and pushed his meal aside. Her throat torn and red, Macy twitched and convulsed as the Genii's virus took hold inside her. With preternatural motion conjured by magic which should have been suppressed, Moor propelled himself to his feet. He opened his arms wide and his skin absorbed the purple light radiating from the thaumaturgic symbols on the floor beneath him. Macy's blood was smeared across his face and dripped down his naked body.

When the light had gone, Moor glared at Denton and his mouth moved. Samuel made out his words clearly this time: *Shall we begin?*

Denton looked back into the observation room with the saddest expression Samuel had ever seen on his old and ruddy face.

'Shit,' Samuel blurted. 'The device ...'

On the elevator platform, the power stones surrounding the sphere began to blaze with violet light. The murky water within the sphere darkened to night. The glass containment box cracked and shattered.

'Denton, get out of there!' Gideon roared.

But it was too late. The glass sphere exploded, releasing a mass of black shadow which instantly filled the warehouse. The view from the Nightshade became obscured, as though a storm cloud had passed before the eye. When it cleared, Fabian Moor and Macy were gone. And so was Denton.

In a shabby one-room apartment above a bakery in the eastern district, Marney lay in bed with Van Bam; naked, tangled in sheets and each other's arms. It was late evening and the fading glow of the sun illuminated the threadbare curtains drawn across the window. In a few hours, Ruby Moon would rise, clouds would gather and the rains would come.

Marney decided – deeply, in every part of her soul – that there was nowhere else she would rather be at that moment than in this apartment, in her lover's arms.

She and Van Bam had cried together, laughed a little, and made love like the end of times began tomorrow. But nothing could fully erase the troubles from their minds. The loss of friends, the things they had seen and done – they hung over the magickers like a nightmare waiting to creep into their dreams. It seemed impossible to Marney that, after all she had been through, she had been an agent of the Relic Guild for less than seven months. Eighteen felt entirely too young for someone who had experienced as much as she had. But that was the truth of it. She wondered if she had become an older woman trapped in a young woman's body.

'It's strange, don't you think?' Marney said, her voice sounding alien in the stillness. 'That we have to keep so many secrets from each other?'

'Lady Amilee has her reasons,' Van Bam replied sleepily. 'I trust in that.'

'I'm not sure that I do. Not any more.' Marney held him tighter. 'Some of things Denton and I had to do—'

'Marney, stop,' Van Bam said gently. 'To disregard Lady Amilee's orders would be to break the trust of the Relic Guild. We have not earned that right simply because we are lovers.'

He spoke only the truth, and Marney hated that. But she was an empath. She could feel the troubles her lover carried, and that they formed a hurt inside him that was personal and nothing to do with any fear he might feel for the secrets he had learned.

'I'm not saying we should break anyone's trust,' Marney told him. 'But we're still allowed to tell each other how we're feeling, aren't we?'

Van Bam thought for a moment before conceding Marney's point with a sigh. 'I keep running events over and over in my mind, trying to find something new, but I cannot see how I could have prevented Angel's death.' He sat up and rubbed his face as though trying to clean away bad memories. 'I keep telling myself I am not responsible – I *know* I am not – yet I blame myself nonetheless.'

Marney absorbed his emotions, felt what he felt. 'You saw her die.'

'She called my name, Marney. The look in her eyes ... Angel was begging me for help I could not give. And ... and she wasn't the only one I failed to save. There was ...'

His voice cracked and he broke off.

Marney traced a finger down his bare back. 'There was *who*, Van Bam?'

'Namji.'

'Namji?' At the mention of the name, Marney quashed a selfish pang of dislike. She had met Namji once and really hadn't liked her – mostly because of her obvious affection for Van Bam. 'What happened to her?'

'I do not know,' Van Bam replied. 'Namji was innocent, Marney. I promised to save her from the war, to deliver her to the safety of Labrys Town, but ... in the end, I had no choice but to leave her behind. I somehow doubt she survived whatever happened next in Mirage.'

Marney embraced Van Bam from behind, wrapping her legs around his waist. 'It's always the personal that blurs the bigger picture, don't you think?' She kissed the back of his neck. 'Nothing ever seems fair.'

'I sometimes wonder if it is the Relic Guild's lot to be defined by our regrets.' Van Bam placed his hands over Marney's. 'And what of you? What *regrets* are too strong for even an empath to stop feeling?'

Marney closed her eyes and told Van Bam all she could.

She spoke about her journey with Denton – though not where they had been or their final destination. She told him how she had seen the war and watched creatures of higher magic fighting – though she spared her lover's feeling by not mentioning that she had glimpsed Buyaal, the Genii who had subjugated House Mirage and murdered Angel. She talked of the moments when she had almost died, when she thought she would never see Van Bam again. And she lamented the people who had died by her hand.

'But do you know the one thing that stands out to me – that will probably haunt me for the rest of my life?' Marney stared at the fading sunlight illuminating the curtains. 'There was an Aelfirian soldier – his name was Morren – and he lost his life helping Denton and me. I mean, I hardly knew him, Van Bam, but after everything I went through, his death stays with me the most. When Denton's finished with Moor, we're going to raise a drink in his honour.'

'Some people simply make an impression, no matter how briefly they affect our lives.' There was a hidden quality to Van Bam's words, and Marney could feel him thinking about secrets he could not share. 'Others die unremembered. At least you and Denton will ensure that Morren is not one of them. We will drink to Angel and Gene and Bryant, too.'

'And Namji,' Marney said, rubbing a finger over her lips. 'We don't always get to choose what we remember and what we don't.'

Marney still felt an absence inside her, as though something was missing, and she was now convinced that her memories of the Library of Glass and Mirrors had been stolen. Had Denton taken them? Did he, like Amilee, have good reasons for keeping secrets from her?

'There is more, Marney.' Sadness rose in Van Bam again. 'In Mirage, Angel and I spoke about my relationship with you. She was of the opinion that life would be easier for us should we stop being involved romantically.'

Marney leaned away from him. 'What?'

'Because of Gideon,' Van Bam added quickly.

'Oh.'

Just the mention of the Resident's name soured the ambience in the apartment. Gideon didn't like his agents having anything other than platonic relationships. He had been meddling with Marney's and Van Bam's duties for the Relic Guild, fixing things so they were kept apart.

'Angel said that Gideon would only get worse,' said Van Bam. 'She reasoned that it might be wise to end our relationship on our terms rather than his.'

Marney felt his sadness deepen, and she dispelled it by emoting love back him.

'No, you can't get rid of me that easily,' she said with a smile. 'Our relationship brings me hope. I'm not giving you up.'

'I feel the same, but ...' Van Bam turned to face her. 'I wish I shared your confidence.'

'Listen to me, Van Bam.' Marney cupped his face. 'Denton and me, we met this secret service officer who said that Spiral is growing weaker by the day. He said the war would be over soon.'

'Truly?'

'Think about *that*, Van Bam. We could use the doorways in the Great Labyrinth again, visit the Aelfir, travel across the Houses together.'

'We could run away – *elope*.' Van Bam kissed her. 'I like this *hope* of yours, Marney.'

The moment broke as Marney became aware of a new presence. Someone had climbed up the fire escape. She had a moment to recognise the owner of the hard, unapproachable emotions before a knock came at the window.

Van Bam jumped from the bed, grabbing his cane of green glass.

'It's Samuel,' Marney whispered.

'Samuel?'

'Something's wrong.'

Wrapping the bed sheet around him, Van Bam strode to the window and opened it.

'We've got a problem,' Samuel's gruff voice said. 'Is Marney with you?'

'Yes,' said Van Bam.

'Gideon wants everyone at the Nightshade. Now.' Marney heard the chill in Samuel's voice. 'Fabian Moor escaped. He infected Macy. He ... He's got Denton.'

CHAPTER FOURTEEN

REUNION

The Tower of the Skywatcher was under siege.

The domed ceiling of Amilee's observatory was alive with grim and silent images of the chaos taking place outside. Great beasts soared through the smoky sky on wings of taloned leather and burning feathers. Countless foot soldiers full of battle lust, monsters of war and death and disease, rushed the tower like a charging herd, trying to scale the sheer walls, while mighty giants as tall as trees pounded on the doors with boulder-sized fists. Organised, subservient, *controlled*. The Retrospective had brought an invasion force of wild demons to Lady Amilee's House, along with final confirmation that Lord Iblisha Spiral was free.

Samuel paced the observatory's glass floor, clenching and unclenching his fists, staring at the hateful images above. Clara and Lady Amilee watched him. Over by the elevator, the Toymaker stood still and silent, illuminated by the many lights shining from the interconnected automatons that formed its framework body. Apparently the Toymaker was now Clara's bodyguard but its presence irritated the old bounty hunter. He looked up at the Retrospective again.

'I hope the defences hold,' Samuel muttered. 'If those demons get inside this tower, there'll be no—'

'Samuel,' Amilee interrupted, softly yet sternly, 'Gulduur Bellow will provide us with the time we need.' She was clearly losing patience with him. 'Perhaps you should accept that and calm down.'

How could he calm down when his magic was a bad, sickening feeling in his gut, preparing him for the many terrible things to come? 'You think Bellow can protect us if Spiral decides to join his ...' He thrust a hand at the domed ceiling. 'His *troops*?'

'Spiral won't come for me – not yet,' Amilee said, also looking up at the images. 'Sending the Retrospective here is a message. He's telling me that he knows where I am, but that I am nothing compared to him. He wants me to watch as he crushes the realms around me. But what Spiral doesn't appreciate is that *I* know he doesn't yet have all the power he requires. At this moment, we are protected from his demons.'

'Not very comforting,' Samuel grumbled. 'How much time can Bellow buy us?'

'Time enough,' Clara stated harshly, and Samuel glared at her.

The Nephilim was in a different part of the tower, working his blood-magic to bolster its defences. Although he had been able to return power to the observatory and prevent the demons from entering Amilee's home, he was not strong enough to return her House to its former glory or reignite the Skywatcher's thaumaturgy.

Patience and diplomacy had never been Samuel's strong points. He didn't know where Hillem, Glogelder and Hamir were and he didn't care. Marney had struggled to regain full consciousness and Namji was with her, administering healing spells. And that left Samuel to deal with the bizarre and overwhelming information that Clara had brought back from her journey into Known Things.

The weight of the Retrospective loomed, as though it might descend from the dome at any moment with the full hate of dead time.

'All right,' Samuel said to Clara. 'Denton's ghost was the avatar, but he's gone now. And so is Gideon. I understand that.' He pointed a finger at her. 'But if you're the Resident, then Van Bam must be in your mind.'

'He is.' Clara cocked her head to one side as if listening to something. 'And he says you should get a grip.'

'Does he? Well, tell him that's easy for him to say.'

'He can hear you through my ears, Samuel. And see you through my eyes.'

'I know how it works,' Samuel snapped, and he continued to pace.

Amilee turned a bemused expression on Clara. 'Is he always like this?'

'Pretty much. Samuel, you're not helping the situation.'

The changeling's voice held the same depth of authority that Van Bam had once commanded.

Clara had changed so much from the awkward, desperate girl Samuel had first met. Having won the war against her own magic, no longer frightened of her own shadow, she had overcome more adversity than

Samuel reasoned he could have dealt with at eighteen years old. Clara stood straight and proud in her dark grey magically enhanced clothes, her short hair streaked with silver, sunshine yellow gleaming from her eyes. And it dawned on Samuel that Clara was now his leader, the head of the Relic Guild, the true Resident of Labrys Town.

'We have time and we have hope,' Amilee said. 'Thanks to Clara, we now know where Spiral hid the Nephilim's prison.'

'Yeah … inside the Retrospective.' Samuel gave a sigh of resignation at the wild images filling the tower's domed ceiling. Two flying demons clashed mid-air and began to fight. 'Explain something to me – *how* did he hide it there? Spiral abducted the Nephilim *before* the Genii War. The Timewatcher created the Retrospective *after* the Genii War, by which time Spiral was locked away in Oldest Place.'

'Divination,' Clara replied.

'Creatures of higher magic are good at playing the long game, Samuel,' said Amilee. 'We Skywatchers can read signs of the future in the skies, but Spiral …' She broke off, and Samuel couldn't decide if her expression was impressed or daunted. Perhaps both. 'But Spiral achieved the impossible. He divined the Timewatcher Herself. He knew about the Retrospective before She even created it.'

'So he hid the Nephilim's prison in a House that he knew the Retrospective would absorb at the end of the war.' Clara shrugged. 'The Falls of Dust and Silver.'

Samuel paused. The Falls of Dust and Silver, the House where the Genii War started. Was that ironic?

'It took a remarkably simple feat of ingenuity on Spiral's part,' Amilee explained. 'Unable to destroy the Nephilim, Spiral cast a protective shield around their prison – much like the barrier the Timewatcher cast during the war to protect the Labyrinth from creatures of higher magic.'

'Not that the barrier stopped Fabian Moor,' Samuel growled.

'The point is,' said Clara, 'when the Falls of Dust and Silver was consigned to the Retrospective, the prison was preserved by its shield.'

'And it's been there ever since.' Samuel rubbed his forehead, unable to decide which point to raise next. He settled on the mass-murderer the Relic Guild had been harbouring in its midst since its formation.

'You say that Hamir has to free the Nephilim, but I don't understand how or why.'

'Actually, neither do I,' Clara said. She stood alongside Samuel and they both faced the Skywatcher. 'What I found in Known Things barely mentioned Hamir, only that Spiral was curious about him.'

Amilee pursed her lips thoughtfully. 'The *why* is known only to the Timewatcher, and trying to guess Her reasons is a waste of time. As for *how*, She bound the fates of the Nephilim and Simowyn Hamir together. It is their curse. To achieve this, the Timewatcher manipulated the thaumaturgy that was used to create the Nephilim in the first place.'

'Hamir's higher magic,' Samuel said, recalling the tale Bellow had told at the Icicle Forest. 'The magic of the Progenitor. That's what Spiral used to trap the Nephilim.'

'Indeed,' said Amilee. 'Spiral himself helped to drain Hamir's power. Unbeknown to the Timewatcher or his fellow Skywatchers, he stole it and used it for his own ends. But if that thaumaturgy can be used to entrap the Nephilim, it can also set them free. To achieve this, the Timewatcher's curse must be undone. And that can only happen when Hamir is reunited with his magic.'

Samuel absorbed that. Doubt rose in him. 'Considering Hamir killed a hundred denizens the last time he had that kind of power, are you sure giving it back to him is a good idea?'

'It's the only *idea* we've got.' Frail and tired as she was, Amilee took offence at his criticism and anger came to her tawny eyes. 'I have spent the last forty years steering us all towards this moment. To find a way to defeat Spiral has cost me everything, but if you have thought of a better way, Samuel, then by all means – do share it.'

'No, he's right, my lady,' Clara said, clearly conversing with Van Bam. 'The Relic Guild never really knew Hamir at all. How can you be so certain he'll do the right thing?'

'Because if we don't trust him, we fail,' Amilee stated. 'To find Hamir's thaumaturgy, you must find the Nephilim. It is the power of the Progenitor that preserves their prison. And time is running short.'

Samuel, too tired to argue any further, looked up at the menagerie of savage wild monsters fighting to gain entrance to the tower. The Lord of the Genii hadn't just escaped Oldest Place; he had merged with the

Retrospective. He was in the mind of each creature, in the very substance of the land of dead time. He would keep building, keep devouring, until he had killed every denizen, absorbed the First and Greatest Spell and swallowed everything – unless the Relic Guild acted now.

'The Retrospective is a big place,' Samuel said. He ran a hand through his short grey hair, feeling dwarfed by the task ahead. 'Do we know how to find the Nephilim without Spiral and an untold number of demons noticing us?'

'Perhaps,' said Amilee.

'We need to do better than *perhaps*. Just the atmosphere of the Retrospective alone will probably kill us the moment we breathe it in.'

Amilee looked at Clara.

'We should talk to Marney,' Clara said. 'Before I woke up from Known Things, she hinted that she knew of a way to search the Retrospective.'

'Then let's go and ask her.'

Samuel strode off across the glass floor, heading for the elevator. No one followed him.

'Samuel,' Clara called. He stopped but didn't look back. 'Van Bam says to be kind to Marney. She's been through a lot.'

An order from the new Resident.

Samuel ground his teeth and entered the elevator.

Hamir had been wandering aimlessly through the levels of Amilee's tower ever since the Relic Guild arrived, hiding, thinking of the time when he had been known as Lord Simowyn Hamir.

A thousand years he had spent exiled to the Labyrinth, and it had not been an easy adjustment at first. Hamir struggled to pinpoint when precisely it had happened, but over the centuries he had come to accept his position as aide to the Residents. He had learned to let go of memories of Mother Earth and a life of higher magic. But those memories resurfaced now. He shuddered to recall his punishment at the hands of the Trinity of Skywatchers, the moment when they left him with only the dregs of his former magic.

Simowyn ... that name felt as if it belonged to someone else entirely now.

There was something about Amilee's home that comforted the necromancer. A kind of serenity permeated the many halls and rooms and corridors, familiar yet detached from any danger. Hard to believe that outside legions of wild demons laid siege to the tower. Hamir felt as secure as he had wandering the Nightshade, but he knew the security couldn't last. He supposed his past was always going to catch up with him eventually, but he wasn't quite ready to face it yet. And so Hamir wandered.

Why had the Timewatcher bound the fate of the Nephilim to their creator? Amilee claimed it was so they carried the shame of Hamir's crimes for as long as he did, but it was so difficult to judge when the Skywatcher was hiding the whole truth. Perhaps she didn't really know. All Hamir had to go on were his suspicions and guesses. He found it difficult to see any rhyme or reason in the Timewatcher's actions. The Nephilim lived or died according to whether Hamir did. There seemed little point to such a curse. Unless ...

Unless Hamir's sentence was never meant to last for ever. Had the Timewatcher foreseen an end to his exile? What if She had protected the Nephilim until a time when She decided that the Progenitor was ready to somehow take responsibility for what he had created? If the Genii War hadn't occurred, if She and the Thaumaturgists hadn't abandoned the Houses, would the Timewatcher have one day returned Hamir to Mother Earth? Given him back his thaumaturgy?

In the distant past, Hamir had known a few Thaumaturgists like himself who had been drained of their power and sent into exile. It was the biggest insult, the greatest punishment a creature of higher magic could suffer. But on no occasion Hamir was aware of had any Thaumaturgist been given back the power which had been stripped from them; he hadn't even considered it a possibility. Apparently there were many secrets the Timewatcher had never shared with Her children.

The denizens of Labrys Town were another example of this. One million humans ... had there ever been a generation which gave its fealty to the Timewatcher of its own volition? The answer was no, according to Lady Amilee. Every human was conditioned by a *splinter* of the Timewatcher's magic, unknowingly subjugated into obedience. And when they died, those splinters returned to the First and Greatest Spell, ready to recycle fresh loyalty into the next generation. But did the First and Greatest Spell also claim the souls into which its splinters were embedded?

Hamir entered the elevator and began descending to a random floor of the tower, his mind fixed on another of the Timewatcher's secrets.

Death was an unknowable journey, and even the Thaumaturgists didn't know the truth of it. They too believed the legends that the Timewatcher had created a paradise on Mother Earth for the souls of the dead. But faith was a powerful ally, regardless of whether or not it was based on a lie. Hamir felt a cold whisper fuelling his doubts, telling him that death's journey – now, always – had never led to Mother Earth; and when he thought of how many magickers he had known who lived and died in service to the Relic Guild, he felt he understood why the Timewatcher – and Amilee – might keep secrets. How could he tell Samuel and Marney and Clara that they had no choice but to serve? That perhaps no paradise waited as reward for their faith and devotion?

As if to underline Hamir's point, the ghost of Alexander materialised in the elevator. The Aelf's gaunt face was amused.

'What do you want?' Hamir muttered.

'Her ladyship sent me with a message.'

'And?'

'She wants you to stop skulking and face your demons.' Alexander smirked. 'Good luck, Hamir.'

The ghost disappeared. The elevator stopped then began ascending. Reaching its destination, the glass door swished open. Hamir raised an eyebrow as he gazed into the hall of satin pillars where Alexander's corpse was displayed.

The big and ugly Aelf Glogelder was watching Gulduur Bellow work his magic. Both had their backs to the elevator and neither noticed Hamir's arrival.

Bellow was crouched before the box of thaumaturgic metal connected to Alexander's remains by a host of thin copper wires. In one hand, the giant held a stone bowl filled with blood which had undoubtedly come from his own veins. Using his large finger as a scriber, he drew spells of blood-magic onto the box. Hamir could see that each symbol caused the thaumaturgic metal to change its state and absorb the blood. Alexander's body jerked rhythmically, pumping clear fluid through the glass tubes that sprouted from his remaining organs and limbs. The fluid shimmered with energy as it disappeared down into the metallic hemispheres on the floor.

Glogelder moved a little closer to Alexander's remains. With grim fascination, he said, 'I've seen some things in my time, but this'll take some beating.'

'The day is young, Glogelder,' Bellow replied. 'But I take your meaning. This is a dark form of magic indeed. Usually forbidden to Thaumaturgists.'

'Needs must, eh?' Glogelder scratched his bald and pitted head. 'So the corpse is like a power stone, and you're giving it more power to stop those bloody monsters getting inside?'

'Close enough,' Bellow said. 'I have already bolstered the tower's defences, and now I am feeding energy into the portal.'

On the other side of Alexander's body, the space within the oval frame through which Clara and the Toymaker had emerged was already criss-crossed by jagged lines of magic.

'And when you've got the portal working, it'll take us into the Retrospective to look for your herd?'

'Once I've been given precise coordinates, yes. We can't exactly go searching the Retrospective blindly now, can we?'

With a shiver, Glogelder looked up at the ceiling as though he could see the hordes of wild demons outside.

'I only wish I knew how to activate those automatons down in the reception hall,' Bellow continued. 'They would make a handy addition to our party, don't you agree?'

'No arguments there,' Glogelder said. 'Are you sure you can't do something?'

Hamir cleared his throat and stepped inside the white satin pillars that ringed the operation. Glogelder looked at him, but Bellow continued his work.

Hamir said, 'The only way this tower and its sentries can return to *full* power is when Lady Amilee regains her higher magic – which won't be any time soon, or so she claims. She and her House are in … *symbiosis*, I suppose. Amilee has been a prisoner in her own home since she walked away from the Thaumaturgists.'

'And she'll die if she tries to leave,' said Glogelder.

'Leave, stay – it makes no odds in the end. Not for her.' Hamir shrugged. 'The Retrospective will find a way to enter this tower eventually. All we can do is buy ourselves some precious time, and let the Skywatcher worry about her fate.'

Still Bellow didn't turn from his work.

Glogelder frowned, looking Hamir up and down with a suspicious eye. 'I really don't like you very much. And I like even less that *our* fates are in the hands of a murderer.'

Hamir blinked, surprised by his own surprise. 'Have I done something to offend you?'

Glogelder hissed out a long breath and shook his boulder-like head. 'Do you even care about what's happening to the people around you? Or do you think you're an innocent victim of this situation?'

'Aren't we all?'

Glogelder loomed, his anger growing. 'There's no reason why Gulduur's people should help us, you know – not after the way they've been treated for centuries. Have you considered that?'

'What I've *considered*,' Hamir said dangerously, 'is that I do not have to stand here and answer to an Aelfirian … *whatever* you are.'

'Thief!' Glogelder snapped. 'Con man! Yeah, that's right – me and Hillem made a living by taking what didn't belong to us, and we've never done an honest day's work our lives. Until now. But we always knew what was right and wrong, and never once did we prey on those weaker than us – not like you and your kind.'

'Insightful.' Hamir denied an impulse to summon his necromantic magic. 'But how little you comprehend.'

'Oh, I don't claim to be clever,' Glogelder said, his meaty hands balling into fists, 'but I know that you're a lucky man. You're lucky that the rest of us made a friend of this one' – he jabbed a thumb at Bellow – 'and learned the truth about his people. You're lucky we're still standing beside you. And if *we* are lucky, the Nephilim will help us, and something good can come from your … *murder spree*.'

Hamir, in uncustomary fashion, was disarmed by this final rant. 'Perhaps you'd like to go and see Lady Amilee,' he said evenly. 'I'm sure you need to make plans for entering the Retrospective.'

Glogelder's cheek twitched but he didn't move.

'Going to see the Skywatcher isn't a bad idea, Glogelder,' said Bellow, finally turning from his work. 'Though I have to say, you know how to make a good point.' The giant's blue eyes flitted briefly to Hamir. 'I will call for you if I need help.'

Glogelder sniffed and nodded at the giant. Without a word, he marched past Hamir, shoulder-checking him on his way to the elevator. He had a final glare for the necromancer as the door slid shut and the elevator descended.

Hamir stared after him, rubbing his shoulder. 'You've made a friend, I see,' he said to Bellow.

'Glogelder is a little rough around the edges but I find him good company.' Bellow resumed drawing blood symbols onto the box of thaumaturgic metal. 'It's quite refreshing, don't you think, to hear someone talk with such open honesty?'

'Clearly you haven't spent enough time around Samuel,' Hamir muttered.

'I try to imagine how it must feel to be a creature of lower magic at this time. Candles in a gale. I try to imagine their fear. Is that empathy?'

'I suppose so.'

'They are so small and powerless in the face of what is to come, yet they find the will to marshal their fear and stand strong nonetheless. *That* is courage.'

'Perhaps.'

Bellow clucked his tongue 'A thousand years you've spent among humans, and yet you don't consider yourself one of them.'

The Nephilim sounded like a teacher talking down to a student. Hamir didn't care for how it made him feel.

'I wonder,' Bellow said, studying the necromancer, 'what should I call you? Simowyn, perhaps? Lord? *Father?*'

'Most people call me Hamir.'

'No, no, no – I don't think that name is sufficient. You are and always will be a monster of legend. I shall call you Progenitor.'

'As you wish.' Hamir resigned himself. This confrontation had been waiting happen from the moment Bellow first entered the tower. 'Tell me – do you believe that I received no punishment for my actions?'

'Oh, I'm sure you received a fitting sentence in the eyes of the Thaumaturgists. But who gave justice to the humans you killed?' Bellow dipped his finger into the blood and drew another symbol. 'We remember them, you know – our mothers. The Nephilim herd grew to almost a thousand over the centuries, but it is we elders – your original one hundred children – who carry the pain and torment and death that our mothers suffered to birth us. We hear their screams in our sleep.'

Hamir had no words, only cold memories.

'And now,' Bellow continued, 'Amilee tells me that your life and death are bound to me and my people.'

Hamir sighed. 'You expect answers from me.'

'Do you suppose that you owe the Nephilim no explanation?' Bellow paused in his work to look back disappointedly. 'We believed you were already dead. Can you imagine how disquieting it is to discover your creator lives, but to find him so much weaker than you? There were so many tales told about the Progenitor, of his greatness, of his power – all of them lies, it would appear.'

'I heard these tales,' Hamir admitted. 'And I hid the truth.'

'There's no place to hide now.' Bellow stood to his full ten-foot height, not facing Hamir but drawing a long breath as though to steel himself. 'I want to know why, Progenitor. *Why* did you create us?'

'I ...' Hamir's voice cracked. He bit back against old memories and the angry heat that flared inside him. 'There is nothing I can say that would not disappoint you.'

'But you *will* tell me anyway,' Bellow stated, raising the bowl of blood for Hamir to see. 'I will not open this portal until I have heard the truth.'

Lines of shining magic criss-crossed the oval frame, an incomplete spell. The almost childish defiance on the giant's face was as unnerving as it was unwavering.

'You were an accident,' Hamir said sadly. 'I tried to use dead time to resurrect the spirits of ... of comrades, friends – those I loved and believed in. I thought I could master the power, but I was wrong ... *so* wrong. I never meant for your mothers to die. I never meant to create the Nephilim—'

'I have no interest in listening to you excuse yourself,' Bellow said with a growl that emphasised his size and power. 'There is a path that led you to the creation of your children, whether by accident or not. Now, tell me your story, Progenitor. Tell me *why*.'

Fear came to Hamir then, threatening to drag him back into a time he had darkened from his mind long ago. 'The story is too long, complicated. We do not have the time to ... to discuss it now.'

The giant sneered. 'Truth or evasion?'

'Why can't it be both?'

Bellow stood statue-still, his stare frozen, as though contemplating whether or not to use his immense magic to torture more information from Hamir.

'You were right to say there is no place left to hide, but time is running out,' Hamir said solemnly. 'I swear I will tell you everything you wish to know once we have defeated Lord Iblisha Spiral.'

Hamir didn't know if the giant found sense in his words, or if he had never intended to carry out his threat – perhaps he was fearful of the truth, too – but mercifully, Bellow finally drew the last symbol of blood-magic upon the box of thaumaturgic metal and his spell was complete.

A distorted noise like glass shattering singed Hamir's nerves. The jagged lines of magic filling the oval frame blazed and imploded, leaving behind the shiny churning black surface of a portal.

'I will tell Marney and Clara that you are ready,' Hamir said shakily, grabbing at any excuse to leave the room. 'They will provide you with an exact destination for the portal.'

'I will not forget your oath, Progenitor.' Bellow's expression was unreadable, his eyes bright and large. 'Your day is coming. The Nephilim will have their reckoning.'

When Marney reached full awareness, she was surprised to feel free of pain. She opened her eyes a crack, blinking against the glare of the ceiling prisms. She was lying on a padded table, and someone had dressed her in black leggings and a dark blue jumper. On a matching table, Samuel's coat had been folded up next to a pair of black leather boots, along with a baldric of throwing daggers.

An Aelfirian face loomed over Marney, oddly heart-shaped, large green eyes filled with concern.

The empath managed a smile for Namji. 'The last time I saw you,' she said, her words croaking from a dry throat, 'I wanted to slap your face.'

'I was fifteen!' Namji laughed. 'And jealous that Van Bam was your boyfriend.'

'A long time ago now,' Marney said.

Namji helped her into a sitting position and passed her a glass of water. It was cold and refreshing on the empath's throat.

'How are you feeling?' Namji asked.

Marney felt a little groggy and stiff but said, 'Pretty good on the whole.'

'Your wounds are healed but I'm afraid you've got some scars.'

Marney shrugged and drained the glass. 'I'll add them to the rest.'

The time Marney had spent in Clara's mind, along with the search through Known Things, were still fresh to her, but the memories were somehow disjointed, out of sync. It would probably be a while before she could order them.

Marney felt Namji's sadness. The Aelf was looking at her with a serious expression. 'I'm so sorry about Van Bam.'

The empath controlled a wave of heartache. And regret. 'Working for the Relic Guild comes with risks that we all try to accept.'

Namji looked a little concerned by that response – suspicious, perhaps. 'All the same, I *am* sorry, Marney.' She wasn't just talking about Van Bam's death.

'Me, too.'

Marney recalled a run-down apartment above a bakery in the eastern district. Her emotional memories still clung to the warmth and happiness she had experienced there, shared with Van Bam – stolen moments of love during a time of hate. They had never officially ended their relationship after Van Bam became Resident, but ... how could they continue as lovers if Marney had to share him with the psychopath in his head, who saw, heard and *felt* everything he did?

Marney didn't know if she had ever really stopped loving Van Bam, or just ... learned to live with his absence. And she was sure he reciprocated. There had been moments over the years when Marney knew that Van Bam was watching her through the eyes on the streets, but he never invited her to the Nightshade – perhaps because he realised that she wouldn't have accepted. Gideon had stood between them, kept them apart, as he had always planned to do.

At least she had got to say goodbye to Van Bam in Known Things. And Denton. But ...

'I should've gone to Van Bam.' Marney whispered to herself. 'We could've stayed friends. Too late now.'

'Oh, I don't know about that,' said a man. Marney hadn't registered him entering the room but she sensed his emotions now – worry, fear, confusion. He approached Marney with a jug of water. 'Van Bam's not gone, remember.' He refilled her glass. 'I'm Hillem, by the way.'

'I know who you are,' Marney said, taking a sip. She might've been hiding in Clara's mind, but she had been conscious of what was going on around the changeling. Sometimes. She knew about Glogelder, too – and Gulduur Bellow. 'I take your point, Hillem. Clara's the Resident now, and I'm well aware who her spirit guide is. But I'm not sure how I'd feel about using her to mediate sweet nothings between Van Bam and me.'

'I hadn't thought of that,' said Hillem.

Namji pursed her lips. 'I worry that Clara's a little young to be Resident.'

'Again,' said Hillem brightly, 'remember her spirit guide has forty years of experience to draw on. I think Clara will do fine.' He appeared to mean what he was saying. 'She'll be a good leader, and you certainly wouldn't want to pick a fight with her.'

Marney studied him. He wasn't that much older than Clara himself yet he spoke with the confidence of someone who had decades of experience. His face was a perfect mask of charming certainty, betraying nothing of the anxiety that Marney could feel in him. In fact, if she hadn't been an empath, she wouldn't have known that he was trying to latch on to any form of hope that he could.

'You can see why he made a good con man,' Marney said to Namji. 'He can't possibly be as wise as he sounds.'

'He is, beyond his years,' Namji replied. 'Glogelder – not so much.'

Hillem laughed. 'Glogelder has got me out of more scrapes than I care to count.'

'As many times as your quick mind has saved him, I should imagine,' Namji said.

Hillem shrugged. 'Brains and brawn – it's a lethal combination.'

Marney didn't need empathic magic to know how Hillem felt about Glogelder. They were loyal, like family. No matter what happened, they would always be able to depend on each other. With a pang of nostalgia, Marney remembered when it had last been that way for the Relic Guild. And how it had all ended.

'Hillem,' said Marney, 'don't ever forget your friendship with Glogelder. Don't ever drift apart.'

'That's right – you'd be lost without me,' Glogelder said from the doorway. He entered the room, followed by Samuel, whose expression was as closed down and borderline angry as always. Glogelder grinned at Marney. 'And someone has to teach him how to talk to girls.'

Hillem laughed. 'Says the Aelf whose idea of romance is ten pints followed by a burping competition.'

'Oh, sure, but you should see me dance!'

Hillem shook his head at Marney. 'Two left feet,' he whispered.

Marney looked into Samuel's pale blue gaze.

'How are you feeling?' the old bounty hunter asked.

'Not bad,' Marney replied. She swung her legs over the side of the table and got to her feet. 'You know, considering we're all about to walk into the Retrospective.'

That statement chilled the mood in the room. Marney felt fear coming from the Aelfir but not from her fellow magicker. From him, only sadness.

'I thought maybe some of us could stay behind,' Samuel said. 'But it's only a matter of time before the wild demons get inside the tower.'

'Wouldn't make a difference if they couldn't,' Namji said. 'We'd go with you anyway.'

'Can't walk away from this now,' Hillem added.

Glogelder nudged Samuel with his elbow. 'Against our better judgement, of course.'

Samuel gave the smallest of smiles. 'Actually, I was thinking we could send Gulduur and Hamir by themselves.' Something close to genuine gratitude emanated from him. 'But I'm glad to hear we're still standing together.' Then his face became stony once again. 'Amilee's asking for us. The portal's working. It's almost time to leave.'

'Come on, then,' Glogelder said, his manner professional. 'No sense hanging around.'

'I'd like to talk to Marney alone first,' Samuel said. 'We'll catch you up.'

Respecting Samuel's wishes, the Aelfir left without a word.

Marney and Samuel stared at each other for a while. He was trying to protect his emotions behind the hard shell he always wore to keep people at arm's length. But he couldn't fool an empath. How like Samuel it was to know what he was feeling while being unable to express it. Marney remembered this man so well, but a gulf of forty years stood between them.

She grabbed the boots from the table. 'I heard you, you know,' she said as she put them on and fastened the buckles. 'Somehow, a part of me heard you telling the others that you wouldn't give up on me.'

Samuel struggled with words at first. 'I watched Denton and then you sacrifice yourselves to Fabian Moor to give the rest of us a chance.' He shrugged. 'I honestly thought I'd never see you again, Marney.'

But he couldn't express his joy for this reunion, Marney could sense. The fiery heartbreak of losing Van Bam burned too deep inside him. She took the baldric of throwing daggers and sat on the edge of the table, looking down at the slender blades.

'During the old days,' she said, 'Denton told me how you came to join the Relic Guild. You had a tough childhood – as tough as Clara's, I imagine. But I understood you better after hearing that story. It made me like you.'

'I always thought you were a pain in the arse.' Marney snorted a laugh and the ghost of a smile reappeared on Samuel's face. 'But I'm glad you're with me now.'

It was a grand admission by Samuel's standards. He sat next to her on the table and Marney felt as though she had deflated.

'I miss Denton, Samuel,' she said, resting her head on his shoulder. 'I miss Van Bam. I miss them all.'

Samuel held her hand. 'Me, too,' he whispered.

CHAPTER FIFTEEN

LORD OF LIES

The Retrospective was supposed to be the means to an end. Not the solution.

The scorched plains of dead time had opened onto yet another Aelfirian House. Through a great rent in the air, trees and fields and cities were pulled into the fiery, poisonous belly of the Retrospective. Countless wild demons slaughtered and fed upon creatures of lower magic, gathering steaming, bloody remains — raw matter, compost — from which new monstrosities would grow. The Aelfir could not hope to stand against this pandemonium, not even if they raised an army of a billion. The Retrospective was inexorable. And soon, the Lord of the Genii would augment its power to new heights with the First and Greatest Spell.

Fabian Moor stood on a hill of volcanic rock, watching, listening to the tumult of a dying House. Beside him, Mo Asajad also observed. Further down the hill, Viktor Gadreel had raised his hands to the spiteful acid sky, revelling in what he saw and heard. Unlike the hulking brute, Moor embraced no joy, for he had been listening at the Sisterhood of Bells; he understood the implications of his lord and master's words. Although they hadn't spoken of it, Moor knew that Asajad was as troubled as he.

We will grow and expand until the only state of existence is a House of blood and dead time, Spiral had said.

There had been a time when Moor had considered himself Spiral's closest confidant. He was certain that Spiral shared every aspect of his plans with him, and his faith in his Lord's methods had been complete. Moor's faith was now blemished by doubt.

How many Aelfirian Houses had Spiral devoured so far — five? Six? It was only the beginning; there would be no end to his pursuit. Not until the First and Greatest Spell had been ripped from the heart of the

Nightshade and the Retrospective had accumulated so much power it would absorb every House, every world and realm, every form of existence to create ... what?

What happens next? Moor wondered.

Before Spiral took the Sisterhood of Bells, he had opened the Retrospective on the Tower of the Skywatcher. He wanted Yansas Amilee to suffer, he had said; he wanted her to watch as the realms burned around her. Yet Spiral had shown no interest in discovering whatever plans the Skywatcher and the Relic Guild were trying to concoct. It seemed that he didn't care.

But Fabian Moor cared. And by the look on her face, so did Lady Asajad. Had Lord Spiral become complacent? Had Oldest Place damaged his mind beyond repair?

Eyes scouring the destruction of an Aelfirian House, Moor was irritated by Viktor Gadreel's childish revelry.

'Look at him,' Moor muttered angrily. 'Did he ever once stop to consider what he is witnessing?'

'You feel sympathy for the Aelfir, Fabian?' Although Asajad's tone was scalding, she had lost her supercilious edge and easy mockery. 'Has it not always been Lord Spiral's design to make them serve us?'

Moor studied her shrewdly. 'Serve *us*?'

They had to be careful. Never once had either of them been given reason to question Iblisha Spiral; and to do so now was dangerous. The Lord of the Genii had become the Master of the Retrospective. He and it were one. There was no telling where Spiral was, or what he could hear.

Choosing her words carefully, Asajad said, 'Spiral's symbiosis with the Retrospective is ... *ongoing*. I suspect there are many things in his new world that he is not yet able to control or see. Consider – perhaps he can only complete the process when he has the First and Greatest Spell.'

Moor looked at the hate and torture playing out on the horizon. In the sky, a flying demon dropped the two Aelfir it was carrying in its claws. Their bodies fell tumbling, screaming, into the writhing sea of monsters below. Gadreel bellowed a laugh at the spectacle.

'Then perhaps while our lord is preoccupied with this latest attack on the Aelfir, he is not listening to us,' said Moor.

Asajad regarded him like the predator she was. 'If you tell me your troubles, Fabian, I might tell you mine.'

'The Retrospective,' Moor said quietly. 'I always reasoned that it would be the weapon that brought the Aelfir to their knees. A deterrent for disobedience.'

'You and me both,' Asajad said. 'Billions of Aelfir will still fight for the Genii's cause. They will march in Spiral's name on the Higher Thaumaturgic Cluster, to a new war that would see him reclaim Mother Earth for his own. But it was not supposed to happen *this* way.'

'Is Spiral creating a new existence?' Moor added. 'The Retrospective will become the future of everything, he said.'

'If that is true, have you wondered what place we Genii will have in Spiral's new design?'

Moor looked out across the broken landscape as the Retrospective finished devouring the Aelfirian House and closed its mammoth maw. The raw blood and matter painting the land red heaved and expanded before Moor's eyes; and even as he watched, fresh demons rose from the red ground. The Retrospective had grown, and so had Spiral's army.

'I will tell you this,' Moor said to Asajad. 'I worry that our lord has no need for anyone now.'

Asajad made to reply, but then a figure materialised on the hillside between them. At first Moor feared it was Spiral himself, having overheard the conversation, bringing wrath and punishment to those who dared question him. But instead, a small, elderly Aelfirian man appeared.

Councillor Tal, the Ghoul, looked exactly as he had at the Sisterhood of Bells, except for his eyes. They had become large pools of deepest black.

'Lord Spiral requires your presence,' Tal said amiably.

Although the Aelf appeared calm and compliant, Moor could tell that behind those black eyes his mind and soul were screaming in agony. Spiral had turned Tal into a plaything, a servant, a whim, a shadow to follow him around. A spy?

'And where might our lord be found?' Asajad asked primly.

'In his great hall.' Tal pointed to something behind the Genii.

Tremors shook the ground. In the near distance, red and black rock cracked and split and collapsed into a gigantic hole, releasing noxious smoke and steam in blistering clouds. A great tower of obsidian rose from the hole with the roar of a thousand thunderstorms. Lightning struck its spire, igniting a shower of sparks. It radiated the power of higher magic and dead time. From all over the land, wild demons flocked to the tower, as though it were a beacon of salvation. At a leisurely pace, Tal the Ghoul followed the flow of monsters.

'Incredible,' Gadreel said, joining Moor and Asajad on the hilltop. He took a moment to admire the vision, clearly energised by what he saw. 'Our lord has *such* strength.' Excited, Gadreel set off for the tower.

Moor and Asajad paused for a moment before following him.

'I do not think Viktor shares our concerns,' Asajad said quietly.

'The fool is besotted,' Moor replied. 'Say nothing to him.'

The screams of dying denizens mingled with the ululations of the infect- ed – blood-chilling screeches caught somewhere between coughs and barks. A child's wail was cut off abruptly and Sergeant Ennis closed his eyes, shaking and hiding from the horror down on the street.

A little earlier, some thirty or more denizens had headed towards Ennis, fleeing through the night from the horde of virus victims chasing them along Resident Approach. The denizens were trying to reach the safety of the central district. Although some of them carried guns and the infected were only half their number, Ennis had known straight away that they didn't stand a chance, and he was unable to help them. And so the police sergeant had hidden, ducking inside a cobbler's shop, heading for the sanctuary of its rooftop.

Hunkered down behind a low wall, Ennis gripped his pistol tightly, waiting for the carnage to end, praying to the Timewatcher that he hadn't been noticed.

A new sound mingled with the cries and screeches: metallic footsteps clanging on stone. Ennis peered over the wall.

To his amazement, he saw an army of automatons charge into the fray. The silver plates on their breasts and faces shone beneath the moon- light. Eight feet tall, fifty of them at least, the automatons moved with grace. The infected, seeing no danger, sensing no flesh and blood in the constructs upon which they might feed, continued to focus their assault on the denizens. They made easy pickings for the huge metal hands that reached for them. Heads were crushed, necks snapped. With merciless efficiency, the automatons slaughtered the virus victims, including those among the denizens who had just been freshly infected.

Ennis watched, his heart pounding.

The surviving denizens – no more than ten – were herded together by the silver warriors. They formed a protective circle around the group, and the sound of the townsfolk's tears sent a shiver down Ennis's spine. He waited on the rooftop as the silver constructs escorted the survivors south towards the central district, leaving the dead behind on the street.

Ennis ducked down and gathered himself.

He didn't know where the automatons had come from but they were a welcome addition to those already fighting the infected. Apparently every statue in Labrys Town had been concealing a secret guardian; and when Ennis and Captain Moira activated the town's defences, the automatons had broken free of their stone shells to rise up and fight for those who had made it to the central district.

Once the automatons and the survivors passed out of sight, Ennis made his way down from the rooftop and onto the street. The clouds had cleared and Ruby Moon was but a red ghost in the cold, rising glare of Silver Moon. Sickened by a stench like rotting vegetables, Ennis picked his way through broken corpses lying on blood-smeared cobbles and continued his journey north along Resident Approach.

The air was still. The temperature dropped.

Labrys Town's worst nightmare had been realised. The virus had finally spread, becoming an epidemic in the north, south, east and west. It happened so fast! How many thousands – *tens* of thousands? – of denizens were already infected? How many bloodthirsty abominations now roamed the streets, looking for fresh meat to feed on? How many had suffered the full extent of the virus and now wandered aimlessly as mindless stone golems?

Ennis tried and failed not to think about it.

In his hand, he carried his police-issue pistol. Holstered at one hip was Long Tommy's strange gun, loaded with two bullets of thaumaturgic metal; on the other hip was sheathed the knife coated with the same metal.

From somewhere distant, the savage cough-barks of the infected echoed.

Twenty-five miles of straight road lay between the police head-quarters and the Nightshade. It would have been faster to travel by tram but much less inconspicuous. The lower regions of Resident Approach were full of businesses and stores, gardens and parks, taverns and eateries – usually an area full of life and activity. Now the violet glow of streetlamps shone down onto a deserted street still wet from the rains of Ruby Moon. Buildings were lightless. Dark, ominous windows like soulless eyes watched Ennis.

He passed an eye device fixed to the wall of a business centre, which glowed as an eerie female voice repeated a message over and over: *This is an emergency. All denizens will proceed to the central district …*

Ennis had already been travelling for a few hours, jogging along Resident Approach, ignoring the sweat running down his back in the cold air of Silver Moon. He recognised the area he had reached and judged that he had passed the midpoint of his journey. He pushed on, willing extra strength into his legs, cautious of every shadow, flinching each time a breeze stroked his damp skin.

According to the avatar, only one Genii remained in the Nightshade: Hagi Tabet. The others had left to free Lord Spiral from Oldest Place and didn't plan to return until their virus had wiped out the denizens. Ennis had one chance to save his townsfolk: get inside the Nightshade and kill the Resident. Only when Tabet had been removed could the distress signal Ennis had activated bypass her magical barricade and reach the realms outside the Labyrinth. With Tabet's death, someone, somewhere, would come to the denizens' aid. It almost sounded simple.

After a further hour of unhindered travel, Ennis felt his energy levels flag and hunger pains nauseated his stomach. He ducked into the first café he found; dark inside, tables and chairs upturned. His magic read the signs: the place was deserted of hiding denizens and lurking infected.

Pouring a glass of water and helping himself to a rice cake from a plate on the counter, Ennis sat to eat his simple meal and rest his aching legs and feet. He watched the street through the broken window.

Ennis reckoned that there were between three and four hundred automatons, thinly spread as they guarded all streets and alleys which led into the central district. But the army of constructs wasn't fighting alone. Thanks to Long Tommy and Captain Moira, the police and the underworld had formed an unlikely alliance to protect their town.

Tram-load after tram-load of food, weapons and ammunition – everything that could be salvaged in time from the warehouses on the south side – had been hoarded in the central district. The majority of denizens were well defended. Labrys Town's strange alliance couldn't do anything to save those stranded in the outer districts, but it might just ensure that hundreds of thousands of people survived the Genii's virus. However, in the end, if Ennis didn't succeed, all that would amount to nothing.

Ennis laid a hand on the holstered gun loaded with thaumaturgic bullets. Spiral was free. The Lord of the Genii had returned.

Finishing the rice cake and swigging the last of the water, Ennis headed outside. He buttoned up his coat against the chill and continued at a jog along Resident Approach.

He made good progress, occasionally hearing cries and shrieks coming from some distant location in the northern district. After half an hour or so, he stopped for another drink of water at an abandoned tavern. It was then that he heard a shout from outside.

'No! Give them back!'

It was a man. He was answered by the telltale cough-barks of the infected.

Sticking to the shadows, Ennis followed the voice as it continued to shout incoherently. He held off priming the power stone on his police-issue pistol lest someone notice its glow.

Before long he saw the man, standing outside a house on the opposite side of the street. The house's door had been smashed from its hinges. The man was frantic, acting more out of desperation than sanity as he looked up and down the street. Apparently he had other things on his mind than the four virus victims closing in on him.

Three headed straight towards him, shrieking as they loped along on all fours, more animal than human. The fourth appeared on the roof above him preparing to jump down on him.

Ennis thumbed the power stone into life and took aim.

His first shot missed but the second hit the rooftop monster in the chest. It collapsed and fell, hitting the ground head first and snapping its neck.

The man paid attention then.

He backed away as Ennis stepped onto the street. The pistol flashed with a low, hollow spitting sound and he took down two more infected with clean head shots. He hit the last in the shoulder. The bullet spun the monster and it bellowed with rage but kept on coming. By the time Ennis's remaining three bullets killed it, the monster had crashed into the man, knocking him to the ground.

The man kicked the corpse away from him and scrambled to his feet. Ennis scoured the area, listening for signs of more approaching infected while loading his pistol with metal slugs. Apart from some distant shrieks, there was nothing. Satisfied, he approached the man.

'My children,' he said, bordering on hysteria. 'They were taken. It broke down our barricades, killed my wife.' Tears filled her eyes. 'I-I couldn't stop it.'

'Calm down,' Ennis said gently. 'Were your children bitten?' He tensed, knowing that an affirmation would equal a death sentence. There was no cure for the Genii's virus.

'It wasn't the infected,' the man said. 'It was the Resident's demon. The Woodsman.'

'The *Woodsman*?'

'It just appeared,' the man wailed. 'Snatched my Daniel and Jade from their mother's arms. They're just babies!'

He cried freely, and Ennis's mind raced to the axe-wielding beast that served the Resident.

His magic nudged his attention and he noticed the single line of blood running from the cuff of the man's shirt, over his hand, dripping from his finger. Ennis's heart froze as his eyes found the rip in the man's sleeve and the bite on his arm. He could see the black veins of infection already stretching from the wound.

The man coughed and retched. 'What do I do?' he begged.

'I'll help you.' There was stone in Ennis's voice as he backed away. 'Do you keep any weapons in the house?'

'My wife has a pistol.'

'Go and get it. We'll find your children together.'

It broke Ennis's heart as a glimmer of hope appeared in the man's eyes. He retched again and then turned to enter the house. Ennis aimed his gun at the back of his head and fired.

The man fell dead without a sound.

Ennis dropped to his hands and knees and vomited up the water he had just drunk.

With a surge of willpower, he got to his feet and staggered on down Resident Approach. As if things weren't bad enough, the Woodsman was still loose in Labrys Town.

Moor remembered how powerful Iblisha Spiral had grown before the war, how he had taken the Pantheon of Thaumaturgists by storm and blinded the Timewatcher to his long game. His passions, his desires, his charisma and strength had given the Genii something new to believe in. But now Moor questioned his lord's sanity. Never had he known Spiral to revel in whims of such ... *grotesquery*.

In a great hall within the obsidian tower, Spiral sat on a grand throne made from smouldering red rock. On either side of the throne sat two creatures in a perpetual state of incineration providing dancing light. On the edges of the hall, beyond thick pillars of flesh, wild demons writhed and hissed from the gloom. Above, a grisly mosaic formed the ceiling: a host of Aelfir, crushed and broken, fused together, their tortured screams and wails dampened to mingle with the moan of a lonely wind.

The Genii presented themselves before their lord, kneeling upon the obsidian floor.

'Rise,' Spiral ordered testily. He was almost slouched on his throne, rubbing at the scar on his forehead as though he had a headache. At the foot of a flight of steps leading up to the throne stood Tal the Ghoul, docile and subservient, his large black eyes staring into nothing.

For the longest time, Spiral didn't speak. Gadreel appeared content to wait for as long as he had to, gazing around the hall, clearly impressed by what he saw. Moor and Asajad shared a meaningful look.

'Many believed that the Timewatcher learned to love humans,' Spiral said eventually. His voice didn't echo in the hall, but was instead absorbed into the hissing of the demons. 'They were mistaken.'

Moor frowned; Spiral seemed to be talking to himself.

'Generations pass, conditioning prevails, origins are forgotten.' Spiral's violet eyes met Moor's. 'Tell me, what became of Simowyn Hamir?'

It was Gadreel who answered. 'We are uncertain, my lord.' There was far too much eagerness in his voice and manner. The fool truly didn't comprehend what was happening before him.

'Explain,' Spiral said evenly.

'Hamir was able to hide from us,' Asajad said, before Gadreel could say anything further.

'Perhaps he had help from Lady Amilee,' Moor added, willing his lord to acknowledge the danger that he had yet to deal with properly.

'Perhaps he did,' Spiral said offhandedly. '*How* did Hamir hide?'

'He entered a room in the Nightshade,' Gadreel answered, 'the door to which we could not open, no matter what we tried. But *I* believe Hamir is still barricaded in that room. If he is important to you, my lord, then ... fear not.'

'Fear?' Spiral's gaze settled on Moor once again. 'I am disappointed. Did I not ask you to either bring Hamir to heel or kill him, Fabian?'

Moor bowed his head. 'You did, my lord.'

'With Simowyn Hamir at our side, we could have made allies of the Nephilim.'

'I apologise, my lord. I ... I thought Hamir to be a secondary consideration.'

Demons hissed. Tal the Ghoul's blank stare never wavered from the Genii.

'Forgive my lack of understanding, Lord Spiral,' said Asajad. 'The Nephilim were always a rogue element in your plans. Surely you have the power to control them or destroy them at will. What purpose would Simowyn Hamir serve?'

'It is not our place to question our lord,' Gadreel hissed. 'Show respect, Lady Asajad.'

'No, Viktor.' Spiral smiled thinly at Gadreel. 'The question is fair. The Timewatcher did so enjoy playing Her clever little games. She cursed Hamir. She cursed the Nephilim – *stitched* their lives together.' He gazed up at the grim mosaic of moaning Aelfir. 'I stole Hamir's thaumaturgy after it was drained from his body. I was able to master it enough to trap the Nephilim, incarcerate them, remove them from my way, but not enough to subjugate their loyalty. And to kill them ... Well, the Timewatcher made damn sure that death was a gift no one could give the Nephilim but the Progenitor.'

Moor and Asajad shared another look. Gadreel wore open confusion on his face.

Spiral studied their reactions. 'But of course, you wouldn't know. Our Mother kept many secrets from Her children. If Simowyn Hamir is reunited with his higher magic, he could claim control over his creations. However, if he dies then the Nephilim die with him.'

'If Hamir is important, my lord, I shall bring him to you,' Gadreel promised.

Spiral shook his head. 'There was a time when I hoped that Simowyn might join us. But on reflection, I suspect, after all these centuries, that he has been *poisoned* by the humans and would not switch his allegiance now. And I sorely doubt he will have forgiven me for what I did to him. As Fabian said, he is a secondary consideration. If Simowyn is hiding in the Nightshade, then he and the Nephilim will perish when I take the Labyrinth. It is better that way, safer.'

Spiral sat straighter on the throne, a sudden passion flaring in his eyes. 'But imagine it had been otherwise. Can you see the possibilities? The Nephilim are Thaumaturgists and humans merged together by the dark perversions of dead time – the greatest blood-magickers the realms have ever seen. And they could have *merged* with *me*. Who better to understand the Retrospective, to understand an entire *reality* founded on blood and dead time? Imagine what we could have created together. The Nephilim could have been my new Genii.'

New *Genii*? Moor thought.

Spiral radiated insanity, and Moor wondered if he had just received confirmation of his fears.

'You would have created paradises, my lord, and you still will,' Gadreel said – blinkered, blind and unquestioningly loyal. 'With or without the Nephilim, no one can stand in your way now. And we, the last of your most loyal Genii, will ever stand by your side.'

'Yes.' All expression drained from Spiral's face. 'That is a comfort to me, Viktor.'

Moor felt the hissing of the demons become a cold chill that blew through the hall.

Spiral rose from his throne, looking around with a disappointed expression, as though what he had created paled in comparison to what would be.

'What are your orders, my lord?' Gadreel asked eagerly. 'Shall we take another House for you?'

But Spiral was no longer listening. Immersed in and distracted by unknowable thoughts, he gazed unblinking into some far-off distance. 'Yet there is much I still cannot see,' he said to himself. He spread his silver wings. 'I must consult the skies.'

With a single beat of his wings, Spiral rose and became a column of swirling smoke that dissipated in the air. The hall, the shadowed demons, the mosaic of writhing torture, the tower itself dissolved to nothing, leaving Moor, Asajad and Gadreel once again standing on the scorched plains of the Retrospective.

Tal had remained behind. Spiral's spy. His black eyes, shining like the shells of beetles, stared at the Genii. He spoke with a genial, unconcerned tone.

'I am to instruct you in Lord Spiral's absence.'

CHAPTER SIXTEEN

OLDER MONSTERS

Clara stood outside the room she had woken up in, eavesdropping on Samuel and Marney's conversation.

'… I never really had much interest in Hamir,' Samuel was saying. 'In the old days, the others were always joking about his origins and secrets, but I don't think anyone would've guessed he was a Thaumaturgist.'

'Sort of seems obvious now, doesn't it?' said Marney.

In the hall outside the room, the Toymaker stood a few paces away from Clara, his many parts interlocked into a single automaton. He never spoke, merely followed Clara around, obeying Amilee's command to protect her. Clara supposed the Toymaker was her bodyguard now. Strange how things turned out sometimes.

'I'll tell you what I'm wondering,' Marney said. 'If Hamir is the Progenitor, and if Gideon's ancestor was a Nephilim … does that mean Hamir was Gideon's great-great grandfather or something?'

Clara heard something then, something she had never heard before: the light and open sound of Samuel laughing.

Marney sighed. 'But Gideon has gone for good now. And so has Denton.'

'Do you think their spirits made it to Mother Earth?' Samuel said.

'I hope so.'

You do know, Clara, Van Bam said in her mind, *that this counts as a breach of privacy.*

Clara smiled. *Can you honestly say you've never listened in on your agents in secret?* Van Bam didn't reply. *Thought so.*

If Clara felt anything strange about having the voice of a dead Resident in her head, it was that it *didn't* feel strange at all. Van Bam's ghost was a smooth, gentle presence, benevolent and calming at the back of her mind – nothing like the harsh, intrusive ghost of Gideon.

Ever since Clara awoke from Known Things, she had felt complete, as though she had been listening to Van Bam's voice her entire life. She didn't know why the Nightshade had chosen her, wasn't interested in discovering what qualities might make her a good Resident; she simply accepted that this had happened because it was supposed to.

Clara, said Van Bam, *given the circumstances, perhaps you should announce your presence to your agents. Lady Amilee and the others are waiting for us all.*

Oh, come on – aren't you just a little bit curious?

'So what have you been doing for the last forty years?' Samuel asked a little awkwardly, as though *having a chat* was an alien concept to him.

'I went back to university after the war,' Marney replied. 'I finished my degree and wound up teaching history.'

'I didn't know you were at university,' Samuel said.

'That's because you hardly ever bloody spoke to me,' Marney chided. 'I was in the middle of my studies when I joined the Relic Guild.'

'Bounty hunting felt like the only thing left for me.' There was a distant, remorseful edge to Samuel's tone. 'I wouldn't like to guess how many contracts I fulfilled over the years. I was damn good at it.'

'And they called you Old Man Sam,' said Marney. 'The shadow, the mystery. I knew it was you they were talking about whenever Old Man Sam was mentioned. You terrified the underworld, you know.'

'I kept waiting for Van Bam to get in touch, to let us know the Relic Guild was needed.' Bitterness laced Samuel's words now. 'But so much changed, and the call never came.'

'Until now.'

'I always wondered what I'd do if I ran into you on the street, Marney. But I didn't see you again until the night Fabian Moor returned.'

'I saw you a couple of times, and I hid,' Marney admitted. 'I wasn't sure how you'd react. It just never felt right to approach you. Does that make sense?'

'Yes.'

In the following silence, Clara considered the history of these two magickers. They had shared so many experiences; how could they have let themselves drift apart as they had?

As if plucking the thought straight from her mind, Van Bam said,

I think it was easier in the long run. The Relic Guild became a defunct organisation after the Genii War. The Timewatcher and the Thaumaturgists left. The doorways to the Houses of the Aelfir were taken away. We had simply lost our purpose, and perhaps with it our commonalities.

But to not even try? Clara said. *Friendship, camaraderie – surely that counted for something?*

If only we had remembered that, Clara.

'I used to hate that we had to keep so many secrets from each other,' Samuel said.

'At least we understand why now,' Marney said. 'Amilee's been plotting for a lot of years, gathering all the pieces that only made sense to her bigger picture.'

'But if only I'd known we'd be needed again, just to give me some ... *certainty*. After the war, I was lost without the Relic Guild.'

'I know how you feel. Though I think being an empath was far easier to hide than, say, being a changeling.'

Samuel huffed. 'And here we are, with a changeling as our Resident.'

Clara stiffened, her attention finely tuned now.

Ah, said Van Bam. *So this is what you have been waiting to hear.*

Clara gave a mental shrug. *It can't hurt to find out how they feel about me.*

Clara, I should warn you—

She shushed him as Samuel continued.

'I don't know what the Nightshade looks for in a Resident,' he said, 'but I certainly don't envy Clara. Do you?'

'Definitely not,' Marney replied. 'Especially not for being in charge of old magickers like us.'

'Do you think she's too young?' Samuel said, not unkindly. 'Do you really think she's up to it?'

Clara, you should understand by now—

Quiet, Clara snapped, her heart in her mouth.

Marney said, 'Without a doubt, Samuel, I believe Clara will be the greatest Resident Labrys Town has ever known.'

'You do?' Samuel was full of scepticism. 'Really?'

'No, of course not!' Marney announced, adding drily, 'But she's eavesdropping outside the door so I thought I'd make a good impression.'

Clara froze.

As I was trying to say, Van Bam said, clearly amused, *I would very much advise against trying to hide your presence from an empath.*

Feeling sheepish, Clara told the Toymaker to wait outside before slipping into the room.

Samuel stood facing the door, his arms folded across his chest, a frown on his face. Marney was sitting on the edge of the padded table, wearing a baldric of throwing daggers like a waistcoat and giving Clara a knowing look.

'She's certainly sneaky enough to be a Resident,' Samuel said.

Marney nodded.

Clara discovered that she had no words. She didn't know how the Resident was supposed to address her agents of the Relic Guild. She just felt like regular old Clara standing before them. Not that that had ever been an easy thing.

Any advice? she asked Van Bam.

Be yourself, Clara, he answered softly. *They are already on your side.*

Clara took a deep breath. 'I don't know what happens next,' she told them. 'But if we live through this, I won't let us become strangers in whatever home we have left to return to.'

Marney grinned. 'Well said.'

Samuel was staring intently into Clara's eyes, perhaps trying to see a sign that his old friend Van Bam was somewhere behind their sunshine yellow. 'Well, as you say, we have to live through this first.'

Van Bam laughed. *You know, I have yet to meet the person who could convince Samuel to see the positive side.*

Clara addressed Marney. 'Before we woke up from Known Things, you told me you'd thought of a way to find the Nephilim's prison in the Retrospective.'

'I have,' said Marney, her face serious. 'And it might be easier now the Retrospective's already here.' She slipped off the table and headed for the door. 'Let's go and see Gulduur,' she called back. 'We need to summon a demon.'

When Ennis caught up with the Woodsman, the demon was under attack.

Ennis hid behind a tree in a small grove that marked the end of the inhabited region of Resident Approach. Across the street from the last building in line – an open warehouse of some kind – fifteen or more virus victims rushed the Woodsman, coughing and barking, clambering over each other to be the first to reach the demon.

The stench of rotting vegetables reached Ennis's nose.

The Woodsman calmly placed the squirming sack it was carrying on the ground and stood astride it. The demon lifted its mighty wood-cutter's axe and faced the horde. The stitches holding together the gashes on its limbs strained as muscles bunched.

The first three infected were cut in half by a single sideways strike and the axe emerged from a torrent of blood, trailing red through the air. Undeterred by the fate of their fellow beasts, the rest of the infected attacked as one, desperate for a taste of the demon's flesh. But the Woodsman was preternaturally fast, freakishly strong, and the axe rose and fell, hacked and slashed, lopping off limbs and heads in a methodical routine.

Hidden behind the tree, Ennis observed with clenched teeth, his pistol clutched in a shaking hand. If the Retrospective came to Labrys Town, the threat of this virus would pale before the onslaught of many more wild demons like the Woodsman.

One of the infected managed to manoeuvre behind the fight and jump onto its foe's back, sinking long teeth into the Woodsman's shoulder. Unperturbed, the Woodsman continued dissecting the enemies before it. The beast on its back fell away, choking and writhing as though it had swallowed the deadliest of poisons. Its skin split and the meat under-neath liquefied, steaming and melting in but a moment to a pool of organic soup around a pale skeleton.

While the Woodsman made quick work of the final few infected, the sack between its legs opened and a young girl wriggled free. She looked to be around ten and was holding the hand of a boy a few years younger.

Daniel and Jade.

Ennis resisted the impulse to call to them as they fled from the Woodsman in their nightclothes, bare feet slapping through the viscous puddle left behind by the poisoned virus victim. But the Woodsman, with no enemies left to fight, saw the children trying to escape and caught up with them in a few long strides. It bundled the pair back into the sack, ignoring their tears and screams.

Feeling sick, Ennis remembered Long Tommy's pistol holstered at his side. He doubted regular ammunition would have any effect on the Woodsman, but should he use one of the thaumaturgic bullets in an attempt to kill the monster and save the children?

Torn, desperately clinging to the greater goal of his mission, Ennis did nothing but watch the Woodsman throw the sack over its shoulder and continued northwards, carrying the axe in its free hand. Only when the demon had disappeared into the unlit gloom did Ennis summon the courage to leave his hiding place and follow.

Buildings and streetlamps were soon left behind as the desolate, most northerly region of Resident Approach stretched ahead. Even in normal times no denizen lingered in this area, as though the street itself had become a forbidden zone, a bridge into unknown and dangerous places. There were no shadows to hide in and Ennis felt naked in the cold gleam of Silver Moon.

Before long, the street narrowed and the tramlines converged into a single track. The street began to dip, cutting into the ground and eventually levelling out like a valley floor, flanked by sheer walls fifteen feet high. At least the walls provided some cover.

The Woodsman, the Resident's *pet*, was obviously heading for the Nightshade, too. There was no chance Ennis could get ahead of it now; he would just have to keep his distance and figure out a way to deal with the demon when the time came.

He picked his way through an area of stone debris scattered across the cobbles. The remnants of the statues of past Residents, he realised, broken and crumbled to reveal the automaton sentries beneath. Amidst the debris sat spherical eye devices, glowing with a violet light as the woman's voice again told the denizens to evacuate to the central district.

Clearing the debris, Ennis stuck close to the wall, continuing as fast as he dared. He only slowed when he caught movement ahead.

Resident Approach ended at a high wall. Beyond it, the gigantic black cube of the Nightshade rose above the street, mysterious and ominous beneath Silver Moon. It was by far the largest building in Labrys Town. Ennis had been this close to the Nightshade on several occasions, normally to supervise the deliveries of cargo that until recently came through the portal in its forecourt. But he had never been inside it.

A tunnel in the end wall led to the Nightshade's forecourt. Ennis watched as the Woodsman carried the sack into it and was almost immediately swallowed by darkness.

The demon's reek of decay and hopelessness carried on the breeze as Ennis approached the tunnel. He checked the way was clear and then crept inside. The walls were slick, dripping with moisture. Nearing the end of the tunnel, Ennis remained hidden and looked out onto the forecourt. To one side, the Resident's black tram sat on its tracks. The south wall of the Nightshade served as a vast backdrop, its dark stone decorated in places with a labyrinth design.

Ennis froze, holding his breath as the Woodsman came into view. It stood before the vast wall on the other side of a line of evenly spaced pedestals, upon which eyes sat and glared with pale light. With the sack still over its shoulder, the demon stepped towards the Nightshade. Shadows stretched from the wall, rising up like a wave, but they reared away from the Woodsman as though reluctant to receive an unwanted guest. Finally, perhaps bidden by the Resident, the shadows descended. The demons didn't flinch as they engulfed him. When they receded, the Woodsman and the children were gone.

Ennis steadied his fear, recalling the words of the avatar. *You cannot enter the Nightshade unless the Nightshade wants you inside. Despite the influence of the Genii, I'm confident the Resident's home will have retained enough of its sentience to recognise a friend.*

Confident? Discovering if the Nightshade would let him inside or not didn't bother Ennis. But he was terrified of what happened either way once he found out.

Wishing his legs would stop shaking, Ennis left the tunnel. The light of the eyes glared from their pedestals as he passed them. He sent a silent prayer to the Timewatcher as the shadows of the Nightshade rose.

In the Tower of the Skywatcher, the group had congregated in the room where Alexander's corpse was energising the tower's defences to keep the demons of the Retrospective outside. For now.

With Amilee on one side of her and Samuel on the other, Clara watched, nervous and fascinated. Marney and Bellow had entered the circle of twisted white satin pillars where the cadaver was displayed and were preparing to summon a demon. Behind Clara, Namji, Hillem and Glogelder kept their distance, unsure and afraid. Hamir skulked at the back of the room.

The Toymaker guarded the door, under instructions to ensure the necromancer didn't try to slip away again. Clara had already sent the automaton out once to find Hamir, who seemed determined to put off facing the judgement of the group for as long as possible; but there was no time left to accommodate whatever shame the former Thaumaturgist was feeling.

Marney sat cross-legged on the floor, surrounded by the wet heartbeat-like sound of Alexander's body pumping blood-magic around the tower. Her teeth gritted, she was using one of her throwing daggers to carve some kind of sigil into the skin of her forearm.

'I'm not convinced this is a good idea,' said Amilee. The Skywatcher's tired face was creased with concern. She looked around the room as if fearful that a horde of wild demons might storm her tower at any minute. 'You understand what you are attempting to do, Gulduur?'

'Please be quiet,' Bellow replied. He didn't speak with disrespect or chagrin; he simply required silence in which to concentrate. With his hand painted red from a fresh cut on his palm, the Nephilim was gently stroking the surface of the dark portal within its oval frame, barely touching it.

'I hope this works,' Samuel muttered.

The silence that followed was broken only by the noises coming from the corpse.

When Clara, Samuel and Marney joined the group earlier, Bellow highlighted a problem heading towards those without thaumaturgic skills. Even if creatures of lower magic could traverse the Retrospective while bypassing legions of wild demons; even if they were able to survive the blistering, acidic environment; even if they could somehow adapt to breathe an atmosphere of purest poison and hate – even then, the chaos of dead time would still crush their minds and pervert their bodies until it left behind nothing more than savage beasts. To enter the Retrospective was to invite a fate worse than death. Dead time was corrosion to lower magic, Bellow said; rust for the soul.

Each agent of the Relic Guild had taken turns to stand before Bellow as he drew glyphs and blood-magic wards upon their stomachs. Using a bowl filled with his own blood and whispering words too fleeting to catch, the Nephilim cast the spells that would protect them all from the damnation of the Retrospective.

'What is dead time, anyway?' Glogelder had mumbled when Bellow finished painting on him.

Clara had taken her place before the giant after Glogelder, raising her dark grey top to reveal her stomach. Kneeling in front of her, Bellow had begun his work with a surprisingly light touch.

When no one replied to Glogelder's question, Clara had looked at Amilee and said, 'I think we're all curious about the answer to that one.'

The Skywatcher had considered for a moment, as though thinking of a way to explain a concept far beyond the understanding of most.

'Time has many forms,' she said eventually. 'Its *unused* substance can be manipulated – *abused*, some might claim – to create great wonders. Known Things, for example, or the Great Labyrinth itself. But the creatures of higher magic who can use time in this way are few.'

'The Timewatcher and Spiral,' Samuel said.

'And me, to lesser effect.' Amilee made a gesture that encompassed her tower. 'Manipulating unused time to create my slipstream stripped me of everything, and perhaps that will help you comprehend how dangerous it is. However, *dead* time, put simply, is time that has been torn and damaged. It can be harvested from a specific era where many terrible things occurred. In the Retrospective's case, the Genii War.

'Every atrocity committed during the war – every crime, every death, every betrayal, all the rage and hatred and heartache – was harvested by the Timewatcher and used as the founding stones of the Retrospective. Dead time is more difficult to master than anyone in this room could possibly imagine.' Amilee had aimed a hard, accusing glare at Hamir. 'Am I right?'

All eyes besides Gulduur Bellow's turned to the necromancer. Hamir faced the group with the same unknowable indifference he used for every situation.

'Dead time is a volatile and unpredictable substance.' His tone had been genial, as unreadable as his face. 'Trust me, the less you know about it, the better. Nothing good can come from its use.'

'Oh, I don't know about that,' Glogelder said happily. 'You're forgetting our new friend here. He and his people might just save all our skins – even yours, if you're lucky.' He grinned unkindly at Hamir.

Hamir had raised an eyebrow, perhaps understanding that while the Toymaker was escorting him to the room, the rest of the group had been discussing him and his relationship to the Nephilim.

Bellow had smirked at Clara as his deft finger drew around her navel. 'I don't know about you, Clara, but I think Glogelder makes an excellent point.'

His artwork done, the giant completed his spell by blowing whispered words onto the glyphs and wards on Clara's skin. She shuddered as the blood dried instantly. Marvelling at the intricate pattern, she confirmed that the spell would remain active if she changed into the wolf before lowering her top.

Bellow had then painted protective spells on the remainder of the group – including Hamir, in what was an awkward moment to say the least, but one that Glogelder relished nonetheless – before standing to his full height and aiming the shining blue orbs of his eyes at Marney. 'My spells will count for little if we have to travel into the Retrospective without a guide. Come. Tell me about this demon you wish to summon.'

Now, as Marney carved the sigil into her arm, her face a mask of concentration, Bellow waited, feeling the portal's surface with his bloodied fingertips. The others watched in a silence that pressed down on Clara.

The heated copper wires that had punctured Alexander's exposed brain sizzled organ tissue and a trail of smoke coiled into the air.

Bellow had connected the portal to the Retrospective outside. He claimed to have opened it just enough for Marney's summons to enter the House of dead time and find the demon she was looking for, but not enough for the host surrounding the tower to come pouring through. Nevertheless, Samuel was ready with his ice-rifle. Glogelder and Hillem had drawn their pistols. Namji, her trust in the Nephilim's magic apparently overcoming her apprehension, stood alongside Lady Amilee, her crossbow hanging from her belt. The Toymaker remained by the door, guarding Hamir.

Clara wondered if she should turn into the wolf as a precaution, but Van Bam told her, *It is important that the Resident exhibit confidence even if she does not feel it. I would advise remaining human. For the time being.*

Marney gasped and dropped the dagger. 'That's it,' she hissed. 'It's here.'

As quick as a striking snake, Bellow's hand dived into the portal. The blackness encompassed his arm to the elbow. The stench and screeches of wild demons filled the room and the group tensed as one. Bellow grabbed hold of something, grimacing as he struggled with it. A moment later, he dragged a small, wriggling form through the portal and threw it onto the floor.

As the portal closed and the tumult disappeared, Marney jumped to her feet, rubbing at the bloody sigil on her arm, backing away as Samuel, Hillem and Glogelder aimed their guns at what looked like a mewling child at Bellow's feet.

Dressed in only a loincloth, the demon manifested as a boy of around five or six years of age. But when it stopped whining and climbed to its feet, its true monstrous form was revealed.

Glogelder swore.

Its fingers were tipped with black talons. Sharp, glass-like teeth gnashed the air. The demon's blood-red eyes, veined with black, bulged as it hissed at Marney accusingly.

This was not the first time the empath and this demon had met.

On the night Clara joined the Relic Guild, she and Samuel had gone on a mission to save a man called Charlie Hemlock. Hemlock was one of Fabian Moor's human henchmen, and he had used Clara as bait to trap Marney, which was how this whole sorry situation began. But prior to Marney falling foul of the trap, she had summoned a demon to separate Hemlock from his master, thus buying the Relic Guild some time to rescue and question him. And now Marney had summoned that same demon once more.

The Orphan, Van Bam said.

Glogelder swore again as the demon's forked and surprisingly long tongue darted from its mouth and lashed the air.

'What a curious and disgusting little wretch,' Bellow said. With thumb and forefinger he picked the Orphan up by the skin on the back of its neck, holding it at arm's length. He chuckled at the talons swinging ineffectually for his face.

Hillem stepped in for a closer look. 'And you've had dealings with this thing before?'

'It's a complicated relationship,' Samuel said, glancing at Marney. 'Some wild demons are older than the Retrospective.'

'They inhabited the Nothing of Far and Deep,' Amilee explained, watching the Orphan thrash and hiss in Bellow's grasp. 'A strange phenomenon, the explanation for which is old enough to have been forgotten.' The others didn't notice, but Clara – and Van Bam – caught the hard and meaningful glance Amilee gave Hamir. 'Wild demons were a problem for Labrys Town long before the Retrospective came and gave them a new home.'

'And this one can lead us to the Nephilim's prison?' Hillem asked.

'With a little luck,' Marney said. She cleaned away the blood on her arm with a cloth Namji had given her. 'The Orphan is more intelligent than your average demon. Gulduur, can you bring it to me?'

Marney sat on the floor again, and Clara could tell by her expression that she was summoning her empathic magic. By this time the Orphan had given up struggling, hanging limp and pathetic as Bellow placed it down in front of Marney.

Earlier, the empath had explained that during her previous experiences with the Orphan, she and it had formed a strange kind of emotional bond. The demon didn't emote with feelings but with shapes and colours that Marney's magic was able to decipher; and she came to understand what symbols would gain the Orphan's attention, especially when made with blood – its favourite kind of food. Evidently, the strange connection between magicker and demon had been made again. The Orphan froze, staring at Marney, and they began a silent but empathic conversation.

I never it realised until now, said Van Bam, *but Marney must have become a vastly accomplished empath to use her magic for summoning demons, and to make a copy of her mind inside yours. Surpassing even Denton's powers, perhaps – and that, Clara, is truly saying something.*

Clara shivered, wondering how it must feel to have the emotions of a wild demon in her head.

'It's frightened,' Marney announced. 'But not of us.' She was studying the Orphan's red-and-black-veined eyes. 'It's frightened of something that's happening to the Retrospective. A change ...' Marney looked as though she was struggling to decipher the demonic emotions. 'It's Spiral. He has ... mixed? No – *merged* with it. Spiral *is* the Retrospective?'

'Just as we feared,' Amilee muttered bitterly. She clenched her fists. 'Time is running out. It won't be long before Spiral devours the Labyrinth and claims the First and Greatest Spell.'

'I think that's the polite way of saying hurry up,' Glogelder said to Marney.

'What of my people?' Bellow asked, a demanding edge to his tone. 'Does this thing know where they are?'

'All of you, give me a minute,' Marney snapped.

A long, tense moment passed before Marney leaned back, narrowing her eyes at the Orphan.

'I might have something,' she said uncertainly. 'The Orphan is talking about a secret place. It's ... it's the wild demons – they're afraid of it. They steer well clear of the area, but ... but it's a hiding place? Somewhere Spiral hides? Keeps hidden? Can't see?' Marney rubbed her forehead. 'I'm not quite sure how to translate the emotions, but I think the Orphan's saying the demons are frightened of it because it's ... *good*?'

The Orphan made a mewling sound.

'That would make sense,' Bellow said, his large face expressing pride. 'The Nephilim would be an abrasive anomaly to something as monstrous as the Retrospective.'

'It might be the prison,' Samuel said. 'What else does the Orphan say, Marney?'

'This secret place seems to be the only area that dead time can't re-cycle.' Marney leaned closer to the demon. 'It holds a power that the Retrospective can't destroy.'

Van Bam said, *Considering the curse the Timewatcher placed on*

Hamir and the Nephilim, it would appear that Marney has discovered our destination.

'It has to be them,' Clara said aloud.

Amilee nodded in agreement.

Bellow straightened. 'Can this wretch lead us to my herd?'

'Oh yes,' Marney replied, raising an eyebrow at the Orphan. 'But we can't trust the little bastard. It'll try to escape as soon as we enter the Retrospective.'

Hamir cleared his throat, stepping forward and engaging with the conversation for the first time. 'Gulduur could bind the demon to us.'

'Indeed I could,' Bellow replied.

Hamir placed a hand on his stomach, as though the blood-symbols were irritating his skin.

Clara wasn't sure that being bound to a wild demon was a good idea but she didn't air her feelings, watching in silence as Bellow crouched, grabbed the Orphan and held it face down on the floor. With the blood already on his free hand, the giant scribed blood-magic onto the back of the demon's head. The Orphan thrashed and hissed, powerless in the Nephilim's grasp; and when Bellow had finished his binding spell, it sat on the floor, shoulders slumped, a murderous scowl on its face.

'No running away for you,' Bellow said. He was talking to the Orphan but looking at Hamir. He picked the demon up and sat it on his shoulder, then motioned for Marney to join him before the portal. 'Now then, little monster, tell my friend how to find this secret place you fear.'

As Marney began questioning the Orphan once again, translating her findings to Bellow in a quiet voice, a ripple of apprehension passed through the rest of the group. The final journey was about to begin and the Relic Guild was looking to its Resident.

Any advice? Clara thought to Van Bam.

Be true to yourself. Be true to your friends.

Clara felt a thrill of fear and excitement. 'We know where we're going, and we know what we have to do.' She was surprised by the confidence in her voice, 'Any questions?'

'Only one,' said Glogelder. 'Is it too late to go home?'

Hillem chuckled at the big Aelf. Namji cracked a smile, and Samuel shook his head.

Amilee expressed nothing but sadness. 'My friends, I have done all I can to ensure the future is uncertain. What happens next is up to you.'

Hamir, still standing apart from the group, was staring at the floor.

'We have our destination,' Bellow announced.

With Marney beside him and the Orphan sitting unhappily on his shoulder, the giant faced the group. Behind him, the surface of the portal lapped in agitated folds.

'Lady Amilee,' Bellow said, 'you are a trickster and a master manipulator, and I haven't forgotten the promises you made me. Nevertheless, once my herd is free, *I* promise that the Nephilim will return to release you from *your* prison.'

The Skywatcher inclined her head. 'I have one or two tricks left up my sleeve, Gulduur. But I hope to see you again some day.'

'Perhaps then you will show my people the road that leads to the Sorrow of Future Reason.'

Amilee smiled, not quite amused. 'A promise is a promise, Gulduur.'

Bellow looked at Clara. 'If it pleases the Resident, I think it is time to leave.'

'I'm not sure *pleases* is the right word, but ... let's go,' Clara replied.

'Come on, sunshine,' Glogelder called to Hamir. 'You're the star of this show.'

Hamir hesitated, his eyes averted, before being encouraged towards the portal by the Toymaker.

Do not forget that Hamir is still your agent, said Van Bam, *regardless of his crimes.*

Clara looked the necromancer up and down. 'Are you ready to do the right thing?'

Hamir's face turned sour. 'Clara, please tell your *bodyguard* that I no longer require a chaperone. And, by all means' – he gestured to the portal, as though to remind her exactly where they were heading – 'do change into the wolf.'

THE FIRE OF THE NEPHILIM

In the Nightshade, Samuel and Van Bam watched Hamir, who was sitting at his desk in his laboratory, brushing a clear, sterile liquid onto a power stone. Working under a magnifying glass, the necromancer's hands were steady as he used a small brush with thin, finely cut hair for the delicate work. Every so often the liquid sparkled with the iridescence of magic.

Fabian Moor had escaped. Macy had been infected with his virus. Nobody spoke of it but they all knew there was no cure for the Genii's disease, no hope for Macy, wherever she was. But there was hope for Denton *if* the Relic Guild could get to him in time; *if* they could find where Moor had taken him. At that moment, as far as anyone knew, the old empath was only a victim of kidnap. How long before that changed?

Samuel could feel his hands shaking with anger and desperation. Beside him, Van Bam was keeping his emotions hidden behind a mask of perfect calm. Marney was in her private chambers preparing for the coming hunt, as was Gideon. And Hamir, maddeningly, was taking the customary slow and methodical approach that he applied to all things. The concept of urgency was wasted on him.

Checking an impulse to shout, *Hurry up!* at the necromancer, Samuel huffed his impatience and said, 'How much longer, Hamir?'

'You are about to go hunting for a Genii,' Hamir said, without looking up from his work. 'I rather think that precaution takes precedence over haste in this situation, yes?'

Samuel was about to retort but Van Bam stopped him.

'I understand how you feel, Samuel, but I have to agree,' he said softly. 'And it is not just Hamir we are waiting for.'

The illusionist was right, though Samuel was hardly in the mood to admit it. Earlier, Samuel had gone to Denton's chamber in the Nightshade and found one of his hairs, which he placed inside the spirit compass. The device was in Samuel's coat pocket now, his hand closed around it. He could feel the ticks of the compass needle as it turned around its face, confused, struggling to lock on to Denton's spirit. Until it did, the Relic Guild had no idea where to begin their search. Samuel refused to acknowledge that the spirit compass might be confused because Denton was already dead and consequently no longer had a spirit to lock on to.

'Fine,' Samuel snapped, and he began tapping the heel of his boot, willing *everything* to happen quicker.

'So glad we're on the same page,' Hamir said as he continued to brush the power stone.

Samuel glared at the back of his head.

He had always been unnerved by Hamir's laboratory. The glow lamp on the desk was barely bright enough to lift the shadows. Papers were strewn chaotically among contraptions of black, twisted metal and glass tubes passed fluid from one jar to another. Shelves were crammed with books bound in cracked leather and bottles filled with dark substances only Hamir could identify. The room carried the sickly sweet smell of chemicals, along with the underlying scents of dust and age. On the desk, Amilee's leather-bound book lay open, filled with the secrets of higher magic written in the language of the Thaumaturgists.

For more generations than anyone could remember, Hamir had served the Nightshade. His laboratory held secrets that Samuel didn't want to know and probably wouldn't understand if he did. It contained the unknown history of a necromancer.

The spirit compass ticked in Samuel's hand and his impatience boiled over again.

'What's that bloody power stone for, anyway?' he demanded.

'You will see.' The magical liquid shimmered as Hamir dipped the brush. 'And I'd have thought by now that you would trust me to know what I'm doing, Samuel.'

'Like you knew what you were doing with Moor's prison?'

'Samuel, this does not help,' Van Bam said.

'Actually, he raises a valid point.' Hamir peered more closely through the magnifying glass. The power stone glinted in the dim light. 'Higher magic is by no means infallible. I can't say for sure why the prison failed, but I think it likely that Moor simply exploited some flaw I had missed. And that is to my regret.'

'No one blames you for what happened to Macy and Denton,' Van Bam said.

Samuel wasn't sure he agreed, but Hamir was uninterested in either man's opinion.

'Of course, there is the possibility that Moor *wanted* to be captured – that he always knew a method of escape.'

'For what reason?' Van Bam asked.

'Perhaps to catch the right person.'

'Denton?' Samuel said.

'It would make sense,' Hamir replied. 'If I were Moor, believing that I could extract the secrets of the Nightshade from a magicker of the Relic Guild, then I would test my theories on the oldest and wisest among us.'

'Surely that's you,' Samuel pointed out.

'Hmm.' Hamir paused in his work, considering. 'Nevertheless, Denton would be a fitting second for Moor's needs. And if the Genii knew he was going to be captured, it would explain why he relied on creatures of lower magic to continue his work.' He applied the brush to the stone again. 'But this is only supposition. Tell me, are you concerned that Gideon will be leading the hunt for Moor?'

Samuel shrugged. 'At this stage, we need everything we've got.'

'Quite,' said Hamir. 'However, if Gideon is preparing for a fight, Samuel, then his *blood* will be *up*. You don't need me to remind you how dangerous he is, do you?'

Van Bam looked concerned, as well he might. But the illusionist had only ever heard stories about Gideon, whereas Samuel remembered him from the time before he became Resident, when he was an agent of the Relic Guild working the streets of Labrys Town. Gideon's blood-magic had made him powerful and unpredictable, and Samuel had seen him use it to do terrible things.

'Samuel.' Hamir's voice was laced with warning. 'I would advise you to follow orders without complaint. Hold your tongue and give Gideon no reason to be angry.'

'What about you, Hamir?' said Van Bam. 'Are you not coming with us?'

'Someone has to remain at the Nightshade. To bolster its defences, you understand, in the event that none of you … return.' Hamir placed the brush down and blew on the power stone. 'Now then, let's see what we can do about picking up the pieces of this catastrophe.'

As Hamir opened a drawer in the desk, the spirit compass gave a solid *click* in Samuel's hand. Fishing it out of his pocket, he saw that the needle had fixed on a southerly direction. The compass had found Denton's spirit.

'Got him!' Samuel said triumphantly, showing the compass to Van Bam.

'Excellent timing,' Hamir said.

The necromancer pulled a pistol in an old brown leather holster from the drawer. He laid it on the table and drew the pistol. Samuel had never seen one like it before. It had two short barrels and two triggers, blocky and heavy-looking, longer and fatter than Samuel's revolver.

Hamir clicked the freshly painted power stone into its housing behind the double barrels. 'I've taken the precaution of charming the stone so only a magicker can activate it. We cannot afford to waste the ammunition it will hold.'

When Hamir passed it over, Samuel thumbed the power stone and it whined into life, but instead of glowing violet the stone shone red. The weapon was as heavy as it looked.

Hamir produced two bullets from the pocket of his suit jacket. As fat as rifle slugs but not as long, the bullets were silver, polished to an almost mirror finish.

'Thaumaturgic metal?' Van Bam said.

Hamir nodded. 'I reasoned that the order for Fabian Moor's execution would come at some point so I prepared these bullets for the occasion. Unfortunately, there isn't time to make more. You have two shots, Samuel – two chances to kill a Genii.'

Deactivating the power stone and cracking the pistol open, Samuel slid a thaumaturgic bullet into each barrel. 'They'll definitely work?' he asked, snapping the barrels shut.

'Yes, according to this.' Hamir tapped Amilee's book. 'But then again, I was certain that Moor's prison would work. As I said—'

'Nothing is infallible.'

'I would recommend a head shot, to be as certain as possible.' Hamir passed Samuel the pistol's holster. 'Happy hunting, gentlemen. I hope to see you again.'

Marney had wrapped herself in magic, deadening every emotion inside her. Except anger. And hate. Those she kept alive like smouldering coals waiting for the wind that would fan the flames of an inferno.

She sat on the bed in her private chamber in the Nightshade, staring at the baldric in her hands and the twelve slim silver throwing daggers it held. She didn't believe that the daggers would have much effect on a Genii, but they reassured her nonetheless; and not just because of the sense of security that came with being armed.

The baldric had been a gift from Denton, shortly before they went searching for the Library of Glass and Mirrors. It almost felt as though she was taking a slice of Denton's confidence with her on the hunt for Fabian Moor.

Marney put the baldric on and fastened it. A comfortable fit, like wearing a waistcoat. She checked herself in the dress mirror, noticing the hollow look in her eyes. Marney knew that if she eased her magic in the slightest, she would succumb to grief and desperation. She would feel lost without the wisdom and guidance of her mentor.

A soft *click* filled the air. The outline of the door appeared on the maze-covered wall and swung open, and Gideon stepped into the chamber. Immediately, Marney had to block the wash of emotions he radiated. None of them was positive.

Gideon's sunken eyes stared at the empath for a moment. 'Lady Amilee has sent a message to the Nightshade.' His voice was detached, somehow, distant. 'The Skywatcher had some ... *encouraging* news. The Timewatcher's armies have begun a mass assault on the Genii. Amilee expects victory over Spiral within the next few days. It seems the war is almost over.'

Marney felt nothing about the news but recalled the words of the mysterious Aelf known as the Ghoul. The Last Storm, he had called it;

a synchronised operation to invade every last enemy House and Genii stronghold simultaneously.

'Of course, celebrations will have to wait until we tie up this loose end of ours.' Gideon looked Marney up and down. 'Are you ready to leave?'

Marney tried not to look at Gideon; at the savage, almost animalistic expression on his face. She noticed that the Resident's scarred hands were covered in symbols and glyphs written in dried blood: a sure sign that he had been cutting himself. Preparing to join the hunt.

'I replied to Amilee's message, informing her of our situation, but she has not responded. Strange, don't you think?' Gideon stepped closer to Marney, and only her magical apathy kept her from backing away. 'Tell me something – during your mission for Lady Amilee, did you and Denton discover anything that might be helpful to us now?'

'I ...' Marney shrugged. 'I don't know.'

Gideon's expression was dangerous. 'Oh, I understand that Amilee swore you both to secrecy, but I think we can agree that everyone's plans have taken a sharp left turn.' His voice became a predatory purr. 'Tell me what you discovered.'

'No, I mean ...' Marney faltered 'I really *don't* know.'

'You believe you're being loyal, is that it?' Subtle anger, barely contained, heightened the threat of Gideon's presence. 'Have you considered that you might know something which will help us save Denton and kill a Genii?'

'You don't understand, Gideon. Denton ... I think he blocked my memories. Or took them away. I just can't remember what we discovered.'

'Is that right,' Gideon whispered, his brown eyes glazing with repressed magic.

Marney quickly added, 'And perhaps Denton did it because he knew I'd tell you everything if I thought for one second that it might save his life.'

Gideon studied her face, evidently deciding that she was telling the truth. He closed the remaining distance between them. He towered over Marney, his emotional energy expanding, filling the room.

'Denton trusts you with all his heart, you know. He believes that you are well on your way to becoming a mighty magicker – the best of us, he says. But me … ?' Gideon pulled an unimpressed face, as though unable to discern what was so special about Marney. 'I really don't know how much I should trust you.'

Marney felt nothing. 'What are you talking about?'

'Your conduct hasn't always been in the Relic Guild's best interests. I'm concerned that your affection for Van Bam will cloud your judgement on this mission.'

Marney clenched her teeth. 'Listen to me, Gideon – I'm focused, I'm professional, and so is Van Bam. I'm dedicated to nothing but saving Denton and getting rid of that bastard Fabian Moor.'

'If you want me to believe you, then you'll swear to me you will end your relationship with Van Bam.'

And there it was, mistimed and spiteful, the Resident's order.

Marney let her anger rise to the surface. 'Now, Gideon?' she snarled. 'You want to deal with this *now*?'

'You will obey me!' Gideon shouted.

His fiery passion was as sudden as it was furious, creating an aura around him filled with madness. Marney matched him with the cold fearlessness only an empath could conjure in an instant.

'No!' she shouted back.

Gideon shook his head, as though to rid it of a bad thought. 'Shut *up*!' He hit himself in the temple, obviously battling against the voice of Sophia, his spirit guide. 'Be silent!' Spittle dribbled onto his chin.

Before Marney could question her actions, she reached out with her magic, trying to latch on to Gideon's emotions and bend his mood to her will, or force him to listen to Sophia's advice.

It was a mistake.

With a roar, Gideon grabbed Marney by the collar and crashed her into the wall, pinning her against it.

'You think your magic can work on me?' He was raging, practically frothing at the mouth. 'You think you can control the chaos in my veins?'

His strength, his fury, his magic – Marney was insignificant compared to the Resident and her empathic defences crumbled before him.

'Gideon, stop,' she begged.

'I am a blood-magicker!' he barked into her face. 'I am descended from mightier stock than *you*!'

'Please …' Marney tried to remove the fists squeezing her throat but the symbols and glyphs covering Gideon's hands singed her skin. 'Let me go.'

'Tell me,' Gideon hissed. 'If you can't obey a simple order, then what good are you to the Relic Guild?'

Marney could feel the insanity crackling through his emotions, the abandon, the power, the vicious desire to snap her neck like a twig. Uncontrollable.

'I'll do what you want.' Marney pleaded, her magic crushed and stamped on, her own emotions torn open, as raw as a fresh bite wound. 'Anything. Please, Gideon!'

'Compliance after threats.' Gideon bared his teeth. His breath reeked of blood and magic. 'A Resident shouldn't have to put the fear of the Timewatcher into his agents—'

Gideon fell away with a howl as someone punched him in the side of the face. He crashed to the floor. Released, Marney slid down the wall, gulping down breaths. Gideon sat up, blood trickling from the corner of his mouth, displaying his anger with a deathly grin aimed at his attacker.

'Hello, Samuel,' the Resident purred.

Samuel had drawn his revolver. The power stone glowed. Marney felt his cold menace.

Gideon dabbed a finger to the blood at his mouth. 'What do you think?' he said, eerily calm. He pressed his thumb to the blood on his fingertip and drew out a viscous red line that sparked with violet fire. 'Is your magic quicker than mine?'

Samuel didn't reply, his face expressionless, the aim of his revolver steady.

Marney had regained her magical defences; her shock and fear were now drowned by apathy. With clarity, she judged the high emotions in the air. The danger posed by Gideon had activated Samuel's prescient awareness; and in that moment, Marney gained an insight into what it was like to be him. She felt the atmosphere pressing in on Samuel like hot needles, dampening his reason and emotions, igniting his survival instincts. One wrong move, one wrong thought from either Gideon or Marney, and the voice of Samuel's magic would roar.

'What's it to be, Samuel?' Gideon said. 'Can you pre-empt blood-magic?'

'Stop it!' Marney rose and stood between them. 'I'll follow your orders,' she told Gideon, before facing Samuel.

But Samuel was looking through her.

Although the revolver was still aimed at Gideon, Marney's chest now blocked a clear shot. She knew that if Gideon attempted an attack now, Samuel would shoot through her. Unless Gideon backed down – unlikely – Samuel would remain locked in his most dangerous state.

Again, Marney reached out with her empathy, using affection, careful to remove any trace of threat from her magic. She seeped through the alien shell of prescient awareness, sliding into the bitterness and sadness of the man beneath, latching on to Samuel's sense of reason. And Marney injected the sound of her voice into her magic.

Think of Denton. Think of everyone who has died. His face twitched as she got through to him. *Let's finish this, Samuel. Let's find Moor.*

Lastly, Marney infused him with calm determination, the will to see the foolishness of the current situation, and finally she broke his state.

Samuel's eyes appeared to see her for the first time. He lowered his revolver.

With a smirk, Gideon extinguished his magical fire. Marney released a relieved breath.

Samuel looked as though he was struggling to understand what had just happened. 'I've got a fix on Denton's location,' he said, sounding disorientated. 'Van Bam's waiting for us.'

'Good.' Gideon remained sitting on the floor, and his smirk had grown. 'Go and wait for me outside. *Both* of you.'

Samuel marched from the room. Marney and Gideon stared at each other for a moment. The fury had left the Resident but the madness still shone in his eyes. Marney hurried after Samuel, struggling to catch up with his quick, long strides down the corridor.

'Samuel, wait,' she called. He didn't respond and kept walking. Marney grabbed his arm. 'Samuel, please ... don't tell Van Bam about this—'

Samuel wrenched his arm free and rounded on the empath. 'You and

Van Bam are idiots,' he snapped. 'And don't *ever* use your magic on me again.'

He stormed off, and Marney watched him go.

As the Resident's personal tram wound through the streets of Labrys Town, heading deeper into the southern district, Van Bam studied the body language and micro-expressions of his colleagues. The situation was stressful enough without the extra tension riding high in the carriage. Bad feeling between Samuel and Gideon was nothing new, but there was something else going on, something that had also affected Marney.

She was sitting on the bench seat next to Samuel, opposite Van Bam. Her every emotion was deadened behind a magical shield of apathy, but Van Bam could still tell she was experiencing more than anxiety over Denton. His lover wouldn't even meet his gaze. Seated next to Van Bam, Gideon's blood was up and he was ready for a fight; beyond that, the illusionist couldn't get much from him. Samuel, staring at the spirit compass in his hand, expressed obvious agitation, but nothing that might explain its roots.

With his green glass cane across his lap, Van Bam looked out of the window at the buildings of the southern district passing by. Clearly, in the short time between leaving Hamir's laboratory and congregating outside the Nightshade, some kind of altercation had occurred between his fellow magickers. Perhaps now was not the time to discover the cause. The illusionist made a mental note to question Marney about it later – *if* any of them survived the night.

The tension continued in the silence.

The tram was driverless, powered by the magic of the Nightshade, which, in turn, was in sync with the magic of the spirit compass. It was at moments like these that Van Bam was reminded of just how big a place Labrys Town was – a two-and-a-half-thousand-square-mile home for a million denizens, divided into five districts. Without the small Aelfirian device to steer the tram's direction, they might never find Denton. And as of that moment, finding Denton was the only chance they had of finding Fabian Moor.

The tram began to slow and Samuel stood up. 'Time to leave,' he said, still staring at the compass.

Marney didn't react. Gideon, however, moved to the end wall of the carriage and laid a hand upon the eye device fixed to it. The milky fluid inside the glass hemisphere glowed in response and a buzz filled the air.

'Yes, I'm here,' Hamir's distorted voice said from the Nightshade.

'We've reached our destination,' Gideon growled. 'If you don't hear from us by morning, you know what to do.'

'Indeed. I will send a distress sig—'

Gideon removed his hand from the eye, cutting Hamir's voice dead. The tram came to a full stop and the group disembarked.

The atmosphere was humid, Ruby Moon a smudge of red light behind thick, dark clouds. They had arrived in the warehouse area of the southern district, close to the boundary wall on a deserted street outside the gates of a metalworks yard. It would rain soon, and already the violet glow of streetlamps illuminated the fine drizzle in the air.

'Well?' Gideon demanded of Samuel.

'The compass isn't showing a firm direction,' Samuel said. 'Denton must be below ground.'

'In the sewers,' Gideon said and he opened the gates to the metalworks yard. 'Follow me.'

By day, the yard was filled with workers who repaired trams and built new ones from the piles of metal recycled from decommissioned vehicles. But now the yard was closed for the night and as deserted as the street outside its gates. The lingering smell of hot grease and oil was borne on the drizzle. Holding his cane tightly, Van Bam brought up the rear as Samuel and Marney followed Gideon over the tramlines criss-crossing the cobbles towards a long, narrow supervisor's hut.

Van Bam didn't suppose that the yard's employees had ever realised that the hut was longer on the outside than it was inside. But it was: at one end, Gideon opened a secret door in the hut wall concealed by a magical charm, revealing descending stairs of stone. The vile odour of the sewers drifted from the doorway.

Gideon ordered Samuel in first with a jerk of his head. Samuel complied, studying the compass, the two-shot pistol loaded with thaumaturgic bullets drawn and primed. Marney went next, her eyes still not meeting Van Bam's, her face a stony blank.

'Hide us,' Gideon instructed Van Bam before following them.

Entering himself, Van Bam whispered to his magic, channelling it through the cane, and the glass glowed with pale green light. It was a concealing light in which the group cast no shadow; and so long as they remained within its sphere, they would not be seen or heard. However, Van Bam wasn't certain that his magic could fool the perceptions of a Genii.

The secret door closed behind them and they began descending the stairs, quickly arriving at a metal grille platform where a caged ladder led straight down into the sewers. The four magickers soon reached the slick cobbles of a walkway which ran alongside a river of foul-smelling waste. Fixed to the black brick walls, grime-smeared glow lamps shed weak light upon this dingy world. The acrid air left an oily film in Van Bam's mouth.

The spirit compass gave a solid click and Samuel whispered, 'Got him.'

The group followed his lead.

The sewers were like a distorted mirror image of Labrys Town. Instead of streets and alleyways dividing the buildings, the river of sewage snaked and weaved through a network of paths and tunnels, flood pools and filter chambers. On numerous occasions it had provided a quick method of travelling around town unseen for the agents of the Relic Guild. Van Bam had known its stink to linger in his nostrils for days.

The compass took the group through a tunnel where moss and luminous fungus grew. Marney's hands were out at her sides, feeling the fetid atmosphere for signs of emotions. Gideon's impatience was evident; he walked close behind Samuel, as though willing his agent to go faster. The symbols of blood-magic that decorated his hands appeared to reflect the light from Van Bam's cane.

At the end of the tunnel they turned right onto a new walkway. Here the viscous rush and burbles of the river were accompanied by the echoing patter of dripping water. The walkway stretched ahead into the gloomy light, bending round to the left. When the group reached the bend, Marney said, 'Wait,' drawing them to a halt.

'What have you got?' Gideon snapped.

Eyes closed, the empath faced the dark sewer ceiling high above her. 'Emotions,' she stated with an empty voice. 'But ... they're weak, phasing in and out of existence.'

'Denton?' said Samuel.

'No.' Marney looked at Samuel with hollow eyes. 'Someone down here is infected with Moor's virus.'

A shriek came from somewhere not too distant. It repeated, coming closer.

Van Bam said, 'My magic hides us from eyes and ears.' He looked pointedly at the symbols on Gideon's hands. 'But our scents will still carry. The infected are drawn to blood.'

'Then by all means extinguish your light,' Gideon drawled.

Van Bam did so and the gloom enveloped the group.

A third shriek activated Samuel's prescient awareness. He shoved the spirit compass into his pocket, holstered Hamir's pistol and drew his rifle, aiming it along the walkway.

Gideon stepped ahead of him as a series of coughing barks approached.

'Hold your fire, Samuel,' the Resident said darkly. 'I don't see why you should have all the fun.'

Eager to use his magic, Gideon gave a flick of his right hand. The glyphs of blood-magic sparked and burst into violet fire, licking the air from his fingertips like the flames of perverse candles.

A moment later, a figure emerged from the gloom, racing for the Relic Guild with an animal's gait. Coughing, barking, shrieking – hateful and desperate to claim the taste of fresh blood.

A chill slithered through Van Bam. 'Oh no ...'

It was Macy.

Marney swore.

In the dim light of glow lamps, Macy came on all fours, a ghoul retaining little of the person she had been. Her clothes were shredded. What remained of her blonde hair was matted to her scalp. The jagged lines of black veins covered her skin like thick cracks in porcelain. A carrier of magical disease, Macy no longer recognised friend from foe; she only saw *food* before her.

Coolly, his hand ablaze, Gideon watched the monster coming closer and closer ... and closer still.

'Gideon!' Samuel hissed, the aim of his rifle steady. 'Deal with her before I do.'

'Hold your nerve,' Gideon spat, as if disgusted by his agent's concern. He waited until Macy was close enough to see her jaundiced eyes, bulging from their sockets with bloodlust, before he unleashed his blood-magic.

The fire flew from Gideon's hand, trailing violet flames like a comet. It erupted as it hit Macy and punched her onto her back, engulfing her. The heat caused Van Bam, Marney and Samuel to move away. Gideon held his ground, however, fire licking at his boots, watching as his magic consumed Macy, silencing her screeches with the finality of death.

The magic ran its course, leaving behind a charred skeleton lying in scattered ashes before the last flames died.

Van Bam stared, filled with sadness and nausea at losing yet another friend. Gideon looked unperturbed by having just killed one of his own agents, infected or not. Samuel, like Van Bam, stared at the remains, his teeth clenched.

Marney's voice, flattened of emotion, broke the moment. 'I can feel something else.' She almost sounded bored. 'There's a residue, like emotional footprints leading through the sewers to ... to Denton.'

'Where?' Gideon snapped.

'Up ahead.' Marney used her chin to indicate the area from where Macy had appeared. 'Not too far away.'

Samuel fished the spirit compass from his pocket and confirmed the direction. He frowned, confused. 'I've lost his spirit.'

'I can definitely feel Denton,' Marney stated.

'Can you sense any sign of Moor?' Gideon said.

Marney shook her head.

'My magic's giving me no new warnings,' Samuel said. 'But Hamir told me that Moor can conceal himself from lower magic.'

Gideon growled. 'Then let's side with caution. Van Bam ...?'

Knowing what was expected of him, Van Bam tore his eyes away from Macy's remains and stabbed his cane down on the slick cobbles. With a glassy, musical chime, green illusionist magic spewed from the cane and rose to form a small ghostly bird in the air. Flapping its tiny wings, the bird sped off, following the line of the walkway, carrying Van Bam's vision with it.

The illusionist could almost feel the wind on his face as he raced through the sewer, seeing what his bird saw. All too soon he found Denton, and had to fight the urge to wrench himself away from his magic; to deny what he saw. But he didn't. Hot tears filled his eyes.

Denton was dead.

The old empath's naked, pallid body was held against the sewer wall by a host of glowing tentacles that had sprung from a cluster of luminous fungus on the floor. There was a fresh and ragged bite wound in Denton's neck from which black veins had begun to spread. He wasn't moving. He wasn't breathing. His head hung limp, his chin tucked against his chest. Van Bam was glad he couldn't see his face.

The tentacles not holding Denton snaked in the air, barely able to hold themselves up, as though life was draining from them. One of Denton's arms was free and his fingertips were covered in wet, glistening blood. Evidently the blood had served as ink, and Denton's last act had been to write something on his stomach. The letters were upside down.

Gideon's voice filled Van Bam's ears. 'What have you found?'

Dispelling his illusion, Van Bam returned his sight to his eyes. Wiping away tears, he told the group what he had discovered. Moments later, they all stood before Denton's corpse.

'Maybe his heart gave out.' The coldness of Marney's tone could have frozen the humid, bitter air of the sewers. 'Maybe the virus was too strong for him.'

Gideon agreed absently, his usual spite and anger replaced by something personal and unspoken.

Samuel, stoic, studied the writing on Denton's stomach, tilting his head to one side to better read the words. Blood had run from the letters.

'I can feel residual emotions here,' Marney said. Van Bam wondered if her empathic magic was experiencing Denton's final moments. 'There's pain. And anger. Whatever Moor was after, I ... I don't think Denton gave it to him.'

'Small mercies,' Gideon murmured.

'It says *recyc portal*,' Samuel told the group. 'A message from Denton?'

'Maybe,' Marney replied, deciphering the emotions she sensed in the atmosphere. 'Could be telling us where Moor went next.'

'There is a portal close to the recycling plant in the southern district,' Van Bam said.

'And it can't be far from here.' Gideon sighed, looking at his agent's corpse. 'Farewell, Denton,' he whispered mournfully. 'Samuel ... let's not leave him like this.'

Gideon stepped away, beckoning Van Bam to join him.

Marney stood statue-still, unflinching, as Samuel aimed his rifle, muttering something that might have been a prayer – or a curse – before shooting a fire-bullet into Denton's chest. With a soft *whump*, the fire bloomed a ferocious furnace orange, incinerating the old empath from the inside out, spreading to the tentacles and fungus, reducing them all to smouldering ashes. Samuel and Marney stared at the remnants of their friend wreathed in smoke that reeked of magic.

Van Bam desperately wanted to hold his lover.

'Concentrate,' Gideon told the illusionist, though his voice held genuine, uncustomary sorrow. 'Let's say Moor is heading for the portal. Is he intending to leave?'

'I do not see how he could,' Van Bam said quietly. 'The Timewatcher's barrier still surrounds the Labyrinth.'

'Moor already evaded the Timewatcher's barrier once to get in,' Gideon pointed out. 'And I wonder – Her spell might prevent creatures of higher magic from entering the Labyrinth, but does it necessarily stop them leaving?'

'Even so, it makes no sense.' Van Bam's sadness was quickly turning to anger. 'Moor gained nothing from Denton, he does not have control of the Nightshade, he has not subjugated the denizens – why leave when he has achieved nothing?'

Gideon considered that. 'What if we hurt his plans more than we realised?' he said. 'What if Moor is fleeing – aborting his mission?'

'If that's the case,' said Samuel, 'he might be gone already.'

'Then we do what?' Van Bam said with heat. 'Just assume he left? Let him become someone else's problem?'

'No.' It was Marney who answered. Her expression was unlike anything Van Bam had seen on her face before. It wasn't an emotionless mask; it was open, murderous rage. The daggers in her baldric glinted in the dim light. 'We find Moor, and Samuel puts a bullet through his head.'

'Agreed.' Gideon gave a deathly grin. The symbols on his hands flared with the energy of blood-magic. 'The war is almost over. There can't be many places left for a Genii to flee to. We follow him.'

The rains of Ruby Moon were falling by the time they exited the sewers. It was the predictable heavy and warm downpour that had fallen every night on Labrys Town for the last thousand years. Marney barely noticed it drenching her clothes and soaking her skin. She had stoked her rage to a magical tempest that burned and devoured every other emotion inside her. Murder was the only instinct driving her feet.

'We need to know the House symbol,' Van Bam said above the hiss of rain. Jogging on slick cobbles, the four of them made their way along a wide street of residential dwellings. 'Without it, we cannot know which doorway Moor travelled to.'

'Have a little faith,' Gideon announced confidently, as though the weather only served to heighten the power in his veins. 'Your Resident knows a secret or two.'

Marney hoped so. The Great Labyrinth was an endless maze filled with countless doorways leading to the Houses of the Aelfir. If Moor had already left Labrys Town, the Relic Guild were dead in the water without the House symbol to summon the shadow carriage that had whisked Moor away to whichever doorway he needed.

Samuel said, 'This street gives me a bad feeling.'

Everything looked normal. There was no one other than the Relic Guild out braving the rain. Lights shone from behind the misted windows of the houses. Marney searched for emotions, detecting those of unconcerned denizens carried on the rain. Snippets of laughter and raised voices came from a small tavern they passed. Normal. But Samuel was right to feel troubled; the street felt almost *too* normal.

A Genii could fool lower magic, Hamir had said ...

Using the image of her mentor's dead body, Marney honed her rage to a point of white-hot determination. She knew that if she acknowledged her grief for but a moment, she would crumble, crash – fall down and perhaps never get up again. She would not let Fabian Moor walk away from all he had done. That Genii was owed his execution.

Up ahead, the street ended at the boundary wall – a sheer, looming canvas of black bricks a hundred feet tall. The street turned to the left, leading to an industrial area where the recycling plant was situated. But directly ahead, just beyond the last of the houses, a large square had been cut into the boundary wall, easily big enough for a tram to pass through. It led to a courtyard filled with a darkness that the glow of the streetlamps couldn't penetrate: a checkpoint where a portal and shadow carriage waited to deliver people to the doorways of the Aelfir.

The group headed straight for it.

Undoubtedly, Moor had already dealt with the police officers assigned to guard the checkpoint in this time of war, but had the Genii killed them outright or left them infected with his virus? Just as Marney wondered this, the group came within twenty yards of the checkpoint entrance and stopped as one.

'Do you feel that?' Van Bam said.

Magic. It permeated the air, sparkling now and then like jewels as rain passed through it. The streetlamps were dead; no lights or sounds came from the houses.

'It is a perception spell,' Van Bam said. 'Designed to conceal this end of the street from the denizens.'

'But not us.' Gideon looked back the way they had come, staring through the translucent wavering wall of the spell to where the street appeared normal. 'Samuel?'

With the rain pattering on his coat and plastering his hair to his scalp, Samuel stood so still he might have been frozen. His thumb twitched and then pressed the power stone on his revolver. It whined into life with violet light. Marney's magic sensed the hard survival instincts of prescient awareness rising in him like a bitter breeze. And then she detected the danger herself.

Emotions phasing and dying ... the aroma of rotting vegetables ...

'Infected,' Marney said.

'And golems,' Samuel added stonily.

Van Bam tensed, holding his green glass cane like a weapon.

Gideon's hands ignited with the fire of blood-magic. 'Where?' he demanded.

'Everywhere,' Samuel replied. 'It's a trap.'

The door of the last house on the left opened, and by the time Samuel had shouted, 'Down!' he was already aiming his rifle at the deformed, lumbering golem that appeared. He shot it through the head before it could raise the pistol in its hand. Even as it fell, hissing with dispelled animation magic, jerking and cracking, crumbling into chunks of stone, two more golems emerged from the house opposite.

As Samuel dealt with them, a window smashed to Marney's right. One of the infected raced shrieking onto the street through shards of glass, crashing Gideon to the ground, burying its face in his neck. The Resident bellowed an indecipherable word and the violet flames of magical fire rose and incinerated his attacker, bones and all. He swore as he got to his feet, holding his neck, waving his hand to clear smoke and ash.

'There're too many of them,' Samuel shouted.

And chaos broke free.

Every window of every house in the area under the perception spell smashed simultaneously. Upstairs and down, a host of golems aimed pistols at the Relic Guild and infected rushed onto the street.

Samuel's rifle flashed and spat. Gideon began uttering guttural words of blood-magic. An instant before the golems unleashed a hail of bullets, Van Bam stabbed his cane against the ground. With a discordant chime, a barrier of green illusionist magic covered the group in a watery dome. But Van Bam wasn't quite quick enough. Bullets and raindrops fizzed harmlessly against the barrier, but the trigger fingers of one or two golems were faster than its creation.

Gideon grunted. He spun around, colliding with Marney, landing on top of the empath as they fell to the ground.

Marney blocked the intense wave of pain the Resident emoted. Her magic couldn't detect golems, for they had no emotions to read; but she could feel the hatred and bloodlust of the infected.

Rolling Gideon onto his back, Marney sat up. The virus victims, savage and animal, crashed their fists against the green dome, baying for blood.

'The barrier will not last long,' Van Bam said, his desperate face staring at Gideon. Already the hail of bullets was putting cracks in his magic. 'It will have to dispel before I cast another and we will be momentarily exposed. What is your magic telling you, Samuel?'

'That those golems aren't running out of bullets any time soon.' Samuel slapped a fresh magazine into his rifle, watching the infected surrounding them. 'How did we walk into this?' he muttered angrily. 'Stupid!'

'Marney,' Gideon grunted.

The Resident had been hit by three bullets: one in the stomach, two in the chest. His eyes lacked focus, lids fluttering. Rainwater flushed blood from his dark green shirt.

'Done for ...' Gideon spoke through gritted, bloodstained teeth, struggling for breath.

'Heal yourself,' Marney snapped. 'We need you.'

'Too late. Bastard bit me.' And the empath noticed the bite wound on the Resident's neck, red and ugly.

No cure for the Genii's virus, not even for a blood-magicker. Marney felt the terminal nature of Gideon's wounds, infection already tainting his emotions, the life slipping from him.

'Give me ... your hand,' Gideon said.

A snap filled the air. Bullets assaulted the barrier. The virus victims continued to pound the magic, frenzied, relentless, hateful, shrieking all the while. The cracks grew and grew.

Samuel aimed his rifle, waiting for the moment the barrier collapsed.

'Marney!' Gideon coughed blood. 'Quickly,' he urged.

She gave him her hand. The fire of blood-magic had died from the symbols on his skin except for a single flame, barely an ember on the tip of one finger. Holding Marney's hand palm up, Gideon began to inscribe a glyph, searing it into her skin. She winced at its sting.

'Will show ... last ... destination ... of carriage.' Blood flowed from Gideon's mouth and down the side of his face. Black veins snaked from the bite wound. He fought for breath. 'Will ... take you ... to Moor.'

Marney yelped as he finished searing the glyph onto her palm and she felt a build-up of emotions in Gideon, as though he was gathering all the hate and madness that he had carried with him for his entire life.

Marney backed away.

With a cry of pain and rage, Gideon barked words of dark magic, blood spraying from his mouth. Red droplets burst into flame in the air as Gideon took control of Van Bam's spell. The green energy of the barrier hardened. It rose, the dome becoming a sphere, scooping up Marney, Samuel and Van Bam and lifting them into the air.

Gideon remained lying on the floor. 'Get the bastard!' he roared and hurled his magic and his agents down the street before the infected pounced on him, eager for a taste of his flesh.

The brief jaunt was dizzying. The green sphere arced and spun through the air, shattering like glass as it landed not far from the entrance to the checkpoint, sending the three magickers sprawling across the rain-drenched cobbles. Marney was the first to her feet, looking back to where they had started.

Golems continued to fire down from the houses onto Gideon, riddling him and the infected with bullet after bullet. And then, just as Van Bam grabbed Marney's arm, trying to pull her to the checkpoint, Gideon's blood-magic exploded.

The Resident's body erupted with wave after wave of violet fire that engulfed his enemies. Marney shielded her eyes. The magical fire kept on coming, blistering paintwork on the houses, setting fire to wooden doors as it spewed down the street towards the group. To Marney, its colour and pattern looked as beautiful as it was terrible.

She stood transfixed until Samuel grabbed her by the scruff of the neck and shoved her through the opening into the checkpoint. Van Bam was close behind them. They pressed their backs to the wall an instant before Gideon's fire reached the courtyard. It raged through the entrance like a great belch from a furnace before receding; before dying.

Smoke filled the air, along with the crackle of burning buildings.

Samuel stared up into the rain and Marney felt his despair.

Gideon had joined Denton, Gene, Angel, Macy and Bryant in death, and the Relic Guild had just lost its most powerful magicker.

'Are you all right?' Van Bam asked Marney.

She nodded, feeling nothing.

Samuel drew Hamir's double-barrelled pistol and gave Marney a meaningful look. 'We're not stopping now.'

Marney walked towards the stone archway of a deactivated portal standing in the courtyard. Before it, a slim pedestal rose from the ground, topped by a stone box filled to the brim with a clear, gelatinous substance. Marney looked at her hand.

They glyph Gideon had seared onto her palm was formed from red welts, depicting surprisingly detailed swirls within a square. Marney laid the glyph upon the pedestal's box.

She clenched her teeth against the pain as the gelatinous substance glowed and sucked the symbol from her skin, leaving no trace of it ever having been there.

The portal activated, its surface churning dark as night within the archway. A grey, smooth disc appeared on the cobbles between the pedestal and the portal: a shadow carriage.

'Well, then,' Samuel growled. He thumbed the pistol's power stone. It whined and glowed with red light. 'Like the man said, let's get the bastard.'

CHAPTER SEVENTEEN

LIFE AMONG THE DEAD

So this was the Retrospective.

Predictably, the portal closed and vanished after it had delivered the group to a huge subterranean passage, a cave tunnel through red rock that stretched into the gloom beyond the glow of the Toymaker's thaumaturgic light. The air was surprisingly cool, though it carried a vague bitter aftertaste, and the only sound was a gentle wind moaning through the passage from somewhere unseen.

Samuel's magic didn't stir. The cave tunnel disappeared into darkness ahead of and behind the group, and there was nothing in the illuminated vicinity that might have served as a magical prison incarcerating nearly a thousand Nephilim. Thankfully, there were no signs of demons, either; no poison and fire, no chaos of dead time waiting to crush and corrupt the Relic Guild. That might have been due to the effects of Gulduur Bellow's protective spells but Samuel suspected otherwise. This place felt very different from what the Retrospective was supposed to be. Perhaps the Orphan was right; perhaps this was somewhere hidden from Spiral's corrosive influence.

The small demonic child was still perched on Bellow's shoulder, scowling, obviously fearful of the calm.

Glogelder grumbled something about missing his spell sphere launcher while checking for the umpteenth time that his pistol was loaded and its power stone charged. 'Anyone like a wager?' he added with forced bravado. 'What odds do you think we'd get?'

'On what?' Marney asked.

Glogelder grinned. 'Winning, of course.'

Samuel knew that they all understood there were no more secrets, no more games to play. Success or failure, Amilee had said. Either way, the end was coming. And clearly they had not arrived in as precise a location as they would have liked.

Clara had changed into the wolf. With the Toymaker close to her, loyal and silent, she stood beside Gulduur Bellow: the new Resident eager to lead the way. For all the wolf's size and power, her head only reached to the Nephilim's waist and next to him she looked no bigger than a pet dog.

Bellow listened to the Orphan's clicks and hisses. It jumped down from the Nephilim's shoulder and stalked to the edge of the Toymaker's light, evidently trying to communicate something. Marney moved up alongside Bellow to decipher what.

Samuel checked his ice-rifle, his magic sensing no immediate danger. He looked from the pistol that Glogelder held to those in each of Hillem's hands, and finally to Namji's crossbow loaded with bolts of vacuum magic.

'You know,' Samuel said, 'bullets and lower magic can't kill wild demons. Not really.'

A frozen moment followed during which Glogelder's face fell. 'You're bloody joking.'

'I wish I were.'

'And you couldn't have told us this earlier?'

Samuel shrugged. 'If they come for you, just ... shoot and run before they come for you again.'

'Not very comforting,' said Hillem.

Hamir cleared his throat. 'If Amilee is right – and let us hope that she is – Spiral will be unaware of our actions. At least for a time.' Hamir studied the subterranean environment with an unimpressed expression. 'And he does not know that one Nephilim escaped him. Gulduur's blood-magic will open his herd's prison, and will also be very effective against any wild demons we happen upon.'

'Any what if they come en masse?' Namji said. 'The demons of the Retrospective are innumerable, or so everyone keeps telling me. Can one Nephilim stand against them all?'

A slight smile curved one corner of Hamir's mouth. 'Stealth and haste are undoubtedly our best weapons here. Before Spiral claims the First and Greatest Spell, of course.'

'Then we'd best get a move on,' said Glogelder. He looked into the cave tunnel's darkness in both directions, adding, 'If we can figure out which way to go.'

Samuel approached Clara, Marney and Bellow. 'Do we have a direction yet?'

'I think so,' said Marney. At the edge of the light, the Orphan continued to speak with eerie clicks and hisses. 'We're definitely in the place that the wild demons fear, but – if I'm reading this right – the Nephilim's prison is further in.' She pointed into the gloom beyond the demon. 'That way.'

The Orphan's voice became agitated, angry.

'It's too scared to take us any closer.' Marney gave Samuel a sour look. 'And it says it'll kill us all if we don't release it from its bonds.'

Clara growled at the Orphan but Bellow gave a throaty chuckle.

'Oh no, my fierce little friend,' the giant told the demon. 'You're with us until the end. Now, lead the way.'

As the Orphan bared its glass-like teeth at Bellow, Marney said, 'Looks like we've got a bit of a hike.'

'And it would be a shame if anyone got lost along the way,' Bellow added. 'Don't you agree, Progenitor?'

Hamir winced, pressing a hand to the area on his stomach where Bellow had painted his protective spell. With a look of shock, he walked forward as though his legs were compelled into action by something other than his own volition, until he was alongside the Nephilim.

Hamir pressed a hand to his stomach again, glaring up at Bellow. 'Did … did you add binding magic to your spells?'

'Only for you,' Bellow replied. 'There's no one else here I don't trust.'

'What did you expect me to do?' Hamir was appalled, his indignation evident. 'Run away?'

Samuel almost felt sorry for the necromancer as he noted the stony looks aimed at him by his colleagues – looks which indicated unanimous distrust. Certainly no one questioned Bellow's actions.

'You and I are already bound together, Progenitor,' said the giant. He gestured towards the Orphan. 'And what's good enough for one monster…'

Glogelder stepped forward. 'So he has to do everything you say?'

The big Aelf was clearly pleased when Hamir raised an eyebrow and rather sourly said, 'Indeed.'

Samuel looked into Clara's yellow eyes. The wolf bobbed her head at him.

'Let's go,' the old bounty hunter said.

With a hiss for the group and misery on its childlike face, the Orphan set off through the cave, clearly much against its will.

The way was uneven, the ground pitted with craters and strewn with boulders of varying sizes. The walls were cracked and jagged, and point-ed formations hung from the high ceiling like stalactites of red rock. Or teeth. Hamir walked beside Bellow, but he appeared to be moving of his own volition. The Toymaker remained close to Clara. The rest brought up the rear as they made their way through a haze of deep gloom.

'We could do with more light,' Hillem said nervously.

'I might have something,' Namji replied. But before she could reach into the cloth satchel hanging from her shoulder, Clara made a low growl at the Toymaker.

Understanding its charge's command, the Toymaker broke apart, dissolving from the head down into a hundred scuttling automatons which spread out around the group, the tips of their tails glowing with the violet light of their thaumaturgic stings. The shadows were lifted considerably, though the extra light revealed nothing other than more red rock and the gloom ahead.

The Orphan made a series of impatient clicks and beckoned them onwards.

Samuel's magic detected no danger but he was suspicious nonethe-less. He was in the heart of the Retrospective, the most savage and unforgiving House ever created. He should at least be experiencing a bad feeling in his gut, warning him that he was walking a dangerous path, but his prescient awareness remained inert. He wondered if his magic would count for much in the end, anyway; for whatever reason, Samuel's prescient awareness would not react to the Genii.

'You know what I'm going to do when this over?' Glogelder said, his thick voice echoing.

'Get drunk, by any chance?' Hillem replied.

'Like I've never been before.'

'Mind if I join you?' Marney said.

'The more the merrier,' Glogelder announced. 'I'll even buy the first round.'

'That'll be a first,' Namji teased.

The jibe induced a few chuckles, all forced and unnatural. The sound of the almost desperate banter, searching for a way to laugh in the face of fear, grated on Samuel's nerves. He focused on the small demon leading them ever deeper into the darkness ahead.

They reached a narrow point in the cave where boulders and sharp protrusions from the walls hindered the way forward, and they had to pick their way through carefully. The cave widened again to reveal a fork, and the Orphan headed down the left path.

It wasn't long before the darkness beyond the Toymaker's light became suffused with an amber glow. The colour was similar to that of a low-burning fire, but the light was still, not flickering. Whatever its source, it spooked the Orphan and the demon hid behind Bellow's legs. The giant picked it up and sat it on his shoulder again.

The wolf looked at Samuel.

'I'm not detecting anything,' he told her.

'I am,' Marney said.

'So am I,' Bellow added, and he set off towards it.

A chittering accompanied the light, and soon the group stood before a great, glowing column. It stretched from floor to ceiling, thicker than any tree in any forest that Samuel had ever seen. The column was formed from a glassy substance, not quite transparent, and the light came from within it: a constant syrupy illumination like sunlight shining through sap. And scurrying all over the column's surface were insects, mites, hundreds of them, similar in size to the Toymaker's component parts, their bodies glowing with the same amber light.

'What an extraordinary surprise,' Bellow whispered, awed.

Glogelder swore, aiming his pistol. 'Are they demons?'

'I don't think so,' Samuel said.

The mites appeared to be secreting more of the glassy substance onto the column, making it thicker, perhaps helping it to sink further into the rock above and below. They were entirely focused on their work, and Samuel's magic sensed nothing dangerous about them.

'They're not interested in us,' he said. 'Marney?'

'There aren't any emotions, as such,' the empath replied. 'They have a drone-like mentality. Maybe a hive mind.'

'What about the column?' Namji asked.

'Now *that* definitely has something emotional about it.' Marney rocked her head from side to side, searching for articulation. 'It's almost sentient, like it's trying to be ... to be—'

'Alive,' Hamir finished. He moved closer to the column and its scurrying mites. 'Considering everything we know about the Retrospective, this formation shouldn't be here.' He peered closer. 'There are nutrients and minerals – this ... this is life – *natural* life – evolving where dead time should prohibit such a thing.'

'What does it mean?' Hillem asked.

'I have absolutely no idea,' Hamir admitted. Clara growled and he deciphered the wolf's prompt. 'But if I were to guess, I'd say that this life has been *seeded* by something.'

'Spiral?' said Marney.

Hamir's eyes moved to Bellow.

'Doubtful.' The giant's gaze was steady. 'But then again, you would know better than I how life might be bred from dead time, Progenitor.'

'Be that as it may,' Hamir replied coolly, 'this formation is not what we're here to find.'

'I agree.' Bellow was watching the Orphan on his shoulder, which was cowering from the column. 'I suspect this is only a taste of what the wild demons fear in the Retrospective.' His eyes narrowed, as though his thoughts were racing. 'There must be more to find.'

He brushed the Orphan from his shoulder and it scurried ahead, leading the way. The group followed, skirting the column and its mites, heading once again into the unknown darkness of the cave.

Samuel felt an alien yet familiar itch inside his head right before Marney's voice spoke in his mind.

Samuel, I just sensed something from Gulduur. His emotions are hard to read – he covers them well – but ... but I think he's hiding something.

I'm not detecting any danger, Samuel replied.

No, it's nothing like that. Marney's pause was contemplative. *It's like he's figured something out, had a revelation. Whatever that column is, it seems to have confirmed a suspicion and it's filled him with … It's hard to explain. Gulduur's almost overwhelmed by a feeling of home.*

Home? thought Samuel. *His home? The Sorrow of Future Reason?*

I don't know. Marney's voice became full of warning. *But we need to tread carefully around him, Samuel. Whatever Gulduur's on to, it's blinded him to the importance of everyone else's well-being – except Hamir's.*

The Retrospective was in flux.

To the east and west, the horizon raged with chaos. Mighty fire tornadoes, each as big as a mountain, shredded the barren ground, tearing poison clouds and bloated flying demons from the sky. In their wake, rivers of molten rock flowed and a new hateful landscape began to form. The Retrospective was recycling, feeding the hunger of dead time, growing, making room for the next consignment of raw material.

Protected from the environment by higher magic, Fabian Moor and Mo Asajad observed a gargantuan rent in the air that had sent the fury of the Retrospective spilling into yet another Aelfirian House. Buildings, entire cities were broken apart as easily as castles in sand – crushed and crumbled to a storm of dust. A countless horde of wild demons slaughtered the Aelfir, destroying life after life, collecting bloody remains as fuel to feed the belly of this damned House.

And somewhere out there among the horde, Viktor Gadreel had joined the slaughter, revelling in the new power he believed his Lord was sharing with the Genii. He was a fool.

At the end of the Genii War, Gadreel had been leading an undersized Aelfirian army at the Burrows of Underneath, a monumental House comprised of a cluster of huge subterranean cities. Gadreel failed to conquer the House, suffering a final defeat when the Last Storm came. Had Lord Spiral not saved him – as he had Moor and Asajad – Gadreel would have died alongside his army. The hulking Genii had never forgotten his defeat or forgiven the House which had given it to him. And now the opportunity to exact revenge had inflamed his desire to fervent heights.

The Burrows of Underneath was sucked into the Retrospective in great plumes of crimson smoke, devoured by the fire of the tornadoes.

All around Moor, the power of the House grew. Its army of wild demons would swell by hundreds of millions with just this latest addition to its mass. How many other realms were to come?

'There is no place for us here,' Moor whispered to himself.

The sky bellowed as new clouds roiled and unleashed a downpour of acid.

'I've not yet had the chance to tell you, Fabian,' said Asajad, watching the acid sizzle and smoke as it hit the dome of thaumaturgy protecting the two Genii. 'When our Lord instructed me to return to the Labyrinth and spread our ... *disease*, I took the opportunity to speak with Hagi Tabet on the way back.'

Moor frowned at her.

Asajad kept her eyes on the rain. 'Hagi learned a thing or two during her connection to Known Things that Lord Spiral does not wish us to know.'

'Oh?'

'She discovered why he is toying with the denizens instead of simply adding them and the Labyrinth to the Retrospective.' Asajad looked at him. 'Spiral cannot achieve his aims unless the denizens die before their House.'

Moor looked out across the chaos of the Retrospective. Spiral's spy, Tal the Ghoul, had accompanied Gadreel into the Burrows of Underneath. Spiral himself was ... somewhere, consulting the skies. It was probable that this conversation remained between Moor and Asajad, but things that Spiral didn't want his Genii to know were a treacherous subject matter.

Moor drew a breath. 'Explain?'

Asajad moved closer to him. 'The First and Greatest Spell,' she said. 'It is currently incomplete. Shards of its magic reside in the souls of the denizens. These shards condition the humans, force them to remain faithful to the Mother who abandoned them. Did you know this, Fabian?'

'No.' Enforced faith? This was a strange revelation indeed. 'You are certain this is true?'

'The Timewatcher Herself made it so,' Asajad replied. 'And according to Hagi, She only ever shared the information with Her Skywatchers.'

But Spiral never saw fit to share it with his Genii …

Asajad continued, 'If Spiral allowed the Retrospective to grind the First and Greatest Spell into the substance of dead time now, its power would be sorely diminished, incapable of helping Spiral to achieve his dreams. But if the denizens die first—'

'Then the shards of the Timewatcher's magic return to the source, and the Spell will be complete.'

'Thus giving Spiral all he needs to change the face of existence.'

Asajad's words made so much sense that Moor felt his resolve, his hope, his faith crumble to lifeless earth inside him. It explained why Spiral hadn't wanted the humans destroyed during the Genii War, and revealed the real reason why he had needed the Timewatcher and Thaumaturgists out of the way before he implemented his plans. It had always been about the Retrospective, this cursed place of blood and hate and dead time. Spiral had foreseen what it could become with the First and Greatest Spell – the most ambitious and powerful creation magic ever cast, spanning a millennium, reaching into all worlds and realms.

'The Timewatcher's greatest achievement will be Her gravest mistake,' Asajad said. 'With Her magic, Lord Iblisha Spiral will rise to a new kind of Watcherhood.'

The Watcher of Dead Time … what manner of anti-life would such a creature breed?

The harsh light of truth banished the last shadows of doubt from Moor. With utter certainty he knew then that there was no place for the Genii in Spiral's remade existence, and Spiral had always known that. Used and betrayed, Fabian Moor, the most trusted of all the Genii, had never been more than a rescuer, a stepping stone, and his part in the long game had ended. But what could he, Asajad and blinkered Gadreel do about that now? There would be no escaping the Retrospective.

As though sharing his feelings, Asajad added, 'Lady Tabet also discovered something else in Known Things. Let's call it *recently added* information of which our Lord is not aware.'

'Clara,' Moor realised with a jolt. 'Known Things took the changeling's memories.' And Spiral had destroyed Known Things before he could read them.

Asajad stepped closer still, her voice barely a whisper as she spoke quickly. 'Hagi wasn't particularly clear, but I ascertained enough to believe that we might not have thwarted Lady Amilee's plans against us after all, and that she hid her true intent from divination.'

'Amilee?' Moor pushed aside his sense of hopelessness.

'Consider what our lord told us of the Nephilim, Fabian, and this prison he created for them. What if Amilee knows of it, too?'

The greatest blood-magickers the realms had ever seen, Spiral had said, perfect creatures uniting higher magic and dead time. And they could not die unless Simowyn Hamir died. If the Nephilim were free, would they be powerful enough to stand against Spiral? Was there still hope for the last of the Genii?

Asajad spoke on. 'Given Spiral's state of mind and that he is so reticent with us while believing that Amilee poses no threat, I am loath to bring this matter to his attention.'

Moor read her underlying meaning. 'I wonder,' he said. 'Keeping information from him is not the wisest course of action, but admitting that we have uncovered his secrets would incur his wrath.'

'Don't get me wrong, Fabian – had it been up to me, I would have stormed the Skywatcher's tower and drunk the thaumaturgy straight from her veins.' Her tone became conspiratorial. 'But consider this – if Amilee has found a way to prevent the Retrospective from reaching the First and Greatest Spell ... well, the contents of Known Things was not meant for us, so perhaps it is best to trust in our Lord's methods and let events unfold as they will?'

'Perhaps.' Moor thought of the Houses and realms to which a Genii might escape and hide. He looked at Asajad's pale face and knew in his heart that for the first time in over a millennia the two Genii were of a single mind.

'We could have been glorious, Fabian,' she said – angry, betrayed. 'Mother Earth was supposed to be ours. It is not enough that we sacrificed so much to reap so little.'

'We should have seen it coming,' Moor replied. 'Did you ever once witness Spiral mourn for the Genii who fell in his name?'

'All I know for certain is that our time is running out. Perhaps one of us should return to Hagi and see if she discovered anything else that might aid our survival—'

She looked up as a cloud burst directly overhead with a roar of thunder. A fiery mass was released which sped down like a meteor, leaving behind a trail of billowing black smoke.

Gadreel materialised within the protective dome. Gore-spattered, he looked confused at having been pulled so suddenly from the razing of the Burrows of Underneath. Tal the Ghoul accompanied him, appearing none the worse for wear.

'What is this?' Gadreel demanded, bloodlust in his eyes.

He received no answer.

Above, the fiery mass morphed into the shape of Lord Iblisha Spiral, borne on silver wings. He passed through the protective magic without hindrance and landed gracefully. His wings rose above him like wicked scythes. His beautiful, terrible face was creased with anger.

'My lord,' Gadreel said, bowing.

Spiral's violet eyes flared and dimmed with insanity. 'Time does not move swiftly enough and the sky is hiding much from me.' He spoke as though he was continuing an argument – perhaps one he'd been having with himself. 'There are things I cannot yet see.' He threw a chittering mass on the ground. 'One of my demons found *this* in a cave.'

It was an insect, some kind of mite. Around the size of a fist, its glass-like body was filled with an amber glow. Moor and Asajad shared a look.

'It shouldn't be here,' Spiral hissed, as though the mite's existence was the fault of someone present. 'You will take an army of demons to where this thing was found,' he ordered his Genii. 'You will destroy any life you find there.' He stamped on the creature, crushing its shell, deadening its glow. 'And then we will return to the Labyrinth and hasten the deaths of the denizens.'

The group travelled in silence.

When the tunnel split into two paths again, the Orphan showed them which way to go, and the passage began gradually rising. Although no one spoke of it, there was genuine fear that it might continue upwards until it reached the surface of the Retrospective.

As the wolf, Clara's courage held fast. She and Van Bam had been talking about Hamir.

Something occurs to me, Van Bam said. *We were given a brief explanation of dead time. We were told that it is a volatile substance, dangerous, and only the greatest creatures of higher magic can master it.*

But Hamir wasn't strong enough to control it, Clara replied. *The Nephilim were an accident.*

But can you not see the glaring hole in the information we were given, Clara? Did you not notice the evasion and hidden meanings that passed between Hamir and Amilee when they spoke of dead time?

He sounded irritated, but not with her. A general aggression pervaded Van Bam's voice. Clara had first noticed the subtle change in his manner when she initiated the metamorphosis. Perhaps her magic had injected a little of the wolf's spirit into the ghost. This didn't displease Clara.

I'm not following you, she said. *What did you notice?*

Dead time encapsulates the horrors of an era. Van Bam's usually smooth and deep tone was more of a growl. *The Timewatcher harvested it from the Genii War to create the Retrospective, yes?*

What's your point, Van Bam?

If everything we have been told is true, then from what era did Hamir harvest dead time to create the Nephilim?

Clara looked at the necromancer. Walking beside Bellow, his calm, unconcerned expression gave nothing away.

What happened a thousand years ago? Clara asked.

The Timewatcher made the Great Labyrinth, Van Bam answered. *It spelled the end of an epoch which the Aelfir refer to as the* Old Ways, *when all the Houses were at war. It was a dark and mysterious time, and little has been written about it.*

So Hamir harvested dead time from the Old Ways? Clara thought about that, unable to see any significance. *Does it matter? He was a*

Thaumaturgist back then – he probably did lots of things that don't have any bearing on what we need to do now.

Understand what I am saying. Van Bam was definitely irritated with Clara now. *The others might believe that Hamir's secrets have been revealed and he has nothing left to hide, but that necromancer, along with Amilee, is still hiding much from us.*

Glogelder tripped and swore. Samuel muttered something about the temperature rising. Clara could taste an increasing bitterness in the air.

When this is over, Van Bam added more calmly, *I would advise you to have a long talk with Simowyn Hamir, Clara.*

'What is it?' Samuel said.

The old bounty hunter was talking to Bellow, who had moved to the side of the cave and was studying a section of the huge wall which reflected light like glass.

'Something is there,' Bellow said. 'Clara, we need darkness.'

With a growl, the wolf ordered the Toymaker to hide its lights. The scuttling automatons swarmed behind a large boulder, where the glow from its many parts was shielded and deflected away from what Bellow was seeing. Silence was broken only by the Orphan's impatient clicks and hisses in the darkness.

Clara bared her teeth.

'What in the Timewatcher's name is *that*?' Namji whispered.

A large, glassy, uneven section of the wall acted like a tinted window, providing a view into somewhere outside the cave tunnel. On what looked to be the bottom of a ravine, a mass bigger than the boulder the Toymaker was hiding behind lay on scorched rock. Like a bloated belly, devoid of chest or limbs or head, it undulated as though filled with something living. Patches of hair grew from flesh tainted with the sickly hue of disease, coiling like small tentacles. No sound accompanied the images.

'Is it a demon?' Hillem asked.

No one answered.

A monster came into view and approached the bloated mass. Stick-thin but taller than Bellow, it moved with an awkward gait, using overly long arms which widened to wicked blades of bone as walking sticks. Its skin was charred and raw in places, its eyes tiny black beads, but its mouth was large and filled with blocky teeth. The nostrils of the monster's flat nose widened to gaping slits as it smelled the bloated mass hungrily.

'Let's hope it can't see us,' Glogelder muttered.

The monster raised its arms and struck. Both blades of bone stabbed into flab, tearing huge wounds in diseased flesh. Blood poured, looking more like rancid melted butter. But following it came something the monster clearly didn't expect. Arachnids. Hundreds of them. The colour of poison, they scurried to be free on armoured legs, quickly emptying the bloated mass to a flaccid sack. They rushed the monster and knocked it to the ground, and in a heartbeat nothing of it could be seen beneath a writhing, feeding swarm.

Hamir said, 'Something is … changing.'

A dazzling blaze of fire shone through the window, savage but soundless, its heat unfelt. Only Bellow and Hamir didn't step away from it. The monster and arachnids were burned away instantly by a blistering wind. The walls of the ravine crumbled and melted to molten falls that became steaming rivers flowing across the ruin of flat landscape.

'The Retrospective,' Hamir said. 'In case any of you needed reminding of what waits outside this cave.'

Noxious gas rose towards a hateful sky the colour of bruises. Spears of lightning stabbed at the rivers, sending great gouts of molten rock into the air. Countless flying demons soared and fought overhead.

'Ever recycling, ever changing.' Bellow's voice was low, whispery. 'An entire House of dead time.'

From somewhere in the darkness, the Orphan hissed angrily.

'Yeah, we should move on,' Glogelder said nervously.

'Come,' Bellow said.

The giant set off after the Orphan and the group followed. The Toymaker joined them again, his lights lifting the shadows once more, and Clara saw the dismay on her colleagues' faces.

Here in this cave, said Van Bam, *it is, perhaps, easy to forget where we are.*

Thankfully, the path began to dip into a steady decline. After a short time they came to a sheer wall which blocked the passage except for three narrow tunnels burrowing into the rock. The Orphan led the way down the centre passage. The group followed single file, Bellow stooping to fit through, the Toymaker's lights dancing. At the end of the tunnel, the cave opened out as wide and high as before. Ahead, the darkness was illuminated by the same amber glow as before.

Bellow quickened his pace towards it, his long strides quickly overtaking the Orphan. The group had to hurry to keep up with him.

Clara. It was Marney's voice, soft and subtle in the wolf's mind. *Can you ask Van Bam something for me?*

Clara acquiesced. For all the empath's abilities, Marney couldn't hear the illusionist's voice, which Clara was glad about; she had no desire to eavesdrop on the chatter between old lovers.

Has he read anything unusual in Gulduur's body language or micro-expressions? Marney asked.

Clara relayed what Van Bam told her, though it wasn't much. Bellow conducted himself with almost perfect stoicism; but, understandably, he was eager to the point of desperation to be reunited with his herd, almost too excited by the prospect to be fearful of his environment. Other than that, the Nephilim wasn't giving much away.

Damn it, said Marney.

Clara didn't like the way the empath's tone felt in her head. *What's the problem?*

I'm not sure. Bellow's figured something out about this place – about what's making that light – and for some reason he's not telling us. I think … I think Hamir's worked it out, too.

Funny, Clara said sourly, *I've just been talking about Hamir's secrets.*

Their emotions are so different, so bloody difficult to read. Marney made a frustrated sound. *I don't think talking to them would do any good, either.*

Van Bam agreed. *Let's see where this leads.*

This time, it was not a radiant column covered in glowing mites that they discovered. It was plant life. Luminous fungus sprouting in clusters along the base of the walls lit a large area of ground covered in a carpet of what looked to be miniature trees with fat, furry leaves.

Marney confirmed that she was picking up the same not-quite-complete emotions as before, battling to find sentience.

'Incredible,' Hamir said, sounding genuinely impressed.

Two narrow paths of black stone divided the miniature forest; and between them was a shallow stream of clear, gently running water that flowed from a spring in the ground. It followed a straight course before disappearing through a crack in a large stone the same colour as the paths.

Clara padded up to the water and sniffed it. It smelled clean, fresh.

I would advise against drinking it, Van Bam said.

'This simply shouldn't be here.' Hamir almost chuckled as he gazed around at the plant life. 'Utterly astounding.'

'I still don't understand,' Hillem said, his curiosity ever present. 'You say this is life, but isn't everything here alive, in some sense of the word?'

'Nothing should form naturally here,' Hamir explained. 'The Retrospective exists by recycling and expanding and remoulding what it already has – or what it claims.' He inspected a patch of fungus on the wall. 'This House is founded upon dead time, blood, *waste* material. But *this* … this is *new*, not native.' Hamir thought better of touching the fungus and straightened, his face troubled as though struck by a epiphany. 'It is everything I was unable to achieve.'

'The Nephilim,' Bellow said wistfully. He produced a curved knife from the sleeve of his robe and cut the end of his finger. He allowed his blood to drip to the ground, whispering fleeting words of blood-magic. His blood sizzled with energy, and where it dripped a new tiny tree sprang up, healthy green leaves unfurling from the buds of its branches.

'Of course the presence of my people caused this life,' Bellow said, as if to himself. 'Some of their magic must have leaked from their prison. I doubt Iblisha Spiral has seen what is occurring down here. And my herd must be close.'

'Or perhaps they're right here,' Marney said. 'Look.'

The Orphan was no longer urging the group to travel further into the cave. The childlike demon was perched upon the cracked stone into which the stream disappeared, hopping up and down insistently.

Bellow strode down the path. Hamir hurried after him, obviously encouraged by the giant's binding spell.

Marney gave Clara a warning glance before following, saying mentally, *We should follow Gulduur's lead, not question him or try to stop what he's doing.*

Agreed, Clara said. *But stay close to him.*

Bellow batted aside the Orphan and studied the cracked stone. Marney hopped onto the path on the other side of the stream and looked for herself. The rest of the group hung back.

'What have you found?' Samuel asked.

'Blood-magic to trap blood-magickers,' Bellow replied.

There are glyphs and wards carved into the rock, Marney told Clara. *They're radiating magic* – higher *magic*.

'This stone is a seal,' Bellow said, his growing excitement evident to all. 'It is a lock. Spiral must believe that only he can open it, but then … he does not know that he failed to trap *all* the Nephilim.'

'The prison must be opened by higher magic,' Hamir mused. 'You are the key, Gulduur.'

Although the wolf couldn't see what the giant was doing, Marney relayed that he was inscribing the symbols with blood from the open cut on his finger.

The Orphan screeched and scurried away as the stone split into two halves. The demon fled into the gloom, its duty served, the magic binding it to the group apparently broken.

Bellow's bright blue eyes held a triumphant sheen as water pooled around his feet. The stream deepened as its flow was stoppered, no longer pouring underground. Bellow, Hamir and Marney stepped back as the stream rose before the broken rock in a veil of shimmering water ten feet tall and five feet wide.

'Bugger me,' said Glogelder.

With his bloodied finger, Bellow touched the water. It parted like curtains revealing darkness beyond. 'A doorway,' the giant said, and he went through, dragging Hamir after him, not waiting for anyone else.

With a nervous glance back at Clara, Marney quickly followed.

The wolf padded down the stone path, Samuel and the Aelfir close behind, the Toymaker's insectoid parts scurrying around their feet.

But as soon as Marney had disappeared into the black, the liquid curtains closed with a splash that sent a wave of magic shimmering through the veil. The doorway collapsed, falling in a rush of water that steamed and hissed on the cave floor. The stream began to boil and froth.

'No!' Samuel shouted.

An overpowering stench of rot filled the air. Namji and Hillem gagged.

The luminous fungus and miniature trees were beset by a preternatural decay that fast reduced them to putrid puddles which were drawn down into the red rock beneath them.

What is that? Van Bam asked.

The wolf's heightened hearing was picking up a sound, a distant rumble made by thousands of running feet.

'Shit,' Samuel hissed.

His face blanked; his eyes lost focus; his body became honed by prescient awareness.

'Listen,' Namji said.

A tumult of voices, echoing, baying, heading towards the group. The ululations of wild demons.

'For a minute there,' Glogelder said through gritted teeth, 'I really thought this was going to be easy.' He checked his pistol and looked at Samuel. 'What's the word, sunshine?'

'Run!'

CHAPTER EIGHTEEN

THE LAST STAND

They came. An endless wave of misshapen beasts.

Ahead of Clara, Samuel turned to run backwards as he fired his ice-rifle, spitting dart after dart over the wolf and into the mass of wild demons the Relic Guild were struggling to outrun. His aim steered by prescient awareness, each dart as hard as crystal, Samuel never missed his mark. But even his sure-shooting couldn't deal with a horde of this size, and he missed the two demons who descended upon Clara from the ceiling.

The first landed on the ground in front of the wolf, the second on her back, causing her legs to buckle. It stabbed hornlike hands into her flanks, the sharp tips digging through her thick pelt, piercing her skin. Van Bam hissed as he experienced Clara's pain. The Toymaker swarmed the demon that had landed on the ground, each insectoid flashing as they administered lethal shots of thaumaturgic venom. Barking and growling, Clara shook the demon from her back and ripped the head from its shoulders with her powerful jaws.

Behind the Relic Guild, the mass of monsters kept on coming – screeching, baying, desperate to tear and rend.

Namji fired three bolts from her crossbow along the horde's front line, which stretched from wall to wall. The vacuum magic slowed the pursuit, crushing and ripping apart any demon that came close to it, but Clara knew the effects wouldn't last long.

'Come on!' Samuel shouted.

Hillem and Glogelder didn't need to be told twice. Namji wasn't far behind them, and Clara brought up the rear with her army of automatons.

If there is any safe place left for us in the Retrospective, Van Bam told the wolf in a growl, *then Samuel's prescient awareness will find it. Don't stop, Clara.*

The thunder of pursuit made by thousands of demonic feet shook the ground.

There was no time to figure out how or why the Relic Guild had been detected, or to worry about what had happened to Marney, Hamir and Bellow. When the demons came, they came hard and fast, pouring down the cave passage like the violence of the Retrospective personified. Blood-chilling cries and bestial roars echoed with the voice of damnation, bringing the stench of age and decay and hopelessness.

Most of the demons were behind the Relic Guild, a vast stampede of perversion reaching back who knew how far; but some had managed to get ahead of the group by burrowing through the red rock around them.

Look out! Van Bam warned.

But Clara was already aware of the danger. The ground just ahead erupted and a four-legged monster jumped for her. It had no face on its conical head, and the smily ebon carapace covering its body looked as hard as stone. It kicked at Clara with its forelegs, its feet more like bony clubs. The wolf dodged the attack, letting the Toymaker take care of the creature.

Hillem cried out in alarm as two more demons appeared from the ground before him. He thrust the barrels of his pistols into their gaping maws and burst the backs of their heads. As he did so, a section of the wall to his right collapsed and a monstrous worm slumped into the cave, hissing putrid breath from the void of its mouth. Glogelder reeled away, pumping two fire-bullets into its huge, flabby body. But neither the big Aelf's shots nor Samuel's ice-darts slowed the worm; in fact, their attacks only caused the beast to rear with anger. Once again, the Toymaker killed their foe with thaumaturgic stings.

The flight continued. The tide of demons remained endless.

Strength and time were running out, and Clara felt they were only fleeing into the jaws of inevitability. But while Samuel's magic continued to lead them, they wouldn't give up. Hillem and Glogelder dealt with the few demons who emerged from the ground and walls and ceiling around them – *if* they got the chance before Samuel and the Toymaker took care of them. Namji slapped her last cartridge of bolts into her crossbow as the group sprinted single file through a bottleneck in the cave. Namji turned and fired at the ground. Demons screeched and died, and the vacuum magic bought a few more precious seconds.

Where's Marney? Clara demanded angrily. *Where are Hamir and Bellow?*

Keep faith, Clara, Van Bam replied. *Pray that our friends have reached a place where salvation will come to us all.*

Clara wanted to laugh at that. She wanted to mock Van Bam's unwavering hope and give in to the wolf's baser instincts, which longed for her to turn around and fight the horde, to face her death with pride. But she kept going. She was the governor of Labrys Town – even though she was probably about to become the shortest serving Resident in history.

Once again, just as it had seemed that they might beat improbable odds, the tables had been turned on the Relic Guild. Perhaps Van Bam was right; perhaps all they could do was hope that their missing friends had found the Nephilim's prison and that salvation was on its way.

The cave narrowed again, shepherding the companions into single file. After Samuel, Hillem and Glogelder had got a little way ahead, Namji turned, shouting, 'Go! Go!' at the wolf and the Toymaker. The small Aelf pulled a spell sphere from her satchel, shaking it until it gave off the glow of angry red magic. As soon as the wolf and the Toymaker had passed her, Namji smashed the sphere on the ground, releasing the spell.

Crimson lines of fierce magic jumped and spat, forming a latticework of crackling energy between the narrow walls and rising high to illuminate the shadows above. Namji sprinted after Clara as the first wave of demons hit the spell. The magic sliced through them as easily as wire through cheese, butchering them into bloody chunks that slapped steaming to the red rock floor.

'It won't last long,' Namji warned, and Clara increased her speed.

The passage widened again, the darkness ahead only lifted by the Toymaker's lights. With a deafening crack, an avalanche of red rock fell from the high ceiling, followed by a demonic giant jumping down into the cavern with an earth-shaking boom.

Thirty feet tall at least, its hair and beard were thick nests of vinelike tentacles that writhed around a broken face with eyes like burning coals. Its arms and legs were as long and thick as tree trunks, its body covered with bony plates of armour. Its roar carried the rage and stench of the Retrospective.

Samuel and Glogelder dived to the ground as the giant swung a boulder-sized fist at them. Hillem darted back, but not far enough to avoid being skimmed by the fist. It smashed one of the pistols from Hillem's hand, spinning the Aelf before he fell into a sitting position. The giant prepared to strike again. Hillem fired his remaining pistol at it with a yell of fear. The bullets pinged harmlessly off the armour of bone.

As the insectoid army of the Toymaker swarmed forward, Namji's crossbow *twanged*. The bolt struck the giant in the midriff. Vacuum magic raged. The spell wasn't powerful enough to devour their foe completely, but the giant's bellow of pain shook the ground as its midsection was crushed and destroyed. The giant collapsed in two mighty cauterised halves, blocking the way forward.

Clara bounded up onto the remains, the Toymaker forming two defensive lines either side of her. Proud and strong, the wolf kept vigil as the others clambered over the giant's body. Glogelder had to help Hillem, whose hand was injured; Namji and Samuel had no trouble, and they all made it safely to the other side. By the time Clara headed after them, the horde of wild demons were teeming down the passage again, and the giant's corpse had begun to steam and melt to raw matter that would feed the Retrospective and create a new monstrosity.

The agents of the Relic Guild continued to fight for every scrap of extra time they could buy themselves, reloading as they ran, killing anything that got in their way. *Pray*, Van Bam had said, but Clara wasn't sure the wolf knew how to.

Their flight became increasingly desperate. Strength waned, ammunition ran low, but the Relic Guild fought on.

The passage ahead was blocked by a great wall, the only way through it a tunnel burrowing into its base. Once the group had entered it, Namji fired yet another bolt of vacuum magic at the opening. With the spell howling like a gale behind them, the group exited the tunnel into a small rocky chamber with a low ceiling … and no other way out.

Namji's magic moaned.

Samuel stood staring at the dead-end wall, breathing hard. Inside her head, Clara felt Van Bam's hope sinking as the ghost studied the old bounty hunter's body language through her eyes.

The end of the road, Van Bam whispered.

'What now?' Glogelder demanded, his voice thick with anger. 'What's your magic telling us to do?'

'It isn't,' Samuel said hollowly. 'This is it. This is as far as the cave goes.' He turned to the group, his old face shining with sweat in the Toymaker's glow. He replaced the spent power stones on his rifle with fresh ones, and his blue eyes fixed on Glogelder. 'What's your situation?'

The big Aelf opened the chamber on his pistol. 'I've got two fire-bullets left.'

Samuel undid his utility belt and threw it to him. 'You'll find more bullets in the pouches. Namji?'

The magic-user dropped her crossbow on the floor. 'I'm out,' she said miserably, then looked inside her satchel. 'I've only got a few healing spells left.'

'I need one of those,' Hillem said, wincing. 'That bloody giant broke my hand.'

Namji removed a sphere from the satchel and crushed it over Hillem's right hand. He groaned as the spell fixed his bent fingers and sealed tears in his skin with the pale glow of healing magic.

You could do with a little healing yourself, Van Bam told Clara.

She carried a few superficial wounds, but they were serious enough to have matted her pelt with blood, and some of them were still bleeding. Calmly summoning her magic, Clara felt the crushing rush of metamorphosis, felt the sting of wounds healing, and then she stood among her colleagues as the human.

Samuel gestured to the small automatons surrounding the changeling. 'Tell them to guard the tunnel,' he ordered.

Defer to him, Clara, said Van Bam. *Samuel's experience is our best bet here.*

Clara nodded. 'Defend us,' she ordered the Toymaker.

The hundred insectoid automatons filled the tunnel, lining the floor, clinging to the walls and ceiling. The thaumaturgic lights on the ends of their tails protruded, ready to sting any approaching enemy.

Samuel said, 'When the vacuum magic runs out, we'll have to pick off any demon that makes it past the Toymaker. Hillem, Glogelder – make your shots count. Clara, save your strength for when we need the wolf. Namji, try to conjure some magic that could help us.'

With Hillem and Glogelder either side of him, Samuel stood at the centre of the cavern, facing the tunnel where the Toymaker glowed.

'Last stand, eh?' Glogelder said as he loaded his pistol with any bullets he could find from Samuel's utility belt. 'Well, then ... shit on it all.'

'You think you've got it bad,' Hillem said. He was loading his own pistol with ammunition from his gun belt. 'The last thing I'll probably ever see is your ugly face.'

Glogelder managed a smirk.

Hillem turned worried eyes to the ceiling. 'You know, there's nothing to say they won't come at us through the rock.'

'Thanks for pointing that out,' Glogelder grumbled. 'Did you think we weren't scared enough?'

'Listen!' Namji snapped. She and Clara had moved behind the defensive line. 'My spell's run out.'

Clara realised that the moan of vacuum magic had stopped, and in its place faint hisses and shrieks echoed down the tunnel into the chamber.

Samuel aimed his ice-rifle, but then shook his head. 'This isn't right,' he announced. 'My magic isn't flaring. The demons aren't coming.'

Hillem crept up to the tunnel mouth. 'I think you're right,' he said, peering through the Toymaker's glow. 'Something's moving down there, but ... but it looks like the demons are retreating. I can see— *Oh!*'

Hillem staggered. He faced the group with a confused expression. A line of blood trickled from his nostril.

'Hillem?' Glogelder said worriedly.

'Get away from the tunnel,' Clara shouted, her heightened senses prickling with a new danger lacing the air.

But it was too late. Hillem dropped to his knees, fighting for breath. Blood streamed from his nose now, and more poured from his ears and leaked from eyes as red tears, drenching his face and clothes. He held out a hand for Glogelder, his mouth open in a silent scream. Glogelder raced to him with a cry of despair, but as he neared an almighty pressure crushed Hillem's head with a harsh *crack*, spraying his friend with a shower of blood.

Glogelder reached his side just in time to catch Hillem's dead body in his arms. 'No!' he bellowed, before a deep *pop* of energy punched the big Aelf to the back of the cavern, where his head struck stone and he fell unconscious.

Namji rushed to Glogelder, making small panicky noises as she searched her satchel for a healing spell.

Samuel took aim at the tunnel, his teeth clenched.

They are coming, Van Bam warned, and Clara knew who he meant.

She stood alongside Samuel, doing her best not to look at Hillem's dead body and the sickening sight of his crushed head. 'They're here,' she said coldly.

She felt Van Bam's fear.

There came a drone. In the tunnel, the Toymaker's lights began blinking out one by one, each automaton deactivating and clattering to the ground. The power stones in Samuel's ice-rifle died next. Clara bent double, groaning as a wave of thaumaturgy hit her and sucked the magic from her body. It hit Samuel at the same time and he sank to his knees.

Fabian Moor walked down the tunnel, picking his way through the now inert parts of the Toymaker. Behind him came Mo Asajad and Viktor Gadreel.

'Please,' Namji was moaning, cradling Glogelder's head, 'wake up, wake up.'

Moor stepped over Hillem's corpse and surveyed the chamber. His cool gaze lingered on Samuel and his face became a mask of hatred. Viktor Gadreel's one dark eye bored into Clara. He looked surprised to find her alive; after all, the last time he saw her, he'd left her to the mercy of the same wild demons that had killed Van Bam.

The changeling felt the ghost of the dead Resident recede further into the back of her mind.

Mo Asajad's expression grew puzzled at the sight of Namji cradling Glogelder and weeping over him, before turning to Moor.

'Well, this is … *surprising*.'

Moor agreed.

'We kill them,' Gadreel stated.

'Not so fast, Viktor,' Moor replied.

Clara, like Samuel, was held immobile by higher magic.

Moor and Asajad locked gazes. Something unspoken passed between the two of them, but there was little point in trying to decipher what it was now.

'Lord Spiral ordered us to kill any life we found,' Gadreel rumbled.

'But as Lady Asajad pointed out, Viktor, finding *this* life is a surprise.' Moor walked to Samuel, lifting his face up by the chin. 'These are magickers of the Relic Guild, and I think Lord Spiral would be very interested in discovering why they are here, don't you?'

— CHAPTER NINETEEN —

FUTURE REASON

Marney was frantic.

The watery portal had disappeared after spiriting her away, leaving behind nothing but the thick red rock of a dead-end wall in another cave
passage. Marney's thoughts were for Samuel and Clara, Namji, Hillem
and Glogelder. She had tried to search for the emotions of her friends,
but all she could pick up on were the alien, indecipherable feelings of a
former Thaumaturgist and a Nephilim.

'We have to get them back,' Marney stated, pleaded. 'There's no telling what the Retrospective will throw at them.' She looked imploringly
at Bellow. 'Reopen the portal.'

'I don't know how to,' the giant replied. It might've been the truth,
but his mind was clearly on something other than the fate of the Relic
Guild.

Marney looked at Hamir hopefully.

'I lost the ability to conjure portals a long time ago,' the necromancer
said in that maddeningly calm and genial way of his. 'And we could be
facing troubles of our own, Marney.' He looked around the cave; huge,
as vast as the passage they had just left and lit by an amber glow that
came from somewhere up ahead. 'Perhaps this is Spiral's doing. He
might have detected our presence in the Retrospective and is on his way
here to deal with us.'

'I agree with you, to a point,' Bellow countered. 'But I believe we were
lucky.'

'*Lucky?*' Marney almost shouted.

Bellow regarded her. 'The Retrospective is ever-shifting, and it is
under Spiral's command. Perhaps he detected us and moved the location
of the Nephilim's prison a moment too late to prevent the three of us
from entering.' Evidently excited, the giant set off towards the amber

light. 'I do not believe Spiral has seen everything, and we have the bigger picture to think about.'

Again Marney felt the overwhelming sense of *home* that Bellow radiated, carrying hints of things that he was keeping to himself. But Marney was reluctant to follow him, reluctant to move from the place where the portal had been and give up on her friends.

Hamir took her elbow. 'I understand how you feel, but Gulduur is right. The best thing we can do for the others is see this through to the end.'

'What end?' Marney snapped. 'I've had enough of secrets, Hamir. What haven't I been told?'

'Come and you will find out for yourself. I would suggest controlling your emotions first.'

Marney was rankled but summoned a shield of apathy and stopped feeling anything.

They followed Bellow, and when they reached the source of the light, they discovered life unlike anything they had yet seen. The red rock had become soft, damp, almost muddy, glowing in places with amber crystals. Luminous fungus and miniature trees sprouted in clusters from the walls and floors. A carpet of soft, ash-grey grass grew underfoot. Warm, clean water dripped from above and humidity misted the air. Marney could hear the clicks and buzzes of insects. If she hadn't deadened her emotions, she would've been astounded to hear the cry of a bird and the distant flutter of wings.

Bellow chuckled – half in delight, half in incredulity – as he trailed his finger over the verdant leaves of a tree sprouting from the wall. 'The Skywatchers really do have a complicated way of seeing the future,' he said. 'If Amilee played any kind of trick, it was to give me the answers to my questions in pieces – to allow me to draw my own conclusions.'

'It's an annoying habit of hers,' Hamir muttered.

Bellow chuckled again, this time with pure happiness. His bright blue eyes welled with tears.

'What are you talking about?' Marney said, her voice emotionless. 'And I want the truth.'

'I've been carrying suspicions,' the Nephilim admitted, 'but now I am certain.' He looked down at Marney, smiling. 'Lady Amilee made promises to me that I believed to be hollow. But now I understand that they were just … more complicated than I realised.'

'Promises?'

'To help me find my home.'

'Consider what you are seeing, Marney,' Hamir said. '*Life* growing in a House of dead time and blood. *Life* encouraged by the presence of the Nephilim herd.'

Marney still didn't understand.

'The Retrospective is founded upon the same principles that birthed the Nephilim,' Hamir continued. 'It's almost as if it was created to be used by blood-magickers – of the thaumaturgic kind, of course. A *perfect* environment for such creatures, in fact.'

Marney looked around at the strange life, still confused. The environment might have appeared peaceful, even borderline tranquil, but outside lay plains of hate and fire and perversion where nothing good roamed.

Bellow said, 'What Amilee failed to mention with her *promises* was that once my herd and me were reunited, we would have to *build* our home for ourselves.'

Marney felt the giant's excitement and screwed her face up, nonplussed. 'In the Retrospective?'

'Precisely,' Bellow said, almost hungrily. 'Come, Progenitor. Your children are close.'

The giant set off again with determined strides, his huge feet crushing short grey grass.

Perplexed, Marney kept pace with Hamir as he was dragged along by Bellow's binding magic.

'The Retrospective is the Nephilim's home?' she asked.

'Potentially,' Hamir answered. 'Dead time, blood, death, recycled matter – it is the very stuff from which I made the Nephilim. If they wrestle control of this House from Spiral, they could transform it into whatever image they choose. Marney, the Retrospective is the Sorrow of Future Reason.'

'Look at this!' Bellow shouted, his tone a mixture of demand and awe.

Magic quickened Hamir's pace. When he and Marney caught up with the giant, Bellow was standing stiff-backed as they approached him, his emotions in desperate flux, threatening to boil over.

'My people.' Tears shone in his eyes. 'My *herd*.'

The giant stood at the edge of a mighty subterranean lake of clear water, glistening with radiance shining from deep beneath the surface. Marney peered over to see the source of the light. Despite her empathic control, a gasp escaped her.

Down in the depths, giants drifted in the lake, curled up asleep in cocoons of transparent glowing amber. Hundreds of them. Perhaps a thousand.

'The Nephilim,' Hamir whispered, and Marney felt a flutter of fear coming from him.

'*My* Progenitor,' Bellow growled. He pointed to an island of black stone at the centre of the lake. From its summit, a deep green light sparkled like a star. 'Your day has come.'

Two bullets and a knife.

The Nightshade knew Ennis. It spoke to him, steered his direction, taught him how to navigate its labyrinthine structure. And it was leading him to the cancer growing at the heart of the Resident's home.

Each corridor looked the same, each new antechamber as dull and uninspiring as the last, and the walls carried a repetitive, hypnotising pattern of tiny mazes. The air felt sickly, as though the very stone of the Nightshade was fighting off the disease of Hagi Tabet's influence. Activating Labrys Town's defences had weakened the Genii's hold, and the Nightshade's magic was seeping through her gangrenous fingers.

Ennis descended and ascended short flights of stairs, passed through antechambers and corridor after corridor, never seeing a single room or window. The Nightshade was as complicated as a three-dimensional puzzle whose thousand pieces were comprised of nothing but a bland cream colour. Yet Ennis knew where he was going, and the building's magic fuelled his courage.

He held the gun that Long Tommy had given him, the charmed power stone primed and glowing red. The sharp blade coated in thaumaturgic metal was safely sheathed at his hip.

Two bullets and a knife ...

If Ennis needed any further confirmation that Hagi Tabet had been weakened, he found it in the grotesque creatures he stumbled upon from time to time, almost tripping over them. Misshapen and pink, their skin hung in folds. With long, thin necks not strong enough to hold up spherical heads, their faces were cursed with smeared features and bulging pink eyes. Monstrous hands dangled from the ends of spindly arms.

Ennis didn't know what they were and didn't care about anything other than that they appeared to be dying. Lying on the floor, either still or weakly failing to pull themselves up by the walls, they appeared to be fading from existence and didn't notice the human passing by.

The Nightshade let Ennis know that he had reached his destination when its guidance drew him to the sound of weeping and the first window he had seen. It was set into the wall, a big clear rectangle in the maze pattern. Ennis stole a glance through it.

A scene of horror made his heart thump.

Her body withered, Hagi Tabet hung on a web of leathery tentacles that had grown from her back to pierce the floor, ceiling and walls. Her face was filled with desperation, anger, hunger. Another tentacle smeared with glistening pink jelly had slithered from her navel and was writhing on the floor.

The Woodsman was there, too, its axe hanging on its back. The demon was holding two children – Jade and Daniel – before the Resident, one in each hand. The sound of their tears was clear to Ennis, as though he was in the room with them.

Tabet's appendage rose above the children like a snake. Its tip inflated, opening a yawning, toothless mouth. Thin, greasy lips quivered.

With an urgent pulse from the Nightshade's magic, Ennis acted. He pressed his hand against the mazes on the wall next to the window. The outline of a door appeared with a click and swung inwards.

'Stop,' Ennis said before Tabet's perverse tentacle could harm the children. His throat was dry, his tongue sticking to the roof his mouth. He stood in the doorway, aiming the pistol. 'Let them go.'

The appendage flailed, flicking pink jelly around the room as Tabet sucked it back into her body, leaving an angry red bud at her navel the size of a fist. She considered the new arrival with watery eyes. The Woodsman let go of Jade and Daniel and blocked Ennis's line of fire.

'Go!' Ennis told the children.

Whimpering, they scurried from the room.

Tabet became agitated. 'Magicker,' she hissed and began swinging on her web. 'Kill it!' she screamed. 'Kill it!'

The Woodsman drew its axe with supernatural speed.

Ennis squeezed the first trigger on the pistol.

With a low and hollow spitting sound, a burst of higher magic shot a thaumaturgic bullet at the Woodsman. But it intercepted the shot with demonic reflexes and the bullet shattered the axe head with a dull clang, sending hot shards into all directions. Ennis yelled and threw himself out of the room, desperately knocking burning pieces of metal from his clothes. Undeterred, the Woodsman stamped into the corridor, cast aside the axe shaft and came for Ennis.

From the floor, he took aim at the dark triangle at the front of the Woodsman's hood and pulled the second trigger.

The demon staggered back as the thaumaturgic bullet pierced the shadows of its hood. A screech came from somewhere distant, like a cacophony of death rattles from a host of wild demons. The Woodsman held itself upright by the frame of the door as lines of dull light cracked its skin. With a final roar it broke apart with a warm, golden glow, as if a burst of sunlight had cleansed the corrosion within the demon. It left nothing of the Woodsman behind.

In the following silence, Ennis got to his feet.

A knife …

He dropped the empty pistol and slid the knife from its sheath. The blade's keen edge glimmering with a pearlescent quality, Ennis stepped back into the room.

'What … what is the meaning of this?' Hagi Tabet tried to appear innocently bemused, but she only succeeded in expressing her madness. 'I am just trying to help the denizens.'

Ennis knew she was too weak to use her higher magic; the Nightshade was telling him so. If he left now, Tabet would most likely starve to death without the Woodsman. Not that Labrys Town could afford to wait for her death.

Ennis moved closer to her.

'Come,' she pleaded. 'Serve me as others have.' She tried to smile. 'The rewards will be great.'

Ennis stared at her.

Hungry ...

Two tears fell from Tabet's eyes.

'You're a monster,' Ennis said coldly. 'And the Nightshade doesn't want you here.'

Tabet's face screwed into bestial rage. She yelled a curse and the tentacle shot from her navel like a spear.

Ennis was ready. He sidestepped the attack and chopped down with the knife. The thaumaturgic blade sliced easily through the leathery appendage, cutting it in half.

Tabet's low roar of pain resounded through the very fabric of the Nightshade. Her wounded tentacle whipped the air, pumping pink blood, spraying the room and Ennis.

Ennis rushed past it and stabbed the knife into Tabet's chest. The thaumaturgic blade met little resistance, plunging through skin and bone as if through wood pulp, and skewered the Genii's heart.

The ensuing silence was abrupt. Ennis staggered, breathing hard.

Tabet's watery, mad eyes stared up at the ceiling before rolling back in their sockets. Ennis retreated further, feeling sick, as the web of tentacles steamed and dried, cracking and popping, turning to brittle stone which crumbled and dropped the Genii to the floor.

Hagi Tabet, the Resident of Labrys Town, moaned once, and died.

Ennis wiped blood from his face.

A drone shook the Nightshade, so low it almost rattled Ennis's bones. The light from the ceiling prisms in the room and out in the corridor died, steeping everything in darkness. Then, one by one, they flickered back into life, a dim glow at first but quickly brightening to a clean silver glare. The drone rose in pitch with the whine of rising power. The Resident's home was waking from a coma to find itself strong and full of rage.

The sound of children crying came from somewhere close and Ennis hurried after it.

In the bowels of the Nightshade, in a room called the Last and Lowest Chamber, the First and Greatest Spell stirred.

Gathering power and momentum, a fat column of purple light danced and crackled with the very highest of magic that could be cast. Finally freed from its constraints, the First and Greatest Spell suffused the Nightshade, pouring out into the streets of Labrys Town, pure and cleansing once more. The column bulged before erupting with a mighty burst of energy that flew into the portal standing beside it.

In the blink of an eye, the energy travelled an unimaginable distance. It reached the end of the portal, smashing a simple wooden door from its hinges. The First and Greatest Spell exploded into many scintillating colours as it filled the cave beyond and then flooded down a mountain-side like lava from a volcano.

Wild demons fled from it. The Retrospective trembled.

The multicoloured power flowed across a bridge that spanned a bottomless chasm. Like a marching army of light, the magic crushed the demons on the bridge, knocking many of them over the sides to fall for ever. Those that escaped did so by fleeing through a rent in the air that led to a House of dead time. The First and Greatest Spell sealed the rent and crushed any demon who remained.

Its light spread up to the sky, turning dreary clouds into majestic mists of uncountable hues. Stars shone brightly and told stories of the future in a vast night sky. Falls of emerald waters cascaded from the surrounding clifftops. Unstoppable, the Timewatcher's magic then flowed into the Tower of the Skywatcher.

Lady Yansas Amilee gritted her teeth as the doors flew open and the spell rushed in. Her silver wings fanning, she bathed in the energy that lifted her from the ground, reignited her thaumaturgy, energised her tower. And she felt the touch of the one who had cast it

'Mother,' she sighed.

All around the hall, automaton sentries whirred into motion, shaking off the dust of decrepitude. Amilee hovered above them, singing her joy so loudly her brothers and sisters might hear her on Mother Earth. She laughed and called down to the sentries.

'It is time!'

And she led her army to the Great Labyrinth.

Perhaps Gulduur Bellow had been right. Perhaps the Progenitor's punishment at the hands of the Thaumaturgists was not enough in the eyes of the Nephilim, or of the humans who had died to create them. Hamir didn't know any more.

'They look peaceful,' Marney said.

She was looking down into the lake's depths where the Nephilim herd lay drifting in amber cocoons. So many of them. Hamir knew that Marney had used her empathic magic to deaden her emotions, to stop worrying about Clara and Samuel and the Aelfir; but the necromancer had decided as soon as they were separated that there was little chance the others would survive whatever happened to them next.

'Their long sleep is almost over,' Bellow said, as if to himself.

The three of them walked along a narrow causeway that crossed the lake to the island of dark stone. The star of green light emanated higher magic from the island's summit, almost whispering Hamir's true name. He knew it was the Thaumaturgy which had been drained from him centuries ago; the power by which Spiral had imprisoned the Nephilim. Curiously, Hamir felt nothing at being in its presence after all these years.

Above, wings flapped. Birds or bats? Hamir stopped to wonder. The cave was so large, it was impossible to see into the gloom beyond the lake's glow. How much life had grown here? How much *could* grow here? What kind of world would the Nephilim create from the Retrospective? Hamir felt the tug of the magic which bound him to Bellow and continued along the causeway.

As they neared the end, Marney said, 'I never expected the Nephilim's prison to be so ... serene.'

'Perhaps it didn't begin this way,' Bellow replied. 'Over the years, I suspect my people affected the environment. It is a sign of their benevolence.'

Benevolence? Hamir thought. How would they react when they woke up to be confronted by their creator? What could Hamir tell them, what reasons could he give to appease a millennium's worth of repressed anger? The herd had grown to almost a thousand, and for centuries the offspring of the Nephilim elders had been listening to lies and myths about the Progenitor. Hamir hoped that the truth would be met by this *benevolence* Bellow spoke of – *if* he could work out how to free them.

As they reached the end of the causeway, the star of green light shone a little brighter, perhaps sensing the proximity of its owner.

How will the Nephilim react? Hamir frowned.

Amilee had given him no obvious instructions as to how he was supposed to reclaim his higher magic; but in the same way that she had delivered Bellow to the realisation that the Retrospective was the Sorrow of Future Reason, Hamir began to understand that the Skywatcher had already given him all the pieces that made up the answer. He just had to assemble them.

'Here we are,' said Marney.

The island had been fashioned like a pyramid, comprising huge individual blocks of black stone. Each level was like a step towards the summit, but they were tall, smooth and sheer, as though crafted for the use of giants. Bellow began climbing.

'You know what you're doing, right?' Marney asked as the giant helped her up onto the first level.

'Personally, I haven't a clue,' Bellow replied. 'But then, I'm not the one we're relying on.'

'I'm sure I can improvise,' Hamir said sourly.

Bellow's massive hand reached down and grabbed Hamir by the collar, yanking him up to stand beside Marney. 'Don't *improvise* too much, Progenitor.'

That name again, that ... *legend*. Hamir shuddered inwardly every time he heard it.

With Bellow's help, they climbed to the penultimate level of the island. Marney looked at the green light shining just above them and then shrugged at the necromancer.

'Good luck.'

'Indeed,' Bellow growled, and he lifted Hamir to the summit.

He stood upon a single great block of black stone. Rising from it was a pedestal of the same dark substance with a smooth bowl carved into its top. In the bowl sat Hamir's thaumaturgy. He had expected its green light to dazzle his eyes, but now he was close by, it dimmed to a dark green glow. A glassy diamond – what other shape would it be? – containing higher magic. Hamir stared at it, wondering why he felt nothing.

'Hamir?' Marney said from below.

'I need a moment to think.'

Bellow hissed out a testy, impatient breath. 'You have had all the *moments* you need. Free my herd.'

'Wait,' said Marney; her empathic magic was obviously sensing Hamir's confusion. 'I think he's telling the truth.'

Truth ... ?

The words of Lady Amilee flowed through Hamir's mind. The revelations, the information, the pieces of a puzzle which now came together as an answer. The Timewatcher had enforced love and devotion from the denizens by implanting splinters of the First and Greatest Spell into their souls. It was impossible for any inhabitant of Labrys Town to deny faith in Her. *You never knew what your punishment was*, Amilee had said; and, with a wry smile, Hamir finally understood.

He had lived for a thousand years among the denizens without his thaumaturgy. Of *course* he would become like them. Over the years, a splinter of the First and Greatest Spell had entered *his* soul, commanded *his* obedience, keeping him trapped.

Did that mean he was ... *hybrid*? Like the Nephilim?

Hamir baulked at the absurdity. 'Gulduur, kindly remove your binding spell. I cannot do this otherwise.'

Bellow's blue eyes glared up at him. 'Spare me your tricks, Progenitor. You're going nowhere until my people are free and you have answered to us.'

'No, you don't understand.' Was that the sting of tears Hamir felt? 'I have to do this by *choice*.'

Because a lowly former Thaumaturgist could never undo the Timewatcher's decree and reclaim the higher magic that had been stripped from him. But he could ensure that it found a rightful resting place. He could take responsibility for everything he had done. He could make the decision that perhaps the Timewatcher had always intended him to make; a decision that would break the curse which had stitched the life of the Nephilim to their creator.

'It's not a trick,' Marney said. The expression of concerned awe on her face suggested to Hamir that she understood what he was thinking, what he had to do next. But how could she? How could any of them? 'Your magic is prohibiting him.'

With eyes narrowed in suspicion, the giant whispered a few words of blood-magic. A light burning sensation on his stomach told Hamir that the binding spell was broken.

'Thank you,' the necromancer said.

After a moment's hesitation, he reached out and took the green diamond from the pedestal's bowl. It felt light and hot in his fist, pliant, gelatinous. Delicate. The higher magic inside called to Hamir. Its light cooled and dimmed, as though nestling into his grasp.

Hamir looked down at the amber glow of the lake, at the Nephilim drifting in their cocoons. Yes – they looked peaceful. Tears misted his vision.

'Hamir?' said Marney, her tone worried.

He smiled at the empath, suddenly remembering with fondness the young and frightened woman who had first joined the Relic Guild. 'Marney, I have been known by many names,' he said, 'and I have seen *such* wonders.' He wiped his eyes. 'But I also survived a time of darkness whose shadow would swallow even the Genii War. It is known today as the Old Ways. Little is remembered of that time, and with good reason.'

He switched his gaze to Bellow, who still regarded him with suspicion. 'There is a book,' Hamir told him. 'It is my ... journal. I wrote it when I was exiled to the Labyrinth at the end of the Old Ways. It was a form of therapy, I suppose you could say, to help me come to terms with my ... *disgrace*. The journal can be found in my laboratory at the Nightshade. It contains everything you wish to know about *why* I created the Nephilim.'

'What is this—' Bellow began, but Hamir cut him off.

'You want answers, Gulduur, and this is all I can offer. But if there is any part of you that can take advice from me, then I warn you to *never* read the contents of that book.' He looked back at Marney. 'It should be burned.'

'What are you doing?' Marney demanded.

'Answering for my crimes.'

Hamir crushed the green diamond in his fist.

The light escaped its gelatinous confines, no longer green but now a deep purple radiance that oozed from between Hamir's fingers to spread up his arms, across his body and engulf him entirely.

From a far and distant place, Hamir heard Marney call his name as the radiance seeped into him through every pore. There was no pain, no surge of power – only a curious sensation that let Hamir know this thaumaturgy no longer belonged to him, but to his children.

His being crumbled to atoms.

He saw everywhere at once: the cave, the lake, the island. A blood-magicker and an empath watched him burst into a swarm of pinprick stars, spiralling with higher magic. The swarm cascaded into the waters, speeding down to the lowest depths, where they scattered, invading amber cocoons and the bodies of sleeping giants. As splinters of the First and Greatest Spell kissed a thousand souls with the essence of their creator, Simowyn Hamir became no more.

And the Nephilim awoke.

CHAPTER TWENTY

BLOOD RAIN

Iblisha Spiral, Lord of the Genii, hovered in the air above a hill of scorched rock. His silver wings gently fanned the hot updraughts radiating from the Retrospective; his beautiful yet terrible face expressed neither pleasure nor displeasure. Below him, endless ranks of wild demons surrounded the hill. Row after row of them, stretching back as far as the eye could see, all observing silently, almost standing to attention. High above, more demons flew beneath a sky roiling with clouds of poison and acid.

Spiral's violet eyes gleamed with curiosity at the remnants of the Relic Guild kneeling on the hilltop.

Inside, Samuel was beset by fear and anger and hopelessness; outside, thaumaturgy had strangled his magic and rendered him so immobile he couldn't even blink to moisten his eyes against the dusty heat. Clara, Namji and Glogelder were held in a similar state. Voiceless and incapacitated, they knelt in a line, staring up at Spiral. Behind them stood the Genii.

Hillem was dead. Marney, Hamir and Bellow were missing. But there was a surprise inclusion at this gathering: Councillor Tal. The elderly Aelf, his face expressionless, stood directly below Spiral, staring with eyes of black – subjugated, possessed. Samuel understood the implications of Tal's presence and felt himself surrendering to the inevitable.

'I'm confused,' said Spiral. His voice was in the ground, the sky, the wind ... a voice that could command universes. 'Did I not tell you to destroy any life that you discovered?'

'You did, my lord,' Viktor Gadreel rumbled from behind Glogelder. 'Lord Moor and Lady Asajad decided that you would want to question this rabble personally.'

'We thought you would wish to decide their fates yourself,' Mo Asajad added quickly. She stood between Clara and Namji. 'We thought they would interest you.'

'Did you now?' The army of wild demons stirred, as though expressing Spiral's displeasure. 'And what do you suppose I might find so interesting about them?'

Fabian Moor, who had been standing directly behind Samuel, moved ahead of the group. He was holding Samuel's hunting knife. 'My lord, this is the Relic Guild.'

'Ah …' Spiral looked down at Tal. 'Do you see, Ghoul? These are the people who you claimed would never kneel to me, who would always *stand* against me.'

Tal remained silent, his eyes expressionless.

'Go on,' Spiral prompted him. 'You know what I expect. Let's start with one of your fellow Aelfir. The brutish one first.'

Subservient, Tal walked to where the Relic Guild's weapons had been dumped into a pile. He selected Samuel's revolver before approaching Glogelder. Glogelder could only stare, unblinking, as Tal pressed the barrel of the gun to his forehead and primed the power stone.

'Wait,' Spiral said, clearly amused. 'I think he wants to say something.'

Spiral dispelled the restraining magic and Glogelder groaned. 'Hillem.' Tears sprang from his eyes and he wailed his friend's name again. 'I'll kill you.' His face was a mask of rage and hatred as he bared his teeth at Spiral. 'I'll kill you all—'

Tal pulled the trigger.

Samuel wanted to close his eyes. To shy away. But Spiral's hold forced him and his companions to watch as the back of Glogelder's head burst with blood and bone. The big Aelf fell on his side, staring at his friends. The hole in his forehead smoked. His blood pooled.

Fabian Moor stared at Samuel in something close to contemplation, turning the blade of the hunting knife over and over in his hands.

'Yes,' Spiral said, as if talking to himself. 'The point has been well made.'

Tal pressed the revolver to his temple and shot himself.

As the elderly Aelf fell down beside Glogelder, Samuel sank further into the oblivion of hopelessness.

The Retrospective began devouring Tal's corpse, drinking his blood, liquefying his body and skeleton into a soup that was absorbed into the rock.

Spiral frowned when he noticed that Glogelder's body remained untouched.

'How curious,' the Genii Lord said. 'Viktor, remove his clothes.'

The hulking Genii stamped over to Glogelder and proceeded to strip him unceremoniously, disrespectfully, ripping his hooded top and yanking it savagely away from his body. Spiral called a halt before Gadreel could complete Glogelder's indignity by removing his boots and trousers.

'What do we have here?' Spiral was talking about the red magical symbols written on Glogelder's stomach. 'A ward of protection?' He scoured the remaining members of the Relic Guild. 'They must all wear them, but ... who among them, I wonder, has knowledge of blood-magic?'

With a flick of his hand, Spiral burned away the symbols on Glogelder's body. Immediately, the ravenous hunger of the Retrospective devoured him, clothes and all, and his last remnants were sucked down into the rock.

Winter descended on Samuel, an icy state that forbade him to care any longer.

'Question this one, my lord,' Moor said, pointing at Samuel with his own knife. 'He's probably their leader.'

Spiral stared at Samuel as though considering an insect before releasing him from the magical restraints. Samuel fell forwards onto his hands, breathing hard, blinking tears and dust from his eyes. His magic returned to him. It was dull, almost dead.

'You and your friends are associates of Simowyn Hamir.' Spiral's tone was all the more disturbing for its friendliness. 'Have you been travelling with him? Did he give you these protective spells?'

Samuel coughed, spitting a bitter taste into the dirt. He looked up, trembling, and his lie came as a nod.

'Where is he now?'

In that icy place that was slowly dying in Samuel, he latched on to the last ember of defiance burning with the fading hope that Hamir could somehow still save the denizens, the Aelfir ... *everyone* – if he was given enough time. 'Hamir is dead,' he stated.

'I think you are lying to me, little magicker.'

To Samuel's surprise, Moor answered for him. 'Perhaps not, my lord.'

'Oh?'

'When we found them,' Asajad explained, 'they had already been attacked by your demons. It is probable that Hamir fell along the way.'

'But we have no way of confirming that,' Gadreel added, almost admonishing his fellow Genii. 'The last we knew, Hamir was barricaded in the Nightshade. Just because—'

'Enough,' Spiral purred. Above, the sky roiled. 'Dear Simowyn is clearly alive and free.'

Samuel spared a glance for Clara and Namji. Still on their knees, they expressed nothing of the fear and turmoil they must have been feeling.

'I know why you are here.' Each of Spiral's words seethed with intolerance for Samuel. 'I understand why the skies have been keeping secrets from me. But no matter what Lady Amilee has planned, she is trapped, and she is not coming to help you.'

Samuel didn't respond, but he noted Moor and Asajad sharing a meaningful look that their lord didn't notice.

'Hamir's thaumaturgy was stripped from him centuries ago,' Spiral continued. 'Even if I hadn't moved the location of the Nephilim's prison, he no longer has the power to open it. But I would like the chance to speak with Hamir – before I kill him.'

Spiral summoned his thaumaturgy and dragged Clara and Namji across the rocky ground, hoisting them into the air to hover just below his feet. Although they couldn't move or speak, Samuel still saw the panic and terror in the eyes of his friends. 'Now, unless you want to watch me feed your friends to the Retrospective, you will tell me where Simowyn Hamir is.'

Samuel felt a nudge from his prescient awareness. It wasn't much, just enough to brighten the dark hopelessness with shadowy light, and it encouraged him to look up at the clouds. The sky was changing, darkening.

'Hamir is with a friend of ours.' With a surge of courage, Samuel decided that on these damned, demonic plains, surrounded by untold numbers of enemies, he would face his fate on his feet, and he forced himself upright before the Genii Lord. 'His name is Gulduur Bellow. He's an elder of the Nephilim herd.'

Clara and Namji fell to the ground, the restraining spell evaporated. They scurried to Samuel's side.

Spiral rose higher into the air. The demons around the hill hissed. The Genii looked up at their lord uncertainly. A dark hole appeared in the poisonous clouds above him. Flying demons fled from it.

'Impossible!' There might have been fear in Spiral's tone. 'There are no free Nephilim.'

Samuel's magic became a warm, oily feeling, soaking into his intuition. 'You were too late,' he growled. 'Hamir and Bellow got inside the prison. The Nephilim are coming for you, Iblisha Spiral.'

'My Genii—' Spiral began, but his wings fell limp and he crashed to the hilltop in a heavy, ungainly manner.

A sudden stillness gripped the Retrospective.

A shout of thunder came from the hole in the sky.

Spiral got to his feet, trembling with rage at the pain he appeared to be feeling. He glowed with higher magic. Samuel, Clara and Namji backed away – as did the Genii, and the wild demons. All of them looked to the sky.

It was raining. Dark, viscous drops of blood pattered down on the group, filling the air with a rusty tang. Each drop glistened with energy as it splashed upon the red rock and seeped into the Retrospective.

The atmosphere crackled. A storm of lightning shredded the clouds and the dark hole widened, turning a deep shade of amber.

'No!' Spiral shouted, and his wings fanned once more.

Figures appeared from the amber light, hundreds of them, bringing the rain of blood. Even from such a distance, Samuel could tell they were giants.

'The Nephilim,' Clara breathed.

Namji whimpered.

With a roar of fury, Spiral beat his wings and vaulted into the air, becoming a tornado of fiery smoke that billowed up to meet his adversaries.

The wild demons broke ranks, countless in number, fighting and scrambling over each other to get clear of the magical rain.

Samuel wiped blood from his eyes to watch Viktor Gadreel summon thaumaturgy and race skywards to join his master in battle. Mo

Asajad had no such intensions, or any interest in her human captives. Whispering the language of the Thaumaturgists, she sliced a hand through the air, causing the dark rent of a portal to appear. She jumped into it and disappeared from the Retrospective.

Namji had lost her mind. She knelt on the ground, spattered in red, covering her head with her hands. Clara was with her, holding her. Samuel made to join them but Fabian Moor yanked him back and held the hunting knife to his throat.

'You're coming with me,' the Genii hissed.

While the sky exploded with fire and infinite colours, Samuel was dragged into churning darkness.

The voice of the Nightshade spoke to the magic in Ennis's blood.

It was as though the building was flexing its muscles, no longer a victim of the Genii's disease, gathering its energy until it was returned to the peak of its power. And it welcomed Ennis, welcomed him in a way that made him feel more a part of Labrys Town than he had ever felt before. And it thanked him for his part in saving hundreds of thousands of lives.

The Resident was dead. Her demons were gone. But Ennis wasn't alone in the Nightshade.

A small army of automatons were prowling the corridors. Wherever they had come from, they appeared to be leaving, perhaps to add their numbers to the automatons and denizens already fighting the infected out on the streets. Ennis wanted to follow them, feeling exhilarated, almost desperate to join the fight. But he couldn't. Not yet. He had two children to rescue from the Nightshade's labyrinthine structure.

A shout came from up ahead, from beyond a right-hand turn in the corridor. Ennis slowed and peeked around the corner. His heart froze when he saw the Genii Lady Asajad.

But she was on her knees in an antechamber, held down by two imposing automatons. Her face, smooth and porcelain pale, paler than the scarring on her forehead, was streaked with lines of dried blood. Before her stood another woman, dressed in purple robes, her head shaved bald. Through slits in the robe, Ennis could make out something silver on her back. Wings? The woman's hand glowed with higher magic.

'Amilee, wait!' Asajad cried.

Yes, the Nightshade whispered to Ennis's blood. *Lady Amilee, the Skywatcher, the patron of the denizens …*

'We were *wrong*!' Asajad's tone was pleading. She appeared frail, painfully thin, exhibiting nothing of a creature of higher magic's power. 'Iblisha Spiral is insane!'

'A shame you did not recognise that fact forty years ago, Lady Asajad.' Amilee's voice rivalled the surging power of the Nightshade. 'Baran Wolfe tried to warn you.'

'You don't understand,' Asajad half-sobbed, half-snarled. She tried and failed to free herself from the automatons' clutches, 'Spiral doesn't wish to merely overthrow the Timewatcher – he will *become* Her, exceed Her power—'

'Not any more,' Amilee interrupted. 'There is blood on your face. It is the blood of the Nephilim. They have sown a seed of dead time in you, and it is destroying your thaumaturgy. You have been cursed by blood-magic.'

'Amilee, please …'

'It is a little too late to be seeking my mercy.'

Amilee's magic became a wicked spike of energy in her palm. Her silver wings spread and she grew taller, more powerful. 'Lady Mo Asajad, usurper, Genii, former disciple of the Pantheon of Thaumaturgists – in the name of the Timewatcher, the Trinity of Skywatchers and the people of Labrys Town, I sentence you to death.'

Held prone by the automatons, Asajad could only begin to scream, 'No!' before Amilee rammed the spike of higher magic into her face.

The Genii convulsed, thrashing in the automatons' vice-like grip. When Amilee dispelled her magical weapon, Asajad fell limp, hanging dead from metal hands, her face a charred and blackened ruin.

'Take her away,' the Skywatcher said dispassionately.

The automatons dragged the dead body down the corridor leading away from the antechamber. Amilee watched them leave and then looked back over her shoulder. Ennis caught a glimpse of the black diamond tattooed onto her forehead before ducking back and hiding.

'The Nightshade's defences are now at full strength.' Amilee's voice drifted to Ennis, perhaps even from the walls and floor and ceiling around him. 'Its magic is once again protecting the denizens and ridding this town of the Genii's filthy virus. This is largely because of you, Sergeant Ennis, and you have no reason to hide from me.'

Gingerly, Ennis left his hiding place and faced her, not knowing whether to feel fearful or humbled that the Skywatcher knew his name; but not even the Nightshade could fill him with the courage to walk down the corridor and join her in the antechamber.

Amilee smiled. 'On behalf of the Nightshade, the Relic Guild and the denizens of Labrys Town – thank you, Ennis.'

He tried to reply but his mouth only succeeded in moving wordlessly. Even from that distance, he couldn't look into her tawny eyes. Lady Amilee was radiant, and her very presence only highlighted the fatigue in Ennis that begged him to lie down and cry and not get up again for a very long time. He was almost glad when another automaton arrived to disturb the moment.

Sitting in the crooks of its arms were the two children. The automaton let them down and they hid behind Lady Amilee, clutching the folds of her purple robe. Their eyes were wide and full of fear.

'I believe you have already met Jade and Daniel,' Amilee said.

They recognised Ennis and hope came to their small faces.

Amilee's long, slender hands rested protectively on the children's shoulders, and they looked up at her. 'Now then, young ones, this is Sergeant Ennis. He is a policeman, and you have my promise that you can trust him.'

Ennis stared at the three of them. The way this creature of higher magic spoke, communicated with these children as *equals* … he found himself wishing that she would speak to him in the same manner.

'Sergeant Ennis,' Amilee prompted. 'You *will* take care of Jade and Daniel for me?'

Ennis snorted a laugh. 'Of course I will.' He felt such relief within him that he sank to one knee and opened his arms. 'I've already helped them once.'

With a little encouragement from Amilee, the children ran to him and he gathered them into his embrace.

'Labrys Town is hurting, Sergeant,' Amilee said as she strode off with the automaton. 'The denizens will need people like you to help them heal.'

The wild demons couldn't escape.

They tried to flee the rain of blood and the fury of the Nephilim but they didn't get far. In their tens of millions the demons died upon the endless savage plains and crashed down from the sky. Their screams were cut short as dead time broke them, crushed them, churned their remains into a soup of blood and meat and bone, forming a deep layer of compost from which strange plant life grew with preternatural speed. Fungi the size of houses; trees as tall as mountains; swards of grass as grey as ash, littered with flowers glowing with amber light. The Retrospective bloomed with the life of the Nephilim.

But the battle was not yet over.

As the House of dead time transformed, a patch of scorched rock erupted on a hilltop. From the depths of a dark hole, a hundred insectoid automatons burst to the surface, their tails lashing with thaumaturgic stings. They swarmed, creating a protective circle around a human magicker and an Aelf kneeling on the ground in each other's arms.

Clara barely noticed the Toymaker's return. Her teeth clenched, she only had eyes for the battle between Spiral and the Nephilim herd. The wrath of incomprehensible power, shouting with thunder, shaking the ground and blistering the air, had turned the sky deep crimson. The blazes of higher magic were so fierce, so bright, that Clara could barely discern the multitude of giants draining the last slivers of control from the fierce storm that Spiral had become: a tornado of flaming black smoke that stretched from morphing ground to bloody clouds.

Namji's mind had snapped. She clung to Clara, sinking into her embrace, weeping and moaning on her knees as though the changeling was her last hope. The blood that had rained down on them earlier had dried to flakes that tingled upon the skin. Clara and Namji were now covered by a shield of energy, a dome of translucent magic that protected them from the battle and the bloody downpour.

Namji needs you, Van Bam said. He sounded as though his teeth were gritted, too. *The two of you could be all that is left of us.*

Marney, Hamir and Gulduur Bellow had obviously succeeded in opening the Nephilim's prison, but where were they now? Lady Asajad had disappeared and Clara didn't know where Fabian Moor had taken Samuel, but Viktor Gadreel was present.

The hulking brute, the only Genii to remain loyal to his master, had been thrown from the battle almost as soon as he tried to enter it, crashing into the hilltop like a bird with broken wings, landing so hard he cracked the rock. Only Gadreel's thaumaturgy had saved him from death; but that power was quickly drained from him by the blood-magic of three Nephilim who had descended to accost the Genii.

Gadreel looked puny as he raged and spat at the two giants holding him down on his knees. The third giant approached Clara and Namji, and the Toymaker parted before her.

Wiry beneath a robe of brown, itchy-looking material, she bore a plethora of pale scars on the weathered skin of her arms and legs. Her dusky hair was tied loosely into a tail. A few stray tangles framed her gaunt face and startling blue eyes. Above her, the sky blazed and shouted.

'My name is Eysha Bellow,' she said, her voice surprisingly clear and calm, betraying no anxiety amidst the tumult of battle. 'I am an elder of my herd, and you ...' She stared, her eyes drifting briefly to Namji's shivering, weeping form in the changeling's arms, before deciding something. 'Your name is Clara, and you speak for your people.'

Clara wasn't sure how to reply until Van Bam reminded her that she very much spoke for humankind now. 'I am the Resident of Labrys Town,' she said, looking up at the Nephilim towering over her. 'I am the leader of the Relic Guild.'

Eysha Bellow bobbed her head respectfully, solemnly. 'We Nephilim owe you and your kind a great debt of gratitude.'

Namji clutched at Clara, her sobbing increasing.

'Your friend is terrified,' Eysha said with sympathy. 'And who can blame her?' She turned her eyes to the battle in the sky. 'This is no place for creatures of lower magic.'

'The rest of my friends,' Clara said, desperation and panic rising. 'They're missing. There was—'

'They are beyond your help.' Eysha spoke with certainty, not unkindness. 'And I suspect that your people need their Resident now. I will return you to the Labyrinth.'

That's it? Clara thought. *We just leave and keep our fingers crossed that the Nephilim defeat Spiral?*

The Nephilim have already won, Van Bam replied. *Look at the sky.*

The smoky black tornado that was Spiral had shrunk, becoming noticeably thinner, its fire dying in the blood rain, beset on all sides by nearly a thousand Nephilim shining with higher magic.

Then we go home, Clara said, realising that she had never expected to be saying such a thing. But Van Bam had other ideas.

No, he growled. *Not yet.*

The ex-Resident directed Clara's vision to Viktor Gadreel.

The Genii had given up struggling against his Nephilim captors. He now stared into the battle, calling his lord's name.

Gadreel's thaumaturgy is gone. The ghost's tone was as harsh as talons scraping the inside of Clara's skull. *He is as mortal as any human.*

Clara had never known the illusionist to exhibit such heat and anger, and she did not disapprove. She drew courage from it, strength.

Gadreel fed me to wild demons, Van Bam said hotly. *And he made you watch!*

Clara felt her magic stirring. *You want me to kill him for you?*

I want the wolf to rip him apart.

Eysha already appeared to know what was going on in Clara's mind and her blue eyes studied Gadreel. 'You wish revenge?'

Clara rose, standing little higher than the giant's midriff. 'I do.'

Namji grabbed at her. 'Don't ... don't leave me,' she begged.

'It'll be all right, I promise,' Clara soothed. Namji wrapped her arms around her body and began to rock back and forth. Clara addressed Eysha. 'For his crimes against my people, Viktor Gadreel deserves to die.'

The Nephilim watched the battle. Spiral's ever-decreasing storm was now shot through with spears of violet lightning. Gadreel called his lord's name again.

'Yes,' Eysha said. 'I understand why you would wish for vengeance.' She drew a shuddery, exhilarated breath. 'Very well. We will not stand in your way.'

Clara instructed the Toymaker to not interfere. Eysha ordered her fellow Nephilim to release their prisoner with a wave of her hand. She then picked up Namji. Eyes squeezed shut, the Aelf wept in the giant's arms.

It took Gadreel a moment to realise that he was no longer being held, and then he stood, suspicious until his one dark eye fixed on Clara and the clear ground between them.

'Little wolf,' he rumbled – seething, defeated. 'You deserved all the pain I gave you.'

Van Bam sighed. *Do as you were born to do.*

Clara summoned her magic.

It came with searing heat that rushed through every inch of her being. Clara's limbs and body morphed and grew, absorbing her magical clothes even as silver-grey hair sprouted from her skin. With a final surge, Clara's face snapped into a long muzzle and she stood on four strong legs.

Snarling, the wolf bounded forward.

Gadreel was big, a brute, quick and strong even without his higher magic. He raised an arm for defence and managed to remain upright when Clara sank her long teeth into it. Gadreel hissed, smashing a meaty fist into the wolf's side. Clara felt a rib snap but she didn't let go. She bit as hard as she could, tearing the arm away at the elbow. Gadreel roared in pain and fell down onto his back, spraying blood. His remaining hand gripped Clara around the throat, trying to crush her windpipe. With impressive strength, he held the wolf at bay. For a moment.

Viktor Gadreel's final curse was lost as Clara's jaws closed around his head. Her teeth sank through skin, cracking bone. The wolf revelled in the taste of his defeat, crushing his head until his skull gave and her teeth speared into his brain. Growling, Clara bit and shook until Gadreel's head was torn from his neck.

Van Bam was silent in her mind.

With the hot, salty tang of Genii blood filling her mouth, the wolf stood astride her foe's corpse and howled victory at the furious sky.

The remnants of Spiral's storm had become thin tendrils of oily smoke hanging from the crimson clouds. One after the other, they dissipated as bolts of purple lightning struck them. The sound of thunder faded into the distance. Blood rain continued to fall. The Lord of the Genii was dead. The magic of the Nephilim flourished and commanded the Retrospective.

'The Sorrow of Future Reason,' Eysha Bellow whispered. She approached Clara, Namji unconscious in her arms. Her blue eyes shone with tears and the power of blood-magic. 'Come then, you magnificent creature. Your people need you.'

THE GREAT LABYRINTH

Marney felt nothing.

The shadow carriage disappeared, leaving her, Samuel and Van Bam standing in a courtyard somewhere in the Great Labyrinth.

Only the three of them left now.

Rising from the centre of the courtyard's cobbled floor was the stone arm of a golem. Held in its hand was an open-topped box made from pearlescent metal, which was filled with the gelatinous substance used to summon shadow carriages. An improvised device, fashioned by Fabian Moor, no doubt. But of the Genii himself there was no sign.

Samuel swore.

He and Van Bam faced a portal on the courtyard's back wall. It was active, churning with the thick, gluey whiteness of the Nothing of Far and Deep. But it was unlike any other portal to be found in the Great Labyrinth; it didn't sit behind a wooden door with a symbol engraved into a metal plaque signifying which House it led to. This portal was a large circle on the wall – another of the Genii's improvisations.

'Damn it,' Van Bam said. 'Moor must have already escaped.'

'Then we follow him,' Samuel stated.

But Marney had detected something in the air. It was vague, yet more than just the emotional residue of someone who had passed this way, and she could barely comprehend its complexity. She projected her voice into the minds of her fellow magickers.

Moor's still here.

Samuel thumbed the power stone on the pistol loaded with thaumaturgic bullets. Van Bam looked at Marney and replied, *Get ready.*

But the empath already knew the drill.

Marney amplified her magical search, locating the source of the alien emotions. She fed what she found to Van Bam, who stabbed his cane against the cobbles, whispering to his magic. Green streaks of illusionism sped from the glass towards an area close to the portal, where they wrapped in spinning lines around a concealing spell. Samuel took aim.

But he didn't get the chance to fire.

Some invisible force punched Samuel off his feet, sending him crashing into the wall. His head cracked brickwork, the pistol clattered from his hand, its power stone dying, and he fell unconscious to the courtyard floor. Just as Marney felt rage rising in the alien emotions, Van Bam's magic coalesced into a ball of liquid green. Briefly morphing into the perfect likeness of Fabian Moor's visage, it became a burning, iridescent light which shot at Van Bam, hitting him square in the face.

The illusionist fell, screeching and writhing on his back like a wounded animal. He tried to scrape the magic from his face, but it sank into his skin. He gave a final scream as his eyes boiled and burst from their sockets, and then he lay still.

Marney felt nothing.

Not knowing if her lover was alive or dead, she snatched up Hamir's pistol from the ground just as Fabian Moor materialised.

Apparently unconcerned by the weapon aimed at him, Moor stood close to the portal, staring coldly at Marney.

'I thought I'd have to retrieve your body from your filthy town to interrogate your soul,' he said. 'I'm glad you found my message.'

Marney saw Denton's dead body in her mind, the words written in blood upon his skin ... The pistol whined as she primed its power stone.

Moor sneered. 'You're coming with me, *empath.*'

Marney pulled the first trigger.

With a burst of higher magic, Moor blurred, phasing out of sync with the real world as his presence slid to one side. The first thaumaturgic bullet cracked harmlessly against the wall. But Marney's magic was still tracking Moor's strange emotional aura. As he rematerialised in front of the portal, she squeezed the second trigger.

Moor groaned. He sank to his knees, looking confused by the wound in his chest. He stared at Marney, perhaps surprised that he had been hurt by a simple magicker. The portal churned whitely behind him. Marney let the pistol fall from her hand. Moor's face creased in pain.

Samuel appeared alongside Marney, his rifle drawn. As Moor

clutched at his chest, his pain increasing, Samuel unloaded a magazine of fire-bullets at him, bellowing his hatred. Marney didn't know if lower magic could add any further injury to a creature of higher magic, but she watched with murderous thoughts as Samuel's magical onslaught blistered the air around Moor.

When the fire subsided, Moor's body lost cohesion; his eyes staring lifelessly, he ripped like paper into pearlescent tendrils that were absorbed into the portal. The primordial mists of the Nothing of Far and Deep churned and crackled with energy as they devoured the Genii. And then, like a slowly closing eye, the portal deactivated, shrinking, disappearing, until only the black bricks of the wall were left behind.

Marney felt nothing.

'We did it,' she said.

Samuel didn't reply. He touched the back of his head, looking at the blood that came away on his hand.

Van Bam moaned.

Marney rushed to her lover's side. She held his hand, trying to soothe his complaints with calming waves of empathic magic. His face was burned, his eyelids fried to withered crisps, and the sockets were dark red holes.

'Get it out ...' Van Bam was delirious. Despite Marney's magic, he began thrashing again and his voice rose in agony. 'In my head ... Get it out!'

Marney gave the illusionist the full force of her magic. It crawled inside him, blocked the pain and confusion, shut down each of his emotions and pushed him back into the depths of unconsciousness. He lay still again.

Samuel stood over them. 'Is he going to be all right?'

'Yes,' Marney said flatly.

She had felt a presence in Van Bam's mind just before he lost consciousness, wondered if she had heard a voice she recognised – a pernicious, spiteful voice, laughing. She told Samuel nothing of this, saying, 'We need to get him to Hamir.'

Samuel holstered his rifle, retrieved the double-barrelled pistol and then lifted Van Bam's limp body onto his shoulder.

Marney walked over to the golem's arm standing in the courtyard.

With a finger, she inscribed three concentric squares into the gelatinous substance, feeling a mild wave of relief as the dark grey disc of a shadow carriage appeared on the floor, waiting to carry them back to Labrys Town.

Samuel locked gazes with Marney, looked about to say something, but his words failed.

'Let's go,' said Marney.

CHAPTER TWENTY-ONE

THE LAST OF THE GENII

The pain was tolerable. As long as he kept very still.

There was a dark spot on Samuel's memory. One moment, Fabian Moor had been dragging him away from the Retrospective; the next he was waking up, returned to the silver cube of thaumaturgic metal at the heart of the Icicle Forest. Stripped naked, bathed in the sterile glow of silver light, Samuel lay in the clutches of a strange serpentine plant-like creature. With writhing tentacles for branches, it grew from the cube's floor and was holding Samuel aloft on his back.

Close by, Fabian Moor stood watching him, toying with Samuel's hunting knife. He looked as tired and defeated as Samuel felt. His pale face was streaked with dried blood from the Nephilim's rain.

As usual, Samuel's prescient awareness couldn't detect any danger in a Genii's presence, but it had become a grim, cold feeling in his gut. The gift Samuel had been born with, which had steered him well through the long path of his life, was now telling him that there was no more path left to walk.

With a gesture from Moor, the serpentine creature raised its captive into a sitting position so he faced the Genii. Samuel hissed a breath through his teeth. Many of the leathery branches had stabbed into the meat of his legs, buttocks and back, manipulating his movements like the strings on a puppet. Two more had punctured his hands, entering through the backs to emerge from his palms and coil round his wrists. Another had pierced the skin at the top of his neck, making Samuel's face feel tight as it slid under his scalp and over his skull.

But there was little pain, as long as neither he nor the creature moved.

Moor stared, unblinking. 'Shall I tell you what I remember most from the time when I *allowed* the Relic Guild to hold me hostage?' His eyes drifted up into memory. 'It isn't the casual insults of your fellow magickers. It isn't the tortures Simowyn Hamir exacted upon me. It's *you*, Samuel.'

Moor began pacing, turning the knife over in his hands. Samuel followed him with his eyes, not daring to move his head.

'Your arrogance was offensive,' Moor said. 'You were so certain that you were *right*, that you were the guardian of *justice*. I understand now that you were subject to your ... *conditioning*.'

Samuel licked his dry lips, too exhausted, too beaten to feel any fear. 'We should've killed you when you first came to Labrys Town.'

Moor looked disappointed. 'How little you comprehend. How *impossible* it is for you to question. Do you honestly believe that the Timewatcher is the most powerful being in the sky? Have you ever wondered if the Labyrinth is *not* the only House to harbour humans? How much do you know about the Old Ways?'

Moor stopped pacing and his eyes met Samuel's. 'All those centuries Hamir spent serving the Nightshade, and yet he never once revealed his origins. And your Residents and magickers never thought to discover it for themselves. Even now, you only know half the truth.'

Samuel watched as Moor began pacing again, studying the knife in his hands.

'I suppose I should show a little gratitude, Samuel – to you and your comrades. Not only did you save the lives of your own pitiful kind, but also mine.' Moor's expression became as dark as his tone. 'I thought Lord Spiral's mind had been torn and damaged by Oldest Place, but the reality is he only ever shared his dreams with himself. I just didn't see it until now. The Genii—'

'I don't care,' Samuel interrupted. And it was the truth. He didn't care about any of it any more. Hamir had been successful, the Nephilim had come, and they could deal with Spiral; they could help his friends. Samuel only wanted to answer the call of the deep fatigue that had been weighing down on him for the last forty years. He wanted to slip into an oblivion where nothing mattered.

The Genii was frowning at him.

'You heard me,' Samuel growled. 'So just get on with it.'

Moor smiled tiredly. Perhaps he was surprised that a lowly human had dared to speak to a creature of higher magic in such a disrespectful way; or was it because he expected nothing less?

'You think I'm going to kill you, is that it?' Moor said. 'No, no, Samuel – well, not entirely, anyway. You see, for the first time in decades, I do not know what my future holds. But I certainly can't stay here.' He used the knife to gesture at the silver walls around Samuel. 'I will travel the Houses, searching for a new safe haven where I can rest, plan, consider my options. Until I find such a place, I will need a supply of blood to keep me alive. *Your* blood, Samuel.'

Samuel tensed. The creature tightened its grip and he closed his eyes until the pain subsided.

'I won't infect you with my virus,' Moor continued. 'I won't give you the sweet release of becoming a golem. I will keep you alive, taking what I need from your veins whenever I need it.'

'No,' Samuel grunted.

Moor approached Samuel, holding the hunting knife across his open palms like an offering.

'I seem to recall that you once threatened me with this weapon, Samuel. You said that you wanted to slit my throat with it. Yet you wondered if that was too quick and easy a death for a *bastard* like me. Do you remember?'

'I remember lots of things.' Moor's intent rekindled Samuel's anger, made him care again. 'I remember Hamir making you scream.'

The Genii's pale, almost albino face displayed some of the merciless anger he had been keeping inside. With a gesture, he ordered the serpentine creature to lower his captive into a prone position. Samuel yelled in pain.

Moor stood over him. 'I don't need your head to keep your body alive.' Loathing laced his every word. 'But I do need your last memory to be the utter certainty that your blood will ensure my survival.' Two-handed, Moor raised the knife above his head. 'Believe the lies if you wish, Samuel, but there is no paradise waiting for you. Any last words?'

A dead, hollow calm settled on Samuel. He fancied that he caught a glimpse of Mother Earth in the silver light reflected from the blade pointing down at him. Van Bam had once told Samuel that he still believed the Timewatcher was out there somewhere, watching, waiting to gather lost souls into Her embrace. Samuel decided that if She interrupted his journey into oblivion, he would slap Her face.

His pale blue eyes glared at the Genii. 'I curse you and all your kind, Moor.'

The knife stabbed down.

There was a fleeting moment of unbearable pain, but the blade quickly sliced through Samuel's spine, and then there was nothing.

With every stab, a sense of loss seethed inside Moor. Each time blood spattered his face, he screamed with vitriol. He struck, over and over, attacking the shattered faith and love he'd once had for the Lord who had betrayed him. His soul darkening with the abandonment of mindless savagery, Moor hacked and sawed until the magicker's head separated from his neck.

He dropped the knife, staggering back, breathing heavily.

The serpentine creature lifted the head clear of the body, raising it high on the end of a leathery branch. Samuel's eyes were closed, his features slack. Moor summoned his thaumaturgy to heal the bleeding neck stump; but not before he commanded another branch to keep the airway open. It wriggled inside, feeding the headless body oxygen. The chest rose and fell rhythmically. Moor felt for a heartbeat. He found it, steady and strong. He then leaned against the silver wall, beset by an ever-increasing fatigue.

Creating the creature, keeping Samuel's body alive, were simple acts of thaumaturgy, yet they had taken much out of Moor. He suspected that some residue of the Retrospective had sapped his strength and he needed to re-energise. How long had it been since he last fed?

Moor's shaking hands were coated in blood. More saturated the front of his cassock. Like a hungry animal, he licked his fingers clean, savouring the blood's life-preserving nourishment. He looked at Samuel's head again, hanging so perversely from the branch, and a sudden laugh escaped him. It came viscerally, unbidden, shaking his shoulders and forcing tears to spill from his eyes in hot floods down his pale face.

Laughter turned to weeping.

All he had done, every order he had obeyed unquestioningly, everything he had sacrificed – and what was it for? 'Nothing!' he screamed at Samuel's dead face.

The release of emotions drained Moor's remaining strength. He placed a hand against the wall, struggling to stay on his feet. There really was nothing. There was no one. Simple survival – that was the only thing of paramount importance now. The survivors of the Relic Guild undoubtedly knew about this cube, and Moor needed to leave, find a safe location, as soon as possible.

It was when the Genii failed to open a portal in the cube's wall that he realised his weakness was getting worse, as if the higher magic was being leached from his veins. He would feed first – drink from Samuel's body and replenish his strength before beginning his search …

A symbol appeared on the portal wall.

As tall as Moor and twice as wide, it tainted the silver metal with coppery rust. Moor's insides froze to ice as he recognised it as an ancient symbol belonging to a dark art. It glowed with crimson light, and Moor understood that his thaumaturgy was dying.

Desperate, the Genii scurried to where he had dropped the knife and snatched it up. He held the weapon before him as the portal opened to allow a giant and a human into the cube.

Rage: it burned in Marney as her sole emotion, a fire stoked by magic.

Standing alongside the empath, Gulduur Bellow whispered the words of an ancient tongue, his lips coated with his own blood. The touch of the Nephilim had sown a seed of dead time into Fabian Moor, and the giant's blood-magic had encouraged it to grow and devour his thaumaturgy. The Genii was now as powerless as Marney wanted him to be.

Soaked in blood, holding Samuel's hunting knife in a shaking hand, Moor looked pitifully weak, almost frightened. He brushed his free hand across his face as Marney's magic invaded his mind. She spared a glance at Samuel's body; the image of his dead face hanging from a tentacle of the serpentine creature hardened her emotions, covered them with spiteful barbs and made damned sure that this creature of higher magic understood what it truly meant to receive the empathy of an empath.

Van Bam! Her thoughts came with the force of a sledgehammer. *Denton, Gideon, Angel, Gene, Macy, Bryant, Hillem, Glogelder ... Samuel!*

Moor dropped the knife and sank to his knees, clutching his head.

They were agents of the Relic Guild, and they died because of you and your master. Marney lessened the force of her thoughts to a growl of thunder. *I want you to remember their names, Moor. I want them to be the last thing you ever think about.*

Moor wiped away the blood that had leaked from his nostril. He remained on his knees, rubbing his chest as though feeling the influence of Bellow's magic. He raised an eyebrow at Marney.

'It seems that you and I have been in this position before.' Moor's tone was resigned, speaking to her as an equal. 'You really are clever. I truly believed I had killed you.'

Marney glanced around the silver cube. She had a vague recollection of the time she had been imprisoned here, a dull memory of the agony induced by Moor as he ripped memory after memory from her mind. Had it all been worthwhile?

You lost, Marney told the Genii. *Spiral is dead.*

'I know.' He looked both saddened and impressed. 'Tell me, throughout the history of the Labyrinth, did the Relic Guild ever play a longer game than this?'

Marney didn't reply at first. Bellow continued to whisper.

No more games. Marney's tone had softened, stripping away all pretence until only the stark truth was felt. *No more plots, no more secrets ... this is the end.*

Tears came to Moor's eyes. 'The Timewatcher always used to be so compassionate and forgiving. But I don't suppose I can expect forgiveness from anyone now. There's nothing left for me.'

You've lost everything. It was sympathy that Marney now injected into Moor's being, and his newfound weakness latched on to it. *Your power has gone, the rest of the Genii are gone – you're alone, Moor, but ... that doesn't mean there aren't any choices left.*

Moor snorted a bitter laugh. 'Choices?'

Think about it. Marney's empathy became a sly snake, coiling around Moor's darker emotions, dragging him further into hopelessness. *Look into your heart, Fabian,* feel *for the right thing to do.*

'Yes, the right thing,' Moor said miserably. He picked up Samuel's knife, studied it. 'Was there ever any other choice?'

No.

And Fabian Moor slit his own throat.

Marney watched, feeling nothing, as the wicked blade severed skin and tendons and arteries with ease. Blood gushed, drenching Moor, pooling on the silver floor around him. Still on his knees, his face expressing only calm defeat, the Genii stared at the red-smeared knife in his hand. He remained that way until his veins had emptied, his eyes closed, and he sagged, lifeless.

Gulduur Bellow barked a single word of blood-magic. Moor's remains collapsed, burning from within with a magical fire the colour of ambient thaumaturgy. The fire spread to the blood on the floor, and in but a moment, the last of Spiral's Genii was reduced to fine ash.

Bellow looked at Marney, his large face and dazzling blue eyes full of sadness. 'I'm sorry we were too late for Samuel.'

Marney glanced at Samuel's corpse and realised that although his head had been severed, his body was not dead. His chest rose and fell with steady breaths, and she didn't want to guess why it had been done to him.

'Please,' she said to Bellow without emotion. 'I don't want to leave him like this.'

Bellow gave a nod of understanding. He moved towards Samuel's body, again summoning thaumaturgic fire to burn the remains and destroy the serpentine creature.

Heat and the stench of magic washed over Marney as she watched the face of her friend crumble to ash. 'Goodbye, Samuel,' she whispered.

And Marney dispelled her own magic, deciding to truly *feel* this moment, to lock it tight inside her, to remember – perhaps to honour each person who had died along this cursed journey that had taken forty years to complete. Marney found devastation inside herself: guilt and sorrow and anger wrapped around a love so profound that she was once again an eighteen-year-old fledgling struggling to make sense of the world, battling her uncertainty.

It was more than she could handle. She tried to stay upright, but she had no strength left and her knees buckled. Sobs came thick and fast. Her back hit the silver wall and she slid down to the floor. The cracks and pops of the serpentine creature crumbling to chips of harmless stone accompanied her wails. Through an ocean of tears, Marney saw the blurred image of Gulduur Bellow approaching her. The Nephilim lifted her into his arms, and Marney fell into his embrace.

'Come, my friend,' Bellow said softly. 'Let me take you home.'

THE END OF THE BEGINNING

The war was over.

In a quiet, smoky tavern in the eastern district of Labrys Town, Marney sat alone at a corner table, getting drunk. She refilled her glass from a bottle of dark rum and sipped, savouring the fiery tang. On the opposite side of the table, before an empty chair, sat a second glass, filled but untouched. The landlord cleaned glasses behind the bar; a few patrons sat by themselves, nursing drinks. They all looked as miserable as Marney felt.

Everything had changed, and Marney found irony in the thought that she was only eighteen and still had her whole life ahead of her.

She hadn't seen her fellow Relic Guild agents since the night they killed Fabian Moor. Samuel was ... Marney didn't know where Samuel was. But Van Bam was in the Nightshade. The presence Marney had felt in his mind that night had been the ghost of Gideon. Van Bam was the new Resident of Labrys Town. And the new Resident's first duty had been to inform his people that they were on their own.

Marney drained her glass and refilled it.

The Last Storm had come. The armies of the Timewatcher had defeated the enemy. Spiral had been locked up in his very own prison House called Oldest Place and the surviving Genii executed. The Aelfirian exiles had been sent home and it was a time of celebration across all the Houses. But in Labrys Town there was nothing but lament.

The Timewatcher and Her Thaumaturgists had abandoned the denizens. Without reason or compassion, She had decreed that the Labyrinth was now a forbidden zone. Every doorway that led to the Houses of the Aelfir had been removed from the Great Labyrinth. The only portal that remained to the denizens was the one outside the Nightshade, to be used for nothing other than importing essential goods; the rest, along with their shadow carriages, had been destroyed and bricked up behind the boundary walls. Now all that could be found among the treacherous alleyways of the endless maze was a cursed place called the Retrospective, a House of poison and damnation where Spiral's Aelfirian armies roamed as wild demons.

The atmosphere suddenly felt too still.

On the other side of the table, the air blurred. At first, Marney thought it was the drink. She frowned through an alcohol-induced haze and watched a woman materialise. Dressed in a thick purple robe, her head was shaved bald and she had a black diamond tattoo on her forehead. She sat calmly in the chair which had been empty a moment before, staring at the empath with tawny eyes.

Marney looked at the landlord and his customers. They weren't moving; they had frozen into poses, mid-action.

Marney looked back at the woman, mildly surprised to see she was still sitting there. 'I thought you'd abandoned us,' she said, struggling not to slur.

Lady Amilee didn't quite smile. 'I have ... one or two affairs to tie up before I leave.' The Skywatcher raised an eyebrow at the full but untouched glass of rum on the table before her. 'Are you expecting someone to join you?'

'No. It's for Denton.'

'Denton?'

'We made a promise to drink to an Aelfirian soldier who gave his life to help us. To help *you*.'

'I see.' Amilee contemplated that. 'But now you're drinking to Denton's memory, too.'

'And everyone else's.' Marney took a slug from her own glass and coughed as the spirit burned her throat. 'What do you want?'

Amilee appeared concerned by the empath's inebriation. 'Do you remember when we first met, Marney? You were so frightened of losing Denton – of having to face the realms without his guidance. You made him proud, you know. He trusted you more than any other person.'

'But he didn't trust me enough.' Marney could hear the bitter bite in her slurring words. 'There were things he stopped me remembering. Things that *you* didn't want me to know, I'm sure.' She poured herself another glass of rum, trying to ignore the tears threatening to come to her eyes. 'What happened at the Library of Glass and Mirrors?'

Amilee pursed her lips. 'Didn't your mentor warn you how dangerous that information is? He was protecting you—'

'I don't care!' Marney slammed the glass down on the table, spilling rum. 'Fabian Moor knew what it was, didn't he? He found out something about me from Denton, and *that* is why he tried to take me with him. Tell me I'm wrong!'

'Marney, calm down.'

'No! Denton blocked my memories and died before he could tell me why. It isn't fair!'

Angrily, Marney wiped the tears from her face. She didn't care any more. As far as she was concerned, every creature of higher magic could get damned.

'Marney.' Amilee's tone was soft, understanding. 'What would Denton say to you now? Would he say that life is rarely fair? That you should hold to your faith and perhaps answers will find you eventually?' She raised a hand, stopping Marney from unleashing a choice retort. 'Have you ever considered that Denton was not only protecting you but also preparing you?'

Marney screwed her face up. 'What does that bloody well mean?'

'That there's hope for the future, Marney.' Sadness filled Amilee's tawny eyes. 'Keep faith in the Relic Guild. Remember the trust you had in Denton. And never forget that all things must be known in the end.'

Marney scoffed. 'Please, I can't stomach any more enigmas, so either speak plainly or go away so I can drink in peace.' Shaking her head in frustration, she looked at the landlord and lonely patrons, still frozen like statues. 'Why did you come here, anyway?'

But when Marney looked back, Lady Amilee, the patron of the denizens, had disappeared. The atmosphere almost sighed as it was released. The landlord continued cleaning glasses and the patrons resumed drinking as though nothing out of the ordinary had occurred.

Marney sat there for a long time, staring into the space where the Skywatcher had been. Her eyes drifted down to the glass filled with rum in memory of Denton. She thought about secrets; she thought about the friends who had died; she thought about the love she could now never share with Van Bam.

She snatched up Denton's glass and drained its contents in one go.

THE RELIC GUILD

It was estimated that almost two hundred thousand denizens had succumbed to the Genii's virus. A fifth of Labrys Town's population – all dead.

But it could have been worse. If the Nightshade hadn't saved its people, if its magic hadn't swept through the town, cleansing the streets, killing those who had been infected, then no one would have survived. The virus would have run its course, eventually turning every denizen into an inhuman golem. As it was, the stony remains of those who had reached the end of the infection's cycle were still being found even three weeks later.

A time of social upheaval was at hand for the Labyrinth. Everything had changed.

Ennis made his way along an alley behind apartment buildings in the central district, carrying a bag of groceries. It was early morning and the sun had yet to clear the boundary wall. A light mist hung over Labrys Town. The shadows clung to the chill of Silver Moon.

Whenever possible, Ennis had taken to avoiding the streets at the busier times of day; he couldn't really explain why. Going back to his old apartment, returning to his old life with the police force, hadn't felt right to him, and it just seemed better to stay out of the way, perhaps to let others believe he was dead. At present, it was very easy to hide among the deceased.

A lot of children had lost their parents to the virus and the orphanages were struggling with the influx. Ennis, however, had managed to get Jade and Daniel into a good place in the western district. They'd be well cared for. Ennis had tried to find Long Tommy after the troubles, but the old crook had become just another name on a long list of casualties, and the part he played in saving Labrys Town would probably never be known. As for Lady Amilee, Ennis hadn't seen her since the night he killed Hagi Tabet, but he suspected that she was long gone from the Labyrinth.

Reaching a black iron fire escape, Ennis first checked the coast was clear and then began climbing the ladder one-handed, clutching the grocery bag to his chest.

Van Bam was dead. The denizens were now calling him Van Bam the Blind. They said he was the Resident who failed his people, who allowed the Genii to return and take control of the Nightshade. Ennis still wasn't sure of the whole truth but he doubted Van Bam had failed anyone. The Nightshade had a new Resident now, and Ennis was happy to hide from her.

Climbing onto the rooftop, he took a moment to enjoy the view. In the distance, far across the dirty old town, the sun had finally cleared the black canvas of the boundary wall. Its golden rays evaporated the mists and glinted upon the metal of silver fighting machines. The automatons that had risen to defend the denizens had scaled the boundary walls and were now perched atop it – ever-watchful guardians, Ennis supposed, waiting for a time when they were needed again.

The air smelled somehow fresher, sweeter; the atmosphere clean and uncluttered. Only in recent days had Ennis come to appreciate how stagnant this thousand-year-old town had been. But now, nothing would ever be the same again.

On that night in the Nightshade, Ennis had wondered if Lady Amilee's presence heralded the return of the Thaumaturgists, the great overlords from myth and legend. But no; the Labyrinth had new overlords now. The Nephilim: a race of giant creatures of higher magic who came from a House called the Sorrow of Future Reason. Ennis had never heard of them before but the town's older generation had, and he'd heard them whispering about how the Nephilim were blood-magickers, dangerous and to be feared. Worse than the Genii, some claimed.

Ennis didn't really understand why the Nephilim had come, but somehow their House had replaced the Retrospective, and thus far they had done nothing to justify such a terrifying reputation. Because of them, the doorways from the old stories had begun reappearing out in the Great Labyrinth. Portals were once again connecting the denizens with the Houses of the Aelfir. The boundary walls might as well have collapsed. The people of Labrys Town were staring into the face of a bright and complicated future.

Ennis stiffened.

The air didn't feel right. He was being watched.

He scanned the rooftop.

Since the end of the troubles, Ennis had been living in a secret apartment that used to be the hideout of the bounty hunter Old Man Sam. Its secret entrance was a hatchway disguised to look like an innocuous air vent. Ennis stared at it now as the tingle of magic brought gooseflesh to his skin.

A woman materialised, sitting on the concealed entrance. Her ears were pointed, her mouth and nose small, but her eyes were large, giving her face an oddly triangular shape. An Aelf. In her hand she held a spell sphere.

'Hello, Ennis,' she said, rising from the entrance. 'Are you going to invite me in?'

Eyeing the spell sphere warily, Ennis wondered if he could drop the bag of groceries and draw his pistol before she could use it.

As if reading his thoughts, the Aelf smiled and shook her head.

'Who are you?' Ennis said.

'My name's Namji,' she replied. 'A friend of mine wants to talk to you. She'll explain everything.' She opened the hatchway and gentured to the ladder beneath. 'Let's go.'

Ennis descended into the secret apartment to find another woman – a human – waiting for him. Namji followed him down, closing and locking the hatchway behind her.

'This is Marney,' the Aelf said.

She looked to be in her late fifties, wearing a short coat with a baldric of silver throwing daggers beneath. Her hair was tied into a loose tail and her expression was unreadable.

'Sit, Ennis,' Marney said.

He felt compelled to follow her instructions, knowing somewhere inside him that she was using magic. It suddenly felt like a very good idea to put the groceries down, pass Namji his pistol and sit on the threadbare sofa. His own magic rebelled against this subjugation but there was little it could do. His solitude, his peace, crumbled to dust.

'How did you know I was here?' he growled.

'You'd be surprised by what we know,' Namji said.

'What do you want?'

'We've been looking for you,' said Marney. 'Thought we'd better have a chat.'

'I haven't done anything wrong,' Ennis said miserably. 'I don't care what you've heard, I just want to be left alone.'

Marney was amused. 'He certainly sounds as defensive as the person who used to live here.'

'All he needs is a rifle on his back,' Namji agreed.

Ennis looked from one woman to the other, unable to decide if they were here to harm him or mock him. He couldn't think straight through whatever spell Marney had placed on him.

'We've been hearing rumours,' Marney said, 'about a police sergeant who went the extra mile to protect the denizens. He likes to keep secrets, apparently.'

'Especially about his magic,' Namji added.

Ennis made to object, realised it was pointless and closed his mouth.

'I understand your need to hide,' Marney said. 'We know all about you, Ennis.'

She stood to one side. Ennis tensed as a low growl came from the bedroom. Whatever courage he might have clung to evaporated when a wolf walked into the room, glaring at him with eyes as fierce as the sun. The beast was huge, its head almost level with Marney's shoulder.

'Don't,' Ennis blurted, dwarfed, panicked, his insides quaking. 'Whatever I did, please don't hurt me.'

To his surprise, the wolf glowed with magic. Shrinking and morphing with bony pops and clicks, the beast changed into a young woman, not even twenty, wearing dark grey clothes.

A name rustled from Ennis's dry throat. 'Clara ...'

The new Resident of Labrys Town. The last time Ennis saw this woman, he had considered her the enemy and treated her as such. Had treated her with contempt.

'I'm sorry,' he whispered.

'A magicker is an illegal presence in the Labyrinth,' Clara said. 'Yet a lot is changing. The Nephilim are watching over us, we're in contact with the Aelfir again – the future is looking good, but we have a lot of hardship to wade through first.'

'Spiral destroyed the Panopticon of Houses,' Namji said. 'The Aelfir have to establish a new governing body and they're as uncertain as the denizens. We need to build bridges.'

'And there'll always be treasure hunters,' Marney added. 'You'd be surprised how clever they are, and how much trouble stolen relics can cause.'

'I may be young, but I have the wisdom of an old Resident in my mind, Ennis.' Clara cocked her head to one side as if listening to something. 'And he tells me that we need to pool our every resource to help the Nephilim hold things together. He tells me that I need you.'

'You ...' Ennis faltered. 'You need *me*?'

'Pack your things,' Namji instructed. 'We've got a room for you at the Nightshade.'

Confused, Ennis stared at the Aelf, and then at Marney.

'You heard her,' she said.

'But ...' Ennis rubbed his face, trying to clear his mind of Marney's influence. 'Why?'

'Because you made a promise to serve and protect the denizens,' Clara said. 'Because the magic in your veins understands why we're here. Because you know deep down that your life is about to become as bizarre as it gets.' She gave him a small, knowing smile. 'Sergeant Ennis, welcome to the Relic Guild.'

ACKNOWLEDGEMENTS

And so this trilogy comes to an end. It's been quite a ride and there are fabulous people who deserve my thanks.

Jack and Marney, my wonderful wife and daughter, who never stop loving me, supporting me, and putting up with my every shade and mood. Dot and Norm and Mum and Dad. My fearless agent John Berlyne, and my marvellous editor Marcus Gipps, who I forgot to tell was the inspiration for the character Hillem. Gillian Redfearn who sees all! Simon Spanton, Sophie and Genn, and the rest of the amazing Gollancz team. My fellow writers who shared the madness and put up with my antics. And special thanks to Joanne Harris who, when this all began, took the time to sprinkle the fairy dust of wisdom on a new and clueless novelist. Thank you for your support, Joanne.

The Relic Guild trilogy was sometimes maddening to write, but the reward of seeing it the hands of readers makes everything worthwhile. So to every reader on the planet, with love and appreciation, thank you. We'd be lost without you.

There are unseen kindnesses in this world. And I am grateful for them.